Betsy

P9-DNQ-585

A Question of Trust

Also by Alexandra Raife

Drumveyn

The Larach

Grianan

Belonging

Sun on Snow

The Wedding Gift

Moving On

Among Friends

Return to Drumveyn

The Way Home

ALEXANDRA RAIFE

A QUESTION OF TRUST

Hodder & Stoughton

Copyright © 2003 by Alexandra Raife

First published in Great Britain in 2003 by Hodder & Stoughton
A division of Hodder Headline

The right of Alexandra Raife to be identified as the Author
of the Work has been asserted by her in accordance with the
Copyright, Designs and Patents Act 1988.

2 4 6 8 10 9 7 5 3 1

All rights reserved. No part of this publication may be
reproduced, stored in a retrieval system, or transmitted, in any form
or by any means without the prior written permission of the publisher,
nor be otherwise circulated in any form of binding or cover other
than that in which it is published and without a similar condition
being imposed on the subsequent purchaser.

All characters in this publication are fictitious and any resemblance
to real persons, living or dead, is purely coincidental.

A CIP catalogue record for this title is
available from the British Library

ISBN 0 340 82624 X

Typeset in Plantin Light by Palimpsest Book Production Limited,
Polmont, Stirlingshire
Printed and bound in Great Britain by
Mackays of Chatham plc, Chatham, Kent

Hodder & Stoughton
A division of Hodder Headline
338 Euston Road
London NW1 3BH

HAMPSHIRE COUNTY LIBRARY	
C013488496	
H J	19/03/2003
F	£18.99
034082624X	

In the last light of dusk the comfortable room, furnished with its friendly relics of the past, welcomed her, warm and quiet. Philippa liked driving home in the evenings at this time of year, when the first hint of lengthening days was discernible. Even if the hilly roads she mostly used were snowy or icy, as they had been tonight, it was much pleasanter not to have to tackle them in the dark.

Then it occurred to her, as she switched on the big reading lamp and went to rouse the fire to life, that she hadn't given a thought to the state of the roads all day. She paused to consider this. It was true. A year ago, in similar weather, a faint anxiety would have nagged about whether she would make it, first up the main road where it climbed above Muirend, then up the even steeper, single-track and little used road on which the cottage stood. But, almost without realising it, she had learned to trust in her battered old Mini, and in her own capacity to keep its wheels turning.

Though she had grown up in these glens, she hadn't had to worry too much about wintry conditions then, since in those days there had been no necessity to get out, no matter what the weather, to earn her living.

This afternoon, safely shut away in that bright, freshly decorated and efficiently heated room, empty except for the two sewing machines whirring busily, the yards of glowing ruby velvet they were working on adding their own warmth to the scene, she had scarcely been aware of the threatening sky or the snow that flurried from time to time against the windows. She had been content to be where she was, doing what she was doing. A friend of a friend, who had turned out to be very agreeable company, had decided to make curtains for the whole house as a wedding present for her son, then hadn't felt quite brave enough to tackle the job on her own.

The fire, banked up several hours ago, woke to life as Philippa disturbed its black crust, rewarding her with a red glow. Another minor skill acquired; in the early days she had often come home to find it out. She propped the small logs she'd left ready round its live heart and, as she began to look through her mail, flames had already started to lick up, their friendly sound dispersing the silence of the room.

A bill from the garage. What was that for? Oh, yes, the new tyres. Wow, Andy had let her off lightly. He'd said he'd get them 'from somewhere' for her, but even so, she'd expected to have to pay more than that.

A card thanking her for looking after two cats and a great-grannie for a weekend. 'We know you said you only expected to be fed and watered, but we're so grateful . . .' A book token was enclosed. How very kind. It had been a painless couple of days in a pleasant house full of books, its three occupants doing little more than snooze gently in the even warmth of sunny rooms.

And here, after much tedious chasing, since she was supposed to have been paid on the spot, was the cheque for the lunch she'd done for that Boxing Day shoot. It had been a lucrative booking, but it had pretty well taken over Christmas, and had involved a horribly early start and too much driving. It hadn't been any fun either, since she'd found herself catering for would-be grand guests on some fancy package holiday, who had been too busy concealing the fact that they'd never shot anything in their lives to address a word to her.

The single message on the answerphone was from Penny Forsyth. 'Hi. At long last I've managed to fix a date for the boys' party. Second weekend in March. Please, please say you're free. They seem to be inviting most of the school, which wasn't exactly what I'd had in mind. Give me a ring and we'll get our heads together about food, mountains of it by the sound of things . . .'

Was that weekend all right? Checking her diary, relieved to find nothing pencilled in which couldn't be juggled around, Philippa paused, examining the pages, with their comfortable spread of entries, with new attention.

She really was busy; the jobs did turn up. When she had decided to come back to Glen Maraich, as the one place where it had seemed possible to piece together some workable existence for herself after everything had gone so terribly wrong, there had been plenty of foreboding voices to advise against it. Pointing out the high level of unemployment in rural areas, they had warned that living in an isolated cottage, on what she could earn from casual and almost certainly low-paid jobs, would not only be lonely but impractical and uncomfortable. They had hinted too that the friends of the past would be busy with their own lives, and that Philippa, now on her own, might not find it as easy to slot in again as she imagined.

Philippa had paid no attention to the last part. The links with friends here went back a long way; she knew they would always be there for her, as she was for them. But the gloom and doom about the difficulties of earning enough to survive on had found their mark, and she had taken every job that offered, no matter how humdrum. Which was why she had found herself battling through that Boxing Day lunch for those awful people.

She played Penny's message again, looking round the room appraisingly as she did so. It seemed to her to offer all she wanted. And outside its thick walls, in the cold and silence of the February night, lay the landscape and the environment in which she belonged and where she felt at home.

Suddenly the moment was significant, as though for the first time since she'd returned she was able to stand back and see how far she'd come.

Minor as the different elements which had produced this moment of objectivity might be, they added up to something positive and reassuring. Even the fact of heading up the glen this evening, sure that if she ran into trouble someone would find her, someone would help her, was progress in its way. More importantly, there was no reason to suppose the flow of work would dry up, and that meant, she decided with satisfaction, that never again would she take on a job she didn't like just because it paid well.

She had found the perfect place to live, and could live in it in her chosen way. She had woven herself once more, almost without being conscious of its happening, into the network of friendships which had been the background to her life and the life of her family for generations. The need to adapt to an alien world, with its different demands and different values, was behind her. As was her failure to find happiness in it.

The empty spaces had filled, the doubts had receded, and with them the deeper fear that the pessimistic voices might have been right, and that after all she might have to capitulate, uprooting herself again in order to find some more conventional means of supporting herself.

But tonight this chance combination of the enjoyable day, the uneventful journey home, the postbag full of good news and another job safely in place – even the fire now blazing brightly in its wide stone hearth – added up to a new and comfortable certainty. She was here, where she wanted to be; she had made this work.

I

An hour after Philippa had taken the climbing road which bored deep into the hills flanking Glen Maraich, when darkness had fully fallen, a second car came that way, a powerful Subaru, driven by a stranger.

In spite of not knowing the road, he pushed on fast, glad to be near the end of his journey, and glad to be clear of Glasgow, where he'd had nothing to do but kit himself out and find wheels while this bolthole was being organised for him.

Hardly a vehicle on the road, hardly a light of human habitation to be seen since he'd left the grey little town of Muirend behind him. Somewhere in this desolate landscape he would be sitting out empty weeks, perhaps months, while negotiations in which he had no part wound tortuously on, setting up once more the operation whose first phase had gone so disastrously wrong.

He'd actually opted for this location, swayed, he knew, by the private dream he kept on hold for the faraway day when the fighting would be over. Though now that he was actually here he could hardly believe the facile image he'd created for himself – retired major, renting a cottage in the glen while he looked for a place to buy. In the disorientated, almost dazed interval after they'd got back, struggling to deal with the abrupt transition from action and the adrenalin rush of danger to aimless inactivity, the fantasy had seemed appealing.

All the same, he must have been out of his mind to choose as his temporary persona that of Major Jon Paulett, RE. His own regiment. That broke every rule in the book. Here, however, he was, Barbour (suitably distressed) on the seat beside him, green wellies in the back, his mind still unable to rid itself of the nagging memory of the betrayal which had so nearly cost them their lives, and the scrambling terror of their escape.

Even so, he could still function at a practical level, and had no need to consult his map. The track to the cottage should appear soon. If he could get up it, he thought sourly, for though the road had obviously been ploughed and gritted at some point today, fresh snow had fallen since.

A turning came up on the right. Half a mile more and he should find the main entrance to Baldarroch estate on his left. There it was, wheel marks in the snow vanishing between stone pillars. A couple of hundred yards more . . . yes, a second drive. A tractor had been using it; that would help.

He put in four-wheel drive and took the unfamiliar track with heedless aggression, anger ready to boil up if anything got between him and his objective now. But the Subaru excelled itself, and he even felt a brief lift of exhilaration at the way it handled on the treacherous switchbacks, exhilaration which died abruptly as it bellied in a drift. But the lights had picked out a small stone building at the top of a bank a hundred yards ahead. He could jump from here.

As he tried to open his door packed snow resisted, and he forced it back with an impatient heave, his temper ready to flare at the slightest check. He reached for his jacket and stepped out into the snow, pausing for a moment to take in the feel of the night. The smell of the air told him that more snow was on the way.

'This is it then,' he said aloud, turning to reach for a carrier bag and 'the major's' leather holdall from the back seat. 'You're here, Jon without the h. And good luck to you, you poncy bastard.'

Taking an Army issue torch from his pocket he set off up the slope, cursing as the snow went over his desert boots. Should have put your wellies on, Major.

Would the door be unlocked as promised? He found it hard these days to trust in any arrangements but his own. The door opened, however, into a narrow corridor, its temperature starker than that of the night outside. Dingy whipcord carpet, a row of hooks, brown varnished doors. The first opened into the kitchen, a striplight laying bare its sterile cleanliness.

He dumped the carrier bag on a worktop and looked round with the disillusioned eye of long experience. But he could spot no obvious deficiencies. The fridge was humming quietly, a box of matches lay on the Calor gas cooker, a dishcloth was draped across the mixer tap, washing-up liquid and dish mop were in the drainer basket. A sticker on a cupboard door said 'Immersion', and as he located the switch and turned it on, he found that the tank was already warm.

He crossed the passage to the room opposite. With the awful blankness of rented accommodation it awaited him, orderly and drab. Four chairs were pushed in round a bulbous-legged table, two armchairs flanked the hearth, a dim watercolour hung above a thirties oak sideboard.

He couldn't imagine this room ever accepting him or receiving the stamp of his personality – of Jon Paulett's personality – yet he had to admit that he had seen far worse. The fire was laid, logs heaped beside the hearth. A small television was pushed back into a corner.

A door led to an inner room, its light shrouded by a tasselled shade. Jon didn't recognise the old-fashioned Scottish three-quarter bed for what it was, only thankful that it would give him room to stretch out. Basic furnishings, mobile gas radiator, the smell of unlived-in air. The rest of the house consisted of a dank bathroom and a second bedroom, its cold even more penetrating.

Shivering, Jon returned to the sitting-room and put a match to the fire, noting, as the first flare and crackle broke the pall of silence, that the kindling was dry and that the chimney drew well.

Back in the kitchen, he tipped out the contents of the carrier bag, intending to cook supper. But even the effort of opening a tin and finding a pan seemed too much. He made a couple of cheese sandwiches, and left the rest where it lay, a carelessness in sharp contrast to his usual neat-handed efficiency.

And that was it. There was nothing else. Without function or responsibility, the days yawned before him for an unknown stretch of time. He was left only with his anger. But releasing it was an indulgence which, alone in this shell of stone set down in its empty landscape, he knew he couldn't allow himself.

He took the bottle of Gordons from his coat pocket, and looked at it for a long moment. Glasses? In the sideboard he found a squad of tumblers, formed up and dressed off by the tidy hand which had left this place so clean and so barren. Taking the first swallow, he closed his eyes, letting the alcohol reach him, setting himself to subdue the impatience still consuming him.

'OK, slow down, you've arrived. You're going nowhere.' The bleakness in his voice against the weight of silence was hardly comforting. His mouth twisting, he raised his glass to the only living thing in sight, the flickering fire.

He slept unmoving for hours, his brain accepting that danger couldn't reach him here. Even the biting cold failed to penetrate his abandonment to exhaustion, to the release of tension, and the effects of the first alcohol he'd been free to touch for months.

Brought to consciousness by his protesting bladder he

came awake at last, alert to strange surroundings, almost startled by the silence. No sound of wind or water, bird, dog or distant traffic reached him through the stone walls. The burn a few yards from where he lay was captured and stilled, the birch branches which dipped into its falls turned into sprays of crystal, the sound of its reduced flow muted beneath a dome of ice.

He slept all that day, waking only to put together a careless meal, falling back into bed afterwards, his body compensating in this almost drugged oblivion for the strain it had been subjected to for so long.

He would have scorned any suggestion that he was close to breaking point, though he had assessed the signs in others a hundred times. It was part of the condition that no one recognised it in himself. But Kramer had known, relieved when Jon had chosen this remote spot to hole up in till they were back in business. On a personal level, Colonel K wouldn't have minded if Jon had disappeared for good. As a second in command, he still had far too much of the regular Army about him, and some highly inconvenient ideas of right and wrong. But they needed him, for his specialist skills, his toughness and experience, and because the men he trained would follow him anywhere.

Jon woke finally to grey light and a first mild interest in his surroundings though, ravenous by now, he took time to cook breakfast before he went outside. Taking time was what this was supposed to be about.

The cottage perched on a ledge above the glaciated floor of the glen, facing south but too close under the western ridge to get any late sun. Behind it a couple of knock-kneed sheds appeared to be held up by the dry-stane dyke at their backs. In one he found logs, a box of split kindling and a gas cylinder. Tipping this he found it was full. He stared at it, arrested by the discovery.

Accustomed for most of his life to having to fight for everything, he was aware of a novel sense of being looked after. In the rented rooms he'd occupied between jobs since leaving the Army, he'd become inured to providing for himself anything that wasn't nailed down. But he rejected the momentary flicker of gratification. He would pay somewhere along the line.

The first job was to shift the car. There was an uneasy feeling of being trapped, even here, as long as it was stuck. He knew he'd have to learn to shed such unease, but it was too soon yet. He found a shovel, and set about the job of freeing and turning the big vehicle.

He made himself go out without locking the house. There was nothing there beyond the guileless major's gear, but the effort lay in leaving his lair unsecured, against all training and habit. No one would know or care but, in denial as he might be about his present mental state, he recognised that it was crucial to leave behind the mind-set of that other world, if he hoped to establish any kind of reality here.

He slithered fast and casually down the mile of track, where light fresh snow covered the frozen ruts, and coming out onto the glen road turned left for Kirkton.

In the village piled snow bordered the street, a lot more snow at this height, Jon observed, than there had been in Muirend. He parked outside a shop window offering a few dead flies and some faded tartan artistically rucked round a notice saying 'Open Easter'.

Already resenting this apathetic scene, he went into the only other visible shop, encumbered by his size and bulky coat in its crammed aisles, and feeling conspicuous under the eyes of the two customers already there. He was served with formal courtesy against a background of attentive silence.

Mindful of his new role, he assumed a plummy accent,

instantly lifting the hackles of all present, as he asked without much hope for gin.

'We've no licence for that sort of thing,' the grey-haired assistant told him reprovingly, though a natural instinct to be helpful made her add, 'You'd maybe get a bottle at the Kirkton Hotel.'

'They're waiting on their order at the Kirkton,' one of the customers interposed.

'Then, unless you were to go away down to Muirend, you'd best try the Cluny Arms.'

'That's up the hill the other side of the river,' the second customer added. 'It's no' far.'

Jon, wishing they'd mind their own damned business, scraped up some fulsome thanks, which made them turn down their mouths as he went out.

'That'll be the tenant Mary said was coming to Keeper's Cottage.'

'Colonel somebody, Alec was saying.'

'Pilot, was it?'

'Some name like that.'

'That's a damp cottage, though . . .'

Jon took the road to the Cluny Arms, past the last straggling houses of the village, then zig-zagging up open hillside. The hotel, once a pleasant, well-proportioned country house, had been vandalised by the addition of a flat-roofed extension to one side and a carpark below the terrace. A porch cluttered with walking sticks and umbrellas, dog bowls and rack of curling leaflets, led into a hall which, opening to the left through an archway, formed a chintzy, slightly down-at-heel but comfortable-looking bar. A grille was run down to a counter faced in buttoned mock leather.

Emptiness, silence. On a table in the hall stood a brass handbell. Beside it a card said 'Please ring', in a shapely confident hand. That writing couldn't have meant anything to Jon; the moment could have had no significance. Yet always afterwards he remembered the scent from the bowl of blue hyacinths which stood at the back of the table, as he reached out and lifted the bell.

2

A swing door at the back of the hall opened with a whoosh, and an untidy girl appeared, a sweatshirt with the hotel logo straining over ample breasts, eyes popping with interest to see this large unknown male appearing so early in the day.

Jon, already forced to accept that options were limited here, took some trouble to be affable as he enquired when the bar would be open.

'It's open now,' she told him, still goggling. 'It always is really. It's just that no one's been in yet.' Coming forward she pushed up the lowered grille, and Jon realised it hadn't even been locked in place.

'So how about a gin and tonic?' His gullet ached to feel it going down. How swiftly, having broken the long abstinence, the lure of alcohol reasserted itself. As the girl raised a glass to the optic he turned his eyes away from the quiver of slack flesh. He needed a drink before he could face that.

'Better make it a large one,' he said, then felt his throat constrict as she put the glass down and swirled the stale water in the ice bucket with the tongs.

'I'll just go and fetch some ice.'

'Don't worry about ice.'

'It won't take a sec. I'll get a lemon as well.'

Jon took some trouble to keep his voice easy. 'How about giving me the drink, then you go and do whatever you have to do.' He even managed a smile, though judging by the look she gave him he wasn't sure she recognised it as one. She slapped away obediently, but Jon, his whole being concentrated on the clean astringency of the first mouthful, barely noticed that she'd gone.

'Hey, there's some new guy in the bar,' Sharon reported excitedly in the kitchen. 'I bet he's the one who's taken the Baldarroch cottage. A bit old, but a hunk. You take the ice in, Lorna, and have a look.'

This second emissary dropped ice into Jon's glass so clumsily that the gin splashed out, following it with a ragged lump of lemon which did the same.

Where did they find these morons? Not locally, by the sound of them. But Jon forced down his irritation. He wanted something today, might want it again in the future, and even in his present state he could still summon self-discipline. In any case, with his glass refilled his sense of urgency lessened, and he exchanged a few pleasantries with this dim little creature before dispatching her to look for her boss.

Ian Murray was a man of few words but an experienced hotelier. As he came through the swing door and saw Jon's big shoulders hunched protectively over his glass, caught the alert turn of his head and his look of almost hostile appraisal before geniality masked it, he summed up his new customer in one word – trouble.

He agreed to sell Jon a bottle of gin in the hope that he would take himself off to drink it somewhere else, but before Jon's glass was empty a muddy Land Rover had parked below the terrace and three local men had come in, two gamekeepers making the most of the slack time of year, and Ross Nicholson, who regarded most times of year as slack. Each took Jon's measure with covert glances.

They'll not shift themselves today, Ian Murray thought resignedly, and that means this major fellow probably won't either.

He was right. It was late afternoon before they emerged into a blue dusk, the muzzles of patient dogs lifting the canvas back of the Land Rover as the men tramped heavily across the gravel.

Uninspiring as their company had been, Jon found himself deeply reluctant, as he followed them down to the village, to face the oppressive silence of Keeper's Cottage again.

He was back at the Cluny Arms by lunch-time the following day. He knew that human contact, no matter how uncongenial, was the only thing that was going to get him through this transition from highly charged activity to the absence of demands of any kind.

A handful of people were already in the bar, among them Ross Nicholson, who had correctly gauged that the major might be a useful source of free drinks. Lorna was on duty, the men ponderously teasing her.

'Is that all you're giving me, lass? What kind of a dram do you call that?'

'I didna see you at the dance on Friday, Lorna. What was wrong, were you afraid Willie might be there?'

Sniggers and muttered asides.

Jon felt a weary disgust to have actually sought such company. When Lorna had scuttled away, cheeks pink, and the men turned to more interesting topics, he half listened, restless and contemptuous, wondering if Ian Murray could produce anything in the way of food.

A door behind him opened. He swung round in instant reflex, managing a reasonable smoothness but aware that it had taken more effort to achieve than it should have done. Coming in, already passing him, was a girl he hadn't seen before.

Impossible afterwards to be certain of how much he took in in that first moment, but some details would always remain vivid – her straight back and light stride, the way she carried herself, but most of all her look of expectancy and pleasure, of confidence that life would be good, a confidence few people in Jon's world shared.

He was struck by the way the mood of the bar changed, the men responding to this girl very differently from the way they'd treated Lorna, straightening up, turning to watch her, smiling.

'And how's Philippa the day?'

'This weather to your liking then?'

'How about a wee refill while you're here? And you'll have something yourself?'

There was friendliness in the voices, but also, Jon observed, a new and apparently genuine courtesy.

The girl was answering them easily, but wasting no time. When she held up a glass to the optic, as Sharon had done, Jon had no inclination to turn away. As she tipped back her head, the light brought out a rich gloss in the heavy, conker-brown hair which fell to her shoulder blades. She was wearing a soft creamy sweater, and well-worn brown cords hugged her narrow haunches. As she turned Jon studied her automatically – part of his trade was reading faces – but he knew that much more than professional interest had awoken in him.

The brown hair swept smoothly back from a high forehead; the face was thin, jaw and cheekbones cleanly defined. Her mouth had a soft droop to it when she concentrated, but widened into a warm smile as one of the men said something which amused her. The kind of face you'd expect with that toff's accent, Jon thought disparagingly. His first comment on Philippa, negative and grudging. But what was someone like her doing behind a bar? He watched out of the tail of his eye, mouth turned down, as she whisked things into order, slid some chits from a spike by the till and turned to go on her way. Though as she went she didn't forget a courteous nod and smile to him, the stranger, esconced with his back to the wall at the end of the bar, his face expressionless.

Going through the swing door Philippa felt a real sense of escape. Who was he? She could see why Sharon and Lorna had been in such a flutter about him. Though his face had been impassive, she had rarely been so aware of a powerful personality in a complete stranger, or felt herself subjected to such penetrating observation.

Unlike the return to more interesting topics after Lorna's departure, this time the men indulged in a small ripple of comment.

'Philippa's in good fettle these days,' one remarked. 'It must suit her to be back.'

'To my mind, she should never have gone away in the first place,' another said censoriously.

'Aye well, after all that had happened . . .'

'But now that she is back, she shouldna' be wasting her time working here.'

'There's no' that many jobs to be had in the glen, nor in Muirend, come to that.'

'She shouldna' be needing a job at all,' Ross Nicholson stated with finality, and muttering, 'Right enough,' and 'Aye, well,' they left it there.

Philippa didn't reappear, though Jon was aware that he was waiting for her to do so. Ordering a couple of rolls for lunch, he took them to the table in the window. From there he could see the vehicles below the terrace. A battered blue Mini was parked askew at the far end. No one drove a Mini nowadays. This was the nineties, for God's sake. Piece of pure affectation, he decided, though he wasn't clear why he was so disgruntled about it.

He stayed where he was until, just after four, he heard the unmistakable roar of a Mini starting on full choke. He found himself listening as the sound faded away down the drive.

Stretched in front of the television at Keeper's Cottage that evening, exasperated by everything on offer, the dire reception and lack of a remote control, in spite of all he could do he found his thoughts returning to Philippa. He saw again the smiling mouth, the hazel eyes which had met his with such friendly directness, and points he hadn't been aware of registering emerged with surprising clarity – the long-fingered narrow hands, the slightness of her shoulders under the soft sweater, and again, the way she moved. She was ten years older, at a guess, than that other dismal pair, a mature and assured woman. Had he wanted then or did he want now to slide his hand up her slender neck and into the warmth of that shining hair?

Cursing, he came to his feet. Maybe he needed a woman, it had been a long time; but that kind of woman he definitely did not need.

Nothing but skin and bone, he told himself as he rolled into his chilly bed. Give me something to get my arms round. But still her smile was there against the darkness as he heaved the bedclothes round his shoulders and sought sleep.

Neither Philippa nor the blue Mini was visible at the hotel the next day, or the next. Jon knew it was absurd to care, or even notice, but he also knew that he desperately needed something, anything, on which to focus his mind. Though he was a man of hard self-discipline, a survivor by instinct and by trade, he knew it would be fatally easy to sink into depression in his present situation, and to be tempted to mitigate that depression by drinking.

If he let alcohol take over he might not be able to haul himself back, and if he didn't he'd come to a sticky end. The bottom line was that he had a contract to fulfil and there was no way out of it. In any case, he wanted the pay-off, one worth having this time. It represented his only hope of getting clear of the downward spiral which gradually, almost without his registering it, had sucked him down and down since leaving the Army. It represented the dream to which his mind so often turned. The dream of one day ending up in that little place on the West Coast which Mackay had said he'd let him have. Was he there now, sitting out the waiting time as Jon was doing? Most likely not. Whenever they'd used the place, as a hideaway on a different kind of job, Mackay had been adamant that he'd never go back.

Unattainable fantasy as it would almost certainly prove to be, Jon knew that its appeal had made him choose a not dissimilar environment now. Which was driving him mad with boredom. The irony didn't escape him.

At this stage, in fact, going to the Cluny Arms was the only thing that kept him sane. Though at this time of year there were few residents, it was a more popular local than the Kirkton Hotel, in spite of its distance from the village, and its evening scene was fairly lively.

Among the regulars three or four girls usually appeared, and they were very much aware of Jon, as they made clear. New face on the scene, cash in his pocket, and an intriguing mystery about what he was doing here. One of the girls sent him some very explicit signals. She was, on balance, the best of the bunch, with a plump but shapely little body, and a quick tongue which noticeably gingered up the lumbering conversation of the men. But Jon was careful to avoid anything which could be interpreted as a response. This pert little Moira sparked no interest in him – and certainly wouldn't have been the type the major would have gone for.

Though to a casual observer Jon might have appeared one of the group, he invariably had the sensation, as so often in his life, of everyone around him being part of the scene, sure of who they were and of their place in the scheme of things, while he belonged nowhere.

Major Paulett, had he existed, would no doubt have had contacts in the area whom he would have looked up. Though he might have tolerated the Cluny as his local, he would have had social resources outside it. Major Paulett would have called at Baldarroch and made his number with the laird. There would have been invitations, doors opening.

But, driving home after another of these unsatisfactory evenings, a sense of futility almost overwhelming him, Jon knew precisely what was adding a keener edge to his bleak mood – one smile, for him alone, had given him a glimpse of something so promising, so intensely desired, that it had hovered somewhere in his mind ever since.

3

Though recognising the dangers of drinking, Jon hadn't fully taken into account the equally insidious pitfalls of inertia. He existed from day to day, finding it hard to motivate himself, his mind unable to free itself of the terrors and traumas of recent weeks – the growing suspicion of betrayal, the hurried moves leaving hard-won weapons and equipment behind, the final mad race to get out, the heart-bursting run under fire, the choking dust whirled up by the rotor blades, the racket of the engines, the panic that the doors would close . . .

He knew there should have been some professional debriefing, even a period of rehabilitation before being pitchforked back into civilian life. He'd seen others return from tough missions under the delusion that they didn't need help, and he'd seen them suffer the consequences. Yet still he couldn't believe this was the case for him, and stubbornly he buried the memories deeper, though he could do nothing about the nightmares that continued to beset him.

Deep as he was in the aftermath of stress, he would be startled each time by the kick of pleasure it gave him when, arriving at the hotel, he saw a muddy Mini parked below the terrace steps. Turning up in the mornings, by this stage he was mostly served and left to himself. Sharon had tried flirting with him but had given up, flustered by his cold stare. Lorna vanished whenever she saw him coming, while Ian Murray had never revised his original opinion of him.

The glen men still more or less tolerated him, since he spent freely, but there was a tension about him, a watchfulness in his eyes, which they could never quite ignore, and they sensed his contempt for them beneath the surface cordiality. 'Yon's a coarse bugger,' Ewart Rhynie, the Dalquhat grieve, commented one day when Jon had taken himself off abruptly without a word to anyone. It was felt this summed him up pretty well.

He didn't mind being alone. It slowed consumption for one thing. He'd switched to lager for the same reason. His surroundings were comfortable enough, food was available, and there was always the hope that Philippa might appear.

On a morning when he'd been sitting there for an hour or so, scanning yesterday's paper in the empty room, he supposed when he heard the swing door open with its now familiar sigh that someone was coming to hint that he paid rent for his bar stool. But it was Philippa, smiling a greeting, putting down the plate she was carrying and pouring herself a glass of orange juice.

'Here, let me get that,' Jon said quickly.

'No, really, thanks, Ian gives us a lunch-time drink. But can I get anything for you while I'm here?'

'You could, thanks.' As always, he watched her neat movements with pleasure. She had a way of whipping through what she was doing, without appearing to hurry, which the others could never match. And with equal speed going on her way – she'd almost caught him out again.

'You're not leaving me on my own, are you?' Intended as easy and friendly, the words sounded crass, and Jon mentally kicked himself. But he'd had to stop her. He knew by now that her appearances here were rare. Apart from collecting residents' bar bills, she had no reason to come in. If someone else had already picked them up she could arrive and leave again without being glimpsed.

She hesitated. 'I usually take my lunch to the office and go on working,' she said.

And if she'd known that the major was in here on his own, she'd have taken orange juice from the kitchen fridge and gone round the other way.

'You must be entitled to a lunch break,' Jon objected.

Wrong again, he realised, as the arched eyebrows went up.

'Entitled? It's not like that. I come in, do what work there is, and when it's finished I go. Simple.'

'Well, stay and have lunch here today. I'd be glad if you would,' Jon urged, though this time, having learnt his lesson, his voice was as direct as hers.

He caught her quick look, and knew she hadn't missed the altered tone.

'All right.' She was up on a bar stool before he had time to pull it out for her. 'Like some of this?' She pushed the plate of pâté and oatcakes towards him.

'That's your lunch. I'll get something later.' Not gracious, but with her he had a sense of being continually one step behind, and he wasn't used to it.

'Why don't we share this and I can fetch more if we want it?' Philippa suggested.

God, what am I arguing about, Jon asked himself, relaxing. 'So this is your job, secretary here? Part-time secretary?'

'One of my jobs. I do all kinds of things, cooking for dinner parties, filling freezers, house-minding, baby-sitting, dog-sitting.'

'And you enjoy it.'

A statement not a question. Rarely had Jon met anyone who gave such an impression of enjoying life, or of a natural contentment with life. Close to her like this, her attention for once solely his, it seemed that he could almost feel the glow of that contentment. He found himself smiling.

Offering him the last oatcake, Philippa caught the smile. How it changed him. As a rule, she found him slightly menacing, and felt too conscious of those unreadable eyes on her whenever she appeared. There was a vigilance about him, an observant response to what was going on around him, which was far from restful. She had stayed now since it would have seemed rude to leave him on his own. Unkind even, because for a second she had seen him as oddly vulnerable, if such a word could be applied to such a man.

But the smile made her forget the latent threat she associated with him. It made him look younger; early forties perhaps? He seemed larger than ever close to like this, but she observed with interest that his hands, brown like his face with the deep tan of a person who has spent time in a hot country, were long-fingered and well-shaped, craftsman's hands.

Jon, determined to spin out the moment as long as he could, asked more about her jobs, and Philippa, finding him easier to be with than she'd expected, talked readily about eccentric households and glen dramas.

Though his face gave nothing away, Jon's eyes took in with pleasure the healthy skin, the smooth fall of hair, the amused light in the green-brown eyes. No beauty, he summed up, face too thin – so why did he feel this intense satisfaction just to be near her, to take in every inch of her? Even the voice which he tried to despise charmed him, soft and warm. Why did he feel that the only thing that mattered was to keep her here beside him for every second that he could? Why did he feel, for the first time for God knew how long, not alone?

Feeding her questions, tucking away any piece of hard information that could be extracted, he found himself once or twice laughing outright, and it struck him that he'd almost forgotten about laughter too.

When the door opened and Ross Nicholson appeared, murderous rage filled Jon. Philippa, with a small rueful smile, was already slipping off her stool. After serving Ross she was gone, and Jon felt as if he'd stepped off a step he hadn't known was there.

He found it disproportionately hard to deal with. He felt as though every need and demand came before his own, not only for Philippa, but for everyone else. He knew it was a situation he'd created for himself but it seemed to be taking him over. He didn't guess, as he sat morose and forbidding in the corner now recognised as his, that in the office across the corridor Philippa was finding it surprisingly hard to concentrate on work.

An hour or so later Jon heard the Mini leave. She wouldn't give him a thought as she headed down the glen and home. Why should she? And where was home? He hadn't taken his chance to ask her any of the things that mattered.

During the next few days he did his best to put in perspective the brief time they'd spent together. It had had no particular significance. In agreeing to have lunch with him Philippa had merely been polite, as she was to everyone. So why did his mind go exhaustively over everything she'd said; why did the image of her persist, however hard he tried to banish it? She wasn't even his type, more like some up-market stick insect – but no whipping up of cynicism could alter the feeling that something good had come into his life, something good was in store for him.

A woman like that? Get real, he mocked himself. For someone like Philippa he wouldn't even exist.

The days ran into each other indistinguishably as he stuck to the pattern he'd established with dogged obstinacy, knowing he could cope with it, not sure he could cope with anything else. Increasingly, he gave off a warning of trouble about to erupt, and the Cluny regulars tended more and more to keep to their own affairs, leaving him hunched, taciturn and apart.

Only Philippa treated him with unchanged friendliness. Her warmth could penetrate his darkest moods, and catching sight of her, no matter how briefly, seizing a moment's talk with her, became the goal of his featureless days. He might recognise the futility of this obsession, but nothing could alter his gut reaction at the sight of her, or the delight which filled him.

Philippa's own feelings were mixed. Jon was an enigmatic figure, whose presence in the glen and lack of occupation and purpose were puzzling. He was also a man impossible to ignore, both for his looks and his brooding personality. But her mind would go back to the glimpse she'd been given of the different man who emerged when his guard was down. What had brought him to this state and this situation? What demons rode him?

All the same, she had no intention of trying to find out, rather the opposite, and on a morning when the hotel was short-handed, and she took a crate of tonic into the bar to find that Jon had arrived while she was in the cellar, she wished she'd been less conscientious. No one else was there, since today just about every male in the glen had gathered for an assault on the Alltmore rabbits – an informal day's sport in which Jon would have been invited to take part had he been more popular.

He came to take the crate from her. 'Here, Murray shouldn't let you do that. It's not your job.'

Pity he always needed to blame someone, Philippa thought, smiling her thanks. 'As it's tonic water and you'll probably drink most of it I accept.'

'I didn't notice your car outside.' It had been a wonderful surprise to see her coming in.

'I brought the bread order up with me, so I parked at the back door.'

'Ah. Want these on the shelf?'

Watching as he brought forward old stock and filled up

with new, rapid and deft, Philippa wondered again what a man like him was doing here.

'Thanks, that was kind.' She slid the crate under the bar and picked up one of empties.

'Hang on,' Jon said quickly. 'You don't have to rush off, do you? How about a drink?'

'Yes, of course.'

'For you, I meant.'

'Thanks, but it's a bit early. Anyway, I ought to get on.'

'I thought you worked at your own pace?'

Did he have any idea how combative he sounded?

'There's a lot to do today.' And I don't have to explain myself to you either.

'How about lunch-time? Surely you could take ten minutes then?'

Philippa glanced at her watch. Thinking up some excuse, Jon thought with quick anger.

'All right,' she said. 'Half twelve?'

He nodded, hardly able to believe his good fortune.

As the morning crawled by he was amazed by the tension building in him. Someone was sure to appear; something would foul things up. Then, even before the time agreed, Philippa was at the door, asking, 'What are you going to have? I'm making myself a toasted sandwich.'

'That'd be fine.'

'Cheese, tomato, ham . . . ?'

'Anything.'

As Philippa vanished Jon felt a novel peace spread through him. She was his. For a brief, finite period she was his. He went behind the bar and poured two glasses of house wine, one white, one red, and took them across to the window table.

'Nice. Thanks,' Philippa said when he offered her her choice. No mention of staff drinks today, Jon was glad to find.

He could feel elation rising simply to be near her. He caught a faintly herbal scent from her hair as she leaned forward, and noted that her lashes, lowered as she concentrated on separating the sandwiches which were glued together with melted cheese, were long and thick.

'Ow, hot. Here, this one's unstuck.' She put it on his plate and he found the gesture intimate and pleasing. You total idiot, he told himself, quite in vain.

He was unaware that Philippa's outward ease, as she lured him onto the safe standby topic of the Army, was merely the product of the kind of manners he usually scorned, for in the sombre mood he'd fallen into lately she found him about as soothing to be with as a live grenade. Enjoying himself, his normal perceptiveness dulled by pleasure in a level of communication he'd never shared with a woman before, Jon didn't notice how at home she was with the references and terminology.

He even found himself, as his ease with her grew, attempting to put into words not only things he'd done but how he'd felt, telling her, when he described the claustrophobic conditions of a tour in Northern Ireland, what it did to you to feel yourself perpetually surrounded by hatred, to breathe it in with the air around you. How have I got into this, he wondered, realising what he was doing. It's history, stuff everybody knows. Lighten up, this hadn't been the plan. But the assurance of real interest, and of being understood, was too beguiling, and Philippa led him on with no trouble to talk about free-fall parachuting, sub-aqua at Bovisand, a joint-services expedition to Borneo, winter survival in Lapland.

He broke off to go and fetch the rest of the white wine she'd preferred, but she would only let him fill her glass once more.

'I'm sorry, I really do have to go.'

'You're not going anywhere, relax.' He couldn't bear it to end.

'Sorry, Major.' She was already on her feet.

'Jon, for God's sake.'

'Jon.' That smile. 'I'd love to stay and talk but there's a pile of mail waiting. Thanks for the wine.'

'We'll do this again,' he said, surprised at how reluctant he felt to let her go. Physically reluctant.

'That would be lovely.'

Too smooth, too cool, he thought, as the door swung behind her. Empty social response. Going over their conversation, he realised that yet again he'd learned nothing about her. Had she, in the nicest possible way, kept him exactly where she wanted him? He swore mildly to have been so sweetly manipulated, but couldn't help grinning. Do him good for once.

It was through Sharon and Lorna that he discovered more. They were cleaning shelves one morning and, since Jon moved to the window table to get away from the rattling and chatter, they soon forgot him and began talking as if they were on their own.

'. . . when he said Mrs Howard I didn't realise at first he meant Philippa. I checked the guest list. He must have thought I was potty . . .'

Jon's head came up.

'Mrs Howard?' Lorna repeated. 'I'd never heard her other name either. Where's her husband then?'

'Somewhere abroad. In the Army. No, the Raff.'

'Doesn't he come home on leave?'

'He hasn't since I've been here.'

'Perhaps they're divorced.'

'No one seems sure. You know what Philippa's like, never lets on about anything.'

Jon found he was crushing the newspaper and relaxed his hands.

'Seems funny, someone like her on her own.'

'D'you think she's attractive then?'

'In a way. A bit skinny though, and she never bothers much about clothes, does she?'

'Not about fashion, but she's quite stylish.'

'Um. Are these bowls meant to be here?'

'We're supposed to put crisps in them, only then you have to wash them up afterwards.'

'Why don't we hide them at the back? Come on, that'll do. Shona said we weren't to be long.'

In the silence Jon sat very still. Mrs Howard. A husband in the Air Force. Divorced or not divorced? He had to know. Useless to tell himself that the Philippas of this world were not for him. Some instinct, which he didn't dare to examine too closely, told him that without Philippa somewhere within reach, without that one source of hope and promise, he wouldn't survive.

Within the hour he learned more. Two or three locals had come in and presently one of them, glancing at the clock, exclaimed, 'Here, that's never the time. I said I'd be at Dalquhat by the back of twelve.'

'You're away to Dalquhat?' someone else asked. 'You can save me a journey then. I've some rabbit netting in the van for Philippa but it seems she's no' coming in the day.'

'Och, I'll drop that off at Achallie, no bother. It'd no' be very handy getting it in the Mini anyway.'

'Not that Philippa would worry.'

Laughing, they went out.

Achallie. Jon reviewed the map. Dalquhat he placed at once, a turreted house high on the road which looped down to Muirend on the other side of the river. He recalled one or two cottages lower down. A blue Mini might be parked outside one of them.

He had another drink, chatted, even made himself have lunch. But he knew what he was going to do.

The Dalquhat road crossed the river by a hump-backed bridge and climbed away. Where it levelled out the first cottage stood, dwarfed by two big larches. No house name, no car outside, but propped trustfully against a weathered shed was a roll of wire netting.

Jon didn't stop, but in the couple of seconds as he passed he absorbed a comprehensive image. A stone cottage, usual door in the middle, window either side, dormer windows above, but with a single-storey addition to the right. He had an impression of a tiny front garden, winter drab, of white paintwork, a stretch of gravel between house and shed, and behind it a lawn sloping up to a fenced vegetable plot. The whole had an unfussy but cared-for air, and he found himself wanting passionately to know this place, be accepted by it.

Aware that it was ridiculous, as he drove on he was filled with optimism, as though something had actually been achieved, and the paralysis which had had him in its grip had already loosened its dangerous hold.

4

Buoyed up by this new optimism, Jon decided, when he heard the Mini come to a swirling halt below the window the next day, that if Philippa didn't appear he'd go and find her in that office of hers. He'd had enough of snatched exchanges and interruptions.

As he sat savouring his anticipation, two big off-road vehicles pulled up outside, and a cheerful group streamed in, obviously very much at home.

'Hi, Ian about?'

'Pippa must be. That's her wreck outside.'

'So this is where you hide out in winter, Ross.'

'What are we having? I'm starving.'

'Drink first, anyway.'

'Shall we ask Ian if he'll do mulled wine?'

'Lovely fire.'

'Let's pull a couple of tables together.'

Jon, glowering at the invasion, and resenting that casual 'Pippa', was put out to find that the new arrivals, in particular a young man whose blond good looks made Jon mutter into his lager, were being welcomed by everyone. Ian Murray hurried in, unusually affable, then Philippa was there, being hugged and kissed on all sides.

Jon would have done better to have left at once, but couldn't bear to relinquish his plan of getting Philippa to himself at some point. His face became grimmer as she was persuaded to join the newcomers for lunch, and everything he heard, as he sat on, increased his sense of isolation and exclusion.

'. . . Aspen was marvellous. Incredible facilities.'

'Didn't Clarinda say it was too commercial?'

Clarinda, for Christ's sake.

'Have you heard how Nita is, Joanna?'

'Oh, yes, when's the baby due?'

'Haven't you heard? It's to be twins. Elaine went into orbit, kept phoning Grannie and saying she'd never live down the disgrace, till Grannie pointed out that having twins doesn't actually make Nita twice as wicked or immoral or whatever Elaine thinks she is . . .'

'I can hear Grannie saying that.'

Jon scowled at the laughter.

'Are they from round here?' he asked Ross Nicholson, who had left the new arrivals to themselves now that he had a few drams safely stacked up.

'The one by the fire is a Munro from Allt Farr, away at the top of the glen. Well, her married name's Drummond, though she lost her husband a while back. The rest are up for the skiing, staying in the Allt Farr cottages mostly. The fair lad, Alastair, runs the pony-trekking here in the summer. He's at the ski instructing now, but he'll be back at Easter.'

Jon didn't like the sound of that. Nor did he like seeing Philippa at the centre of this cheerful crowd.

Forget it, he told himself. You've always known she was out of your league. But that didn't help when, urged by Ian to forget work for today, she left with the rest – even though she gave Jon a smile all for himself among the general goodbyes.

She had been conscious of him the whole time, tempted to draw him in, but afraid that he would find an invitation to join a noisy crowd of strangers both surprising and unwelcome. She barely knew him; they weren't on those terms. Yet his smouldering presence on the fringe of the scene was unsettling, and she was rather relieved to go off with the rest when lunch was over.

Torpor settled in their wake.

'Joanna's looking better these days.'

'Aye, getting over things a bit now.'

'Alastair's a good lad.'

'He is, right enough.'

'A great hand with the ponies.'

There they stuck.

Jon, bored as he was with them, nevertheless couldn't face the alternative of the empty cottage. Eaten by jealousy of the confident crowd who had swept Philippa away as of right, he was still there when the evening drinkers began to drift in, Moira among them.

He came awake reluctantly, somewhere before dawn, cramped and frozen. Where the hell was he? In the car, yes, but where? His head throbbed in a leaden rhythm as, wincing, he tried to unlock his stiff limbs. He was in the lane outside the row of cottages where Moira lived.

Last night's events began to come back – the bash that had developed at the hotel and later, though he had no recollection of driving anywhere, finding himself in Moira's crammed little living-room, chilly as the output from the storage heater sank to nothing. He remembered a gaudy throw slipping down the dingy moquette of the sofa, the crackling acrylic of Moira's sweater, the messy spikes of her hair, her unsubtle scent, and how slack and cushiony her body had after all felt.

Then, thankfully, he remembered pushing her away and escaping to a freezing bog, its black cistern and pink glossed walls streaked with condensation – and not going back. He checked there, wanting to be certain. But yes, he had come out with relief into the stark cold of the night. Thank God he hadn't tried to drive.

He was barely fit to drive now, but this was Kirkton, the road home was the glen road; he could make it. His thoughts as he drove weren't pleasant. He had let his anger at seeing Philippa surrounded by her friends, ignoring him, tempt him into drinking so much that he'd actually gone off with someone like Moira. A familiar disgust filled him. There could be something so sluttish about women, their bedrooms and bathrooms, their squalid dressing-tables, which offended his soldier's sense of order. Then he thought of the state of his own cottage. It was more than time to sort out the way he was living.

Walking groggily into his kitchen, the first thing he saw was the corpse of a mouse in the trap under the sink. He disposed of it, then turned on the tap. The water was barely lukewarm. He banged the immersion switch on, the small setback almost enough to rock his good intentions. Who was there to see or care if the place was a tip? Who would come visiting here, up the snowy track? But his disgust at what he'd done had been real. Head pounding, he set about some basic tidying while the tank heated, and presently, clean and somewhat restored, fell thankfully into bed and let his hangover take over.

Outside, snow began to fall, and as the day passed a bitter wind came in from the east, strengthening during the night, whining over the small stone dwelling on the hill with its solitary unconscious occupant, shaping a new landscape as it went.

After sleeping the clock round Jon woke to find the storm had died. Standing at the window, shading his eyes against the brilliant light bouncing off the drift which came clear to the sill, in spite of everything he felt his spirits rise. Getting out of here today was going to be a nice little exercise.

Almost brisk, he shaved, made coffee and toast, changed

the bed and sorted out a bag of laundry to take to Muirend – should he ever be able to get there. Opening the door to fetch kindling, he found a waist-high drift against it. The sun glowed gold through its delicate crest as it held its shape for a moment, then it curved silently over and collapsed at his feet.

He laughed, because it took him by surprise and because it was beautiful. Looking down the glen, where today the sun brought out vivid contrasts of tawny larch and green conifers, he wondered how Philippa had fared in the storm. The thought of her made him groan. How could he have let jealous anger push him into drinking like that – and ending up at Moira's, for Christ's sake? Why had he let it get to him so badly? But, he reminded himself, nothing had happened, so nothing had changed. He would see Philippa again; they would talk. Though it would be easier to achieve if she had some recognisable timetable.

Timetable? You don't even know what day of the week it is.

It took him a couple of hours to clear snow, bring in logs and get down to the road on foot. Sun and exercise and the crisp air combined to produce an almost forgotten euphoria. The snowplough had been up from Muirend, and Jon walked at a swinging pace on the scraped white surface speckled with grit. Between road and river a tractor traced a circle, followed by a line of sheep. On the road nothing moved.

Cross-country would be good in this terrain. Skiing. Jon's thoughts went again to the strangers who'd come swanning into the Cluny, and so to Philippa. As if his thoughts were ever far from her. Agreeable fantasies shaped themselves – sunlit snowfields, coming down in the dusk to that cottage of hers, a big fire, a couple of bottles of plonk . . . But he didn't pursue the images to their obvious conclusion, memories of Moira returning. He must have been out of his mind.

He didn't stop when he reached the village. He would pick up supplies on the way down. Heading for the hotel he saw that, though the council plough had turned at the last house, beyond it a smaller blade had been at work. The Subaru would have had no trouble. Then he heard a car behind him and stepped hastily onto the banked snow so that it wouldn't be forced to slow down. But even as he turned he knew it was the Mini. He was impressed that it had got this far. Would it make the hill? Philippa being Philippa, however, she couldn't drive past.

Shaking his head at her folly, elated at the mere sight of her, Jon went round to her window.

She was looking pretty happy herself, her face glowing, hair all over the place, as if she too had been engaged in some strenuous exercise.

'Isn't this glorious?' she greeted him, beaming.

Jon definitely thought it was. 'What are you proposing to do now?' he enquired politely, indicating with a nod the snowy slope ahead.

'Um.' Philippa studied it dubiously, then looked over her shoulder. 'I'll back a bit.'

'Good idea.'

She laughed. 'Will I make it to the hotel?'

'Probably not, but you're clearly going to try.'

'I've got front-wheel drive.'

'Really.'

'Oh, well, I'm going to have a bash.' She felt carefree, reckless, startled by the effect his teasing grin had on her. He was without question the best-looking man she'd ever seen. 'I don't suppose you're brave enough to risk a lift?'

Jon straightened up and went round to the passenger door. The day was improving by the second.

'You wouldn't like to drive by any chance?' Philippa asked as an afterthought, as he fitted his bulk in beside her with some token muttering. Goodness, he was big. For a second she found it almost alarming to have him so close. He seemed to fill the car.

'I wouldn't dream of it,' he assured her. This was going to be interesting.

'Fine.' She rammed into reverse and rocketed backwards.

Jon took a grip of the dashboard. 'Get your tin hat on, Paulett.'

'Don't make me laugh or we'll never get anywhere.'

'There might be something to be said for that.' Jon let his body give an exaggerated jolt as she pulled up then surged forward again.

Philippa giggled, but he saw from the way she settled in her seat that she intended to give this her best shot. He liked that. The Mini flew the course like a willing pony, as Philippa took the hill with a confidence she might not have felt without such an impressive supply of pushing and digging muscle on hand. In spite of snow blown in on a couple of corners she kept going, swinging round the tail of the drifts regardless of anything which might be coming down, faltering only as she turned into the hotel drive and felt the back end go wide.

Jon reached a quick hand to the wheel. 'Keep going, don't ease up. Give it some wellie, you'll make it.' She kept her foot down and the Mini straightened out and clawed its way up the final rise to the empty carpark.

'We made it!' She turned to Jon exuberantly. 'I never believed we would. I was sure we were going to bottom on that second corner.'

For a heady moment Jon thought she was going to hug him. 'Well, I did think of baling out once or twice.' He failed to sound repressive.

'Good job nothing was coming.'

'Oh, you took that into account?'

'Well, not at the time. And I'd definitely have gone into that gatepost if you hadn't grabbed the wheel.'

Intoxicated by success, the sparkling day and tonic air, but most of all by Jon's shedding of his usual dour reserve, she felt wildly, absurdly happy.

'What about this box? Is it going in?'

She dragged her mind back to business. 'Oh, yes please. I'd forgotten all about it.'

Ian Murray appeared at the door. 'And what do you think you're doing, Philippa?' he demanded, shaking his head. 'Nothing in the glen's moving today.'

'Road's fine,' she said airily.

'Oh, aye.' Ian reached to take the box from Jon.

'No, you're all right.' Jon held on to it. He'd stick with the workers and see where that led.

Ian grunted, holding back the door. He hadn't much time for the major, but since he'd arrived with Philippa Ian supposed he'd have to make the best of it. So Jon, to his satisfaction, presently found himself at the kitchen table with the Murrays, Sharon, Lorna and Philippa, drinking coffee and eating warm baps and heather honey in an agreeable atmosphere of normality suspended.

'You got out all right then,' Ian was saying to Philippa.

'Yes, Ewart came by early with the tractor and blade. Once I'd dug as far as the road I just rolled down in his tracks. Not sure how I'll get back though.' A year ago it would have worried her. 'Perhaps the plough will have gone round by the time I go home.'

'I don't think you should stay too long,' Shona put in anxiously. 'The forecast was for more snow.'

'More to come, that's certain,' Ian agreed.

'I thought I could take some of the work home with me,' Philippa said.

'Ach, you're daft,' he told her kindly. 'There's nothing that can't wait.'

'And that,' Philippa reminded him, unmoved, 'is why you have a secretary.'

'Well, I wouldn't argue with that. Let's pack up what you need, then, and you can be on your way.'

'I'll do anything urgent while I'm here.'

Ian gave up. 'You'll suit yourself, I can see.'

'Jon, want a lift when I go down?' Philippa asked as they stood up. 'Or was once enough?'

Jon is it, Ian noted dourly.

'I think I could stand it,' Jon said. And then what? A day like this could bring anything.

The sun had vanished by the time they left, and the sky was grey and lowering, but Jon was too mellow after a couple of lagers by the bar fire, with the prospect of leaving with Philippa ahead, to notice or care.

In the shop they ran into Ewart Rhynie.

'That you away home, Philippa?' he asked. 'I'd best come behind you in the tractor and make sure you get up. Yon brae's no joke the day.'

'Oh, Ewart, would you?' Philippa said gratefully. 'I'd been wondering if I'd make it.'

'Don't leave it too long,' he warned. 'That sky's full of snow.'

'I'll drop you off at the end of your track,' Philippa said to Jon, but Ewart cut in.

'You come wi' me. I can put you all the way up.'

It was a kind offer but, jouncing in the tractor cab, trying to keep his mind off what might have been, Jon was glad that conversation was impossible. He would have been surprised to know that Philippa wasn't grateful either. She was fairly certain that, whatever good sense dictated, she and Jon would not have parted at the Baldarroch track. It would have been good to meet him on new ground. He'd been a different man this morning; for the first time she'd felt truly at ease with him.

For two days the returning storm clamped down on the glen. The plough from Muirend got no further than the Dalquhat turn, and apart from tractors little moved. Jon and Philippa were cut off in their separate cottages.

Jon soon exhausted possible jobs and the books he'd bought in Muirend, making do with a deteriorating television picture until it vanished for good on the second day. Then he idled the hours away thinking about Philippa. He'd sat out plenty of time in worse places, and with less pleasurable thoughts to occupy his mind.

Philippa cleared paths, brought in coal and logs, split kindling, polished off the hotel work, took oranges out of the freezer to make marmalade, caught up on letters and read *Framley Parsonage* in luxurious chunks.

She also thought a good deal about Jon. What was he doing in Glen Maraich? She had her doubts about the 'major' bit, she didn't like the way he drank, and she knew he could be both arrogant and truculent, but she couldn't pretend that she wasn't enormously attracted to him, in a way quite new to her.

In her relationships to date, which amounted to a couple of brief but enjoyable affairs and an equally brief but less enjoyable marriage, Philippa had 'loved' chiefly in response to finding herself loved. She had needed that, and needed to trust in it. She had also 'loved' where, whether she was aware of it or not, she had been sure that everything would unfold according to the rules she understood. One of those rules had been that the man made the moves. Now she found herself acutely aware of the physical impact of a man she hardly knew, a stranger who had shown little more than a casual interest in her, a stranger from a world very different from her own.

She didn't learn that Jon had spent the night with Moira until the storm was over, and she was able to get to her various jobs again.

Back in the hotel office, after the topic had been aired by willing tongues at coffee break, she leaned against the door, struggling to get her feelings under control, furious with herself for minding so much. How she regretted the light-hearted episode of tackling the snowy hill in the Mini, afraid she had shown too openly her pleasure to be with Jon.

And, though common sense told her Moira might be the sort of woman he would go for, and that she should look on the whole thing as a timely warning and put it out of her mind, she was shaken by jealousy of a kind she had never imagined herself capable of feeling.

5

It was unfortunate that their next meeting should be a confrontation, though on a very different matter.

Rumour had it that Jon had bounced a cheque at the village shop – a fact he hadn't imagined would be so swiftly or so widely known – and Ian Murray, who had been making his own calculations as to what the major spent, had said no more cheques were to be accepted from him.

Jon wasn't too concerned about funds running low. He had his Army pension, his retainer would be paid in soon. He never worried about a temporary shortfall. Cash was a commodity, always available somewhere.

As soon as he was able to get out from Keeper's Cottage, courtesy the Baldarroch snowplough, he took the precaution of stocking up. Arriving at the hotel with his wallet empty after a trip to Muirend, to find that the Murrays were away at the cash-and-carry, he didn't imagine he'd have much trouble working his charm on Sharon or Lorna. Both, however, though Lorna slipped him a drink on the house, and Sharon was silly enough to lend him a fiver, stuck to the rules, leaving him to his own devices as soon as they could. With the fiver already in the till and the bar empty, since most people were busy repairing the ravages of the storm, he was glad to hear the Mini arrive. Philippa had not only been very friendly at their last meeting, but she had access to the cash.

Jon gave her time to settle in, then went in search of her.

The peremptory knock made Philippa jump. If there had been a dozen cars parked outside, she would have known who it was. She was thrown into a flurry, remembering what good company Jon had been the day she'd given him a lift, then swept again by the revulsion she'd felt when she'd heard he'd slept with Moira. She had never wanted to see him again, ashamed of the feelings he aroused in her, yet a spontaneous pleasure she could do nothing about filled her to see him coming in with his prowling stride.

A pleasure which was swiftly extinguished. From his too-ready smile, and the hearty tone as he said, 'Ah, Philippa, the very person I wanted to see,' she saw that he was in 'major' mode, and she hated that. She also saw that the smile wasn't matched by the wariness in his eyes.

'Jon, how are you?' That was all right, cool, bland, giving no hint of the turmoil going on inside her.

'You got home safely the other day?' In spite of his impatience to get hold of funds, Jon congratulated himself on having penetrated this sanctum at last, noting that the office was also a sitting-room, with a couple of chintzy armchairs in front of a fire at the far end.

'Yes, thanks. You survived at Keeper's Cottage?'

'Survive's about the word.' But Jon's mind was so clearly on his next move that Philippa braced herself for what was coming. 'I gather I've missed Ian,' Jon went on breezily, cheque book in hand, patting his pocket for a pen then reaching for one from the desk.

So it was to be the offhand approach, hustling her into doing what he wanted, as females always did. Her cheeks beginning to burn, Philippa waited quietly.

'Ian and I have a little arrangement. He cashes the odd cheque for me to save me going down to the bank. Now, let's see, the date is . . . ?'

Laying the cheque book across the corner of the desk and holding the stubs back with a broad thumb, he glanced around, very much at ease, for a calendar.

Not like him to make a mistake like that, Philippa thought. It shouldn't be too hard to work out that I'd know about any such arrangement – and about any new ruling on it that Ian had made.

'I'm afraid I can't help you,' she said quietly.

'Oh, I'm sure Ian gives you that much authority.' Deliberately misunderstanding her, his voice smooth, Jon scribbled in the hotel name.

Philippa watched him. All right, if he wants to waste a cheque.

'What can you manage? A hundred? Fifty?'

'I'm sorry, I can't cash that.'

'Are you telling me you don't have enough in the safe? How about the bar till?'

'There's plenty of money in the safe.' Philippa spoke evenly, her tone as courteous as ever, but she met his eyes with resolution; and saw them harden.

'So? You're saying Ian doesn't trust you to—?'

'Ian trusts me. I frequently cash cheques for people. I'm not going to cash that.'

She faced him calmly, though she didn't feel calm. He was very large, and more than daunting in this mood.

'Why not?' His face had altered, the jaw muscles ridged, cheekbones more pronounced, the compelling grey eyes openly hostile, urbane role-play forgotten.

Had he made it a request, to someone with whom he was on ordinary friendly terms, Philippa would have explained that she was following instructions. But she didn't respond well to being browbeaten. She said coolly, 'Because I assume it will bounce.'

For a tense moment, as he menaced her with his height

and size, she thought he was going to lose his temper, and the prospect was alarming.

'What the hell are you talking about?'

But Philippa stood her ground, her eyes meeting his angry stare with apparent equanimity, adding nothing, explaining nothing, and Jon had enough sense to realise that he was going to get nowhere.

'That's bloody ridiculous,' he blustered, ramming his cheque book (and Philippa's pen) into the pocket of his Barbour. 'Do you people want the business or not? I shouldn't think Murray will be too happy when he hears about this.'

It was the merest face-saving, and Philippa didn't trouble to reply, waiting, hip pressed against the desk to steady herself, until she heard the slam of the terrace door and was sure that he'd gone.

'Um,' she said aloud, her voice wavery. 'I don't think the major was too impressed with that.' Trembling, she dropped into one of the shabby armchairs, feeling as though she'd fought a war not a battle, so powerful had been the antagonism Jon had generated in the small space. 'I don't expect I'll be hearing from him again.'

On a personal level, she meant. No need to worry any more about being so disturbingly attracted to him. The problem had solved itself.

Jon, on his way back to Muirend to see if he could do better there, knew he was angrier about having tangled with Philippa than about failing to acquire some spending money, a fact which would have surprised her. She would have been even more surprised to know how often his thoughts returned, with reluctant and even amused admiration, to the way she had so calmly out-faced him.

'Andrew, I've just had the oddest conversation with Philippa.'

As Penny Forsyth came frowning into the study at Alltmore

her husband turned from his computer with a mixture of relief and mild irritation at the interruption.

'Why, what's wrong with her?'

'That's just what I don't understand. When I phoned last night to tell her about the job in the Gallowhill estate office she couldn't have been more keen. She was going to get in touch right away, and I know they'd have jumped at the chance of getting her.'

'And?' This had been last night's conversation, and momentarily glad as Andrew had been to be distracted from his accounts, they still had to be dealt with.

'Well, she hasn't done anything about it. It's so unlike her. She always does what she says she'll do. And she'd seemed really keen. Hours more regular, better pay, pleasant surroundings, not too far to drive, and she knows Heggarty the factor quite well, and liked the idea of working with him. Apart from all that, it would be a much more *suitable* job.'

This final consideration, Andrew knew, represented Penny's view rather than Philippa's. Suitable. A word which had mattered more, surely, in their parents' era than it did now. But Penny, though not all that many years older than Philippa, increasingly seemed to belong to a different generation, and to her the thought of – how would she phrase it? – one of their own circle serving the odd drink in a bar or carrying in luggage for hotel guests was both puzzling and hard to accept.

Feeling disloyal, Andrew suppressed the brief spurt of impatience. Penny, he knew, only wanted to see Philippa happy and secure again, the disasters of the past safely behind her, and preferably living in circumstances as close as possible to those in which she had been brought up. Wanted in short to see her married, to someone like, say, Alec Blaikie, someone they all knew and liked, someone – again that word – suitable.

'So what's gone wrong?'

'That's what I can't work out.' Penny sounded genuinely

worried. 'It can't be the hours because it would still be part-time, so she could carry on doing her different jobs for people. We'd mind if she wasn't available, anyway, none of us would want that. But she waffled on about how good the Murrays have been to her and how she doesn't want to let them down, then she said she rather liked the variety in a hotel and that working in an estate office might be a bit samey. And staid. I don't know what she means by that.'

Andrew hid a smile. Staid, though she would have hated him for saying it, was increasingly a description which could apply to Penny herself, with her conventional country clothes, her unchanging hairstyle, her orderly life and well-run house, the pattern of each busy year repeating the last, with the annual rituals of school holidays, half-terms, weekends out, glen events, birthdays, shooting guests, fireworks party, not to mention the now traditional Alltmore barbecue on the first Sunday after the Twelfth.

'Well, it was just a thought,' Andrew said comfortingly. He sympathised with Penny's wish to help and protect Philippa. They all did. 'If she's happy with the way things are . . . You told her about the opening. That's all you can do.'

'I suppose so.' Penny clearly wasn't happy to abandon the plan. 'But don't you think she's been a bit strange lately? Behaving differently somehow?'

'In what way?' Andrew was itching to get back to his accounts by now.

'Oh, just in small ways. As though her mind's somewhere else. When we finally got together about the cooking for the boys' weekend she seemed to want to race through it rather.'

And Penny, Andrew knew, would have wanted to wallow in it, giving up hours to the indulgence of planning and discussion. No wonder, as she'd been pretending to complain, that half the school wanted to come when an Alltmore weekend was in prospect.

'I'm sure it will be perfect, as it always is.' Andrew, who had never, before or since his marriage, had to worry about a single domestic detail, could say this with absolute assurance. His eyes went back to the screen, and his brain locked onto the truly terrifying figure for this quarter's repairs and maintenance. Was there anything there he could reasonably capitalise?

Penny's mind continued to turn over her vague concern about Philippa, hardly noticing that Andrew's attention had been withdrawn. Why had Philippa appeared so ready, keen even, to abandon the hotel job yesterday, then come round full circle today? It wasn't like her; she was usually so clear about what she wanted, even though it must be said that some of her choices had baffled Penny in the past.

'Yon road's like glass this morning.'

'The gritter's never got this length yet, and it's supposed to be before the school bus.'

'That bend by the Cluny burn was where Jock went over last year, and he was in the hospital for weeks.'

'Someone'll be away up to help, surely?'

'Andy's away just now.'

'Did they send for the ambulance?'

'Philippa would be racing, likely, off to one of her jobs . . .'

Jon, shopping for a few basics, his retainer at last in the bank, paused with a loaf halfway to his basket.

'. . . there's nothing to that wee car of hers.'

'Turned it right over, by what I heard.'

Jon tossed the bread back onto the shelf, dumped his basket and pushed past the women without apology. They stared after him resentfully.

'Minded he's owing me, I shouldn't wonder,' Annie sniffed from behind her counter.

'He's owing at the garage too, Andy was saying.'

This topic was almost more rewarding than the drama of Philippa going off the road, though they would certainly have returned to the latter had they realised that Jon had headed up the glen, hastily reviewing the map from memory, pin-pointing the spot where the Cluny burn crossed the road a mile or so north of the village.

He didn't question why he was going, or what Philippa would think when he turned up. His mind was filled only with images of fragile spindle limbs, smooth skin and the shining hair into which his hands so often itched to slide.

Should he have made sure the ambulance was on its way? In spite of wondering this, he was unprepared for the lurch his stomach gave to see the garage Land Rover pulled to the side of the road, a van tilted precariously beside it and, at the foot of a steep drop, the blue roof of the Mini. At least, thank God, it was the right way up.

He tucked the Subaru in past the bend and walked back, his face expressionless. He noted the gouge where the Mini had gone down, the snow packed into its grille and plastered along windows and trim, the folded-back side mirror, the crumpled wing. God, it must have gone over after all. But the roof had held and no windows were broken. Relief as weakening as his previous fear flooded through him.

Andy, the mechanic from the garage, was down the bank surveying the angle at which the Mini had come to rest, giving its wheels the odd kick to aid his thoughts and shaking his head dubiously. With him were two other men, the van driver and a farm-worker whose tractor stood on the far side of the burn. Philippa was standing with her shoulder against the Mini, hands driven deep into her pockets, and even from this distance Jon could see that she was taut with held-down shock.

Philippa, catching a movement, glanced up and saw him on the lip of the bank. Against the blue sky he seemed to tower above them, a source of certain strength and competence. Relief filled her. She felt no surprise to see him there, just a thankful conviction that now everything would be all right.

Jon came leaping down to join them, his expert eye assessing angles and leverage. The men gave him half nods. Andy and the tractorman had run into him at the Cluny Arms and didn't much like what they'd seen. The van driver, whose sole concern was not to be blamed, for anything, ever, had never set eyes on him. Even so, without a word being said, all three accepted that Jon was now in charge.

'You OK?' he asked Philippa in a quick undertone.

She nodded, lips tight, not minding the way he minutely examined her face. The men, seeing that she had got out unharmed, had turned their attention to the more interesting question of getting the car out of its snowy bed. Their concern for her had taken the form of telling her how close she'd come to getting herself killed or, as a poor second, maimed for life.

Jon, however, read the signs – her compressed lips, her pallor, the elbows clamped to her sides, the fists jammed into her pockets – and he wanted more than anything in the world to wrap his arms round her and soothe away her shock and tension.

'Come on,' he said briskly. 'Not much you can do here. Forget the car. No damage that can't be dealt with.'

Andy found this approach far too prosaic. 'My, you were lucky to miss those rocks, Philippa. A couple of feet either way and it could have been nasty.'

'Anything you need to take?' Jon asked Philippa, ignoring him.

She focused her mind with a visible effort. 'My bag. Nothing else matters.'

Jon turned to the men. 'Ignition's off, I presume?'

They rushed into defence and recrimination.

'Wallie, I made sure you'd have thought of that.'

'Me? I didna' touch anything.'

'It wasn't my place to see to it.' The van driver only wanted out of here; he'd deliveries still to do.

'I switched it off,' Philippa said, and missed the satisfied gleam in Jon's eyes.

'How about exchanging names and addresses? Thought of that?' He didn't hide his contempt for the men.

'Oh here, we'll no' need to go that length, will we?' the van driver protested hurriedly. 'There's no' much harm done after all.'

'We don't know that yet,' Jon pointed out. 'And there's the cost of hauling the damn thing out. You obviously shoved her off the road.'

'No, no, it wasnae like that,' the driver cried, round-eyed with alarm at the way this was going. 'I was just coming to the bend, no' going fast at all, then what with the ice the wheels just went from under me.'

Philippa intervened. 'It wasn't anybody's fault. Really,' she insisted, seeing Jon's dissatisfied frown. 'And no one's hurt.'

'Well, if you say so.'

Philippa gave him a grateful smile. She knew he wanted to look after her, but the last thing she felt fit for at the moment was a lot of acrimonious hassle.

Jon could understand that. 'Right,' he said, 'no sense in hanging about then. Leave the keys with Andy. Any you're going to need on that ring?'

'God, yes, the house key. And the one for the hotel office. Thank goodness you reminded me.' Ashamed of not having thought of it herself, she fumbled to prise open the stiff ring, but found her fingers were trembling.

'Here.' Jon took it from her. Her hands were icy. 'This one? And this?' He detached the keys with ease, and Philippa looked up at him with a grimace of rueful apology for her uselessness.

Startled by what the brief touch of their hands and that small private look did to him, Jon turned hastily to Andy. 'We'll need a winch for this job.'

'Aye, right enough, I'll fetch the winch.'

'And we'd better get you back on the road before you start up,' Jon added to the van driver, who took offence at his tone, but said nothing because he wasn't looking forward to getting into his seat, let alone driving away.

With a final regretful comment on Philippa's lucky escape, since it meant he had no further excuse to stop work, Wallie got himself across the burn and back to his tractor. Philippa gave a last look at her forlorn little car and turned to follow the other men up the bank. To her dismay she found her legs wouldn't support her. As she took the first step up she promptly swayed down again.

Without turning, Jon, deep in technicalities with Andy, reached a hand to her, and she was grateful for the smooth output of strength as he drew her up behind him. She made a pretence of helping to push the van onto the road, but in truth couldn't have pushed open a door.

It seemed to be taken for granted by everyone, including herself she later realised, that she would go with Jon. She didn't enquire where, or even what had been decided about the Mini, for by this time shock was catching up on her.

Jon put her into the Subaru and she leaned back in her seat with weak relief as he went round to get in. Saying nothing, he started up the glen, noted where Andy would have room to turn the Land Rover, and drove on until a bend took them out of sight. Then he reversed into a field gateway and switched off.

In the silence he turned to look at Philippa. 'Not too good?' he asked, his voice gentle.

Philippa drew a deep breath. 'If anyone had said to me once more, "Another few inches and you'd not have walked away," or, "You were lucky that roof didn't cave in," I'd have—' She had tried for lightness, but finding her voice quavering ominously broke off.

Jon put his big warm hand on her clenched cold ones for a second, then took it away again, waiting quietly as she stared out of the window, her face turned away from him, biting her trembling lips.

'Hurt anywhere?' he asked after a moment.

'Everywhere!' she exclaimed between a wail and a laugh. 'Elbows, knees, this shoulder – all the corners, in fact. And I think I must have bumped my head on something.' She turned towards him with the simplicity of a child, pointing to the place with a slim finger.

Jon carefully lifted aside the heavy hair. It was not as he had imagined first touching it, he reflected wryly, locating a rising lump. Yet in its way the moment was just as intimate, just as significant. It occurred to him that never in his life before had he minded about someone else's pain like this, as though it were his pain. Fleetingly, a more cynical part of his brain wondered when Philippa would remember that their last encounter had been less than cordial.

'Skin's not broken,' he said, with some effort keeping his tone impersonal. 'I suppose I'd better not say you were lucky.'

Philippa laughed, more naturally this time, and he saw colour was returning to her cheeks and that her air of holding herself together was relaxing a little.

'You were wearing your seat belt?'

'I was.'

'And not going too fast?'

'Not after sailing out of the Dalquhat road-end without stopping,' she assured him, and laughed again as he groaned at the picture. It seemed entirely natural that he should question her like this, and that he had been the one to take her away from the scene.

'So where were you heading?' he asked. 'Can I take you wherever it was? Or would you rather go home?'

'Oh, not home,' she said quickly. The idea of being alone and unoccupied had no appeal. 'Come to think of it, where *was* I going?'

'Well, unless you were lost, not to the hotel.'

'I'm going there later. I know, I was on my way to Alltmore, collecting stuff for the silent auction.'

'You can still do that if you want to. I can take you.' More than anything Jon wanted to prolong the time together, with this new footing between them which she seemed to accept so readily. Unless of course it was the result of a bang on the head, he amended sardonically.

'I'm not sure I could face it,' Philippa admitted.

'What you need,' said Jon, making up his mind and starting the car, 'is a large brandy.'

She raised no objections. 'You're right, suddenly I do need something. But where were you heading for?' it at last occurred to her to ask.

He grinned. 'The usual place. Then I heard in the shop that you'd gone in the ditch.'

Philippa digested this in silence. Glancing at her covertly, guessing that the reference to the hotel had reminded her of their last meeting, Jon wondered how she'd react. He would mind a return to cool formality more than he could have believed possible.

'It was really good of you, Jon, to come and see what had happened.'

To his relief her voice was warm and grateful. Not ready for the inevitable fuss and explanations at the Cluny Arms, he drew in, Philippa making no protest, at the Kirkton Hotel, where in short order he had her tucked into a corner table, a brandy in front of her and his broad back turned with an uncompromising message to the room.

'This is all very conventional,' Philippa remarked. 'Even to the rescuer needing brandy too.'

'At least I'm not downing yours as well.' But yes, he had felt in need of a stiff drink; there had been one or two unfamiliar emotions to contend with this morning.

He let her talk, when she was ready, about the crash, knowing the compulsion to do so, making no comment as she described the sight of the van sliding towards her out of control, the jumble of thoughts in the instant before impact, the slow-motion, horrified realisation that the Mini was going to roll. He watched her minutely, his experienced eye gauging the clutch of her hands on her glass, the flush in her cheeks and the sparkle in her eyes produced by warmth and alcohol. Soon she was laughing about the van driver's alarm at the very idea of being held responsible, and the fact that Andy had been more concerned about the Mini's subframe than her own.

'I suppose I should go and do some work,' she said presently, not pretending to be enthusiastic about it.

'I'll run you up,' Jon offered, though he had seen through the window Andy backing out the breakdown truck, and had every intention of keeping an eye on him. As they went up the hill he debated raising the matter of the cheque. It would be good to get that small unpleasantness out of the way. And, with Philippa amenable and slightly off-balance as she was, this might be as good a moment to choose as any.

'By the way, you'll be glad to hear that I'm in funds again,' he remarked casually.

Philippa turned, frowning. 'That wasn't the point, though, was it? You tried to bulldoze me. And were angry because I said your cheque would bounce.'

Going arse over tip down a thirty-foot drop hadn't done

her wits much harm, Jon reflected, winded by this unhesitating letting fly with both barrels. But he grinned in spite of himself.

'So you're not going to forgive me, even after that socking great brandy?'

If he'd reverted to his patronising major's voice he would have found himself in trouble again, but Philippa had caught the grin. In fact, she was glad he'd referred to the incident. She hadn't liked it lying between them. Jon had used the word forgive, whether he'd been semi-joking or not, and she was ready to accept that as an acknowledgement of having been at fault, if not an actual apology.

She smiled at him, glad to have this much at least out of the way.

The matter of Moira was something else again, to do with Jon's life, not hers. There was no need for it to affect ordinary everyday contacts between them. She was ashamed to remember how, for the space of twenty-four hours, she had been determined to go after the Gallowhill job and abandon poor Ian without a qualm, for no better reason than to avoid running into Jon. Surely she could handle meeting him as a regular hotel customer.

So she told herself.

6

Jon had an agreeable time helping Andy to raise the Mini from its resting place. Sunshine and frosty air, a nice little technical problem to solve, some strenuous exertion for a change, with images of Philippa drifting through and behind everything else – can't be bad, he thought. What would she have done if he'd put his arms round her, standing here, as he had so much wanted to do? Her white face had looked nothing but skin and bone as she gazed at him, not risking words. How thin and cold her hand had been in his, and how weightless she had felt as he'd given her a pull up the slope.

If the car had to stay in the garage tonight, as it almost certainly would, he could offer to take her home. That neat little cottage of hers, so different in aspect from his own . . .

But gradually his thoughts became more sombre. He knew he could hardly hope she wouldn't have heard that he'd gone down to Moira's that night. His car must have been spotted outside. There were eyes everywhere in a place like this. No one was likely to believe he'd slept in it, either. His face darkened.

He hadn't considered the episode in relation to Philippa before, mainly because nothing had happened and he'd there-fore put it out of his mind, but also because it was so far removed from her life, or the way he thought of her. To him, chatting up someone like Moira was part of the faraway past – meaningless, affecting no one but himself. Even the two women with whom there had been anything approaching permanence, June, his wife, and Ulrike, the golden-limbed bimbo whose Helsinki flat he'd shared for the duration of a lucrative 'security' job, had meant little more.

When, for instance, had he ever had anything approaching a conversation with June? His mouth tightened as he remembered the slanging matches, the rows about money, about the child, about his longer and more frequent absences. Oh Christ, all of it, the dragging-down non-marriage he'd insanely hoped would fill at least some of the yawning gaps in his life.

And Ulrike – he didn't recall ever wasting much time chatting with Ulrike.

But Philippa was different. She had principles and opinions of her own, a quick intelligence and sense of humour which he found immensely satisfying. She had guts and energy, and something else he'd never before found in a woman, a quality which fascinated him perhaps more than anything else about her – not only the ability to communicate with ease and directness herself, but the ability to relate to whatever he talked about.

He'd come across this once or twice in the past, with men he'd trained with, fought with, survived with, brought close by shared interests, shared hardships, and ultimately by shared danger. What did it add up to? Not having to spell things out, laughing at the same things, being sure of where the other person was coming from? No, it was more than that. It was trusting someone else to know where you were coming from.

It was amazing to find it with a woman, especially one who belonged to a world so remote from his own. Not even his physical type, either. It made him realise how completely he had come to relegate women to a sexual and secondary role. When had he stopped hoping for anything more? Impossible to say. Years ago, anyway. He had always liked to get up and go, that much was certain. The aftermath of sex, the tangled bed, the littered room, had no appeal for him, and the squalid state of the Helsinki flat had caused many a flare-up with Ulrike. At least with her quarrels had had a certain relish to them, unlike the nagging, dragging rows with June – and they had always ended gloriously, now he came to think of it.

Until today, though acutely aware of her and undeniably attracted to her, he hadn't seriously thought he stood a chance with Philippa. But looking back over their various encounters, few and fragmented as they had been, he knew how much they'd meant to him. Even when she was putting in the boot about that damned cheque. Amusement briefly lightened his dour face. Today he'd felt very close to her, and he was fairly sure she'd felt the same. Whatever she'd heard about Moira, surely she had enough sense to realise that, however much or little had actually happened, that was an altogether different ball-game?

He'd give it a go, he decided, following the breakdown truck back to the village, and his spirits rose at the prospect. Better furbish up the old major image, though. He'd been letting it slip lately.

A familiar bitter and rankling sense of injustice threatened his optimism for a moment, but he resisted it. He was an officer these days, and even if it was only in some damned toy army he'd be a colonel next time around. When they went back in. Fear seized him, as powerful and debilitating as any night-time terror, and he found he was shaking.

'Get a grip, for God's sake,' he said aloud, pulling over and taking a few deep breaths. 'Sort yourself out.' There was no need to think about all that yet.

He let down the window and was grateful for the cold air on his face. Here he was 'the major', and he should be more consistent about it. Normally meticulous, since survival could depend on it, about any assumed identity, he knew he'd never properly applied his mind to this Paulett character, scrambling him together because he had to be someone, too beaten and too cynical to care.

Andy had the Mini on the lift by the time Jon reached the garage, and he took the chance to have a good look at it, as much to put down a marker for future jobs which could be dealt with by a skilled engineer with time on his hands, as to assess how long the work would take today. He was sorry to see that there was remarkably little damage. Andy would hardly be able to make that last overnight.

At the hotel he went in by the side door and straight to the office. No harm in establishing a few precedents. Philippa was relieved to hear the damage report, and warmly grateful for Jon's concern and help. She had also waited to have lunch until he appeared.

Now that's friendly, he thought, trying to be casual, but aware of a small glow of pleasure that was new to him.

'Why don't I hang on and run you down to the garage when you've finished work?' he offered, when lunch could be spun out no longer. There was always a chance that the Mini wouldn't be ready and he could take her home.

'That's kind, Jon.' Philippa would have liked nothing better. 'But Andy will come for me, or run me home if necessary. He's very good about that.'

'Well, let's see how things pan out,' Jon said, as he took himself off to the bar to wait for her. And when in due course Philippa stuck her head in to say she was making coffee, he felt he was still in with a chance.

Stretched comfortably in front of the office fire, while Philippa dealt with a telephone booking, he turned over in his mind the best approach to asking her out. What would 'out' mean to her? Dinner, probably. He'd better get her to suggest somewhere. Good thing his bank account was healthy again.

'This is very civilised,' he said as she put the phone down and came to join him. 'You'll have to turn your car over more often.' He missed the quick look she gave him, alerted not by what he said but by his tone and manner.

Jon had no difficulty in passing himself off as a credible officer. He had the looks and bearing, as well as the professional skills and most of the required personal qualities. The Army would have promoted him long ago but, having made WO1 with impressive speed, he'd hung there frustratingly, in spite of repeated recommendations for commissioning in his confidential reports. These were turned down every time, and every time for the same reason – attitude. In one interview, when the CO had begun by saying that the problem could be summed up in three words, Jon had felt a stirring of hope that there would be something he could put right. But the three words had turned out to be 'attitude, attitude, attitude'.

It was an indication of how far he still was from normality that he failed to realise that any form of pretence would cut no ice with Philippa. It was unlike him to make a misjudgement so basic, yet once more, in spite of acknowledging that she was different from any woman he'd ever known, he blew a promising situation clean out of the water.

Waiting in the bar earlier, he had promised himself that next time they were together he'd get her to do more of the talking. Since conversation between them had always flowed with such disarming ease, it hadn't struck him for a while that Philippa invariably drew him on to do most of the telling, so that he came away with very little in the way of hard fact. He would have been disconcerted to know that she did it deliberately, not only preferring reticence about herself but seeing him as a lonely and for some reason embittered man, and thinking it might help him to relax his watchful hostility occasionally.

In spite of his best intentions she did the same now, very

gently and nicely, and before he knew what was happening
he'd launched into an anecdote about hauling out a three-
tonner which had landed in an ornamental pond in some old
lady's garden, having first passed through her conservatory
to get there. Philippa didn't mind his stories, he told them
well, but she did mind the fruity voice to which he'd reverted,
and the manner that went with it. She didn't watch him as he
talked, feeling exasperation grow. Why did he do this? He'd
been so different this morning, understanding and natural,
and she had felt as if she'd known him for ever.

It was an unwelcome reminder of how disastrous it would
be to get involved with such a man. Inviting him in here for
coffee had been a bad move. She should have waited till Andy
called and then the day's dramas would have been over.

Even as she thought this, the phoney accent goaded her
beyond endurance, and she exclaimed almost involuntarily,
'Oh, Jon, for goodness' sake don't!'

'Don't what?' he asked in surprise, reviewing what he'd said
in bewilderment.

'I hate it when you—' Philippa broke off, seeing his brows
come down. She couldn't leave it there, however. She felt
apprehensive at the thought of Jon's reaction, but if they were
ever to establish any ordinary friendly footing between them
they must get rid of this maddening façade. She mustered
her courage.

'You aren't really a major, are you?'

'What the hell are you talking about?' It was the last thing
he had expected to hear, and his anger was immediate and
automatic.

Well, she hadn't supposed he would make it easy for her.
'I'm sorry, Jon, I don't want to have a fight about it, but I
loathe it when you – put on this act—'

If Jon had been in anything like normal control of himself,
or able to summon his customary ability to read voice and

body language, he might even then have saved the situation, holding on to his temper and fobbing Philippa off with some acceptable prevarication. But he felt he was under attack, and attack moreover from a quarter where he had felt himself uniquely safe, and he responded with both defensiveness and truculence.

'Just what do you mean by that?'

He had jerked out of his lazy sprawl and come to his feet with an explosion of energy which was definitely intimidating.

When threatened, however, Philippa was capable of mustering considerable surface coolness, as Jon should have known by now.

'I think that for some reason you're pretending to be an officer,' she said quietly.

'So what am I then?' he demanded, his voice ugly with contempt. 'And what do you know about it?'

Not a wise move to give her such an opening. 'Oh, Army certainly,' Philippa said, still managing unruffled coolness. 'I have no difficulty with that. One of the more physical regiments. The Paras, perhaps? And an NCO? I'm only guessing, of course.' She hadn't cared for the sneer. 'Po-ossibly' – thoughtfully drawn out – 'a warrant officer, though a staff sergeant seems more likely, or even a sergeant.'

Jon hid surprise under swift bluster. It wasn't difficult, hot as he was with the indignation her measured and astute assessment had fanned. 'And I think you don't know what the fuck you're talking about.'

'Well, that certainly *sounds* like a sergeant,' Philippa observed, pretending to weigh the matter. She hadn't set out to be so provocative, but hadn't enjoyed his bullying response.

'Are you calling me a liar?'

Did he have to push it to this, she thought resignedly. They were both on their feet, he towering over her, holding her eyes with his, which were full of warning, daring her to go further.

For an instant of crackling tension Philippa felt actually breathless, then a memory came of his voice that morning, asking, 'Not too good?' and of the comfort and perceptiveness there had been in that simple question. There was something good in this man, something more than the inconsistent façade and the short fuse of aggression. If she backed down now she would never know.

'Yes,' she said.

After that it didn't much matter what he said. It was abusive but pretty well meaningless, covering his exit as he snatched up his jacket and made for the door.

'Oh, dear, I did make him cross,' Philippa remarked in the ringing silence after his departure, attempting a little facetiousness, but her voice wasn't very steady. Rows, accusations, abusive language, slammed doors weren't part of her life. Clearly they were meat and drink to Jon. Did he have any idea how such a scene shook her, and how drained and wretched it left her? Of course he didn't, but he need never know either. So much for getting things into the open.

Write it off, forget it, she ordered herself, gathering up the coffee mugs. She wouldn't wait for Andy to phone. She would walk to the village and she would go now. The prospect of time alone in the cool afternoon air was definitely attractive, after the tension which still seemed to linger in the office.

And Jon, banging shut the door of the Subaru, muttered vengefully, 'She can bloody well walk home. Serve her right.'

Each was foiled by Andy, who did what he had intended to do all along, which was to finish the work on the Mini and take it up to the Cluny to fetch Philippa.

Jon, coming fast down the twisting road, met him on a bend and only just pulled over in time, swearing with concentrated fluency, glad to have a legitimate focus for his anger.

Philippa, gulping down the first delicious draught of peace

and coolness as she came down the terrace steps, sighed to see the Mini appear, but pulled herself together sufficiently to thank Andy as they started down the hill.

Achallie seemed a much-needed haven after the turmoil of the day. Though it was hardly surprising, she told herself, if she felt washed out after tipping a car over, swigging down unaccustomed brandies, and then racing through a pile of work.

Oh, please. Who are you trying to fool?

She knew, going to run a bath as the most immediate solace to hand, that if all that had happened twice over it couldn't have left her feeling as she did.

7

Jon did his best to fan his anger with Philippa. By putting her finger so accurately on the fact that he wasn't an officer, she had touched on the one failure of his life which deeply mattered to him. His mind turned back with fresh bitterness to the years of seeing young officers, with a fraction of his knowledge, ability and experience, sail on leaving him behind. Though he might not have admitted it, it had been the determining factor not only in his leaving the Army, but in all the decisions since which had led him almost inevitably into the dubious career of bearing arms as a mercenary soldier.

Even so, by the morning after Philippa's accident, he found it hard to raise a spark of real resentment against her. What had she done after all but call his bluff? And call it with an uncanny accuracy. Of course, she had service connections. Her husband, or ex-husband, was Air Force. All the same, bloody hell . . .

He couldn't face her yet, however, disgusted with himself for his crass handling of the situation. Why hadn't he fed her some glib story and left it at that? He knew he'd been careless about the Paulett cover, unable to believe that anyone involved in the recent debacle, either directly or acting for the shadowy agencies who wielded the real power in the background, would seek him out here.

There would have been no reason for Philippa to doubt any explanation he chose to give her. But now that she'd challenged him and he, by losing his temper, had only confirmed what she suspected, how could he expect anything further to develop between them?

He took himself off to Muirend to make sure he didn't run into her, but was unable to get her out of his mind. He should have been phoning this morning to ask how she was, consolidating yesterday's progress. Instead here he was, hacked off and alone, with the frustrating knowledge staring him in the face that he'd slammed shut all the doors, and had no one to blame but himself.

And suddenly there was Philippa coming towards him, carving a way through the groups of drifting shoppers with her floating stride, with that look of cheerful purpose which was specially hers.

God, she's lovely, he thought with a pang of spontaneous delight, and in the same instant remembered the events of yesterday, wondered what she'd do when she saw him, decided to pretend he hadn't seen her, decided to brazen it out, and – more powerful than any of the rest – was startled by a knot of trepidation in his gut which he had known once or twice before in his life, but never, never because of a woman.

Philippa had spotted him and, incredibly, her face had lit up in an immediate smile of pleasure. Jon checked, unable to believe it, then saw doubt take over as she came up to him.

'Jon?' Her voice was uncertain, but the single syllable told him what he wanted to know. The antagonism of yesterday had been his alone, and she was wondering if he was still angry. He felt a big, ridiculous grin spread over his face.

'Come and have coffee somewhere,' he said.

It sounded more like a command than an invitation, but Philippa guessed that the brusqueness cloaked an uncertainty matching her own. She didn't attempt to hide her relief, but reached out impulsively to touch his arm, a quick light gesture which warmed his heart.

'I'd love to,' she said.

Jon glanced up and down the street. He could only remember the pubs.

'I know a nice place,' Philippa said.

She had a marvellous facility for smoothing the way, Jon thought fatuously, then hastily pulled himself together. She lives here, for Christ's sake. She could hardly help knowing where to go for coffee.

'Let's have that basket,' he said. No plastic carrier bags for her. Had to be this antique thing no one else would dream of lugging around. But he failed to raise a sneer.

Philippa led him down a passage into a cobbled court-yard, at the back of which stood a tall stone building with narrow windows and double doors. Without comment, Jon followed her into the yeasty odours of a shop crammed with robust-looking health food. Just the sort of place her lot would fancy, he decided resignedly, as Philippa went through the shop to a high-raftered room with a log fire in a massive stone fireplace. A collection of unmatched tables and chairs occupied the flagged floor, and a trestle-table along one wall held baskets of scones and rolls, and a couple of earthenware jars of dried grasses and seedheads.

Jon looked about him, his face carefully blank. 'You get a nosebag in here, I suppose?'

'I'm sure they'll provide one if that's what you prefer,' Philippa said amiably, nodding a greeting at one or two people but not pausing to speak. She felt extremely, irra-tionally happy. She had been thrilled to catch sight of Jon so unexpectedly, his big bulk standing out among the throng of shoppers, the dark hair no longer in its trim military shape, his face sombre as he prowled along. She hadn't expected his anger to have cooled so soon, and had been grateful for the way he had overleapt explanations and apologies.

Oddly, she felt that suddenly she knew him better; that by coming in here together, naturally and without discussion, they had not only proclaimed a truce but taken a crucial step forward.

'Philippa, hi! Lovely to see you.'

'Hi, Edina.'

Another of them. Jon turned to find a tall girl in a striped butcher's apron beside them, her untidily piled hair making her look even taller, a basket of rolls supported on one scrawny hip.

'. . . ages since I saw you. Penny was in yesterday, and I was asking her what had become of you . . .'

Philippa introduced Jon, who found himself shaking a bony hand.

'Sorry about the flour,' Edina said cheerfully. 'So, what are you going to have? These are just out of the oven. Or there's gorgeous fruit tart, new recipe. Oh and Pippa, the pesto's in at last, don't forget to take it when you go.'

Pesto yourself, thought Jon. Get lost.

Edina brought them strong, freshly brewed coffee, they sampled the fruit tart, and Jon felt, as he had felt before with Philippa, an irresistible sense of peace overtake him. She bore no grudges, her friendliness was ready and real, and in her company there always seemed an added layer of richness to quite ordinary things.

'Yesterday,' he began abruptly. It couldn't be swept under the carpet, tempting though that was.

Philippa's head came up. 'Yes?' She waited quietly for him to go on, but he sensed her tension as he cast about for the right words.

'I said some pretty hard things,' he went on after a moment, deciding on a brisk note, as though taking for granted that this was something no one would want to make a big deal of.

That hadn't been what she'd minded, Philippa inwardly protested. Was he going to dodge the real issue? But she didn't interrupt.

'I'm a bad-tempered bastard,' Jon went on, still sticking to the matter-of-fact approach, but finding it surprisingly difficult to meet her eyes.

'Yes,' Philippa agreed equably, drawing a small grunt of amusement from him.

'Are you going to forgive me then?' Contrite and cajoling; they all fell for that. But her direct and candid gaze reminded him that Philippa was not like all the rest. She was alarmingly astute, and whatever he came up with had better be good.

'For the bad temper?' Philippa enquired. 'Yes.'

She surely did put it on the line, Jon swore to himself, backed into a corner before he'd begun.

Typically, however, she helped him out, though in fairly downright terms. 'Look, Jon, you no doubt have some reason for pretending to be something you're not, and I don't need to know what it is. But leave it at that. Don't lie to me. I hate it.'

She looked unhappy at having to spell it out, but resolute, and Jon knew he must accept that nothing less than honesty would do for her, now or at any future time. He also found he was sure of something else – Philippa wouldn't discuss this with anyone.

Jon hadn't trusted many people in recent years, and lack of trust and a growing fear of betrayal had been the most corrosive element of the weeks leading up to disaster and flight. His face darkened at the thought, and Philippa's heart sank. But he knew with certainty that he could trust this girl and, pushing away the horrors, feeling tension ease down as he remembered where he was and with whom, he registered something even more miraculous – she hadn't wanted to chew over the whole issue, capitalising on her moral victory.

He held out his hand and Philippa thankfully brought hers up from where it had been tightly clenched out of sight, and put it into his. He was watching her intently and she met his eyes without evasion. Although she knew he would make no promises, she was satisfied.

Then in no time, it seemed to Jon, almost before he'd had the chance to savour the new and promising understanding between them, she was looking at her watch and saying she must go, she had work to do.

'I thought you rolled up at these jobs of yours whenever it suited you,' he objected, knowing he was being absurd.

'Wouldn't work too well for dinner parties,' Philippa remarked, already on her feet and winding her scarf round her neck.

'Dinner's hours away,' he argued.

She laughed at him. 'You stay. Have more coffee.'

'Where is this job?'

The need to hang on to her company by any means took him by surprise. Watch it, he warned himself. She's getting under your skin.

'Oh, here, in Muirend.'

'Well, I can at least take grannie's basket to the car for you.'

'Cheek. No, honestly, Jon, thanks all the same. I'm parked here, out at the back. And I've a couple of things to pick up in the shop.'

'Don't forget the pesto.'

Was he losing it, to feel actually gratified to share this trivial detail of her life? Even a couple of minutes more with her seemed precious. The day yawned ahead empty and purposeless, and the days beyond it, to the unknown time when they would be recalled, when the painstaking business of recruitment and training would start up again, and then – what?

For a second Jon's mind rushed forward in something like panic, with an obscure sense that now there was something to lose, where before there had been nothing. Disconcerted, he pulled his mind back to the present, paying the bill, following Philippa into the shop, picking up cheese and bread and some posh kind of chutney for himself. How could the equilibrium he was only now beginning to claw back be destroyed like that, in a second, just because she had to go? But the coil of fear had been real and unnerving.

They ran into more of Philippa's friends on the way out and there was a brief hubbub of confident voices which set Jon's teeth on edge, unfocused resentment beginning to eat into him once more. He hung in there, however, carrying the basket out to where the Mini was parked, tight against the wall in a narrow vennel, tucking away from habit the fragment of local knowledge.

Then Philippa was gone, and he was walking alone down the alley to the High Street, feeling murderously thwarted. What he would have liked more than anything at that moment was a good scrap. Well, perhaps not more than anything, he amended, with the glint of a smile.

Where in Muirend had Philippa gone? What time would she get home? And where, come to that, did time with her go? What did they talk about in that effortless stream of words? Well, for starters, yesterday she had called him a liar. He gave a snort of amusement. And today she had smiled at him across the shopping crowd as though he had been the one person in the world she wanted to see. He knew it was a moment he would never forget.

What was the story about the husband? Had he gone for good? Even if he had, there had to be some bloke. A woman like Philippa couldn't be on her own. What if she'd been with someone when he met her today? His fist balled in his pocket. And, apart from a bloke, there were these endless friends of her, the jobs, the busy framework of her life. He turned into the first pub he came to.

Philippa drove to Northmount House reviewing her menu and wishing that today's cooking could have been for anyone but Amy Semple, so anxious and precise, regarding every dinner party as some kind of art form.

What good company Jon was when he relaxed and stopped putting on that ghastly act. But he could be a bit overpowering too, with that way he had of concentrating his attention on her, shutting out the rest of the world. The grey eyes could be so calculating and assessing, then a gleam of humour lighting them would turn him into a different person.

Oh, please! Philippa thumped the steering wheel with her fist. Get your mind on this damned dinner. Lamb cutlets *en cuirasse*, for God's sake. No one but Amy wanted that sort of stuff nowadays. Almond soup; that couldn't be done till the last minute. Then a choice of puddings, for eight people, because Peter Semple refused to do without his marmalade sponge, a tradition which, in Philippa's opinion, had become seriously outworn.

Northmount was not a house you walked into without formality, though today she longed to go in by the back door and get stuck in as she would anywhere else. Here you rang the bell and were affectionately welcomed by both Peter and Amy, who had known your parents and your grandparents, then drawn into a perfection of polished furniture and carefully arranged flowers, a birch log fire blazing on the neatly swept hearth, the portly yellow labrador colour-coded with the rug.

Amy offered Philippa sherry, at the same time conveying with the courteous authority of her generation that she had expected her to arrive before this. Philippa thought a sherry would have done her a lot of good, but there would have been no question of escaping to the kitchen with it, and she couldn't face Amy's controlled anxiety as more time dripped away in small talk.

It was hard to concentrate. Usually Philippa accepted the elaborate fussing tolerantly, knowing it meant almost as much to the Semples as the dinner party itself, and was possibly more enjoyable. But today, as Peter decanted port at the kitchen table, extolled the virtues of the wines he'd chosen and polished the glasses for a third time, and Amy, her face pinched with doubt, suggested yet another change of plan, Philippa found her patience considerably strained.

She could probably have cooked adequately with thoughts of Jon running like film behind her brain, but to have to make a detour round Peter every time she turned, perform sleights of hand to conceal from Amy the fact that she'd brought frozen pastry from Tesco's, and discuss every step of her preparations, threatened disaster.

Concentrate, she told herself grimly, get your mind off this womaniser, drinker and phoney with a chancy temper into the bargain. She giggled at the lack of impact this catalogue made on her, and Amy looked at her with wounded disapproval. She couldn't help thinking that for once Philippa seemed strangely uncommitted to their shared enterprise.

It was a long day. In the end Philippa found herself seriously resenting the amount of time and effort required to produce four courses of elaborate food, plus cheese, coffee and *petits fours*, for eight elderly people, all of whom were probably more than happy with a poached egg on toast for supper at home.

Cooking in this frame of mind doesn't go well, and she was exhausted by the time she headed thankfully up the icy glen road, leaving the guests at Northmount House, uncomfortably bloated, their jaws aching with suppressed yawns, wondering how soon they could get to their longed-for beds.

8

In the end, Jon found it surprisingly simple to invite himself
to Philippa's cottage. He had worked out various approaches,
hardly able to believe he was making such a meal of it, but
convinced his usual take-it-or-leave-it attitude would get him
nowhere. He had plenty of time to evolve some strategy, since
he didn't see Philippa for several days after their encounter in
Muirend.

Losing track of her, he even telephoned, not sure it was a
good idea, since it gave her the chance to fob him off, but
driven by a feeling he could neither rationalise nor dismiss,
that without her calm good sense to tap into his life would fall
dangerously apart. He was almost relieved when there was no
reply, then at once began to wonder jealously where she was
and what she was doing.

On his way to the hotel the following morning, he met the
Murrays on the hill. Weekly shopping trip. Good, Philippa
would be in. But when he heard her arrive, he was startled
by the pleasure it gave him merely to know she was in the
building. Familiar with the routine by now, he checked the
spike by the till. The chits were still there. When she came
to collect them he'd persuade her to have lunch with him,
organise a bottle of wine . . .

As a planned moving in on a target it was a fiasco. They
achieved consecutive conversation for two minutes at a time at
most, as Philippa got up to answer the phone, was side-tracked
by other customers who didn't see that the major had any

exclusive call on her, saw off departing guests and dealt with a persistent female rep eager to interest her in a new tampon vending machine.

Jon didn't attempt to hide his irritation when Philippa came back for the fourth time.

'That food must be stone cold by now. Get Sharon to put it in the mike for you.'

'It's fine,' Philippa said. 'I'll no doubt have to keep leaping up. It would only get cold again.'

'The others should be able to look after things.'

She smiled, not troubling to answer.

'You ought to be able to have your lunch in peace,' he persisted, ignoring warning bells which reminded him that Philippa didn't see things in this light.

About to say that he could see for himself that everyone was busy, Philippa realised in time that he seriously minded the interruptions.

'It's always like this when Ian and Shona are away,' she said peaceably. 'But I'm sorry it's spoiling our lunch, when you'd so kindly bought wine. It was nice of you to think of it.'

Reviewing during the past few days the ugly spats which had flared between them, over issues no bigger than this, she had wondered sometimes if Jon could be hiding away here to recover from some sort of breakdown. His behaviour could certainly point to something of the sort – the swings from taciturnity to rage, the solitary hours of drinking, the defensiveness. But there had also been something he had once or twice let her glimpse, which was very close to need, and anything like an appeal could always reach Philippa.

'We should go out somewhere,' Jon said abruptly. 'Talk properly, without all this crap going on. Or you could invite me to your cottage.' He hadn't meant to plunge so crudely, and failed to hit the easy note he'd hoped for. It mattered too much. He was astonished to feel his stomach clench as he waited for her reply.

But Philippa only gazed at him, frowning, for moments which seemed to Jon to stretch unbearably. Just as he'd decided, unable to hide his anger, that she was going to turn him down, she made up her mind.

'Yes, that would be a better idea. Do come.'

But Jon hadn't waited long enough, and as she spoke he was already sneering, 'You're not afraid I'd leap on you, are you? No chance.'

He would have given anything to be able to snatch the words back, but before he could try to repair the damage Philippa was called away to deal with an enquiry about a shooting package Ian was putting together.

She was surprised, when she came back, to find that Jon hadn't stormed out. But there he was, not too promising of aspect it had to be said, still at their table. Perhaps it would have been better if he had gone, and the whole idea had been forgotten, she thought wryly. But she couldn't pretend she wasn't pleased to see him there, or deny the instinctive compassion he aroused in her, driven as he seemed to be by some strange compulsion to wreck any chances that came his way.

She slipped into her seat and smiled at him. 'It's hopeless here, as you said. Do come to Achallie, if you'd like to.'

He stared at her, caught on the back foot. Maybe she hadn't picked up on his crude remark. But, hell, what was he waiting for?

'Right,' he said. 'When?'

'Oh, any time really.' Philippa wasn't being vague on purpose. It wasn't easy to piece together the plot of her various activities at a moment's notice.

Jon wasn't having any of that. 'Tonight?' he demanded, with a belligerence he failed to tone down.

'I shall be in this evening,' Philippa said calmly. Lucky she was. It was clear that with him in this mood any apparent hesitation would be fatal.

Fatal? It was even more clear that it would be fatal if he came. Putting together some sort of life for herself, back in the glen after the break-up of her marriage, hadn't always been easy, and she had no wish for everything she'd achieved to be destroyed. The most passing involvement with this man promised nothing but conflict, emotional upheaval and grief, all of which she could do without.

During the afternoon she actually came back to the bar, nervous but determined, to tell Jon she'd changed her mind. But he'd already left, having no intention of drinking all afternoon if he was going to Achallie later. Also, an accurate instinct had warned him that Philippa might easily think better of an invitation he'd more or less dragged out of her.

Going into her quiet cottage at dusk, Philippa couldn't believe she had agreed to risk its precious peace. She didn't exactly expect Jon to turn up and pick a fight with her. Having got his way he would no doubt be on his best behaviour. It was her own feelings she didn't trust. She knew she'd never felt anything approaching this level of attraction for a man before, an attraction which had nothing to do with reason or good sense, but the warnings were sounding loud and clear at the prospect of letting an explosive commodity like Jon Paulett into her life.

And when would he turn up? She should have given him a definite time. He was sure to arrive, having already eaten, just as her own dinner was ready. Damn, damn, damn; what an idiotic situation to have wished on herself. And what could she give him to drink? She should have remembered gin. And what in heaven's name were they going to talk about? There were no handy escape routes here, as there were in the hotel. Then again, what would Jon have read into her invitation?

That crack about leaping on her. His rules were bound to be different from hers. The whole thing was going to be a total nightmare, and she had no one to blame for it but herself.

Jon had been firm that he mustn't arrive too soon. As nothing had been said about a meal he must give her time to eat, and he knew in Philippa's case that wouldn't be early. All the same, he found himself rolling down the track well before he'd planned, without quite knowing how he'd got there. He tried to drive slowly, but some magnet drew him inexorably towards Achallie.

Philippa heard the car, headed for the kitchen door then checked. Would Jon think he should go to the front door? She never used it in the winter. No one did. It was draught-proofed and curtained and probably stuck fast with damp. She worked up a swift uncharacteristic annoyance about this, before getting her nervousness under control.

In fact, Jon had taken one look at the mossy path and the line of leaves against the front door, and come round the end of the house. Philippa heard his step on the gravel with some shame at what her momentary flurry of doubt had revealed. He looked bigger than ever smiling at her from the doorstep, his pose relaxed and confident. But she saw the wariness in his eyes and her own tension evaporated. He knew he'd pushed too hard for this, and was uncertain of his welcome.

All Philippa's natural warmth and kindness came rushing back at that, and she beamed at him as she stood aside to let him pass.

Elated to be here, and relieved at his reception, which a long afternoon at Keeper's Cottage had given him far too much time to worry about, Jon found it hard to settle down when Philippa took him through to the sitting-room. He roamed about examining his surroundings with frank interest.

'Was it your idea to knock the two rooms into one?' he asked, giving the arch his professional attention.

'I suppose you're going to tell me that was a supporting wall.' Philippa sighed exaggeratedly, doing her best to
subdue her fizzing delight to have him here, his presence
and personality taking over the room, dispelling its ordered
self-containment at a stroke.

'Someone's mentioned it already?' He grinned at her. How
good she looked, here in her own setting, and how attractively
the thin face broke up as she laughed.

'It's held up for a few years now, anyway,' she told him
cheerfully. 'The last occupant but one did that, and thank
goodness he did. The rooms must have been horribly poky
before. But you should have seen what the last owner did
with it.'

'What did he do?' He was ready to listen to anything she
chose to tell him. He was here, he'd made it.

'He filled in the gap again with what I think is known as
a room divider. A monstrosity' – substituted in time for 'a
monstrous erection' – 'with green dimpled glass and cunning
shelves and nooks and strip lights—'

'In here?' Jon looked at the deep-set windows in the thick
walls, the simple slabs of granite framing the fireplace, the
stone hearth. 'Vandal. Probably got a kit out of a Sunday
supplement.'

'That's exactly what it looked like. And he put a varnished
mantelpiece with cubbyholes round the fire.'

'Glad you had that taken out.'

'I did it myself. Messy but satisfying.'

Big job. Good for her. But Jon's approval was shot with a
faint resentment. What was that about? He found he wanted
to have done the job for her. Something very odd seemed to
be happening to him.

'Nice room now, anyway.' He appraised it at his leisure, his
heels on the hearth, his backside warmed by a log fire nicely
taking hold. Not the sort of room he was used to, but he felt

a sense of recognition just the same, as though it represented some ideal he had never precisely defined to himself. Its furniture was large-scale for a cottage, and shabby. There was a deeply buttoned chesterfield, its faded cover patched on the arms, but as welcoming a sofa as he, with his long back and long legs, had ever seen. A winged armchair across the hearth was almost as tempting in its generous scale. He looked with pleasure at a handsome dining-table showing the honourable scars of long use, and at the tall corner cupboard where Philippa was pouring drinks.

'Jon, dismal failure I'm afraid,' she said over her shoulder. 'I forgot gin. Could you bear whisky for a change – or wine? Or there's lager in the fridge.'

'Lager would be fine.' Whisky did too much damage too fast.

Fetching the lager, Philippa knew she was happy. She had wanted this. And Jon in his present relaxed mood was a marvellous person to be with.

'By the way,' she said as she came back, 'there was also a flicker-log electric fire in here. I wouldn't want you to miss any of the finer points.'

'Go on then, what else?' He took the pewter tankard from her (her husband's? – where was the lucky bastard?) and sank into the embrace of the big sofa.

Philippa, pouring wine for herself, elaborated obligingly. 'Two different wallpapers, one striped and one patterned with bamboos – or was it bulrushes?'

'And?'

'Kitchen wallpaper coffee pots and carrots. Lilac and lemon bathroom. Oh, and you should see what the fretwork king produced upstairs.'

Jon resolved on the spot that one day he would.

'What admirable restraint,' Philippa teased, having seen too late the opening she'd given him.

Jon laughed. 'So what did he build upstairs?'

'A huge bed, for one thing,' she answered, looking him in the eye. 'A permanent edifice, since the stairs are so narrow. It has a headboard with a gothic arch and barley-sugar twists and—'

'Mirrors?'

'No mirrors,' she said firmly. 'I was going to rip it out but it's so hideous it's almost splendid, so in the end I left it.'

He would see it, and the rest of the house and everything in it, Jon felt suddenly, calmly sure. There was no hurry. In fact with this woman hurry would ruin everything. For now, this was enough and more than enough – to be here with her in this comfortable room, lit by a couple of reading lamps and the light of the fire, with her books and possessions about them, and nothing to drag her away from him. He consciously savoured a contentment he didn't intend to spoil this time.

Before long, though, he must make it clear to her that, whatever she'd heard, he hadn't slept with Moira. He needed to have that out of the way. But a wise intuition told him it wasn't a matter to raise tonight.

Why had she worried over what they'd talk about, Philippa wondered a couple of hours later, when she had pointed Jon towards the bathroom and was in the kitchen foraging for supper.

Jon found a bathroom unexpectedly luxurious and warm, with pretty tiling and a splendid Victorian claw-footed bath. Even more importantly, for him, it held no messy clutter and smelled delicious.

'Nice bog,' he commented from the kitchen doorway.

'Faced with a bath panelled in quilted mauve plastic what could I do? However, I can promise you there's no extravagance *de luxe* to equal it anywhere else.'

'And not a shred of carrot wallpaper left in here.' He looked approvingly round the small kitchen: whitewashed walls, oiled and waxed wood surfaces, colourful earthenware on open shelves, and some definitely antiquated kit by way of fridge and cooker. He watched, at peace, as Philippa loaded a tray with Stilton, a jar of chutney labelled in her flowing hand, a pat of yellow butter which didn't look as though it had ever seen the inside of a shop, and a big brown loaf. The smell of percolating coffee made him suddenly ravenous. A general sharpening of the appetites, he decided.

'Is there a boyfriend on the scene?' he asked, not even knowing he was going to put such a question.

'No,' Philippa said quietly after a moment.

'Oh, come on, there must be somebody.' He tried to sound rallying, but didn't succeed.

'No one.' She had her back to him, reaching down plates from a wooden drying rack.

'How come, gorgeous woman like you?'

'Unanswerable,' she said lightly.

'It must be by your own choice then.' If he had hoped to make his probing more acceptable by offering a clumsy compliment he didn't have much success.

'Yes,' Philippa agreed, with a lift of her eyebrows. 'Would you take the tray? I'll bring the coffee.'

Back off, he warned himself. She's answered you. Leave it. Was she more formal now, or did she merely seem so because she was hospitably busy, pulling a table up to the sofa, pouring coffee, cutting bread? He resisted offering an apology.

'The extension to the side of the house, where the kitchen and bathroom are,' he said instead when they were both supplied, 'that looks even older than the rest.'

'It was an earlier dwelling, I think, then became the byre.' Jon heard the relief in her voice at the change of subject. 'My room's at the front end of it.'

'Not brave enough for the monster upstairs?' His determination to see it faded.

'Too daunting altogether.'

They had no trouble in picking up the thread again on neutral topics but, driving away not long afterwards, Jon realised that for all his pleasure in the evening he still hadn't learned much about Philippa's life. There was no appearance of reserve, yet she gave little away. How good it had been, though. When had anything last been that good? Thinking back, he knew that nothing had.

Philippa went for a walk. It was a crisp night, the sky crowded with stars, and the tingling air as she saw Jon off, combined with her own mood, stimulated and alive, made sleep unthinkable. She went up the silver ribbon of the road where walking was easy, but her efforts to calm down were quite in vain.

She checked once. Her comments about flicker-log fires and hideous wallpapers – she'd been so sure Jon would laugh with her, yet she hadn't an idea of his taste. In fact, thinking back to NCO's married quarters she'd seen, these horrors might well have been exactly what he'd go for. But something had told her she was on safe ground. He had liked what he'd found at Achallie, and she knew it. In spite of all the differences between them, and the feeling of walking on thin ice emotionally which being in his orbit gave, Jon never felt alien to her, and that was both surprising and reassuring.

9

Jon rang Philippa just before nine the next morning, liking the feeling that now he had every right to do so. He had woken early, happier than he'd been for a long time, but had made himself wait to phone, pleased with his own considerateness and restraint.

Philippa had been gone for an hour. Jon listened to the ringing tone in frowning disbelief. She'd said she wasn't working today. Where the hell was she? It was a moment of balance. On present form such a setback was enough to make him profitlessly dissipate the entire day. But last night he had briefly felt in touch with a world more generous and more promising than his own, and he wasn't willing to lose sight of it. With an oath, for he'd spent the last hour elaborating on what he'd say to Philippa, and indulging in agreeable fantasies about where the conversation would lead, he slammed down the phone and went back to his bedroom. Well, the fantasies had included images of himself as fit and active, so at least he could do something about that.

Keeper's Cottage was perched on the ledge left by ancient glaciers as they scoured down the trough of the glen; this should provide reasonably level running for starters. It was just as well it did, for he was far from as fit as he'd supposed. He possessed an excellent physique, and prided himself on a high level of stamina, developed by years of hard training, which was never much affected by his occasional excesses. But he was in his mid-forties now, and the weeks of idleness and drinking since he came here had done him no good. Christ, he couldn't afford to get out of shape like this.

He shook off the unwelcome reminder. He had other things to think about today. Thumbing through last night's images – Philippa smiling at him over her shoulder as she offered him a drink, the length of the slim leg she stretched out to push a log into the fire, the coppery light the flames gave to her brown hair as she leaned to put the coffee pot on the hearth, the lift of her neat breasts as she turned to reach down plates from the kitchen rack – he came inevitably to her cool reticence when he'd asked if she had a man in her life. She'd said she hadn't. He found it hard to believe, but knew that one of the chief things he had to learn with her was to trust.

God, what am I doing, even thinking of a woman of her sort, he asked himself in a burst of angry frustration. Think of her, yes, how could he help it – those long, fine-boned limbs sprawled on a bed, the candid eyes gazing up into his – but think of her in terms of a relationship? He must be out of his mind. And he was still married, a technicality so remote these days that it seemed actually irrelevant. He never gave a thought to the slice taken out by direct debit from his Army pension, long used to its vanishing before he saw it.

He had married early, needing two things – freely available sex and a home of his own. Though he might not have admitted it at the time, the latter had been the more important. He knew nothing about his parents. Childhood had been care, a word which held for him resonances quite distinct from its original meaning, and a succession of foster homes. He had been an active, well-developed, rebellious and destructive child, and until he was in his teens he was never tolerated anywhere for very long. Then, unexpectedly, for he had been by this time in an age group and category notoriously hard to place, he'd been sent to the Hinks family. The name could still make him shiver.

He knew he'd been lucky. That was the worst of it; he always had to concede that. He'd been well fed, well provided for in every material respect, and above all given a good education. But the bile could still rise in his throat to remember the cold, cold temper of that house, and the holier-than-thou motive for taking him in – bearing witness, suffering the cross of his presence – and to remember the distinction made, every minute of every day, between the way they had treated him and the way they had treated their own precious son.

It astonished Jon, looking back, that at thirteen he'd had the sense, and the fortitude, to stick it out. Side-lined at every turn, rarely spoken to except in reproof, denied every treat or trivial pleasure, he had hung in, mute and dogged, recognising this as the one chance he was going to get, and learning to take refuge in reading, something he would later appreciate as an incomparable gift. He should have stuck it out longer in fact, got more exams behind him than a few paltry O levels, tried for a commission – that bugbear which would forever dog him – but he'd been too lonely, too desperate to get away, and he'd gone into the Army as soon as they would take him.

There he had found his natural home, his abilities recognised and put to good use, his belligerence channelled, and a trade provided for which he had exceptional aptitude. All with the bonus of the first sense of belonging somewhere that he'd ever known.

He had still been in basic training when he met June, one of the usual couple of hunting birds in a club, eyeing up the lads as they came in, knowing who they were. Opportunities to get off camp had been limited but he'd wasted none of them, and when he was posted for trade training he'd persuaded her to follow him. She had been a pretty little thing then, always nicely turned out, spending every penny she earned, as a receptionist at the local health centre, on clothes and make-up. He hadn't been able to get enough of her soft, round little body and her willing acquiescence to his demands, or take in the amazing fact that someone actually cared about him.

In those days there hadn't been a long wait for married quarters, furnished down to the kitchen clock, and they had been married as soon as Jon (only he was Jack Holcombe then) was posted to the regular regiment. For a while it had given him the greatest gratification he had ever imagined, to walk in at his own door and find his own woman there, and two fingers to the harridans who had clouted him out of their way in their kitchens when he was small, to the warped and sanctimonious charity of the Hinks, and to the impersonal social services which up until then had regulated his life.

Then June had got bored and begun to whine. She had missed her job and her friends, and hated housework. Jon had had a surfeit of her body by this time, and was beginning to realise that he'd made an appalling mistake. He had started spending off-duty time running or down at the gym, and put his name down for every course on offer.

With enough sense, however, to recognise the classic downward spiral, he had made some effort to halt it. He had taken out a mortgage on a slit of terraced house in a nearby village, with the support of a CO who had seen, behind Holcombe's sometimes turbulent off-duty behaviour and the references to insubordination which peppered his reports, obvious officer material of the future.

Since June had hated the restrictions of living in quarters, Jon had hoped that providing her with a place of her own would make her happier. But for him the fact of ownership had been even more compelling: his house, which no arbitrary ruling by strangers could take from him. In the years that followed, paying off the mortgage on that basic little property had been his inviolate priority.

He had honestly believed that he would spend more time at home once they'd moved in; had had vague ideas of tidying up the strip of shaley ground at the back, working on the car on Sundays, frequenting the local. But June had soon been as discontented as ever, and the state she'd let the house get into had driven him mad. The whole scene had been too restrictive, too slow, at a period in his life when he'd had energy to burn.

He had soon made lance corporal, concealing a deep, defiant satisfaction at having passed the first hurdle. He had taken any work-related course the Army offered, but had also seized every opportunity to indulge in white-water rafting, diving, hang-gliding, orienteering, skiing, climbing and free-fall parachuting, finding in these pursuits an outlet better suited to his independent cast of mind than team sports. He had never spent a leave with June, which had caused more friction between them, thus completing the cycle by driving him to seek out other ways to escape.

When he'd been posted to Germany on promotion to corporal she had refused to accompany him, and that had suited him perfectly. When she'd written to say she was pregnant he had had the traditional batter with his mates but hadn't gone home. In fact he hadn't gone back to Thornton until the baby was six months old, and he couldn't have expressed to anyone the mixed feelings that fatherhood had stirred in him.

He would swing from a resolve to give his son the stability and security he had never had, to a violent rejection of the idea of forming a bond with the child of the sort of woman June had turned into. She had become to Jon, by this time, terrifyingly like the sluttish foster mothers of his early years, and he had dreaded her capacity to drag him back into the hopeless, dead-end existence he'd fought so hard to get clear of.

Approaching the house, he had in spite of himself felt a tentative eagerness. His son. It seemed to mean a lot to other men. Would some deep-rooted instinct wake when he saw him? Would this baby provide another hold on that being part of things which other people took for granted, one more radical even than owning a house?

A sour smell had assailed him as he'd opened the door – the smell of his childhood. His gorge rising, he had gone in to find the television on and June supine on the sofa, the baby with a dummy in its mouth in the crook of her arm, a cigarette between her fingers. The littered room had pulsed with heat from the electric fire.

The puny baby, endlessly whimpering or squalling through the one night Jon had spent there, had seemed to have nothing to do with him. It had been June's, a vocal and repugnant part of her. Jon hadn't been able to bring himself to touch either of them. He had walked out of the house the next morning with two things clear in his mind. June wasn't going drag him back into that world; but she would never be able to say he'd behaved as the people who belonged in it did. He would provide for her and the child if he starved in the process; and the house, talisman for the future, would always be there.

Although capable of recognising that the emotional baggage he carried had had as much to do with his rejection of this scene as June's slide into indolence and squalor, it had been relatively easy to put them out of his mind. He had had a tour in Northern Ireland, by now one of the youngest sergeants in the regiment, then had applied for the SAS and been accepted for training. However, and it was something he never talked about, he hadn't made the grade. Although he had had the required guts, endurance, competence and bloody-mindedness, plus a useful flair for languages, he had not when it came down to it been a team-player. He'd been returned to unit, and his chagrin at this, after the glimpse he'd been given of a new and challenging world where he had felt he could succeed, had made a profound impact on him, and would affect all later actions and decisions.

He dragged his mind back to the present. Why beat himself up dwelling on June when he could think about Philippa? Because you happen to be married to June, in case you'd forgotten. So what exactly do you have in mind?

He had never believed in love, regarding it as a cop-out like religion, as propounded *chez* Hinks, or on a par with tenuous abstract concepts like honour. As far as he could see, people were only looking for security when they used the word, afraid of being alone, needing reassurance, elevating the need for physical satisfaction into something a bit less basic, or obeying some inexplicable urge to reproduce their kind.

But once or twice, in rare moments of opening up with an oppo he'd got to know well, stuck in a snow-hole for hours or sharing some cramped bivouac, he had heard a man talk about loving a woman, not in meaningless barrack-room terms, but out of some depths generally labelled the heart, and had glimpsed what it might be like to feel that without one particular person life was meaningless.

You stupid bastard, he told himself. He'd been to Philippa's house once, spent a few enjoyable hours with her, and he was as far from her as he'd been on that first morning when she'd come swinging into the bar and given him her courteous smile-to-a-stranger.

Back at the cottage, drenched in sweat, gasping as raucously as a recruit after his first training run, he propped himself against the kitchen worktop on splayed hands, letting the pain in his chest subside. He yearned for a long sluicing shower and made do, muttering, with a tepid bath.

The last shreds of his waking good humour, threatened by both Philippa's absence and thoughts of June, were blown to the winds when, sitting in the window seat at the Cluny that afternoon, avoiding the big rounds which had been succeeding each other at the bar for the last couple of hours, he saw a Land Rover drive up with Philippa in it, beside that damned ski-instructor chum of hers. Alastair, wasn't it? Jon's stomach tightened in helpless jealousy.

He watched impassively as they came hurrying in, shivering, demanding warmth and alcohol, the group at the bar opening to include them.

'Get it finished, then?' Ian Murray asked.

'We did, and it looks like a palace.'

'It doesn't smell like one,' Philippa added. 'And it's probably damper than ever after the water we've sloshed round it today.'

'Ach, it'll be cosy enough,' Ross Nicholson said, easily reassuring since he had a snug cottage whose expenses were met by the efforts of others.

Alastair raised his glass to Philippa. 'Couldn't have done it without you.'

'That's true.'

Jon, from the other side of the room, where everyone had been only too ready to leave him to his black mood, watched with a festering sense of exclusion. She hadn't even spoken to him. Well, she hadn't seen him, as he knew perfectly well. But he couldn't help feeling she was inaccessible once more; that any imagined link between them last night had existed in his own mind.

Philippa's eyes had gone to Jon's usual corner when she'd come in, disappointed not to find him there as the noisy group engulfed her. Her thoughts had been on him all day as she'd scrubbed out the mildewy little caravan, a promise of help she had much regretted when she'd woken after a restless night. She had done her best to keep the facts clear in her mind: Jon was a transient here, looking for no more than a passing affair; she knew next to nothing about him, and what she did know would scarcely bear examination. But somehow her mind had kept floating off in happy speculation, and all afternoon she had found herself looking at her watch.

Easing out of the crowd to go and clean up before starting on the sandwiches Ian had gone to fetch, she was startled to meet Jon's eyes fixed on her across the room, and to read in them something very close to dislike. Even so, there was no question about her pleasure at seeing him. Beaming, she raised a hand in greeting and received a grudging nod in return. Coming back from the loo, she was about to go and say hello when Alastair pointed to the waiting sandwiches, scooping her back with a long arm.

Jon wanted to punch his head in then and there, have a go at Philippa and anyone else who got in his way, and walk out. But Philippa, with a quick word to Alastair, was freeing herself and coming over.

Jon's wrath sank down and dissolved, though as she smiled at him he didn't for a moment guess the pang she'd felt to see him like this, isolated and dour. Last night they had been together, enclosed and at ease in her quiet room, and here he was once again suspicious and apart.

'Jon, how nice.' Her voice was balm, gentle, for him alone. 'I didn't see you when I came in.'

He nodded, his eyes feasting on her, indifferent to the ravages of the day's work, the cobwebs clinging to her sweater, the wet patches on the knees of her jeans.

'I enjoyed last night,' she said.

'I tried to phone you.' His brain wouldn't come up with words. What had she been doing all day with Alastair; what would be a cosy place?

'Nice of you, but I was off early. Like a fool I'd promised to help muck out Alastair's caravan.'

'I thought he lived in the hotel?'

'He did last summer, but now that he's getting married he and Jenny want to be on their own.'

'Married?' Jon floundered, his burning jealousy abruptly surplus to requirement. 'So why isn't she doing the cleaning then? Why should you do it?' he demanded, urgently needing something to cavil about.

'It's a surprise for her. Horrible job, though. I've told Alastair he needn't expect a wedding present.'

'I should bloody well think not.' But Jon could feel the tide of good humour flooding back.

Philippa laughed at him. 'Look, I'd better go. Ian's kindly feeding us. Then I'm afraid I have to shoot off. Friends coming to dinner, and I haven't done a thing about it yet.'

'Will you be here tomorrow?' Clutching like a fool at something, anything, to hold on to.

Already turning away Philippa looked back at him, alerted by something in his voice, and caught a look in his eyes which he couldn't hide – simple need.

Impossible for her to disregard such an appeal. She made no conscious decision. 'No, day off tomorrow, I'll be pottering about at home. Look in if you'd like to.'

'Yes?' Jon's eyes narrowed, his look probing her, as though he needed to be convinced she meant it.

'Yes.'

Receiving only a brusque nod in reply, Philippa turned away and Jon saw Alastair pull out a stool for her. Good luck to you, mate, he thought magnanimously, a warm, amazed complacency filling him.

Are you mad, Philippa wailed to herself as the Mini scudded down the glen. Her solitary days at the cottage were precious to her, the staple of her hard-won peace. She knew she'd be on edge all day, wondering when he'd show up. If only she didn't have to rush round now cooking dinner for the Napiers and Alec Blaikie. But perhaps it would be a good idea to be occupied, and anyway, she'd enjoy it once they were there.

Then she laughed and groaned at the mental chaos which two minutes' conversation with Jon could create.

'Damn the man,' she protested aloud, taking the Dalquhat turning far too fast.

But through all the talk and laughter of the evening, fun and satisfying as it was, a new thread of anticipation hummed like an electric wire.

These close friends could hardly help being aware, as Penny Forsyth had lately been in contacts with Philippa, that something about her was different. Pauly Napier, who, though some years younger than Philippa, had acquired an almost instant family at Drumveyn after her marriage, and was so busy looking after a teenager and three small children, a big house still needing attention after many years of neglect, various pets and her adored Archie, that at dinner parties she had a tendency to fall peacefully asleep after the pudding, was the least analytical about it. Blissfully happy herself, warm-hearted and generous, she wanted the rest of the world to be as happy as she was. She had only known Philippa since the latter had returned to Glen Maraich, but she knew her story, and knew how concerned all her friends were about it, so she wished her the best that anyone could want – to meet someone as nice as Archie, have lots of children, and preferably live somewhere in the neighbouring glens so that they could get to know each other better.

Archie, like Philippa in his early thirties, had known her since childhood, and looked a little deeper. As other friends had done, he had observed in her when she came back a new, though always courteous, always smiling, reserve, along with a quiet resolve to create a fresh life for herself with the means now at her disposal. The message had been clear; she was not repining, and didn't want anyone else to repine on her behalf. He respected her courage, her independent spirit and the way she had tackled the challenges of a return to home ground in such altered circumstances – not only in the jobs she had taken on, many of which she could surely not have found congenial, but in the way she had settled into this cottage and turned it into a home which seemed to suit her and was certainly welcoming for her friends.

There might even be one or two among them, he thought with a rueful twist of a smile, who envied its comfortable simplicity, and longed if only temporarily to be free of the relentless struggle to maintain large unwieldy houses designed for a different age, and estates daily more weighed down and ensnarled by legislation, falling markets, wage increases and the rest of it.

He shook the thoughts away. This was supposed to be an evening for putting work and responsibilities on hold. And, to return to his starting point, it was a pleasure to see Philippa back on something like her old lively form, whatever the cause.

For Alec Blaikie, however, awareness of the change in Philippa brought reactions both more complex and harder to deal with. It was no secret that since their teens she had been the object of all the passion a shy, inarticulate, bumbling male such as he was could feel. He had mooned after her, dreamed about her, been teased remorselessly about her, and gone through agonies of delight and trepidation on the rare occasions when she had agreed to be his partner for some party or event within their tight-knit circle. For his own part, he had rarely been tempted to venture outside it, and his imagination had carried him little further than the joy of collecting Philippa in his treasured Morgan, arriving at some well-known house with her beside him and, however little he might see of her in the interval, being allowed to take her home again afterwards.

Settling, as the years slid by almost without his noticing their passage, into the undemanding, unchanging, masculine routine of life alone with his father at Torglas (had his mother seen this future all too clearly when she had taken her departure the year he went away to school?), he had let himself believe that one day, through some mysterious agency which had nothing to do with his own actions or resolve, Philippa would be his. She would move into Torglas and life would go on in much the same way, only it would be happier, more satisfying and complete. He wasn't specific about what 'complete' would mean. What mattered was that he would have achieved what everyone else seemed so effortlessly to achieve, without having to worry ever again about what exactly it was or how it came about.

The series of shocks he had received when Philippa's life so dramatically changed and she left the glen – and when the later news came that she was married – had numbed him. He had talked to no one about his groping sense of life being suddenly empty, the future frighteningly blank. He had gone on from day to day, as it was after all quite easy to do, doing exactly what he always did, and even his closest friends had never guessed his despair. They had moved on in any case, their lives changing, their horizons widening; no one was going to pause long enough to wonder whether good old Alec still carried a torch for his adolescent love, now vanished from the scene.

And then, suddenly, almost without a word, Philippa had come back. Alone. There had been a flurry of comment about where she had elected to live, questions (which remained largely unanswered) about what had gone wrong with her marriage, then she had been reabsorbed into their lives again almost without a ripple – though for several friends bringing the added bonus of an extra pair of competent hands at busy times and in emergencies. It was lovely to have her back; the new pattern merged seamlessly into the old.

For Alec, still trying to adjust to the unexpected death of his father a few months earlier, there had been a few days of disorientation about which he could later remember little. Then, with surprising swiftness, it had begun to seem as if Philippa had never been away. Helplessly, confused inner protests barely shaping themselves into words, he found himself precisely where he had been before, shaken to realise that after all this time Philippa remained his ultimate fantasy, and that he had no more idea of what to do about it now than he'd had at sixteen. Then, imperceptibly, it became normality once more; and so did doing nothing about it.

As he had found after losing his father, it was all too easy to let the uneventful routine and virtual torpor of life at Torglas roll him along as it had for so many years. And Philippa was clearly back to stay. There was plenty of time to get used to things again.

Tonight, for the first time, dimly sensing a change in her but unable to define it, the thought crept across his brain that perhaps it wasn't going to be that simple. Catching, though he would much rather not have, one of the drowsy, loving smiles that Pauly sent Archie, her smooth skin warm and peachy in the light of the old brass oil lamp on the table, her generous curves and glowing happiness creating a heady aura of sexy contentment and promise, these fears finally coalesced into the appalling question: what if Philippa fell for someone else? But who? Alec's mind went round their familiar circle. Everyone he could think of was married. No, there was Max Munro; but it was safe to count him out, Ann Logan would never let him out of her clutches. A few Hays from Sillerton were still on the loose – there was such a clan of them there always would be – but none was the right age for Philippa.

A newcomer then? Some entirely unknown quantity? But no one 'of their sort' had recently moved into the area. Not that Alec would have used the phrase, or any similar one, but that was what he meant.

Though the drama of Philippa putting the Mini off the road had been the first topic when he and the Napiers arrived, Philippa had merely said, in answer to a query from Archie, that 'one of the Cluny customers' had run her up to the hotel afterwards. The Cluny Arms was not a place that any of her guests tonight frequented on a regular basis, though they went there from time to time, and it was a natural assumption to make that one of the glen men had obligingly given her a lift.

No suspicions were aroused on that point, and no further questions were asked, but on the way home Archie commented to Pauly, 'I had the impression this evening that Philippa has finally put the past behind her, didn't you?' While Alec took the longer road to Torglas with a perturbed feeling that all was not going to be quite as simple as he had begun to take for granted it would be. Perhaps, alarming idea, it was time to have a look at his life and see what needed to be done about it.

IO

Jon had not anticipated that the day's entertainment at Achallie would include digging a drain. He had, very reasonably, decided that Philippa wouldn't want to get up too early on her day off, particularly if she'd had people in for dinner the night before, yet once more he found himself haplessly driving down the track soon after breakfast, with that tightness in his gut which no other woman had ever been able to put there before. Well, maybe he could give her a hand with the chores, fetch in the logs, split some kindling. She'd be glad of the help.

As he pulled in behind the Mini Philippa came down the slope of lawn towards him, smiling her wide heart-lifting smile, mud on her face, mud on her jeans and mud on the front of her sweater. She was clearly well into her day. She didn't waste time on greetings – or even on an offer of coffee.

'You couldn't have turned up at a better moment,' she told him, adding another streak to her forehead as she pushed back a straggle of hair, and Jon felt tension melt away. He no longer cared what the day brought. Seeing her come smiling towards him with that free, graceful walk of hers, which could turn him on even when she looked such a total scruff, made him forget doubts. He was here; he was with her. That was all that mattered.

'You're a bit clean,' Philippa said, sounding more doubtful now. 'You don't happen to have boots with you, do you?'

Jon gave a resigned chuck of his head, eyebrows raised, and plodded sighing round to the back of the Subaru. Good job he'd chucked them in at the last minute – the major would never have gone anywhere without them. Cut the crap, he warned himself, she hates it. But in this moment of elation the reminder made no impact.

Philippa grinned at the long-suffering bit, trying not to look too dizzily happy. She hadn't dared to hope he would appear so early. Better get on with some nice sobering digging.

'Drains,' she said.

'Swearing at me already? What have I done?'

She laughed. 'Come on.'

She led him up the molehill-dotted winter lawn, past a fenced patch bare now except for a couple of rows of curly kale putting out new green, to a bank overhung by leafless fruit trees, the pure white and green of snowdrops pushing through the pale stalks of last year's nettles and hogweed.

'This is the first time for ages the frost's been out of the ground,' Philippa explained, briskly practical. 'I want to get this done before it's time to sow stuff in the vegetable garden. Any heavy rain pours straight off the hill and washes the whole lot away.'

They stood together on the lip of a half-dug trench, and Jon observed that it followed the best available line and appeared to have the necessary run. He also noted that any sizeable stones which had been dug out had been piled along one side, earth neatly heaped on the other.

'Who did this for you?' he asked, and never knew how close he came to being given coffee and sent home.

Catching her expression as he turned, he hastily revised the question. 'Did you do this yourself?'

'Don't you mean "all by yourself"?' she mocked.

He made a show of examining the work, squatting to assess the fall of the ground, looking up the hill and down the garden, while Philippa watched him with a warning look in her eye.

'Might do,' he announced finally, deadpan.

'*What* a relief to know that.' She handed him a shovel, took the pickaxe and jumped into the hole.

He'd taken it for granted he'd have the pick. Philippa knew he'd taken it for granted he'd have the pick. She began neatly and efficiently to break up the ground round a mammoth stone and scrape it aside.

'You can see why I said you'd arrived at just the right time,' she said.

Jon stood for one second watching her, rearranging a few preconceived ideas and tasting a rich amused pleasure he scarcely recognised, then with a grin he began obediently to shovel aside the loosened earth. And he'd thought he might chop a few sticks for her. His spirits soared, and he was aware of a sharper edge to all his senses. The day had the first true feel of spring about it, or more a relaxation of the hold of winter, and he was aware of the faint, delicate scent of the snowdrops, the calls of finches and tits, a new softness in the air.

The big stone, when fully revealed, presented them with one of those primitive, strenuous challenges which turn into a stubborn determination not to be beaten. For Jon, though he might not have recognised it, there could have been no better therapy than to get his hands on such a job, everything else for the moment forgotten, and enjoy himself. When the upended monster finally fell with a squelching thud precisely where they intended it to go, Philippa threw herself down on the damp ground beside it, muscles trembling and knees rubbery.

Jon surveyed her with a feeling rare for him – pure affection. This mud-caked and aggressive Philippa was a far cry from the composed, courteous girl he saw at the hotel; and a far cry from any woman he'd ever fancied.

'Get up, you idiot, that grass is soaking.' He reached down a hand and was impressed, though he didn't show it, by the way she gathered herself from her pithless sprawl and came easily to her feet at his pull. 'Isn't there such a thing as a tea-break on this job?' he enquired, doing his best to sound hard done by in order to quell some decidedly out-of-hand feelings.

'Tea-break? *Tea-break?* It's not dark yet.'

'Bloody hell.'

'Oh, well, if you insist.'

They heeled off their muddy boots on the doorstep and padded into the kitchen to stand companionably at the sink, sharing the nail brush and sluicing off mud.

'I'd never have shifted that brute without you.'

'But you'd have tried.'

'Oh, I'd have tried. I'd probably have been there for a week and ended up underneath it.'

'What are you planning to do when the trench is dug?'

'Line it with polythene, half fill with stones and backfill,' she said, reaching for the towel.

'Ah,' said Jon, giving his nails another scrub. Ask a silly question.

'Will that be right, do you think?' Feminine, anxiously deferring.

'Get lost.' He wasn't accustomed to being wound up and he liked it, from her. 'Get the kettle on. What kind of woman are you anyway?'

'I think I need a bigger kitchen,' she remarked as she filled the kettle, glancing at him looming behind her, his head nearly touching the ceiling. 'We'd better go through to the sitting-room, though the fire's not lit yet, I'm afraid.'

'Where would you sit? In here?' He nodded to the stools tucked under the table against the wall. 'There's room for both of us, isn't there?' He had a childish need for everything to be as it usually was. Futile bugger, he told himself amiably.

'Try it for size,' Philippa said.

Jon tucked himself into the corner. 'Fine. Excellent even, since now I can't get out.'

'Huh.'

The coffee wound its fragrance up into the slanting sunlight. The little house was quiet around them. Time had no meaning.

It intruded again presently, however, as Jon began to wonder, after a couple of hours of shared effort and peaceful, sporadic exchanges, whether Philippa would give him lunch, whether he should take himself off so that she could have some herself, or whether, which he was beginning to fear was most likely, she was going to dispense with food altogether. He could suggest taking her somewhere for a pub lunch. Have to be Muirend. The Cluny Arms was definitely out today.

'God, is that the time?' Philippa exclaimed, just as he'd got to this point. 'Poor Jon, you must be starving. Why didn't you say? Come on, that's enough for one day.' She scraped mud off the shovel with the side of her boot, and reached to unhook her sweater from the branch of a damson tree, and Jon told himself he should learn to stop worrying; she had never failed him yet. Except in the small matter of supplying him with cash. He grinned as he gave the pick a polish on a clump of couch grass. By now that little clash seemed to belong to another life.

Washing in the bathroom this time, he lifted her towel from the heated rail and held it to his cheek, its warmth and the faint scent of her instantly arousing him. Yet he knew he had no plans for getting her into bed at the first possible moment, as he so much longed to do. Why? His give-away-nothing eyes stared back at him from the mirror. Even to himself he'd hardly formulated the answer to that. Because he sensed there was so much more to discover about this woman? Because he valued the whole package? Or because, try as he might, he couldn't rid himself of a feeling that one day, just conceivably, there might be many good things to share with her?

Cursing, he turned away. He was here, and it was good. Be satisfied with that. Going back to the kitchen he knew he'd rather dig over the whole damned garden than risk what he'd already gained by one false move.

'Hi. Want to stir this while I set the table?'

Standing over the soup pan, Jon smiled to himself. Yes, the ground rules were different here.

For relaxation after a morning with pick and shovel Philippa suggested a walk when lunch was over. From the field gate beyond her shed a track meandered away at an easy gradient. She went straight up the hill.

Jon long remembered that first walk with her. Not for the beauty of the day, snow still on the hills and the sun bringing out vivid colour from last year's dead bracken and the yellow-brown larches on the lower slopes; not for tender passages or intimate exchanges. He remembered it for something he had almost forgotten – fun. And the severe rattling of his self-esteem.

Halfway up the field, which rose steeply to the dry-stane dyke enclosing it from the hill, he awoke with disbelief to the fact that Philippa, taking the slope with her leisurely looking stride and chatting easily to him over her shoulder – *over her shoulder* – was a good deal fitter than he was. His wind was obviously going to let him down long before hers did, and he was not responsive as he forced himself level and tried to stay there, eyeing the lift of hill above the dyke with new attention.

The dyke was as high as his head and beautifully built. His eye picking out a route via the solid corner stones, Jon turned to offer a hand to Philippa, and saw her boots going past his head.

'For fuck's sake—'

He heard her giggle as she went down the other side. Well, it is her back garden, he reflected, then swore again to find himself making excuses. She was kind enough to wait for him before floating away up the hill again. She was one fit woman, and he was going to have to admit the fact. But he'd be running every day from now on, he privately vowed.

Philippa certainly knew the ground. She led him, at that pace which appeared so unhurried but which was punishing because she never changed it, across bog and corrie, heather and scree, without ever seeming to look where she was going. Once or twice Jon suspected her of winding him up deliberately, but in the end had to accept that she was merely out for one of her customary afternoon strolls. His competitive dislike of being shown up soon gave way to professional appreciation. Philippa didn't carry an ounce of surplus flesh, had an excellent eye for terrain and a stamina he'd like to test out of simple interest. Later. At present she'd very sweetly make mincemeat of him.

They leaned shoulder to shoulder at the cairn (Jon making a fierce effort to quieten his breathing), and watched the shadows creep up the high snowy slopes, turning the apricot glow of late-afternoon light to an eerie electric blue in the steep corries. The sky was the colour of a duck's egg, empty and cold.

'I hate going down.'

'Me too.'

He felt the light weight of her against his arm, the rare and peaceful certainty of a mood shared. Going down, back to reality, would break it apart. Unendurable.

The bleak thought was dispelled as Philippa giggled.

'I've just thought . . .'

'What?'

'The drain.'

'What about it?'

'You – a Sapper – plowtering about in my silly little ditch.' She seemed to find it very funny, then stopped laughing to ask in pretended consternation, 'That is, of course, if you are in the Royal Engineers, any more than you're a major? I hadn't thought of that.'

'Watch it,' he growled, 'cut it out,' as she giggled again, but his hot resentment when she'd first challenged him on the point seemed far away now. Also the teasing light in her eyes told him that being huffy would get him nowhere.

'Come on, Jon, tell me truthfully, have I had a highly qualified engineer howking stones with me?'

How could he resist that smile? 'You have,' he said resignedly. 'One of the best in the world, if it makes you feel any better.'

'Oh, it does,' she assured him, clasping his arm with both hands for a second, before leaping away shouting, 'Come on!' and taking off down the hill at a pace which startled him. Swearing, he went after her.

We're behaving like a couple of kids, he had time to think as he paid attention to where he was putting his feet – *not* the moment to take a purler. But what did it matter? This sort of light-heartedness had been missing from his life for far too long.

Today he found that, with Philippa, even the reluctant coming down from height and space and solitude could have its compensations, as they went in out of the now cold air, sharing the domestic intimacy of dragging off boots, lighting the fire, switching on lamps, drawing curtains, making tea. But the curls of smoke and pale flames of the fire had barely begun to redden when Jon's agreeable musings about a large gin and tonic, a meal cooked by someone else, and an evening with his legs stretched out on that inviting hearth, proved premature.

Philippa was glancing at her watch. 'Jon, I'm sorry, I don't want you to rush away but I ought to go and change. I'm going out for dinner and it's a longish drive. But you stay where you are, have a drink . . .'

'Tell them you can't go.' Jon's voice, his face, his whole self, altered. 'Say you're ill.'

Philippa's heart sank. How like him not to enquire whether I want to go or not, she thought, trying to temper dismay with irony.

'I'm sorry, Jon, I can't do that.' She looked at him appealingly but his eyes were hard.

He couldn't help himself. He hated his own jealous anger, but felt defeated by all the things that could so easily take her from him. He didn't even wait to finish his tea, aware that he was being boorish, but unable to sit on by the fire knowing their day together was over.

'Thanks for your help this morning,' Philippa said at the car window, but he only shrugged, putting what they'd done into perspective as trivial, absurd even, and forcing her to step back as he reversed rapidly out.

'You bad-tempered so-and-so!' she protested, turning back to the house, minding very much that the contented time together had ended on a jarring note.

Her disappointment in his reaction didn't improve a tedious dinner party at Carrhill. The Heriots were long-standing friends of her family, but she had little in common with them nowadays. They continued to invite her, she knew, because she was on her own, and that didn't make her feel any better about it. The evening was somewhat redeemed, however, by the presence of Max Munro of Allt Farr, clearly asked as her opposite number since the rest of the guests were paired off. Max, though notorious for his lack of patience with fools, could be good company when he chose, and having known Philippa since she was a child he put himself out on this occasion to entertain her. That helped, and she was grateful to him.

Jon, driving fast, was almost past the Baldarroch track when at the last moment he swung in. He could face no company but Philippa's tonight. Keeper's Cottage looked even less inviting after the friendly comfort of Achallie, but he had sat out more time in worse rooms. He watched a cheerful programme on open-heart surgery, and assuaged a new loneliness with carefully timed drinking. He'd made more than one good resolution today.

His last waking thought was of Philippa pouring herself up and over that head-high dyke as fluidly as a weasel. He was smiling as sleep engulfed him.

I I

After this day together a state of wary skirmishing established itself between them. Each still felt in control of the situation. Philippa was determined that Jon wasn't going to destroy her peace of mind, and let herself believe that as long as they stayed out of bed that wouldn't happen. Jon, who had no idea how Philippa felt about him, was determined to do nothing to risk ground gained so far, aware that finesse was needed but confused by some unfamiliar signals.

He knew he mustn't lose sight of the fact that Glen Maraich was a temporary bolthole. Though it might take months for their force to regroup in sufficient numbers for training to be resumed, technically he could be recalled at any moment. Deeper still lurked the knowledge that the operation could end in disaster, as the initial stages had, and he would find himself wishing heart and soul that he hadn't committed himself to the contract. Yet the stakes were high. It had looked like exactly the chance he'd been waiting for.

Even so, he couldn't stay away from Philippa. She and her friends didn't on the whole drop in on each other without warning, being busy people, and Philippa tended to cling jealously to any chance to be on her own at home. There was plenty of work to be done on both house and garden, so callers for whom work had to be abandoned, herself scrubbed up and food produced could be a pain.

Jon, however, came cruising up the hill whenever he

thought there was a chance of finding her in, and every time she heard the car the same clutch of excitement would make itself felt. She was indulging in a form of cheating, she knew – fooling herself that if she was vague about her movements this kept Jon on the level of a casual acquaintance. Jon too, though often frustrated by her elusiveness and the amount she packed into her days, told himself that the uncommitted approach was best. At least it meant he didn't have to show his hand to someone as certain to turn him down as Philippa was.

All the same, he kept tabs on her, and enjoyed rolling up to find her puttying windows, dragging rubbish from an old ashtip, knocking together a cold-frame, uprooting nettles. He would come strolling across to see what she was doing and make one or two patronising observations, and in no time his jacket would be off and he'd be deep in whatever project was on hand, slipping into conversation with the same ease.

He liked the way Philippa tackled jobs, but liked even more getting stuck into those that were beyond her. On one occasion he arrived to find her on the roof, trying to net the chimneys against the persistent jackdaws, who had taken them over while the cottage was empty.

Jon subdued an unfamiliar lurch of panic as he shouted up, 'What do you think you're doing?'

'Being defeated,' Philippa called back in frank relief to see him. 'I've discovered I need two hands to fasten the wire and one to hold on with.'

'Hang on.' With great satisfaction he joined her on the roof-ridge, balancing easily where she hadn't had the courage to let go her hold on the chimney. He stepped round her and fixed the netting in place with a few deft turns, ticking her off as he did so for not waiting for him to do the job in the first place. But he was impressed that she'd had a go, and he valued the moments they spent, legs astride the ridge, enjoying the sunshine and the new view a housetop affords.

He pushed back one or two loose slates while he was about it, and spotted a couple of cracked ones he could replace with the spares he'd noticed in the shed at Keeper's Cottage.

On other visits he sealed leaking gutters, rehung a door, and freed the axe Philippa had driven, immovably it seemed to her, into a knotty root, splitting the latter apart with a what's-the-problem look she chose to ignore.

Tucked into 'his' corner of the kitchen one day, making inroads in a freshly baked batch of scones, he commented, 'That centre light isn't very handy, is it? Wouldn't you be better off with one over the cooker and another over the sink?'

'Can't run to luxuries, I'm afraid,' Philippa said cheerfully. 'Wow, look at those cobwebs.'

'Want me to do it for you?'

Her eyes widened. 'Jon! Could you do that?'

'It's not black magic, you know.'

'It is to me. But how would you manage it? It's all stone in here, isn't it?'

'Do you mind if I don't try to explain,' he said wearily. 'Just decide where you want the lights.'

'Oh, Jon, you are wonderful,' she breathed.

'Belt up.'

Altering the kitchen wiring at Achallie gave Jon more satisfaction than any job he'd ever done, and no amount of telling himself he was a fool did any good. It seemed ironic that he'd undertaken such chores with reluctance in the Thornton house, motivated by nothing more than a wish to increase its value.

He enjoyed working on the Mini too, though a drawback was that Philippa then disappeared to do other things. Also her comments could be less than rewarding.

'There, listen to that,' he would order, and she would obey earnestly but with a look of doubt.

'Well?' he'd demand impatiently.

'I'm sorry, Jon, is that better or worse?' she would ask apologetically, trying to look solemn.

'God in heaven, woman, you're hopeless,' he'd explode, slamming shut his tool box, hiding his grin.

She was so unlike the girls he'd always gone for, but he found that an intense physical awareness of her had grown in him, of a kind he'd never known before. He would find himself almost unbearably moved by some detail which would have meant nothing in the past – the thinness of her wrists as she wrestled with some heavy object, the soft hair at her temples lit by the spring sunlight, the co-ordination of her muscles as she swung the pick or negotiated some obstacle on the hill. He would get a hard-on just watching her. But apart from this emphatic and unsubtle reaction he discovered another which was even more telling – her body, and the beauty he saw in it, had become precious to him without his ever having touched her. He felt he could feel with her skin.

This aside, he was in a much more stable state these days. Less time spent in the bar, more fresh air and exercise, returning fitness and an absorbing fascination with a woman, with everything still to play for, couldn't fail to produce results, and observers at the Cluny Arms began to think he was halfway human after all. They weren't too keen about his interest in Philippa, but were prepared to be more tolerant if she approved of him.

Jon's hold on good humour was still fragile however. If he suspected that Philippa was shutting him out he could swiftly revert to his dark mood. Once he lost track of her for a day or two, finding Achallie deserted, and ranged the glen and Muirend looking for her, though angry with himself for being so dependent on seeing her.

By the evening of the third day he was eaten by resentment.

He'd spent some hours in the Cluny bar, withdrawn and silent, sufficiently self-disciplined to regulate his drinking, but the aura of contained anger around him warning off all contact. Ian Murray, sure he'd end up with a fight on his hands, was thankful when he took himself off soon after eleven.

Without conscious decision Jon found himself heading for Achallie. The Mini was there. Relief filled him to see it. No light was visible; Philippa must be in bed. When had she got back, where had she been? Jealousy stabbed again, but less sharply; she was here now. He pulled into the gateway below the hill track and switched off lights and engine, wanting to absorb the fact of her nearness. He imagined her in bed, asleep in the downstairs room he'd never seen, the relaxed limbs and smooth warm skin, the spread of hair.

Christ, I want her, he thought with a rueful honesty. It was so much more than sexual longing; it was a wrenching need for a completeness to life, a meaning and rooted permanence he knew could never be for him.

Steps on the road. Reaching for the lights he caught Philippa stilled like a rabbit in the beam, an arm up, long fingers shielding her eyes. Then she had recognised the car and was coming to the window, smiling.

'Jon, what on earth are you doing here?' She sounded more pleased than surprised. 'Coming in for coffee?'

She really is something else, Jon thought. Here I am hanging about outside her house like some damned stalker, and she asks no questions, draws no inference.

'Coffee would be good,' he said, hoping he sounded as casual and ordinary as she did.

In the kitchen she asked, 'OK in here?'

'Fine. When did you get back?'

Her bag and big basket were on the table.

'Half an hour ago. I was getting a few gulps of air

before sorting this lot out. Look, loot. Your timing's as good as ever.'

She began unpacking tupperware containers, prising off lids.

'Did you make these?' Tiny *vols-au-vent*, crab patties, curry puffs, sausage rolls, cheese straws.

'Every, every one,' Philippa lamented. 'And a few hours ago I wouldn't have believed I'd ever want to see them again, but now I'm starving. Um, a rather travelled look to one or two. Never mind. Plates, please.'

'Some party,' Jon commented, reaching down plates. He still couldn't bring himself to ask where she'd been, hating the unknown people who had claims on her.

'Wedding,' Philippa replied briefly, spooning coffee into the percolator. 'Hard work, too. Oh sorry, Jon, I should have asked if you'd prefer a drink.'

'Coffee's fine.' Alcohol, when he was with her, was unimportant, which he found reassuring. But was she fobbing him off with these uninformative answers?

'Actually it was fun,' Philippa went on, oblivious of undercurrents. 'The great thing about being worker as well as guest is that you can rush off to do something urgent when some bore corners you, like old buffers who danced with your grandmother and want you to think they knocked her off as well.'

Jon laughed. How could he cling to a sense of grievance when Philippa was so natural and welcoming? God, if only he could stay. He felt the inevitable physical response at the thought of it, yet as clearly as if she'd posted the rules on the wall he knew it was out of the question. How did she do it? Her courtesy, the trust implicit in her openness, created their own defences.

All the same, in spite of his frustration, Jon was a lot more contented as he drove home. He had expected nothing when, restless and lonely, he had come up this road an hour ago.

He felt confident as he took it again the next afternoon, and it was a severe jolt to find another car parked behind the Mini. He drove straight past.

The car remained for the next five days, during which Philippa appeared only once at the hotel. While there, she made a point of coming to find Jon, explaining that she had friends staying and inviting him to meet them. He curtly declined.

The day Philippa's guests were due to leave he drove to the Cluny Arms with anticipation filling him, sure she would come in, feeling as deprived by now as if he hadn't seen her for a month. Sharon and Lorna were laying up the dining-room as he went in, calling to each other as they slapped down silver, the door to the hall open.

The first words stopped Jon in his tracks.

'Fancy Philippa getting up at six to come here.'

'I know, when she's still on holiday. Barmy.'

'I suppose she knows Ian won't have touched a thing, and the work will be piling up.'

'Just as well he doesn't touch it. He can't add two and two.'

Giggles.

Jon stood very still, unnoticed by them and out of sight of anyone in the bar.

'What's he called, anyway?' Sharon asked, as they started to rub up the silver.

'Who?'

'That man she stays with. The one with the cottage on the West Coast.'

'Haven't a clue. You'd think she'd go somewhere decent, though, wouldn't you? Not Scotland.'

'Where would you go?'

'I dunno. Majorca or somewhere.'

'It's Mayorca, you waste of space.'

'Mayorca, then . . .'

Hours later Jon negotiated the Subaru with exaggerated care out of the carpark of a Muirend pub. A stone wall bulged towards him, receded, and he was out in the street. A car flashed at him. Police? Christ, no, his lights. He hunched forward in his seat, concentrating. He could barely remember now where this had begun. His mind groped back. Philippa, of course. Always Philippa, damn her.

Muirend was left behind; the road climbed.

Across the glen he saw the light on the hillside but it was a moment or two before he registered that it could only be at Achallie. What did that mean? Philippa was away, had gone away without telling him, to stay with some bastard on the West Coast. Someone she'd never told him about. But she'd left a light on. To scare away the burglars? Lot of good that would do if her car wasn't visible outside for days on end.

As the Dalquhat sign appeared, Jon remembered how, that last time he'd parked by the field gate, she had materialised out of the darkness and come smiling to ask him in. In a sliding tailskid he made the turn.

Philippa, tired out and about to go to bed, checked, listening. That sounded like Jon's car on the hill, but hardly like Jon's driving.

It had been a long day, and a long week. She had found the Telfords, not specially close friends who clung to Achallie as a convenient holiday base, heavy going this year. When Jon hadn't been keen to come and help her out she hadn't tried to persuade him, but she had missed seeing him more than she'd expected to, and had regretted her offer to go and settle the Telfords into Alec's cottage for the remainder of their holiday. She had offended them, she knew, by refusing to stay the night as originally planned, but she couldn't wait to get back. And she'd kept quiet about putting in a couple of hours at the hotel this morning before they were up, or they'd have made even more fuss about her driving back.

Hearing the grind of gravel, and the Subaru's engine race and die, she turned back along the hall, flurried but elated. Then, at a heavy thump a moment later on the kitchen door, she frowned. Something was wrong.

Jon looked rough. Philippa's heart sank at the sight of him, and at the memories it brought back – memories of watching her handsome, charming father drink away all they owned, and ruin his life and health in the process. She knew Jon was capable of heavy drinking – there had been plenty of stories going the rounds about the major's excesses when he first came to the glen – but she had never seen him like this. He seemed larger than ever, looming on the step, and actually menacing. Philippa felt a frisson of alarm. How absurd to think she could keep a man like this at arm's length with a few odd jobs and walks.

But she faced him steadily, in spite of his truculent opening: 'I want a word with you.'

'All right, but I don't think this is quite—'

She saw his face darken, and knew her tone had been wrong. Too light and social. Patronising, to him.

He propped a hand against the wall and leaned closer, so that she felt overpowered by his bulk, and had to resist an impulse to duck under his arm and escape.

'Had a nice time with your chum?'

Jon hadn't taken time to work out that, since Philippa was back, he no longer had anything to be angry about. In his mind, through the morose hours when only some inner core of discipline had kept him from drinking himself into oblivion as he'd longed to do, jealousy had built an elaborate and detailed structure out of the few chance words he'd overheard.

Philippa had no clue to this. She simply saw that, much as she dreaded a confrontation with Jon in this mood, it would be irresponsible to let him drive away.

'You'd better come in and have some coffee,' she said, and realised helplessly that whatever she said sounded prissy and self-righteous.

She wasn't surprised when Jon snarled, lowering his arm sharply so that she was literally trapped, 'Coffee, that's about all that's ever on offer, isn't it?'

She didn't want to think what he meant by that. 'I'm sure it's what you need right now, anyway,' she said firmly, and wasn't sure whether she was relieved or dismayed when, with a grunt of ironic contempt, he straightened up, saying, 'Coffee it is, then.'

'Come into the sitting-room.' If she could get him into a chair she might feel less threatened, she thought, then she could calm down while she made the coffee.

He followed her in.

'Come on, Jon, sit down.'

He ignored her, standing with legs braced, head thrust belligerently forward. 'So where've you been?'

'To Arisaig, with the friends who've been staying here.' It was none of his business. Yet she couldn't suppress an irrational satisfaction that it mattered so much to him.

'Friends. Lots of friends, haven't you, Philippa? That's all you've got a clue about, isn't it?'

She had no way of knowing that this taunt, pretty well meaningless, was all he could dredge up as he took in the simple explanation for her absence, and worked out that it had only lasted for a day. He still felt she'd treated him badly, though he couldn't quite pin down how. It made him want to hurt her, to pierce by any means her impervious armour of good manners and self-control.

'You should grow up, Philippa. Come down from your ivory tower, find out about real life. Because as it is you're nothing but a cocktease. Ever heard the word? Not very pretty, is it? You don't like that, do you?'

But Philippa didn't wait for more. After one rigid moment of shock, she turned and went out. Shaking, she stood in the kitchen doorway, then, unconsciously doing just what baffled and distanced Jon most, took a grip on herself. In spite of his taunts she must make coffee. She couldn't get rid of him until he'd sobered up.

But when she went back to the sitting-room, hiding a real nervousness, she found him prone on the sofa, asleep. This was where the caring female was supposed to take off his boots, cover him with a rug. Tough. Philippa put down the tray and left him to it.

A few minutes later, however, she came back with the duvet from the spare bed. Sheila Telford had stripped the bed and neatly folded the sheet and duvet cover. Did she think that proved her a good housewife? Did she put her own sheets into her washing machine *folded*? Philippa concentrated fiercely on this irritant.

But once in bed it was impossible to hold off tears. Was that really what he thought of her? Those times together had seemed so good, she pleaded, to whom she didn't know. She had been sure he'd enjoyed them as much as she had. Now she had to face the truth. This was the real Jon. How naive he must think her, how inexperienced and boring and immature.

Soon after dawn she jolted awake. Footsteps had woken her, footsteps coming to her door. She lifted on one elbow, listening tensely. After an aching pause she heard the steps retreat towards the kitchen, heard the back door slam.

The Subaru started up, reversed with a roar into the road, and headed down the hill.

Philippa, eyes tightly closed, buried her face in her pillow.

12

It was unlucky that on Philippa's next visit to the hotel, having, as she imagined, got her defences in good order after days of strenuous work in the garden and long head-down solitary walks, the topic being aired at coffee break was the major's most recent exploit.

'Well, all I can say is, the state he was in, he was lucky not to be picked up on the road from Muirend.'

'He gets through cases of gin in that cottage of his, by all accounts.'

'He'd do better to stay there then, and no' come messing up my rooms when I've done them,' Ailie, who came in daily to clean, said tartly. 'Lucky I went in to check the radiator. I nearly died when I saw him.'

'Did he help himself to the key?'

'I just wish the lads didn't think it clever to keep slipping him drinks,' Ian Murray put in grimly.

'Ross Nicholson didna' think it was so clever when he found himself flat on his back.'

'And maybe Moira didn't when she found herself flat on hers,' Ailie sniggered coarsely.

'Was Moira with him?' Sharon asked, agog.

'Ach, you'd never believe what he'd get up to,' Ailie said, suddenly cagey. The reference to Moira had been based on nothing more than a wish to add spice to the drama.

'Now, how about getting back to work, the lot of you,'

Ian interposed hurriedly, having caught sight of Philippa's face. She and the major had been getting very thick lately. Shona would never have let the gossip go this far if she'd been present.

As they scattered Philippa stood up, pushed in her chair, put the lid on the biscuit tin and her mug in the dishwasher, walked collectedly to the office and sat down at the computer. Numb and composed, she embarked on a long sequence of error and confusion. Escape and abortion exercise, she thought as she struggled on, but was unable to lighten her mood. She managed to achieve something like order before she left, except for two booking letters put into the wrong envelopes, which would soon go on their way to raise gratuitous panic.

I knew about Moira. I haven't heard anything I didn't already know, she told herself as she drove home. She had been telling herself the same thing all day.

But that was before.

Before what?

Before – nothing that could be put into words. Before she had felt as she did. Before she had known Jon felt as he did. Known? Yes, known, a stubborn inner voice insisted.

Don't be a fool. Just be glad it's over, without more pain than this, before you gave yourself away. Very comforting, she thought, back in her cold empty house.

The car on the hill, the knock at the door. Not a thump this time, but her heart jolted in trepidation all the same. If he'd been drinking on a daily basis since she last saw him what frame of mind would he be in by now? If she didn't open the door what would he do? Batter it down? Though if he turned the knob it would work equally well. The glimmer of humour braced her.

Jon didn't speak when she opened the door; he just stood

there watching her, presenting himself as it were. He looked very scrubbed and brushed and tidy, the aura of the penitent hovering around him.

Hollow and shaking with nerves, barely recovered from a protracted hangover and dreading his reception, he saw, unbelievably, after a moment of frozen tension, a gleam of amusement appear in Philippa's eyes.

'You do look clean,' she remarked, and the amusement reached her mouth, warmed her voice.

'Oh, Philippa.' He ached to put his arms round her, gather her up, obliterate every moment of his life till now, and above all wipe out the mountain of words which would inevitably have to be climbed.

There was one second more of hesitation. Philippa knew that if she was going to make the kill this was the moment for it, swift and clean. Jon had left her in no doubt as to how he rated her friendship: he was still seeing Moira. And drinkers, as she knew from bitter experience, merely went from one bout to the next and never changed. There was nothing to decide. But, looking into Jon's eyes as she braced herself to tell him squarely that she thought it better he didn't come to Achallie again, for one fraction of a second she saw behind their watchfulness the genuine need he couldn't hide. Then she saw it masked, his face hardening, and she knew he was about to say something defensive and probably destructive beyond repair.

'Come in,' she said quietly, and was glad he didn't attempt to conceal his relief at the words.

Without speaking they went through to the sitting-room and without speaking faced each other, standing in front of the fire. All the things that had to be said reverberated in the silence.

'Thanks for – asking me in,' Jon said at last, and had to clear his throat and have a second go at it.

Philippa nodded an acknowledgement, her face strained and unsmiling.

'Look, I can't really remember much about – the other night,' Jon plunged awkwardly. 'I know I must have been – I probably said a lot of things that – anyway, I apologise for crashing in on you like that.'

'Crashing out,' Philippa amended equably, and his mouth relaxed a little. It was good of her to be ready to make even so small a joke about it.

'I thought you'd gone away. That's what I'd heard, anyway.' It seemed incredible to him now that this one tiny shred of news had rattled him enough to set the whole disaster in train.

Philippa frowned. What did that have to do with anything? 'I'd expected to be away for a night, but I changed my mind.' And came back hoping to spend time with you, you fool. Except that I was the fool, to have altered my plans for such a reason.

Jon knew he shouldn't put the next question, but it was out while he was still warning himself not to ask. 'What about the bloke?'

'The bloke?' Philippa was nonplussed by this, and though Jon winced at his own crassness he saw that he had to explain himself now.

'I thought – I gathered – that you were at somebody's cottage.' Jesus, he swore inwardly, was he saying this, as maladroit as any teenager? But where Philippa was concerned he seemed to be victim to a helpless jealousy he would have glibly mocked in anyone else.

'Ah.' Philippa studied him thoughtfully. She was not accustomed to having to give an account of herself. 'I borrow it from time to time.'

Jon knew from her tone that that was it. She'd done as much explaining as she was prepared to. The silence stretched as he rejected one opening after another.

Philippa decided to help him out. 'You fell asleep on the sofa. Do you remember that?'

'I remember waking up there,' Jon said cautiously. His memories weren't too clear about the events of that night, but there were some details he sincerely hoped he had wrong.

Philippa nodded. He would also remember coming to her door. What had his thoughts been?

'Did I – was I out of order?' Surely he'd recall it if he had been? But he had to know.

'Did you try and get your leg over, do you mean?' Philippa asked sweetly, and raised her eyebrows in affected surprise at the reaction this produced. She shook her head. 'No, you stuck to being abusive.'

'Oh, God.' He laid his arm along the high granite mantel-piece and put his head down on it.

'I'd offer you coffee,' Philippa went on without any special emphasis, 'but you seem to object to that.'

His head came up. So now to the accusations, the due exacting of penance. Then he saw that, unbelievably, she was teasing him. She wasn't going to wallow in the whole thing, or hammer him into the ground.

'I objected?' he asked, feeling his way.

'You did.'

'So now I don't get coffee?'

'What a nerve.'

Suddenly Jon, in spite of all that was at stake here, gave a little snort of laughter.

'What?' Philippa asked.

'The way you said, "You do look clean," when I showed up just now. It was the last thing I was expecting.'

'All that was missing was a great vulgar florist's bouquet creaking with cellophane.'

'Hell, I forgot that . . .'

They laughed; were thankful to be released into laughter.

'You know what I'd really like?' Philippa asked.

'What?' It wouldn't be what he'd really like. Was it too good to be true? Had she only been leading him along, and now meant to put him through hoops after all?

'I'd like proper, knees-under-the-table dinner. The whole bit. I feel as though I haven't eaten properly for days and by the look of you you haven't either. Or is it too soon for you to face food?'

'Watch it.'

She felt light-heartedness surge back. 'I've had a brilliant idea – we'll nick a steak and kidney pie.'

'Nick? As in pinch?'

'Well, they're not strictly speaking mine. I made a batch for Lady Hay. But I can make her another. Come on, you peel the tatties while I do the skilled work, like putting the pie in the oven and getting vegetables out of the freezer.'

'Oh, yeah?'

But Jon knew he was happy as he ran water over the potatoes. He hadn't seriously expected to get a toe across the threshold again, and here he was . . .

'Did you sleep with Moira?'

Knife between the shoulder blades. Fortunately, however, Jon took time to register the tone, empty of everything but straightforward enquiry. A lifelong habit of defensiveness when his personal privacy was threatened had to be dispensed with on the instant. Nothing but the simple truth would answer here.

'No,' he said quietly, not moving.

'Did you go to her house?'

'Yes.'

'Since you saw me last?' Even harder to ask, and he heard that in her voice.

He dropped potato and peeler into the bowl and turned. Not only the controlled inflexion but the question itself had told him something crucial. Head down, her back to him, Philippa was trying to prise a chunk off a solid lump of frozen broad beans. Driven to ask these questions by a compulsion she hardly recognised, she was appalled to have done so.

Jon took a step towards her and, careful to make his touch light, turned her to face him. She abandoned the beans, raised her chin and met his eyes.

'No, love,' he said gently. It was the first endearment he had used to her.

She was unable to speak for a moment, then she nodded. 'Right.'

One simple word, but it was a moment Jon would never forget. He had told the truth and had been believed.

'I did go to Moira's cottage, once, a while back. Nothing happened. That's not –' a memory of the mean room came back, but he could hardly put into words, or expect Philippa to understand, how fundamentally the squalor of such surroundings offended him '– that's not my scene. I slept in the car. Nearly froze to death too,' he added with feeling, remembering.

Philippa, who had not missed the look of distaste which tightened his face, grinned at that conclusion, and seizing the bag of beans with new zest whanged it against the edge of the sink. The hoary lump broke apart.

Jon smiled at her with a look of immense affection which she didn't see.

In honour of the 'proper' dinner Philippa opened a bottle of Chateauneuf, laid the elegant table in the sitting-room with care, and offered Jon sherry.

'Is this a celebration?'

'Perhaps it is.'

'I must get drunk more often.'

'Don't push your luck . . .'

But this was another subject, as they were both aware,

which couldn't be swept under the carpet, and though they left it for now, in an unspoken agreement that dinner shouldn't be spoiled, they inevitably came to it in the end.

'You heard at the hotel that I'd been on the batter?' Jon asked abruptly, when they'd left the table and were sitting by the fire.

'Yes.' Philippa put down her coffee cup.

'Well, it was – I mean, I don't know if this makes it any better, but it was a continuation of that bout in Muirend. I just couldn't handle the idea that—'

'Jon, no, please,' Philippa interrupted. 'Before you say any more I ought to explain. I should have told you before. I get upset about drinking because—'

'I don't drink,' Jon said.

Philippa gaped at him. '*What?*' Then she began to laugh, and in a moment he was laughing with her.

'No, but seriously,' he pursued when he could speak. 'I really don't—'

'Please don't say it again,' Philippa begged.

'What I'm trying to say is, the drinking's not out of control. I know you've seen me the worse for wear a couple of times, but it was always for a reason. My choice, if you like. I can cut it out whenever I want to. It's not a problem.'

Philippa looked serious enough now, and dubious. He could hardly blame her.

'Look, I'd been having a bit of a rough time, before I came here.' His voice was brusque; it went against the grain to touch on the subject at all, let alone here, with her. He hated to think of the ugliness and brutality of that world reaching into this peaceful room. 'I hadn't had a drink for months, so when I kind of – let go, it had more effect, that's all. I want you to believe me. I'm not an alcoholic or anywhere near it. Though I suppose any alcoholic says the same,' he ended, with a spurt of bleak self-contempt which Philippa didn't like.

'It's none of my business anyway,' she said.

Jon frowned; that wasn't good enough.

'It's just that,' Philippa hurried on before he could speak, 'it's been a problem in the past.'

'Your husband?' Jon was suddenly alert. He had often wondered what had broken up the marriage.

'To an extent.' She still found it hard to believe that she, of all people, should have laid herself open to the same repeated and hated cycle. 'But it was my father who—' She found after all that she couldn't go on, and reached for the percolator. 'More coffee? No, this isn't hot enough. I'll make more.'

He let her go. He had never seen that disillusioned expression on her face before. But the little she'd said had told him a good deal. In time he would hear more; would make a point of hearing more. She needed to talk this out, that much was clear.

When she returned, Philippa changed the subject with a vengeance. 'By the way,' she asked, refilling his cup, 'am I a cocktease?'

Jon, replete in the big chair, heels on the hearth and boot soles nicely warming, confident that disaster was averted, gasped. 'Bloody hell, Philippa.'

'Only I'd like to know if I am.'

He drew in his long legs, hitched himself up in his seat and surveyed her, perched on a favourite leather pouffe with her back against the sofa-arm, her face, carefully expressionless, half shadowed by her hair.

'Hey,' he said softly.

She gazed at him gravely, hooking her hair behind her ear. The firelight traced the delicate line of her jaw.

'If I said that —' never had he so much dreaded being clumsy, choosing the wrong words '— it only meant that I wanted you. Want you.'

'I don't mean to be, you know.' He had never heard her

sound so vulnerable, and it moved him to a new, fierce protectiveness.

'Philippa, I know you don't. But you must realise, you do make a man feel – I mean, you're so open and friendly—' And warm, generous and perceptive. Qualities which had ravished him.

'So is that how it appears? To you?'

'No, never, not for a second. Believe me. As far as I'm concerned, you've made it clear all along exactly where we stand.'

He wanted to tell her how much it had meant to him to learn to enjoy a woman's company without sex as the sole or primary object, but he was afraid of putting it badly and doing more harm. 'That doesn't mean I don't want you like hell, though,' he said again, with a grin that stripped the years away.

'Good,' Philippa said, briskly if ambiguously, reaching for her cup.

Jon settled back into his chair. 'That it, then?' he said, matching her casualness, amused but satisfied. She certainly didn't let things fester out of sight.

With the comfortable feeling that much had been put right, Philippa talked more readily about her life that evening than Jon had ever known her do before, though she still kept to a mainly anecdotal style. Listening as she talked about hind stalking one severe winter he asked, 'Where was this? Here? Somewhere in Glen Maraich?'

At the question Philippa paused then said, as though coming to a decision, 'One day I'll take you there.'

Jon tucked the promise away, token of time to be.

Only one thing seemed wrong to him as their talk flowed on. He sat here and she sat there. But he let it stay that way. He knew that if once he touched her he wouldn't be able to trust himself. And if he got it wrong there wouldn't be any second chances. Not with her. So the time passed in a strange duality of contentment to be, against all the odds, where he was, and the effort to subdue the different, more insistent messages of his body.

It was hard to leave. Going out to the car in the soft air under a starless sky he protested, since he couldn't complain about what he really minded, 'What have you done to me, woman? I came here to grovel and swear that I was a reformed character, and you've poured sherry and wine and whisky down my throat.'

'Don't worry, you ate far too much for them to have any effect.'

He laughed. 'Come here.' He rationed himself, he didn't know how, to one sensuous, dreamy hug, then pushed her away. 'Get into the house and lock the door or I won't be responsible.'

'Jon.'

'What?' Don't hope, don't hope.

'You thanked me for letting you come in but – I want to thank you for being brave enough to appear in the first place.'

He reached out to take her arm in a brief grip, finding nothing to say in reply. But, driving away, he was shaken to find how much those simple words had moved him. She had known what it had taken to come here tonight.

13

Philippa sat in the sunlight pouring through the wide kitchen windows at Tynach House, high above the snowy field running down to the loch. It had been an early start and the sort of drive, for the fifteen miles of unswept single-track road from the ferry anyway, which you only realised had been tense when it was over.

She loved Tynach House and loved this kitchen. When she'd come here as a child to stay with Sue it had been the billiards-room, of no interest to two small girls. The kitchen had been the dankest and darkest of any she knew, quite a distinction, and miles from the dining-room. When Sue had inherited the house she and her husband had revamped it to suit their needs, and now mostly used the rooms looking south and west over the sea-loch and the hills beyond.

The new kitchen was the heart of the house and, walking into its midday quiet to the welcome of Hecla, the Gordon setter, finding Sue's note of mixed greeting and cooking thoughts, covering three sheets in idiosyncratic abbreviations, Philippa had felt a sense of homecoming – followed at once by a new tug of loneliness.

Questing for something to eat, she found in the fridge a terrine of pâté with a note propped against it. 'Hind's liver. Not bad. You must eat something you haven't cooked yourself!'

With Hecla pressing affectionately against her knee, for a lot of luggage had been about today, but staring aloofly into the distance to deceive her into thinking he wasn't concentrated heart and soul on the pâté, Philippa had a quick lunch and tried to turn her mind to cooking. Half drowsing in the warmth coming through the glass, all she could think of was how much she would have enjoyed sharing this with Jon. The drive wouldn't have been tense with him there.

No, of course it wouldn't, she told herself, because he'd have been doing the driving. He wasn't the passenger type. Her thoughts drifted. She was recalled by the gulps of the setter trying to deal with its saliva.

'Not a hope,' she told him, getting to her feet. He bore her no ill-will, but escorted her kindly to the room in the tower, where Sue had put bowls of greeny-yellow wild daffodils to welcome her. Philippa dropped her bag on the floor, and looked at the enormous bed up its two mahogany steps, built high so that its occupants could enjoy the view. Feeling the clutch of physical longing which only Jon had ever aroused in her, she was suddenly impatient with her own self-discipline, wanting to have skipped the preliminaries and to have plunged already into glorious sex.

Get cooking, she ordered herself. But as she rattled down the spiral stair, not pausing to unpack, Hecla at or on her heels, she knew it had made an enormous difference to her in the past few days to know that Jon had never slept with Moira. She would do her best to be sensible. He'd gone to Moira's house; he was capable of chatting up that sort of woman. Then she would see again his look of distaste as he said, 'That's not my scene.' She knew she trusted it.

Walking through the bright white landscape a couple of hours later on her way to meet the school Land Rover, Hecla furrowing the snow in joyous circles around her, she thought of skiing with Jon a couple of days ago. They had had to go high and there had been no long runs, but the snow had been perfect and the sun actually hot for a while. Spring skiing at its best. How much fitter Jon was looking. He'd virtually stopped drinking, only appearing at the hotel on the days when she was there and then only to have lunch with her.

The Land Rover emerged from behind the larch plantation and Philippa reached the drive end as it stopped. Mariana and Neil jumped down with shy, beaming faces, slightly formal with her at first, reserving their warmest welcome for Hecla, but quite happy to accept her presence. Also school had been exciting today so they were soon chattering.

'We made a *monster* slide, the longest slide we've ever had the whole time I've been there,' Neil, aged five, told her in awe.

Mariana was more interested in the drama of the minister's fox terrier, who had been seen through the window scattering the teacher's hens, so that sums had been abandoned as everyone poured out to give chase.

Would Jon really have liked this, Philippa wondered, as they took hay to the ponies, fed some very boring rabbits, and spent an energetic hour whirling down the field on hay-filled fertiliser bags, where she and Sue had hissed on a heavy wooden sledge with high runners. The equipment and technique might be different, but the exquisite terror of over-shooting into the dark waiting waters of the loch remained the same.

But Jon didn't seem to object to the odd bit of domesticity. Rather to her surprise, he clearly preferred quiet evenings at Achallie to taking her out. And he was willing to get involved in the most mundane of jobs. That day, for example, when he'd arrived to find her hacking her way into the unwieldy roll of carpet Michael Thorne had given her for the hall, he'd wasted no time in getting to work . . .

She listened with half her attention to the children's voices taking on the sing-song intonation of the village school as they did their reading homework, honoured tradition by letting them make their own eggy bread for supper – Neil spreading his with syrup – and helped them to mix Hecla's dinner, then packed with them into one armchair to read *The Story of an Exmoor Pony*, enjoying handling the familiar copy again. She was perfectly happy to be where she was, she told herself.

Jon felt more lost with Philippa away than he could have believed possible, but took the chance to do some much-needed work on his car, and to pursue a rigorous fitness programme. Both occupations gave him plenty of time to think about her, however, and he would find himself – often to keep his mind off thoughts of another kind – going over once more the facts by now gleaned about her past. Boarding school, yes, that probably went without saying, but then the finishing school in Switzerland – did they still call them that or was she winding him up? He had learned to his cost that she could look him in the eye with the most innocent look, while telling him a load of total rubbish. When she thought he needed putting in his place. But the smile would give her away. She could control her mouth, but not her eyes. That mouth was beautiful though, especially the sexy droop to it when she was serious . . .

In self-preservation, he would force his mind to change direction. After the year abroad, it seemed there had been various travels. But not on Daddy's cash; she'd worked her way. She had never mentioned her father again after the reference to his drinking, and never spoke of anyone else in her family. Jon had dug for no further information; she would tell him when she wanted to. With her, in spite of the ever-present awareness that holding here could end at short notice, there was a strange sense of time having a different dimension, of being prepared to let events unroll at their own pace.

Everything was different with her. She was under his skin and he knew it. But where in his life was there room for someone like Philippa? His life. The gnaw of fear would make itself felt, the sick reluctance to have to go back to that other world, making it impossible to project his mind forward to any 'afterwards'.

It was just as well, his thoughts would circle, that Philippa was so determined to keep him out of her bed; or, more bafflingly, gave the impression that she had no idea that he wanted to get into it. Well, that kept things simple.

Oh yes?

In spite of all there was to do, the days at Tynach seemed long to Philippa, a problem she wasn't used to. On the second night more snow fell, and she woke to panic at the possibility of not being able to get back to Glen Maraich, then was annoyed with herself for knowing that meant get back to Jon. He probably hadn't given her a thought since she left.

But a mild wind shifted new snow and old, and when she went to meet the children after school the road was black and gleaming, a strip of grass green on either side, the larch plantation a vibrant orange in the sunshine. Sue and Nick would get back without difficulty. She was ashamed of herself for being so relieved.

They arrived just before eleven, sitting down to start at once on the supper Philippa had ready for them, recounting the mixed fortunes of Cheltenham, passing on news of mutual friends gleaned there. It was after two when Philippa, with the drive home in mind, made a move, and Sue, reeling and yawning, went up to her room with her to say goodnight.

'It was so good of you to look after things, Pippa. I'm really, really grateful. The children love having you, and I always relax when I know you're with them.'

'I enjoy it. And anyway, they look after me.'

'You're a love,' Sue said, hugging her. 'And tomorrow I can be deliciously idle with my full freezers and we can do some proper catching up.'

'About tomorrow – would you mind terribly if I slid off early?'

'Oh, no! Why? It's such ages since I've seen you. Don't say you've got to rush off to another job?'

'Not a job.' Wishing she wasn't so inconveniently honest, Philippa found herself blushing.

'A man?' Sue demanded, waking up suddenly as she saw the blush. 'Who is he? Why haven't I heard about it?'

'He's nobody. I mean, it's nothing.'

'So tell me.'

'Sue, we can't start on this now. It's nearly three in the morning. Anyway, there's nothing to tell. No past, no future and very little present. He's trouble, hassle, disaster. There, now you know.'

'Fascinating. You're not going to leave this house till I've heard all about it.'

'There's nothing to hear,' Philippa protested.

'See you at breakfast.' And Sue whisked off to share the titbit with Nick, for Philippa's friends had been concerned over her new inclination for solitude and independence, and this sounded promising.

How to explain Jon? Lingering over breakfast after Nick and the children had left the next morning, Philippa found herself strangely tongue-tied. 'He's good to be with,' she wound up, having conscientiously enumerated his manifold faults.

'It's more than that, though, isn't it?' Sue asked, looking at her closely.

'Lust too, of course,' Philippa said cheerfully.

'Nothing wrong with lust.'

'Oh, good, that's fine, then.'

They laughed, letting it go at that, but Sue wished as she saw Philippa off that they lived nearer to each other.

As Philippa was filling up with petrol at Kirkton garage, Andy took it upon himself to come out and tell her with sly relish that the major had been in trouble yet again. He'd got himself into a fight, been beaten up, and had ended up in Muirend hospital, where he still was.

'He's gone too far this time,' Andy said, not attempting to hide his satisfaction. He hadn't appreciated Jon's ministrations on the Mini, taking away work that by rights belonged to the garage. 'Must have been out of his skull. Some mess he's in, so they say.'

Philippa supposed afterwards that she had made some suitable response. Certainly she didn't remember driving home, numb with shock – and disillusionment. Less than three weeks since that last episode which had so nearly ruined everything between them. And he said he didn't drink. Fighting as well this time. Violence, upheaval, melodrama, these were Jon's natural element. He deserved all he got.

Methodically, trying to ignore the fact that her hands were shaking, Philippa unloaded the car and began the process of stirring the house to life. She lit the fire, switched on the immersion heater, opened her mail, though everything it contained seemed oddly remote and irrelevant, watered the plants, unpacked her bag and loaded the washing machine. Finding she was actually looking for the next chore to occupy her, she made herself go through the post with more attention. A note from Penny had been in the box with the rest.

Would Philippa phone as soon as she could; a friend of a friend living in Giffnock wanted to talk about a silver wedding celebration.

Giffnock? I'm not going all the way down there, Philippa thought with irrational anger, not clear-thinking enough at present to realise that what was annoying her was Penny's underlying message, care, concern and, as Philippa read it, a determination to draw her back into the fold. That final sentence too – 'I know Alec's been trying to get in touch, do put the poor thing out of his misery and phone when you get back' – was hardly something Philippa wanted to think about now. With an exasperated exclamation she tossed down the note and went to put on boots and jacket. She'd do some work outside; that was always good therapy.

She had got as far as the vegetable plot, fork in hand, before she registered that, in spite of the day having been so mild in the west, here the ground was still crusted with snow. In an uncharacteristic spurt of temper she threw down the fork, left it lying, and took herself off at a punishing pace up the hill.

He was nothing but a con man. It had suited him to have somewhere to go besides the Cluny Arms, a fire to sit by other than his own, even a few jobs to fill his time. He had easily fooled her into thinking he was attracted to her, and all the time must have been laughing at her for falling for it. No matter how outrageously he behaved, he knew he only had to appear on her doorstep looking contrite and she would let him in. How could she have been so gullible? What a fool he must have thought her.

But as she came out onto the ridge and the keen air cooled her cheeks, and the familiar beauty penetrated her abstraction, her anger, always short-lived, began to subside. Jon had been hurt badly enough to end up in hospital. She had thought she cared about him – no, she *knew* she had found something good with him which she'd never found with anyone else – yet her only reaction on hearing what had happened to him had been to feel let down and angry because he wasn't the person she wanted him to be. How seriously had he been injured? Beaten up – that could mean anything. It had happened last night, according to Andy, so he hadn't been fit enough to be patched up and sent home. But a drunken brawl, how could he? Then, realising that she was using clichés to fan her indignation, she concentrated impatiently on facts.

Jon was a stranger who had appeared in the glen for reasons which probably wouldn't bear close examination. He and she had been drawn to each other in an off-and-on, skirmishing sort of way, but there was nothing that could remotely be called a relationship between them. They might enjoy each other's company, but both clearly saw nothing more would ever develop. And, for now, he was in no danger, was being looked after. It would look pretty odd if she rolled up at the hospital asking after him.

This isn't about you, she reminded herself in sudden fury. What does it matter how it looks? There's no one else to go. He might need things, or need someone to take him back to Keeper's Cottage. He's been hurt, for God's sake, he's alone. Turning, she started down the hill at a reckless pace, slowed by lingering drifts, slithering on patches of mottled ice. How could she have wasted so much time? How could she have been so callous?

Telephoning the hospital, speaking to the ward sister, she found she was trembling again.

'Ah, yes, Major Paulett. We were needing to find some contact for him.'

'How is he?'

'Who's this I'm speaking to?' Not a friendly voice. The voice of someone ready to raise difficulties, ready to think the worst.

Philippa was having none of that. 'Mrs Howard. His sister.'

'Are you his next of kin, or is there a Mrs Paulett we should contact?'

Good question. But Philippa replied with a firmness she hardly felt, 'I am the only member of the family within reach.'

The voice didn't appear to think too highly of this. 'Well, he was admitted last night, you realise. However, I can't discuss his condition over the phone.'

Why not? A chill spread through Philippa.

'It would be best for you to come in.'

'Now?'

'Just as soon as you're able.'

14

Driving down to Muirend as fast as she dared, Philippa was appalled at her inhumanity in not having telephoned the hospital the moment she reached home. But thoughts of herself were wiped out when she saw Jon, alone in a side ward, immobile as an effigy, his face battered and discoloured, an ominous frame over his legs.

'The concussion's the main problem.' Sister Mackintosh gave the impression of having no time to waste. She thought poorly of relatives, a breed in her experience unlikely to offer intelligent response and essentially unhygienic. 'His ankle's broken and he has two fractured ribs, contusions to the body and, as you can see, superficial damage to the face, but that doesn't add up to much.'

Philippa, her throat tight, thought it added up to a great deal.

Sister Mackintosh lifted Jon's eyelid, buried in purple flesh, with a firm thumb. 'It will be a while yet before we know if the concussion's serious or not. What's needed is someone beside him when he comes round. We're far too busy to keep an eye on him all the time.'

Why did she sound so accusing? 'Could you tell me what happened?' Philippa asked, getting her voice under control with an effort.

'Humph, I should think you could see for yourself what happened,' was all Sister Mackintosh vouchsafed, as she took herself off with her heavy slapping walk.

Waiting numbly in the featureless cube, hospital sounds muted behind the door with its observation panel like a cell, Philippa felt no more doubt as to whether or not she should be here. Nor did it matter how Jon had got himself into this state. She looked at the mangled face, the stillness of the big body, and felt only an aching, loving compassion. Once or twice a nurse looked in to ask, 'Everything all right?' more or less on the wing, but for the rest of the time Philippa sat in frozen silence, her thoughts fugitive and formless.

When the night staff came on the new sister was a welcome relief after Sister Mackintosh. About Philippa's age, thin and whippy with a friendly intelligent face, Sister Rennie was perfectly ready to answer questions.

'If he's been like this since last night, that's serious, isn't it?' The gnawing fear could be voiced at last.

'Not necessarily.' Sister Rennie's manner was reassuringly direct. 'The important thing is that someone he knows is here when he wakes. Let me know when he does. If he's lucid that's good, but don't let him talk. He should be kept calm. You're his sister, I gather?'

'I'm not, actually. I wanted to cut corners.'

'Ah,' said Sister Rennie. 'How wise.' Her smile made it clear that they understood each other. 'The old man he rescued is doing well. He was able to tell the police what happened and we'll be letting him go home in the morning.'

'Rescued? The police?' Lurch of apprehension. 'What old man? I haven't heard yet what happened.'

Sister Rennie frowned in quick annoyance. Not, Philippa supposed, with her. 'Some lout attacked the pensioner who'd been tidying up at the bowling club after a whist drive. Taking the tea money home, you know the sort of thing. Major Paulett waded in but several more of them piled out of a van and gave him a good going-over. Broke his ankle with a crowbar. Nice clean break though,' she added with professional detachment. 'Shouldn't give him much trouble.'

Philippa had difficulty with her next question. 'Was he – had he been drinking?'

'He'd had a couple.' But luckily Sister Rennie caught the expression on Philippa's face. 'No, I mean literally. The police will want to talk to him as soon as he's able, but they already know who was involved. Not a pretty sight, is he?' she went on cheerfully. 'And he'll look worse before he looks better. Won't be able to shave for a while either. Not bad on his day, though, I should think?'

She gave Philippa a friendly sidelong look.

'Not bad,' Philippa said neutrally.

Sister Rennie laughed. 'Why don't you go and get yourself something to eat? It could be a long night.'

'No, I'm fine.' She couldn't bear to leave him.

She had no idea how long it was before at last Jon muttered, stirred, stilled with a wincing sharpness, then with a visible effort opened one eye and struggled to focus it.

'Jon.' Philippa's voice was a wisp of sound she could barely hear herself. She sat on the bed, careful not to jolt him, so that she was in his line of vision.

'Philippa.' His voice wasn't surprised, only full of a tired satisfaction. The battered eye closed for a short rest.

Remembering instructions, Philippa pressed the bell. As Sister Rennie appeared Jon opened his eye again. 'For a skinny female you're bloody heavy,' he remarked, his voice thin and reedy.

'Sounds fairly normal to me,' Sister Rennie commented, checking his pulse.

Philippa, on the other hand, was unable to say a word.

'He'll sleep now. Why don't you go home and get some rest yourself?'

But still Philippa wouldn't go, obeying an instinct she was too tired to analyse. And Jon woke again, saying, 'Philippa,' before his eye was even open. This time he began foggily to piece together what had happened, and kept asking if she was 'back'. She talked to him quietly and he seemed satisfied, drifting into sleep while she was still speaking, and at last she slipped away and headed for home.

Less than twenty-four hours ago she'd been at Tynach, assuring Sue that Jon meant nothing to her. She must take some kit down for him. And where was his car? The water ought to be turned off at Keeper's Cottage if he was to be in hospital for long. The nights were still cold. In fact, it was freezing now, as she was reminded when the car went wide on a bend. Better concentrate, Jon wouldn't be too pleased if she wrote off the Mini. Briefly amused to find herself thinking this, she knew she was ready to put everything else on hold for the moment. Penny could wait. Alec could wait.

Not surprisingly, constraint returned when she found herself once more at the door of the side ward that afternoon. She'd been too busy all day to wonder whether or not she should come, having, after a brief sleep, gone to the hotel, knowing work would be accumulating. There she had put right any misconceptions about the major's latest escapade, adding by her unwonted terseness considerable zest to the gossip. No one commented on it, however, at least not to her. Philippa could be daunting when she chose.

She had thought of asking Michael Thorne for a key to Keeper's Cottage, in order to collect things Jon might need, but had realised in time how much Jon would dislike such an invasion of his space. So she had gathered up what she could from her own resources and bought the rest.

Now she hesitated. Would he regard even this as an intrusion? Without going in, she could see that he was lying very still. Perhaps he shouldn't be disturbed. She could leave what she'd brought and go. But Jon stirred as she went in.

'Philippa?' His voice was weak.

'Hello, Jon. How are you?'

'Fine,' he said politely, lifting his hand an inch to indicate his prostrate form. How could he joke? The smile she managed was tremulous. He was watching her intently out of his functioning eye. Did he remember that she'd been here last night?

She lifted her carrier bag. 'A few things you might need.' She heard the hospital-visitor brightness in her voice and winced.

'Thanks.' He was still watching her, the gleam in the grey eye as arresting as ever, in spite of the puffy flesh surrounding it.

'You seem much better.' It was true. Battered as he was, he was himself again.

'Nothing wrong with me,' he said laconically.

'If there's anything you need please say. Though I don't suppose you know yet how long you'll be in. I was wondering about the car. Do you remember where you left it? If you want it moved somewhere I could see to that for you if you like. Do you have the keys?'

'Not on me.'

Philippa laughed in spite of her anxiety, hearing by contrast with his dry brevity her own anxious gabble.

'That's better,' Jon commented. 'Less of the deathbed air.'

'How can you be so cool? Don't you feel ghastly?'

'Gha-astly,' he agreed solemnly.

'But just look at you!'

'Not the best day out I ever had,' he conceded.

Philippa began to feel immensely cheered, though that seemed the wrong way round. Joking was the last thing she'd expected him to be capable of.

'I can't stay long, I'm afraid,' she said. 'I just brought – I mean, I wanted to find out how you were. Only I'm going to Allt Farr for dinner so I—'

'Philippa.' Even in this state he had authority. 'Did I dream it or were you here last night?'

They stared at each other. For a moment Philippa was tempted to say no, afraid of what he would infer from the fact that she'd come.

'Were you here?' The husky voice was insistent.

'Yes, I was.'

His eye closed, as though the effort of extracting this answer had exhausted him. He shouldn't be talking, she thought with quick concern. He lay without moving, and she hoped he was drifting off to sleep again. Then he mumbled something and she leaned closer to hear.

'Why did you come?'

She knew he meant last night. She'd never been good at prevarication. 'I was told you'd been hurt.'

The room was very quiet. Then Jon turned his hand palm up on the covers, and Philippa without hesitation put hers into it, wincing as she saw the bruised and grazed knuckles as his hand closed. He felt her fear of hurting him, and tightened his grip, saying, 'Leave it there.'

'Sweet talk, huh?' said Philippa.

His face contorted. 'For God's sake don't make me laugh!'

'Sorry,' she said contritely, and they were silent, glad of the simple, comforting contact.

'I wasn't drunk, you know,' Jon said abruptly, and Philippa heard in his voice how much this mattered to him.

'I know. The night sister told me what happened.'

'Mm.' Pause. 'Must be getting past it.'

'There was a vanful of them, I gather.'

'The old boy must have made quite a story of it.'

'He's home again, did you know? A bit bruised, but that's all.'

'Those bastards. He didn't look as though he had the price of a pint on him.' Jon moved fretfully, anger returning.

Philippa thought he probably shouldn't be talking about it. 'Jon, I really ought to go.'

His hand clamped more firmly round hers. 'Not yet.'

But his voice was tired, and he was sinking into sleep whether he liked it or not. Philippa stayed till he dozed off, half woke to ask once more if she'd been there in the night, then fell asleep in earnest.

So much for not getting involved, she thought with irony as she headed for home. She was going to be late getting to Allt Farr. She didn't care – though she would have preferred to be going to almost any other house tonight. Max Munro was not a person easily fooled, and his mother had the sharpest eye and most sardonic tongue of Philippa's acquaintance.

The next day she was at Sillerton doing lunch. Though Lady Hay invariably said, 'Something simple, don't you think?' Philippa had long ago learned this never meant less than three courses. It was mid-afternoon before she headed down the tree-clad twists of road into Muirend.

Jon had been moved to the main ward. Though this must mean he was making good progress the discovery threw her. She had expected the privacy of the side ward, where a sense of emergency kept reality at a distance.

Jon had told himself, as the wave of visitors surged forward and subsided round the beds, that he should have known she wouldn't be there. It had seemed natural, in the cloudily remembered hours of pain, that she should be nearby, even that yesterday she'd come because she knew he needed kit, but ordinary life had taken over now. He was on his own again, nothing ahead but being stuck in that god-awful cottage, bored out of his mind.

The man in the next bed, relieved because his wife hadn't

turned up but gloomily certain that she soon would, glanced at Jon's grim face and thought better of a chatty comment about nobody giving a toss for them.

When Philippa came swinging down the ward Jon felt a release from rancour and self-pity as sweet as orgasm. She looked like someone from a different world, unselfconscious in her old waxed jacket and boots, a big smile lighting her face as her eyes found him.

'Jammy bugger,' muttered the man in the next bed.

Jon couldn't speak, didn't even realise he wasn't speaking. He could only gaze at her, with a feeling of having arrived somewhere after a hazardous journey.

'Um,' remarked Philippa, surveying him with interest. 'More mustard and khaki today, less aubergine and plum. Hardly an improvement, though.'

'What the hell are you talking about?' He didn't care what she said. She had come; she was here.

'Suffering hasn't sweetened you, I see, Major.'

The man in the next bed looked away, then turned back and looked some more. That was one fancy bit of gear.

'Been at the hotel?' Any words would do.

'No, cooking boring lunch for Lady Hay. Which reminds me.' Philippa fished in her worn leather satchel. 'Invalid food. Shall I hold the spoon for you?'

'What is it?' he demanded, not trusting the solicitous tone, but watching her with a greed which had nothing to do with any goodies she'd brought.

'Try it.' Some kind of fruit mousse of a quality and flavour Jon had never tasted in his life.

'Not bad,' he admitted grudgingly. 'Wasn't it this Lady Hay's pie we ate? Got something against her?'

Yes, she made me late for visiting time.

The only problem, as they fell into talk with the old ease, was that Philippa kept making Jon laugh, then was filled with remorse to see his wincing agony. The only problem, that is, until she told him Michael Thorne had gone up to Keeper's Cottage to turn off the water.

'He had no right to,' Jon objected instantly.

'It is his cottage,' Philippa pointed out reasonably, glad she hadn't gone over to do it herself. 'Anyway, you should be grateful. You'd be liable for any damage if the pipes froze.'

'Yes, well, maybe. Though I'd have thought,' Jon complained, changing tack, 'he might have shown up a bit sooner. Welcomed me in and so on.'

Philippa raised her eyebrows. 'You're recovering, I see.'

'Well, I've been in the place for weeks.'

'Michael has called, as a matter of fact,' Philippa informed him. 'More than once. Though I told him he was wasting his time, because you're such a bad-tempered bastard that you're far better left alone.'

The man in the next bed wondered what they were laughing about, and wished someone would speak to him in the tone in which Philippa was apologising, 'Oh, poor Jon, sorry, that must hurt dreadfully.'

Before she left she asked again about the car.

'I could leave it with friends, if you like.'

'Not worth it, I'll be out of here soon,' Jon replied ungratefully.

'But you won't be able to drive, will you?'

He groaned at the complications ahead, his mood deteriorating.

'I'm afraid I won't be able to come tomorrow because I—' Philippa began as she rose to go.

'Why not?'

'Because I'm doing a job at—'

'Say you can't go.'

'You're impossible.'

'Come on, Philippa, give me a break. I can't even read, flat on my back like this.'

'The day after tomorrow,' she promised.

'Bloody woman,' he grumbled in farewell, but shut his tired eyes to keep safe the smile she gave him.

Philippa, at Kingussie the next day doing a buffet for a christening, had planned to stay the night. She and Gilly Mainwaring had shared a couple of lively seasons as chalet birds and didn't see enough of each other these days. Also it was the kind of gathering she liked best, the preparations part of the party, with people in and out of the kitchen all morning, lending a hand, being dispatched for last-minute items, wandering around with piles of plates, glasses of champagne and other people's babies, everything cheerfully behind schedule. Once safely at the church it was discovered that the godfather – the local vet – was missing, but he turned up, smelling agreeably of horse and still in the jacket and breeches he'd set out in that morning, in time to shoulder his proxy aside. But Philippa knew she wouldn't stay.

'You promised,' Gilly wailed. 'I kept a room, fended off all comers. And we've had no chance to talk.'

'Sorry, Gilly, another time.'

'But why must you go?'

'A friend's in hospital.'

'Oh well, in that case. But who is it, anyone I know?' Then more alertly, looking into Philippa's face, 'Who *is* it?'

Philippa hesitated. Three days ago, to Sue Balfour, she had said 'nobody'. Now she said, 'His name's Jon Paulett. He's staying in the glen for a while.'

'And?'

'Gilly, I'm not sure. If I had any sense it would be "and nothing".'

'I was beginning to think there'd never be anybody ever

again.' Gilly gave her a hug. 'Bring him to see us when you get to the stage of sharing him.'

Philippa laughed but was grateful. The simplicity of friends.

Jon, trying to shut out the sights and sounds of evening visiting time, was angry with himself for counting the hours till Philippa could appear. His ankle, now in plaster, gave him no pain, the tenderness of kidneys and back was fading, but his head ached ferociously and his ribs were sore because he'd insisted on sitting up.

'Hey, wake up, mate, I think this one's for you,' a voice said.

Jon opened his eyes and there she was, smiling at him but looking oddly uncertain. He felt himself melt at the sight of her.

'I thought you said you couldn't come till tomorrow,' he said grouchily.

'Now that was worth tearing myself away from the party for,' she mocked, her smile deepening.

Disgusted, the man in the next bed replayed the scene in several sentimental variations till he got it right. That major didn't know when he was well off.

15

The next question was obvious, though it didn't occur to Philippa till Sister Rennie, catching her on her way out, asked, after making some encouraging comments on Jon's progress, 'He lives on his own, doesn't he?'

Philippa nodded. 'Yes, in a cottage a mile up a track. How soon do you think he'll be able to drive?' Practical realities came crowding in.

'The plaster will be on for six to eight weeks. We'll give him a walking plaster as soon as possible, but most people don't attempt to drive in them.'

'Most people.' A brief shared grin acknowledged that Jon didn't belong in this category.

'Strictly speaking,' Sister Rennie went on, 'we ought to discharge him as soon as possible. He doesn't need hospital care and we need the bed. The headaches are the main problem and the ward's not ideal in that respect. But he can't look after himself.'

Her eyes met Philippa's, who recognised the moment of struggling on the hook but still hoping not to be reeled in. 'I'll have to think.'

'I wasn't sure how you and he . . . Sorry if I've put my foot in it.'

'No, it's all right. I just need a bit of time.'

'Well, don't forget if he does go back to his cottage the nurse will call, home help can be arranged. The system's there to look after him. But in that case we'd have to keep him in till he's more mobile.'

Philippa knew how Jon hated being penned up here, but domestic considerations were not the only ones she had to think over. 'You won't say anything to him?'

'Of course not. And he's still in pretty bad shape, remember. He's not expecting to go anywhere yet.'

Philippa found it impossible to weigh pros and cons objectively. It was hard to remember by now how things had stood between Jon and herself before he was brought into hospital. She thought of the inconvenience, at all levels, of having him semi-helpless at Achallie, and of the interpretation he would put on an invitation to convalesce there. But she knew it was going to happen. As so often where Jon was concerned, she seemed to be careering along oiled rails to a certain destination.

The next thing was to put the idea to him. Having spent a wakeful night planning her approach she was thrown, on arriving at the hospital, to find him in a mood surly to the point of hostility. With him in this frame of mind the mere thought of inviting him to Achallie seemed so outlandish that she kept to any trivia she could dredge up till he interrupted her brusquely.

'This crap about you being my sister—'

Philippa fell silent, startled. They had laughed over it as a brilliant way to foil Sister Mackintosh.

'You'll get yourself into trouble, starting rumours like that.' Jon, attempting jocularity, only succeeded in sounding disgruntled.

'What do you mean?' His tone wasn't reassuring.

'Sister Mackintosh thinks you should take big brother home with you, that's what I mean.' The idea had rocked him, and knowing it was out of the question had filled him with a desperate frustration.

Damn the woman. Now, whatever she said, Philippa knew Jon would believe she'd been pressured into it. But at least the proposal had been aired. That was something.

'Look, you don't have to say anything,' Jon said harshly as she hesitated. 'The bare idea's a joke.'

If that was how he felt . . . Taking a relieved breath to agree with him, Philippa looked up in time to catch the doubt and hope in his eyes, swiftly hidden as they were. Petty anxieties vanished.

'Jon,' she said quietly, 'you're more than welcome to stay at Achallie until you can manage on your own.'

He stared at her penetratingly. But the quiet tone, the simplicity of her words, convinced him. No protestations about its being no trouble, no persuasion and, above all, a businesslike absence of emotion. That's my girl, he thought with admiration and gratitude.

'That's a hell of a big thing to offer,' he said, speaking as directly as she had.

'I know,' Philippa agreed calmly.

Jon laughed, relaxing. The man in the next bed was glad to see that the dismal bugger had at least got hold of her hand.

'Just till you're mobile again.'

'Of course.'

'Don't let the idea go to your head.'

'Of course not.'

'And no calling me a cock—'

'For God's sake, Philippa!' She had the clear, carrying voice of her kind. Heads turned at her peal of laughter at Jon's hasty protest.

'You're sure?' he couldn't help asking when she got up to leave, and he took her wrist in a hard grip.

'Oh, I expect I'll have second thoughts,' she answered honestly. 'But I think it will be all right. We can work out something else if it isn't.'

He nodded slowly, accepting that. But when she'd gone

he found himself almost light-headed with anticipation and incredulous thankfulness.

It was Jon, however, who had the second thoughts. Philippa suppressed the qualms which inevitably attacked her because she felt she couldn't let him down now, but Jon had far too much unoccupied time in which to convince himself that she'd been dragooned into making the offer, and that nothing this good could ever be for him. Anyway, it would be humiliating to be in her house in this state, dependent on her for everything.

'Look,' he said without preamble when she arrived, late and apologetic, the next evening. 'Forget the whole idea of my coming to Achallie, right?'

'But why?' Philippa was rebuffed and puzzled. She had spent a harried day thinking through practical aspects, at the same time feeling guilty for not concentrating on what she was supposed to be doing.

'Because it was a ridiculous notion, that's why,' Jon said savagely, consumed by longing for this marvellous chance now that he'd thrown it away.

'Fine,' said Philippa. Did he imagine she was going to try and talk him into it?

He glowered at her, caught out as he so often was by her. In his book, women always had to run a subject to death, and he knew he'd expected her to persuade him to go; in fact had banked on it. Instead of which, she was explaining why she was late and asking him about his day as though she thought he was here on holiday.

His bluff called, Jon responded in surly monosyllables, but Philippa was having none of it. She kept up her flow of small talk until, without exactly knowing how it had happened, Jon found himself telling her about the old man he'd helped coming in to thank him.

'Must be mad, coming all the way out here just to see me in person,' he wound up, his mood still dour.

'Quite,' Philippa agreed.

Jon felt reluctant good humour creep back.

'So why did you decide against coming to Achallie?' she enquired, when he had thought that door closed for good, his golden opportunity lost.

Taken by surprise, he had no reason ready. But one thing was clear – if he didn't give her a straight answer this time there wouldn't be another chance.

Philippa waited, outwardly calm, inwardly churning with apprehension. Good sense had warned her to leave things as they were, but she couldn't forget the vulnerability, or the flash of hope, which she'd caught in Jon's eyes yesterday. It wasn't hard to imagine the doubts which must have assailed him since. This couldn't be easy for him.

Jon gazed at her for a moment, his face tight. 'Christ, Philippa,' he said helplessly, 'you must know.'

Because he hadn't hedged she was quick to help him. 'Sorry, Jonnie, I shouldn't have asked. You don't have to explain. Coming to Achallie would have got you out of here. That seemed to be the most important thing.'

She had called him Jonnie once or twice in the confused hours when he was still concussed. He found it comforting out of all proportion that she did so now.

'All the hassle,' he muttered.

'I think I can cope with that.'

'I'll pay my way.' He was suddenly truculent, unable to express his real reservations.

'Good,' she said.

'You're to say if you want to kick me out.'

'I shall.'

He gave a little huff of laughter. He could probably count on it. She made things blessedly simple.

★

They didn't seem simple to Philippa, frantically rushing around getting ready on the day she was to fetch him from hospital. She must have been out of her mind ever to have suggested this. Jon would have been taken care of perfectly adequately without her interference. He would read her invitation as a blatant signal that yet another female idiot was ready to run round after him. On a more mundane level – and she couldn't believe she hadn't thought about this till now – how much would he be able to do for himself? And how was he going to fill his time?

But she knew these concerns were trifling. They weren't the real problem. He was virtually a stranger. And half the time a stranger she didn't even like. He was bad-tempered and arrogant, probably had a criminal background and, if not, was at the very least involved in some unsavoury and suspect enterprise. Whatever the truth of that, it was certain that he created chaos every time he turned round.

Set about the mouth and tense about the shoulders, she drove to Muirend far too early, wondering how best she could back out at this stage. Propose some alternative? Take Jon to Keeper's Cottage, and go over each day? But the water wasn't on; the place would be freezing. Well, those were problems that could be dealt with.

But when Jon was wheeled out to the car doubt and panic vanished. He looked so pale where the skin wasn't discoloured or covered by beard, and he went through the painful business of being stowed into the Mini with such docility, that selfish worries were forgotten, and she only felt unbearably moved to see him like this.

'You took the seat out,' he said, grateful for the forethought. He'd been sweating all morning at the prospect of crushing himself into the small space.

'Andy did it for me,' Philippa said, as briskly as she could.

Jon let that pass. He didn't have much choice.

'It's a bit unsociable though,' Philippa remarked as she fastened her seat belt, but still her voice wasn't as steady as she had hoped it would be.

'Philippa? Hey, what's this?' As she had turned her head he'd seen to his astonishment tears on her cheek.

'Nothing, what do you mean?' she demanded, sniffing and leaning forward to wipe the windscreen with her sleeve, as though that would help her vision.

Jon reached to put a hand on her arm. It struck him, as her hand came up to his for a second in response, that he could never before recall experiencing such a sense of optimism and buoyancy.

Philippa found it disconcerting to drive like this with him behind her shoulder. She also felt lost and unsure, the temporary footing established between them in hospital knocked away, ahead the new untried intimacy of being together at Achallie.

Jon, after a couple of rough gear changes and some rather uncoordinated cornering, took note of how tightly she was gripping the wheel and how rigid her shoulders looked. He was sure she didn't normally drive like this. In fact, he knew she had something of a reputation for the way she buzzed about the glen in all weathers. Also she must know this road like the back of her hand. He found himself unexpectedly moved by the anxiety she'd revealed, and wanted to dispel it if he could.

'Look, pull in somewhere,' he said, adding hastily as she glanced round anxiously, 'I'm OK, but there are a couple of things I think we should sort out before we go any further.'

She didn't argue, swinging promptly into the entrance to a farm track they happened to be passing.

Jon grinned but made no comment.

'Thank God to be out of that place,' he remarked for openers, as Philippa switched off and turned to him. 'And now that I am, don't forget that we can work out any arrangement that suits us.'

She gave him an enquiring look but said nothing.

'Come on, Philippa, no sweat. It's just the two of us now. We can decide whatever we like.'

'It feels so odd,' she said helplessly.

He wasn't sure what felt odd, but thought he should deal with the point most likely to be bothering her. 'Look, if we do stick to the plan, you can be sure of one thing – I can't leap on you in this state.'

'I did ask Sister Mackintosh about that,' she confided. 'Just as a precaution . . .'

If she was joking there wasn't much wrong.

'We'll take it as it comes then, yes?'

The mere fact that he'd read her nervousness and taken the trouble to allay it helped, and Philippa felt a lot better as she drove on. There was trouble at once, however, when Jon found she'd given him her room.

'Don't be so idiotic,' she protested. 'How do you imagine you'd get up and down those awful stairs?'

'I don't want to turn you out.'

'There's nothing wrong with the spare room.'

'I didn't want to cause hassle.'

'You're causing it now. Everything's arranged.'

'You know what I mean.'

'Yes, you're refusing to get into my bed.'

'That'll be the day.' But she'd taken the heat out of the argument, as she usually managed to do, and in truth he was too tired to fight her. Apart from a brief practice session when the physio had brought the crutches, and a few painful trips to the bog, he hadn't been out of bed. Dressing in the clothes Philippa had taken down for him had been an effort, and the trip up the glen an ordeal. His head was pounding and there was a stabbing pain behind his eyes. His ribs were sore and his back ached.

'Come on, Jonnie, let me help you.'

He wanted to show her that he could manage alone, but knew it would be an agonising struggle. Having longed so fiercely to be out of that damned hospital bed, he was dismayed to find himself now longing to be safely back in it. He turned towards Philippa with a weary acquiescence very telling in a man like him, though Philippa was for the moment more concerned with the mechanics of helping him to get his clothes off as painlessly as possible.

But it was she who winced when he unbuttoned his shirt and she saw the discolouration round his ribs.

'That looks awful. Shouldn't it be strapped up or something?'

'Supposed to heal better without.'

'How brutal.' Philippa was disconcerted to find tears close again, and concentrated resolutely on the job in hand.

Jon undid his belt and unzipped his jeans.

'Sit on the bed.' Philippa knelt to ease them over his plaster. She had unpicked the seam this morning but not far enough, she realised. Jon watched her with a small smile he wouldn't have dreamed of letting her see. She looked so serious and intent.

She went to hang the jeans in the walk-in cupboard which formed the back wall of the room and turned to see Jon on his feet, unable to do anything about a most emphatic erection.

'Sorry about this,' he said, trying to look penitent, but grinning broadly.

'I suppose you could call that a cocky smile,' Philippa

commented, twitching back the duvet. 'Wrong again, Sister Mackintosh.'

'Don't make me laugh,' he pleaded, as she helped him into bed. 'Anyway, look on it as a compliment.'

'Shut up and go to sleep.'

After the hospital mattress Philippa's bed was welcoming beyond belief. The down pillows were a dream of softness for his throbbing head. As his muscles relaxed Jon deliberately let go, with a sensation of security rare for him in recent years. He was asleep before Philippa had tucked the duvet round his shoulders.

She stood there watching him for a moment, tasting the strange, deep satisfaction it gave to see him there. Her earlier worries seemed remote and unimportant. Then she drew the curtains and went quietly away.

All his life Jon would remember waking in that room at Achallie, and the feeling of peace which washed through him as he realised where he was. No hospital noises – in fact hardly any noise at all. He had to listen to pick up the faint sound of the river at the bottom of the hill, a vehicle on the main road beyond. But the most magical thing was to feel no sense of urgency or frustration. He was here, in Philippa's cottage, in Philippa's bed, being looked after in a way he'd never have imagined possible. It seemed as if, for the first time in a very long time, he wasn't in automatic contention with everyone and everything around him.

He looked round the room, where he had so much wanted to be in the days before he'd had his head just about stove in. Afternoon sunlight glowing through pink-lined curtains warmed the white roughcast walls and the soft colours of the faded carpet; there was a kidney-shaped dressing-table with a frilly skirt, a packed bookcase. He saw that Philippa had stripped away her personal belongings for his occupation, and wished she hadn't. But it was a passing thought. Nothing could mar his profound contentment. All he had to do in the world was lie here in this incomparable bed, and sooner or later Philippa would come walking in.

16

'But who is this man? Where does he come from? No one seems to know anything about him.'

Penny seemed increasingly ready to make heavy weather of things these days, Andrew thought, noting in passing how the lines in her rather plump, pleasant face were becoming more pronounced.

'I expect we'll meet him soon enough,' he said. 'After all, Pippa's hardly making a secret of him.'

'She certainly isn't, bringing him home to Achallie! There must have been some other solution. And how's she going to look after him when she's working? Or perhaps she'll give up her jobs for the time being.' Thank goodness the boys' weekend was safely behind them.

'Well, it's her business, I suppose,' Andrew said, giving his *Times* a brisk flap to hint that the topic could be left there. In fact, he was mildly concerned about Philippa himself, having picked up the odd comment on this Paulett character from Michael Thorne and others – though not from anyone who had actually met him – and not much caring for what he'd heard.

'But where did they meet? How long has she known him?' Penny wasn't going to let it go.

'Philippa's been away from the glen for a while, remember. And she's thirty-something and divorced.'

'But imagine not telling us.'

'She has told us. She phoned specifically to let us know what was happening.'

'You know perfectly well what I mean. And she said nothing to the Munros when she was there for dinner, though Joanna said she arrived terribly late and Grannie ticked her off about it.'

Well, if Philippa had survived that she'd survive anything Penny could say. Still, it did seem a bit extreme to have this man at the cottage. Lucky bloke.

'And what about poor Alec?' Penny demanded.

'Might focus his mind a bit.' Andrew hadn't a lot of sympathy for Alec who, if he wanted Philippa as anything more than an agreeable thought in his mind while he continued to enjoy his bachelor comforts of freedom and independence, should get his act together.

'I don't think you ever realise just how much he cares about her,' Penny protested. 'It's been going on since long before you arrived on the scene . . .'

Andrew stopped listening. He had heard more than enough, in over twenty years of marriage to Penny, of the tight-knit bonds of the circle in which she'd grown up. Alltmore had belonged to her family, the Gilmours, not to his, and he could still wonder at times whether it had been a mistake to take it on when Penny had inherited it, during their engagement. She had never lived anywhere else, and could still, though he knew she'd be horrified to hear it, occasionally make him feel an outsider.

'I think we should pay Philippa the compliment of trusting her to know what she's doing,' he said firmly, and Penny knew the subject was closed.

Philippa herself, in her shed splitting kindling, was far from sure that she knew what she was doing. One thing only was clear: with the dramas of accident and emergency over, and

Jon here because there had seemed no sensible alternative, relations between them must return to the strictly matter-of-fact.

'The strictly out of bed, you mean,' she muttered, clouting a bit of broken plank on a knot so violently that it flew out of the door. Jon had no intention of getting involved, was liable to vanish at any moment, and when he did would never be heard of again.

Philippa had been shattered by the break-up of her marriage, and by Richard's casual attitude that they'd given it a go, it hadn't worked, forget it. In his words: 'Marriage is just a piece of paper – if you don't like it tear it up.' But she had never felt for Richard, or for anyone else, what she knew she was capable of feeling for Jon. When attracted to other men in the past she had, she saw now, however happy she'd believed herself, always remained essentially a separate entity. With Jon, even after so short a time, she no longer felt that, and it was a startling discovery. Would she be able, in this situation she herself had so rashly created, to maintain her usual cool independence? She found that she'd chopped a very large pile of sticks.

Jon, wakened from a light doze by the stealthy opening of the door, felt the familiar skin-brush of fear. Then he remembered where he was and the adrenalin sank down. He lay still, savouring the exquisite relief. Against the light from the hall he saw Philippa in the doorway. Then saw her, obviously deciding he was still asleep, start to close the door again.

'The service was a damn sight better in hospital,' he remarked.

'Don't worry, I can easily take you back,' she retorted, coming in. 'Did you manage to sleep?'

'I did.' And sleep naturally, he realised, for the first time in weeks.

'Want to be left in peace?'

'Nope.'

'How about some tea? Though, knowing hospital, you've probably had breakfast, lunch and supper already.'

'They struck me off the lunch list,' he told her pathetically.

'Honestly? Poor Jonnie. Jon, I mean—'

She turned hastily away to open the curtains, letting in slanting late-afternoon sunshine.

So Jonnie had been for the bruises and kicked ribs. He let it go for now. 'Of course in hospital they bring round the menu the day before,' he informed her.

'So what did you choose yesterday?'

'Jelly. And custard. Custard with everything.'

'Too bad, no custard here.'

Tea over, it was natural to talk on as dusk filtered into the simple little room, Jon comfortably propped with extra pillows, Philippa on a dumpy chair pulled up to the bed. It came as a jolt to Jon when she said, 'Will you be all right on your own for a while? I have to go out.'

'Out? Where?' Affability peeled away as he had a swift vision of himself stuck here bored and alone, while Philippa smiled into the eyes of some Hooray Henry across a dinner table laden with candles, wine and posh food.

'Must I say?' she asked with affected surprise.

But Jon refused to be rebuked. 'You're not going anywhere. You're staying here, with me.'

Philippa switched on the bedside lamp, deliberately dispelling the intimate mood.

'I'm going to see Bessie.'

'Who the hell's Bessie?' Jon demanded, exaggeratedly shielding his eyes.

'You know who she is. She lives just up the hill, and as she's partially blind and likes company I look in most days if I can . . .'

'Well, today you can't,' he said.

'. . . and I've been neglecting her lately,' Philippa went on smoothly, 'because I've been spending most of my time racing up and down to Muirend.'

Clash of blades. Jon liked it when Philippa, usually so amenable, refused to be pushed around.

'Hey,' he called as she turned away with the tray, 'don't be too long.'

His changed tone won him a smile. He smiled himself when he heard the Mini start up. Normally, he guessed, she wouldn't have dreamed of taking the car so short a distance. Now that she had gone, though, he could tackle the urgent business of getting to the bathroom.

It was a bad moment for Philippa when she came back and found the bed empty. He's done a bunk, she thought blankly, though common sense at once told her he couldn't be far away. In the loo, you idiot. But as she tidied the bed she knew her reaction had been revealing.

She went along to the bathroom door. Silence. Was he all right? How awful to have someone come checking on him. Worse than hospital. But what if he was flat on the floor? What if he'd hurt himself somehow?

Determined that Philippa shouldn't do anything for him that he could manage himself, Jon had decided to have as thorough a wash as possible. God knew how long it would be before he could have a bath. It wasn't easy but he did his best, until he made the mistake of leaning forward to splash water on his face. The pain in his ribs, already acute after so much movement, specifically warned against before he was released from hospital, stabbed excruciatingly, and he knew he was close to passing out. Snarling with frustration, he hung onto the basin, making a violent effort to calm and order his protesting body.

Dimly, he was aware that Philippa had come to the door.

She mustn't know he was in trouble or she'd insist on helping him next time. But the dizziness threatened to overpower him, and in the end he was thankful to hear her call, 'Jon, are you all right?'

He drew a deep breath. 'Not entirely. Come in.'

'Oh, *Jonnie.*' Pure concern, no fuss or reproaches. No embarrassment either as she said, 'Come on, back to bed,' and helped him there with a tenderness which made the whole frustrating episode almost worthwhile.

Bliss of smoothed sheet and cool pillow, the extra ones gone, the lamp turned away from his eyes. His jangled body thankfully abandoning effort, Jon kept his eyes on Philippa's concerned face as she pulled the duvet round his shoulders. I'm being tucked in, he thought with amused disbelief and said, like a child, as he had never said as a child because there had been no one to say it to, 'Don't go.'

'All right.' She didn't talk, just sat quietly by the bed, and when he reached for her hand gave it at once, watching the lines of pain smooth away from his face as he relaxed. She didn't feel too relaxed herself. The sight of his big, powerful body, battered as it was, had been disturbing in a way quite new to her.

Not surprisingly, she didn't sleep well.

Nor did Jon, chiefly because he was cold. He'd found hospital stifling, and had welcomed the spartan level of heating in Philippa's room when he'd first arrived, but now it seemed little short of miserable. Also the duvet, in any case too short for him, had ridden up and caught on his plaster, and he'd given his ribs more grief trying to free it. Hating his helplessness, he groaned to contemplate the difficulties ahead. How would he cope once back at remote Keeper's Cottage? More importantly, how soon could he hope to get fit again? If he was recalled before he regained effective mobility . . . He felt the sweat break out on his skin at the thought, then chill unpleasantly in the cold air, and he lunged again at the duvet, rewarded only by a fierce pain in his ribs.

A light in the hall; Philippa was in the doorway. Coming down to make a hot drink to help her sleep, she had checked at his door and heard his restless movements.

'Jonnie, what's wrong? Can't you sleep?'

'Bloody duvet . . .'

'Oh, poor love.' She sorted it out, frowning. 'How long has it been like this? Your feet are like ice. You should have called, I'd left the doors open on purpose. There, is that better? No,' in a different tone, 'I am *so* stupid. Hang on a minute.'

'I'm not going anywhere.' Jon was already hauled out of his pit of despair by this delicious cosseting.

Philippa was soon back. 'I can't believe I didn't think of this in the first place,' she said, plucking away Jon's duvet and throwing over him, still warm from her body, the big double one from the bed upstairs. For Jon, as its light and generous expanse enveloped him, it was a moment of supreme benison. 'There, that's better. Now do you think you'll sleep?'

'Stay and talk to me,' he mumbled, but only heard a laugh as he slid into heavenly warmth and drowsiness.

He woke to faint sounds in the kitchen. The windows were just-discernible patches of grey. Then he heard the light slap of slippers, not coming in his direction.

'Philippa,' he shouted indignantly.

The slippers turned back. She pushed the door wider. 'I thought you'd be asleep. How are you feeling?'

'Is that a mug in your hand?'

She sighed, martyred. 'All right, you can have it. I suppose I can make myself another.'

'Bring it in here though.'

'I was going to drink it while I dressed.'

'At this hour? It's barely light.'

'I do have more to do than run round after you.'

'Bring your tea in here and tell me about it.'

When she came back he demanded, more aggressively than he'd intended, 'So what's this important stuff?'

Philippa eyed him thoughtfully. How much was she ready to let him get away with? 'Earning my living.'

Good answer, but he still couldn't bear the prospect of her being away for the entire day. 'What, a cocktail party in a castle or a piss-up in a palace?'

'Not bad,' she conceded.

'Come on,' he growled, getting impatient. 'Tell me where you're going.'

'Well, for starters I'm going to the hotel.'

He grunted, recalling the hours he'd spent there hoping to see her, and how it had changed the day when she appeared. 'And then?'

'And then I shall come home and give you lunch.'

That sounded all right. 'And then?'

'Well, then, I suppose,' with another long-suffering sigh, 'give you tea and dinner.'

'You're going to the Cluny and that's it?' Jon's spirits soared, and he didn't attempt to hide it.

'I could always find something else to do.'

'Don't you dare.'

It was a long morning but he didn't wish it away, not reading or listening to the radio, glad of the chance to review the events of the last couple of weeks, and take in the astounding fact of being here. Not fit enough yet to fret too seriously against restricted movement, he lay half-dozing, remembering, agreeably fantasising.

Away from the hospital environment, he could appreciate how incredible it was that Philippa had come to look for him there. At the time, drugged and in pain, it hadn't seemed at all strange that she, the only person who mattered to him, should appear at his bedside, bring the things he needed, even deal with his car and make sure his cottage was all right. Now it seemed amazing; and even more amazing, in view of the way she had previously kept him so determinedly at arm's length, had been the offer to bring him here. Particularly when he'd pulled such stunts as fooling with Moira, and turning up the worse for wear to pick a fight with her because jealousy had led him to believe she was off somewhere with another man.

His thoughts floated, disconnected memories surfacing. After she'd rolled the Mini that day it had seemed so natural to look after her, and she'd appeared to think so too. How close he'd felt to her. How easy it had always been to talk to her. She'd fairly torn into him about the old major business, though. This reminded him of something he'd rather not have thought about just now: the inescapable fact that he and she belonged to different worlds. Well, did he fancy such a collection of bones anyway? Skinny women had never done it for him. Then he pictured the infinitely delicate line of her thigh, the way she moved – Christ, yes, he fancied her.

But, this time, he knew he wanted so much more. Time spent with Philippa had a quality to it, a satisfaction and completeness, which he hadn't even known existed. And there and then, lying in the peace and security of her room, he made up his mind that he would wrench his life apart if that was what it took to hold on to it.

A woman like that, for you? a cynical inner voice persisted. But he could answer, I'm here, aren't I?

His thoughts were interrupted by a vehicle pulling up outside. Heavy feet crunched on the gravel. But as Jon began to sweat about being found here – what had Philippa told people, or wouldn't she want anyone to know? – the feet returned, and craning to look out of the side window Jon caught a glimpse of a navy jacket. Postman. Why was he panicking? Of course no one would call.

He was all the more rattled when the next car arrived,

feeling trapped in a way that went against both instinct and training, as he realised Philippa had left the door unlocked and that this person was actually in the house. He swore at his own vulnerability, but his concern was for once partly on someone else's behalf. He could imagine the gossip that would fly round if he were discovered here, in Philippa's bed. Hearing the door close again, steps pass and the car leave, he swore with fresh anger to feel sweat trickling down his spine.

Penny thought she'd been rather heroic to come and go so discreetly. She hadn't realised that Philippa would be working when she came with the promised plants, and it had been odd to be in the house knowing some strange man was lying a few feet away. But she admitted to herself, as she drove away, that her original doubts and, be honest, disapproval, had been succeeded by the wistful thought that Philippa's life certainly seemed more eventful than her own.

'Did Penny come in and say hello?' Philippa enquired, returning soon after twelve.

'Don't be a damn fool,' Jon snapped, beginning to suspect he'd been one himself.

'Didn't you call to her?'

'What would she have thought, finding me here?'

Philippa looked at him in surprise. 'Thought? Nothing. She knew you'd be here.'

'You told her? You don't mind people knowing?' He regretted the question as soon as it was out.

Philippa gave him a level look. 'If I minded people knowing, you wouldn't be here. Now, lunch according to hospital regime, or is it a little early in real life?'

OK, so he'd been out of order. Shut up, Paulett.

17

With the pressures that began to build, Achallie was frequently like a simmering kettle with its lid jigging in the days that followed. The chief problem was that Jon wanted Philippa there all the time. She would have been quite happy to stay at home, but wasn't prepared to let people down. Also, instinct warned her not to let Jon disrupt her life too radically.

Another issue was Jon's insistence on paying his way, which Philippa found hard to accept in the end.

'We had a deal,' he reminded her.

'You're a guest,' she objected, knowing she was being silly.

'You mean you'd have invited me to stay if I hadn't ended up unconscious in a Muirend gutter?'

Philippa had to give in. After all, wasn't the idea to keep matters business-like?

'That's settled, then,' he said, adding with a straight face, 'only it'll have to be a cheque,' so that the argument ended in laughter anyway.

However the world couldn't be entirely shut out, and Jon resented every intrusion, scowling in the background when Philippa invited Ewart Rhynie in for a dram after he'd brought down some seed potatoes for her, or when a newcomer to the area came to discuss menus and stayed for an hour unfavourably comparing winter in the glen with the safe known world of Esher. It didn't make for a restful atmosphere.

Philippa's friends, whatever they thought, saw no reason to change their normal behaviour, and continued to phone for a gossip whenever they felt like it and to invite her to all the usual things, courteously adding, 'Bring your friend, of course.' Jon's immobility provided an obvious excuse for turning down the invitations, but Philippa felt guilty all the same. The comprehensive, unquestioning welcome she'd been given when she returned home had meant a lot to her, and she often found herself wishing that she could explain her temporary absence from the scene more fully. She felt especially guilty about Alec Blaikie, and would have felt even worse had she known the lengths to which he was about to go on her behalf.

Alec, hearing of Jon's presence at Achallie from Pauly Napier, who could be alarmingly scatty at times, had actually gone to the length of driving over to Alltmore with the express purpose of unburdening himself to Penny. She was easily the most stalwart of his friends, and also, though he was not sufficiently self-analytical, or astute, to see it, the most maternal.

The unburdening had not been a swift process. Penny had been obliged to put several pressing jobs on hold, and even, so that Alec could be sure he had her undivided attention, abandon a final attempt to patch a disintegrating pair of jeans which her younger son Barney passionately refused to give up. She had also had to provide him with lunch before he could bring himself to articulate a tiny part of the dismay and yearning which consumed him.

He had finally managed to outline the plans he had formulated, not without immense mental anguish, and received her blessing, plus a quantity of practical advice. He didn't question that the time had come to revamp his life, for even he could see how fatally easy it would be to drift on as his father had done, until one day his abused liver carried him off in exactly the same way, but he had not been a confident man as he took the hilly road home to Torglas.

Meanwhile, until his magnificent plans could be put in train, he intended to keep a toe in the door as far as Philippa was concerned, and in fact made contact far more often than usual. Since he could never think of much to say during these phone calls, it fell to Philippa to do most of the chatting, and as Jon always guessed who she was talking to, they irritated him extremely.

The resultant squabbles, not something Philippa was used to, released some tension but did nothing to take the edge off their growing sexual need for each other.

Jon still spent the mornings in bed, moving to the sofa in front of the fire once the sitting-room had warmed up. Philippa, smiling and friendly, kept her distance, and Jon, reminding himself that it would be inconvenient to find himself out on his ear, resigned himself to watching her night after night curled up in the big chair opposite (she looked surprisingly small folded), or leaning against its arm on her favourite old hassock with her legs stretched across the hearthrug.

They compensated by talking endlessly, but for each there were areas still avoided. Jon felt a nagging compulsion to find out about Philippa's marriage, though knowing he risked hearing details he might not care to have lodged in his brain for ever afterwards.

'I made a mistake,' Philippa said once, when he questioned her. 'I should have known better. I wasn't the right person for him.'

'What was he like?'

She lifted her shoulders, gazing into the fire. 'Insecure,' she said. She hadn't talked about Richard to anyone since she came back. She had brought him to Glen Maraich when they were engaged, and had read with wry accuracy the courtesy with which he had been welcomed. But she had been adrift in those days – home, parents, her familiar way of life lost to her, struggling to adapt to new surroundings and new values.

She had accepted Richard at his own estimation, for within the service environment he had been self-assured, popular and relatively successful. Since he had fallen for her with flattering speed, and pursued her with the blind determination of the true egotist, she had believed that he loved her. More significantly, in spite of his outward assurance, he had once or twice let her glimpse vulnerability, and for Philippa that was fatal. Once they were married, however, his underlying insecurity had soon convinced him, in spite of anything she could do or say, that Philippa saw him as her social inferior, and he had become defensive and touchy.

Some of this Jon elicited, but Philippa never told him what had done the final damage, afraid that he might react much as Richard had.

But Jon did arrive at another key factor which was almost as significant, annoyed with himself that it had taken him so long to slot this into place.

'He started drinking?'

'He certainly had the sort of mess bill the station commander reviewed each month,' Philippa said dryly.

Odd that he'd told her so, it occurred to Jon.

'How long were you together?'

'A year and a half.'

'Um. You poor old duck.' He hadn't realised it had been over so soon. That was rough. He reached out a hand. 'Bring that thing over here.'

Without argument, she stood up and toed the pouffe nearer and settled beside him. He slipped a hand under her hair and caressed her neck. Each, from their own standpoint, reviewed what had been said.

Philippa was briefly tempted to spill out the whole story. In this mood he made her feel very secure. How was she going to bear it when he went away?

She should have a man to look after her, Jon decided, not some wimp needing his ego massaged. Although talking about her husband had produced a strained look he'd never seen in her face before, he couldn't regret having probed for more details. For one thing, if he hadn't he wouldn't be stretched out comfortably with her so close, the silky warmth of her hair spilling over his hand as he had so often longed to feel it.

Less welcome thoughts began to intrude. He shouldn't leave it much longer to put straight the facts about June. Philippa hated lies, and he knew that his marriage was one thing above all he couldn't risk deceiving her about. He'd told her it had been washed up years ago, and knew she would have inferred, as at the time he had meant her to, that he was divorced. But the situation was different now; he was sure, beyond any doubt, that once he was clear of his present contract, if he survived, he'd be coming back.

But wouldn't it be better to tell her about June when he could also tell her he'd put his divorce in hand? He should have done it years ago. June wouldn't give a monkey's either way so long as she got the house.

The next day when Philippa was out Jon helped himself to what he needed from her desk, hardly looking at anything, and wrote to June. He hesitated from ingrained habit over giving Keeper's Cottage as his address, but could see no alternative. Having handed the letter to Postie, thankful it didn't have to be addressed to Mrs Paulett, he tried to put the matter out of his mind. But inevitably associations had been stirred up. It was a shock to work out that his son Brian was older than he had been when he married. The image of him brought back all the old guilt and distaste, and Jon could hardly believe he'd let the whole wretched situation drag on for so long.

The length of his stay at Achallie was somehow never discussed. His headaches had almost gone, the plaster on his leg was no more than an inconvenience and his ribs were mending, but he knew from a persistent pain in his kidneys that he'd suffered more from that systematic kicking than he had at first realised. He could probably have coped with day-to-day living in his cottage, but had no wish to be trapped there, unoccupied and alone, dependent in any case on someone bringing supplies.

He was all too clearly reminded of how little he was fit for when Philippa, as he had so often vainly fantasised, needed his help and he was unable to give it. Recent wild winds had given her old shed a ruthless battering, working loose the corrugated iron sheets of its roof so that their flailing woke him in the night.

Philippa, the perfect hostess, decided to get up there and hammer in the bolts. Jon, annoyed not to be able to do it himself, was even more annoyed that she'd chosen an evening when he'd been alone all day and had been looking forward to company.

'But the forecast's for more wind,' Philippa urged. 'Another hour or so on your own won't matter, will it? Better than being kept awake all night, surely.'

Now Jon could faintly hear her banging away, and he could also hear the wind gathering force. But just as he hobbled through to the bedroom to bang on the window and yell to her to give up, the hammering stopped.

Seen sense at last, he thought with satisfaction, then heard the screech of the ladder against metal, and a dull thud which made his heart jerk and pound. Dot and carry, he went with cursing haste along the corridor, and was relieved to hear the back door open and slam.

In the kitchen he found Philippa, face ashen and eyes closed, leaning against the door, her right hand clamped round her raised left wrist.

'In Christ's name what have you done?' Jon demanded with the roughness of the badly shaken.

'Ladder slipped. Caught my wrist on the edge of the roof.' Her eyes were still shut as she tried to deal with the tearing pain.

He thought of the twisted edges of corrugated iron and his stomach contracted.

'You shouldn't have been up there in the first place. I told you to leave it. Come on, let's have a look.'

He managed to draw her to the table and get her onto a stool, where she sat with her body hunched round the source of pain. 'Come on, love.' Perching beside her, he persuaded her to straighten up and drew the arm away from her body. 'Let me see, sweetheart, let go a minute.'

Gently he uncurled her stiff bloody fingers and, finding the elbow undamaged, laid her forearm along the table. Down the thin white inner arm ran a jagged tear from which he was glad to see the blood welled but did not pump. 'OK, hold on to it again.'

He wrapped her fingers back over the wound and, steadying her as best he could with one hand, reached for a couple of clean tea-towels from the drawer. He swiftly produced a pad and made her press it in place, raising her arm against her chest. 'Hold it there. Lean forward a bit. Are you going off?'

'Quite possibly,' she said muzzily but politely, and even at such a moment Jon found himself grinning.

'Hold on, love.' If he pushed her head down she'd probably end up on the floor and him with her.

'There's a field dressing in the cupboard. Middle shelf left. Polythene box,' Philippa said helpfully.

Keeping an eye on her, Jon went to look.

'OK, got it.' He ripped open the packet without giving a thought to its familiar markings.

'I'm current for tetanus,' said Philippa, who seemed to be one step ahead in the manual, to his amused pride. He didn't question that for the moment either.

'I'm not going to be able to stitch you up, though, am I?' he retorted as he expertly secured the pad.

'Doesn't need stitches.'

'Since you seem so clued up, you must know damn well that it does.'

'It'll be fine.'

'Don't be so bloody stupid.'

Frustrated beyond measure at not being able to put her in the car and drive her straight down to the surgery himself, Jon cast about for a solution as he hobbled to put the kettle on.

Philippa, reviving after swallowing the sweet tea he made, which she ungratefully pronounced foul, argued stubbornly about going to the doctor's until Jon, who was suffering from shock himself, roared at her to do as she was told.

Startled, she blinked at him, and he sat down and put a careful arm round her, saying in exasperated apology, 'Don't look at me like that, I'm not really angry, but you know that arm has to be dealt with right away. How about asking one of your friends to take you down?' He didn't like having to suggest it, but saw no alternative.

'I can drive,' Philippa said instantly.

He nearly roared at her again, but seeing her wan face and tremulous mouth he relented, drawing her close. 'I can't let you go off on your own,' he protested. 'I'd go demented wondering if you were all right.'

She turned her face into his shoulder, breathing in the smell of him, glad of his comforting bulk and his arms round her. 'If I were here on my own I'd drive down.'

'So you'd have decided it needed stitching?' he asked slyly, and was glad to hear her laugh. She was amazingly resilient. That control of hers, though inconvenient at times, had its good points.

Philippa continued to lean against him, never wanting to move again.

He suggested calling an ambulance, but she wouldn't hear of it. 'It's only a cut. Nothing's broken.'

He let her go in the end, hating not to be able to look after her, but knowing he'd only add to her problems if he insisted on cramming into the Mini and going with her. She seemed to be away for a long time, giving him ample opportunity to register that never before had he been reduced to this state of anxiety about another human being.

She came swanning in at last, stitched and bandaged, and, recognising her state of post-shock euphoria, Jon groaned to think of her behind the wheel.

'They gave you a shot? Why in God's name did they do that when you were driving?' he demanded angrily, as he helped her as best he could towards the sofa.

'Told them I wasn't. Lied,' announced veracious Philippa, spinning in carelessly among the cushions.

'Just look at you,' Jon said, hiding his joy and relief to have her safely back. 'What a shambles.'

She was even more of a shambles when she insisted on getting supper ready, and helped herself to a couple of hefty swigs of sherry in the kitchen to steady her hand. Jon took one look at her as she came swaying in with a tray whose contents clashed and slid, and hauled himself hastily to his feet.

'Don't tell me you've been drinking!' He rescued the tray but nearly lost his own balance as Philippa leaned confidingly against him. 'Watch out, you'll have us both on the deck.'

But she was irresistible in this squiffy, feckless state, and in her willingness to cuddle up to him for comfort. Supper never appeared, and it was Jon who eventually went scrounging for cheese and fruit. He had no objections to an evening with Philippa tucked up beside him just where he wanted her to be, boneless as a jelly, self-discipline forgotten, but beyond a few sleepy kisses he didn't exploit his advantage. When he and Philippa made love, as they surely would, she was going to want it as badly as he did. He wasn't interested in having her drowsy and passive and drugged to the eyeballs. He wasn't entirely convinced that she knew who he was.

In the morning he was sardonically entertained to see her exhibit the classic symptoms of a thumping hangover, including wary doubt as to what had actually taken place. She brought in his tea as usual but didn't meet his eye, turning away to open the curtains.

'Where's yours?'

'I thought I'd go back to bed for an hour or two. No work today. Do you need anything while I'm here?'

So they were to pretend the lovely closeness of the evening had never existed. The armour was back in place.

'No.' You beside me. Some hope.

Philippa glanced at him, disconcerted by the harsh mono-syllable, then went out, saying nothing. It hurt more than Jon could have believed.

Upstairs and down, the occupants of Achallie failed to get back to sleep. Jon swore to himself that they'd talk about this; he wasn't going to let her fob him off any longer with the maddening contradictions of open affection and hands-off chilly good behaviour.

Philippa, struggling to unravel confused memories of the evening, could hardly believe she'd so recklessly laid herself open to the very problems she'd been trying so hard to avoid. Her arm throbbed and so did her head. She couldn't imagine how they'd get through the day.

Help came in a form which, in bringing Jon's temper to explosion point, could have proved disastrous. Philippa was in the garden attempting some shaky digging, and Jon was struggling into his jeans, when a Range Rover turned in behind the Mini and a powerful female voice, certain of its welcome, called for Philippa.

Jon was strongly tempted to get back into bed, but almost at once Philippa was at his door.

'Jon, can I come in? Oh, good, you're up. Look, please help me out, come and meet some people.'

'It's not me they've come to see.'

'Oh, Jonnie.' She came further in and pushed the door to, lowering her voice. 'I really, really need you.' Would he refuse in this mood? 'Maria Ramsden is torture. And she's brought masses of food so they obviously intend to stay all day. I can't cope without you.'

'Huh. What would you do if I wasn't here?'

'Suffer.'

How could he resist that smile?

There were other compensations. He definitely relished the hastily adjusted expressions of the guests as he came stumping out of Philippa's bedroom and was introduced to them with no editing.

It was the start of a long day. 'Why didn't they let you know they were coming?' he asked Philippa as they made the first round of coffee together. 'I thought your lot were pretty hot on that sort of thing.'

'Maria thinks everyone's always thrilled to see her.' Philippa found her spirits recovering in spite of the state of her head. Jon had relented; a quarrel was averted; she could face anything. 'She brings so much stuff with her that you can't complain about not being warned, and if she finds anyone else here she thinks they're jolly lucky to be included in the treat.'

'Can't her husband keep her in order?'

'See for yourself.'

Far from keeping his wife in order, Lionel Ramsden was barely capable of completing a sentence. The poor creep had probably never finished one since his wedding day, Jon decided. The Ramsden offspring, two resentful teenagers, were polite enough to Philippa, but were frequently goaded into contemptuous insolence to their mother, which sparked uninhibited family fights.

It was a new experience for Jon to feel so protective as he observed Philippa, white-faced and trying to safeguard her bandaged arm, look increasingly tense as the full-scale operation of lunch was launched.

'Now, I know your kitchen's too tiny to do anything ambitious so I brought the simplest of picnics. These drumsticks only need to be put in the oven and the soup heated up. I'll make the dressing for the salad, shall I, I know just how it goes. Oh, Portuguese olive oil, how unusual. Well, I suppose it will be all right . . .'

Jon, willing to get stuck in but accepting that with his bulk and his plaster he'd be more hindrance than help, could hear every word from the sitting-room, and was glad when the Ramsden daughter turned on the television. Lionel was warming his backside in front of the fire, raising himself gently up and down on his toes and humming, as if wishing to distance himself from whatever was going on. His entire existence was based on this hope, Jon assumed, at once amending, never mind him, what's happening to me, as he discovered he was actually happy to be laying the table. It was a moment of novel gratification when they sat down and he found himself at one end, with Philippa smiling at him from the other.

Every piece of silver, glass and china in the house appeared to have been commandeered, and washing up was even more of an undertaking than preparing the 'picnic'. It was clear that if Jon and Philippa hadn't been walking wounded they would have been left to get on with it.

'Cooks are usually let off, you know,' Maria boomed, not quite joking, squirting such a protracted jet of washing-up liquid into the sink that the kitchen drain had a white mound over it all afternoon. 'I say, Pippa, this plate's a bit dicey. Shouldn't risk it if I were you,' and she snapped across her knee a beautiful ironstone plate which had done duty for a hundred years. Philippa caught the expression on Jon's face and was almost repaid for the loss of the plate.

As the mandatory sortie round the garden was being organised she took the chance to whisper, 'You stay here, no need to join the entourage for inspection.' But she was pleased when he came, scowling darkly at Maria's pronouncements as to what Philippa should prune, move, discard, drain, split, burn, uproot and kill.

A sticky half hour by the fire followed, the young writhing while their mother made Philippa write down the name of a firm who would clean the carpet, worked out the cost of installing central heating and gave dire instances of the disasters which had overtaken people rash enough to ignore her advice.

'Now, I shall leave you the leftovers,' she announced at last, and her stupefied audience stirred in hope. 'Philippa's always jolly glad of these little extras,' she confided to Jon, without bothering to lower her voice. He lifted his lip at her.

Goodbyes seemed to take for ever, only cut short by Lionel, in his one resolute act of the day, perhaps of his marriage, rolling up the windows and driving away with Maria still mouthing and gesticulating.

'God almighty,' said Jon weakly, leaning against the gable end and gazing at Philippa in disbelief.

'Isn't she truly appalling?' She laughed but looked weary to the bone.

'Come on.' It seemed natural for him to transfer both crutches to one hand and put an arm round her, and for her to drop her head gratefully against him. A couple, Jon thought, not caring how fatuous he was, a couple going back into their house together. The fact that he'd been a married man for twenty-six years didn't occur to him. The constraint of the morning was forgotten, high as the price had been.

18

It was probably the first time in Maria Ramsden's life that she left improved relations behind her, but in the days following what Jon called the Ramsden Offensive he and Philippa returned to something like their earlier footing together, and he had enough sense to enjoy what was on offer and let anything else wait. Also, he wanted to be certain of June's reaction to a divorce before he made any more explicit move. He already knew, with a deep private certainty, that when he finally made a play for Philippa there would be nothing casual about it. Everything must be properly in place.

Although he didn't at once recognise it for what it was, Philippa now gave him a signal far more significant than the kind he was used to from women. After the spell of blustering winds and chilly nights, with even a brief return of snow, April had brought the first real warmth. The kitchen door stood open all day, sweaters were shed by ten, and a dozen garden jobs it had been unthinkable to start a week ago all clamoured to be done at once.

Breakfasting in the sheltered corner by the back door on yet another morning promising a perfect day, shadows razor-sharp across the dew-furred grass, the calls of peewits and oystercatchers mingling with the voices of garden birds, Jon remarked, lifting his face luxuriously to the sun, 'What a place to live. You people up here really have it made.'

'I love it,' Philippa said simply. She remembered with a momentary shiver how bleak the years of exile after her father's death had been. 'I've always loved it.'

Jon, acutely tuned by now to any nuance in her voice, turned his head to look at her. 'You've never told me where you used to live.'

'Not in this glen.'

He took this as one of her polite evasions, and though mildly piqued was ready to shrug it off, when she said, 'I'll take you there if you like. Today.'

'OK,' he said, surprised at the offer, so abruptly made, but at once intrigued. 'Where?'

'Not far. Will you be all right in the car?'

'Sure. But where are we going?'

'Come on, let's get moving, before I start thinking of all the things I ought to be doing in the garden.'

Jon frowned at the way she was blocking his questions, then, as she jumped up and began to gather plates, he caught something in her face, a look of – what? – excitement, resolve, apprehension? Wiser with Philippa than he'd ever had the inclination to be with anyone else, he decided to let matters take their course.

As she drove up the glen he looked across to his own cottage, tiny and isolated on the face of the hill. In his mind it had become a grim and gloomy place, chillingly lonely. Soon he would have to go back to it.

Philippa went through the village, and past Alltmore took a narrow road winding into a small-scale landscape of humped hills and small fields, with lichened birches overhanging mossy dykes and full burns. On the way up Glen Maraich they had been light-hearted, arguing every time Jon changed gear to save Philippa's wrist. Now Philippa fell silent. Glancing at her as they came to a high stone wall, backed by tall non-native trees, Jon saw that her face was beaky, almost plain, with the abstraction of a person facing something dreaded.

He did his best. 'Who lives here now, in this place? Wherever we're going.' He wondered belatedly if he was going to have to face some Maria Ramsden clone.

'No one,' Philippa replied briefly.

The wall fell back in a semi-circle, with tall granite pillars and an empty gateway.

'What's it called?' Jon asked.

'Affran,' Philippa answered, such loving nostalgia in the single word that he asked no more.

They turned in past a forlorn gate lodge, grass growing from the rones, flower-beds claimed by weeds. The drive, narrowed by the encroachment of leaf mould, swept up between straggling rhododendrons backed by chestnuts and sycamores just coming into leaf, beech and birch trees still slender-budded, larches misted in new green and towering wellingtonias topping them all. There was a flash of vibrant colour as a squirrel whisked behind a trunk; rabbits and pheasants took to the undergrowth. There were birds everywhere. Planned with expert care, views opened from time to time – of sunny fields, a sheet of daffodils just ready to flower sweeping down to a loch, a glimpse of snow-streaked peaks. Impressed, Jon opened his mouth to comment, but noting Philippa's set face, the ridged muscles along her jaw, held his peace. A sense of expectancy grew, however, about the splendours, decayed or otherwise, to which this climbing, untended drive might lead them.

Trees gave way to ornamental shrubs and bushes, neglected but still putting out leaf and blossom. On the right appeared the remains of a formal garden, terraces with stone balustrades smothered in climbing roses running wild, flights of steps where moss and grass spread from the cracks. Some place; there must be a caretaker here at least?

The Mini dived into a tunnel of laurels, which led to a courtyard surrounded by shuttered buildings. Here all was order, doors and windows sound, paving slabs swept and, unusually, padlocks everywhere. Philippa pulled up with a jerk that made Jon wince, but for once she was oblivious of him. She folded her arms on the steering wheel, looking at the blank buildings, very still, and Jon waited, tension taking hold of him too, the silence of the place seeming all at once eerie, almost hostile.

Who or what was she afraid of finding here?

Abruptly, Philippa appeared to come to a decision. She got out of the car, still not speaking, and stood for a moment gripping the top of the door, as though mustering her forces, forgetting to offer Jon help. Her unawareness of the effort it took to heave himself out told him more clearly than anything else could have done that there was something here which mattered to her very much. It also made him wryly aware of the level of attention he'd come to take for granted from her.

Seeing Jon balanced and ready, Philippa went towards an archway where a path vanished into the shadows of the laurels. Jon followed, raising an eyebrow. From her, the briefing was usually better. As she reached the arch she checked, and turned to take his arm, giving a little grimace of apology or appeal.

'OK?' Jon asked, out of his depth, shifting both crutches to one hand.

Philippa nodded, managed a brief smile and, still clutching his arm, went forward to the blaze of sunshine ahead. As they stepped into its blinding glare, Jon saw that, instead of the imposing house everything he'd seen so far had led him to anticipate, there was nothing but space and light. With a genuine shock of disorientation, he checked where he was. They were standing on a level platform where the remnants of extensive foundations indicated that a big building had once stood. He felt an odd sense of loss, almost of being cheated, at this unexpected emptiness, then became aware that Philippa's hand on his arm was trembling.

'The house was here? Your home?'

She nodded, not risking words.

'So when was this – why?' Jon floundered. 'Why didn't you tell me?' Then, perceptive as he could be where Philippa was concerned, he guessed the rest. 'You haven't been back? You've never seen this?'

'No.' One tight word as she turned her head into his shoulder to shut out that unbearable emptiness.

Jon let his crutches fall and put his arms round her. 'My poor sweet, come here.' The scented air, the heedless birdsong, the warmth of the sun on his shoulders in that high bright space, the supple body in his arms accepting his comfort, meshed in a moment he would never forget.

Philippa lifted her head to give him a wan smile of gratitude, tears on her lashes.

'Tell me about it,' he said. 'Talk to me.'

She nodded, and they crossed the terrace to a curving flight of steps. She settled in its sun-filled shelter with a familiarity Jon didn't miss, and which struck him as almost more poignant than her tears.

He lowered himself beside her and drew her comfortably against him. 'Come on, tell me about it.'

She had never talked to him like this before, rapidly, absorbedly, in low intimate narrative, about the deeply felt past. She told him of her mother's death from unexpected heart failure when Philippa was sixteen; of her father's increasingly frequent absences as his existence became centred on his addictive gambling; of the silence and emptiness of the big house when she was left there alone. With her father's gambling had gone the alcoholism which had killed him at

forty-five (Christ, thought Jon), and it was then that the scale
of his debts had been revealed. The estate, already mortgaged,
had been bought by a syndicate of Dutch businessmen, who
wanted the shooting and stalking but not the house, which
they soon pulled down, preferring to adapt the factor's house
for their use.

'When did this happen?' Jon asked. He wasn't greatly
interested in anything which didn't concern Philippa directly,
but he recognised her need to talk out her grief and was ready
to sit there all day if necessary.

'Oh, a while ago. You must think me a terrible baby for not
having faced up to it before.' Jon said nothing; he would find
out in due course why she had done so today. 'It took ages to
sort everything out after Father died. I almost did come, after
it had been knocked down. I felt I ought to, you know. But—'
She broke off, looking down the elegant curve of weedy steps
to the ragged grass of the terrace below.

'But?'

Philippa hesitated, then went on swiftly, not looking at
him. 'Richard and I were up on leave, staying with Penny
and Andrew Forsyth at Alltmore. He was keen to come and
have a look. Said he wanted to see where I'd grown up and
so on. But at the last moment I couldn't face it with him.
He was – well, pretty angry about it.'

Jon hid his satisfaction at this information.

Philippa's face was sombre, remembering that day. Preparing herself resolutely for what they would find, glad to
have company to see her through it, she had realised as they
were about to set off how completely out of tune with her
feelings Richard had been.

He had wanted to go to see how grand Affran had been.
But whereas, all too frequently, he had resented anything
which revealed how different Philippa's upbringing had been
from his own, in this case, it had dawned on her, he had felt

secure. He would have been quite happy to visit an Affran razed to the ground, knowing he would never have to appear there as a guest, never feel he was on trial or had to measure up. Worse, Philippa had had the impression that he actually relished the fact that, no matter in what surroundings she'd grown up, she now had less in the world than he did.

He had nagged all day, but his interpretation of her sudden change of mind had shown her how accurate her instinct had been. He had believed that, when it came to it, she hadn't wanted him to see what had happened to her home because it would have spelled out her changed circumstances. Not for a moment had he paused to imagine how it would make her herself feel to see it.

'Perhaps it was too soon anyway,' she said, relating some of this to Jon. 'Or perhaps there was no need to come. But the thought of it has haunted me. I felt I had to see for myself that it had gone for ever but, cowardly or whatever, I haven't been able to face coming alone.'

'How about your friends in the glen?' He would really have liked to ask why with him, but didn't want the present to obtrude just yet.

'But they'd been part of it,' she said at once. 'They would have minded too much. And they'd have been kind – I'd have found that hard to deal with.'

Jon gave a small involuntary laugh. So much for some flattering reason for choosing him.

But Philippa was serious. 'You know what I mean. You're unsentimental. I felt I could handle it with you here because, though you can be abrasive at times, I was sure you'd understand. In the things that matter you're very clear-thinking. I'm grateful that you came.'

He knew as he hugged her close that no compliment had ever meant more. 'We'll chase away the ghosts,' he promised, and found his voice unexpectedly husky.

Presently they forsook their sunny corner and wandered on, along the sleeping terraces, past the spongy, rank-grassed croquet lawn to the trapped warmth of the walled garden, and down the tangled paths of an ornamental glen, once beautiful with waterfalls and miniature bridges and the exotic plants brought back by an ardent Galbraith botanist of a century ago. They went slowly, pausing, looking, absorbing, talking.

'You will say if you're bored?'

'I'm not bored.'

'You can't imagine how good it is to talk about it at last.'

'Talk away, fine by me.'

It was, and watching her relax, hearing a more cheerful note creep into the reminiscences, Jon knew that he was content. It suited him, he was honest enough to admit, as it had suited her husband, that she no longer belonged to the sort of out-dated splendour Affran once had represented. Not much chance of her doing Murray's books for one thing if she had. But that was only part of it. Knowing she'd shared with him something so close to her heart, he would give her all the time she wanted.

They ate the picnic they'd brought in an absurd summer-house complete with arrow slits and battlements, well sited to enjoy a huge view and maximum sunshine.

'They knew what they were doing,' Jon acknowledged, though he sounded rather grudging about it.

'Oh, pure chance, surely,' Philippa said blandly, and he grinned, glad she was teasing him again.

Afterwards she drove slowly along the familiar tracks and drives of the estate, until she felt she'd seen enough and was ready to go back to Achallie. She could return here or not as she wished. There would always be deep feelings tied up with this place, but never again the dread of pain. Nothing would bring back her quiet-voiced mother or her once fit and handsome father, whom she had latterly known as a grey, shambling figure with shaking hands and an uncertain temper, but there were many good memories to hold on to too.

'We could go home now,' she said to Jon, as they leaned on a gate enjoying the sight of pairs of lambs tucked up against each other in engaging poses in the afternoon warmth.

Jon smiled, putting out a hand to ruffle her hair. 'Therapy worked?'

'You've been so good.'

'Any time,' he said, but he was more than satisfied. Optimism filled him as they turned into the glen road.

But back at Achallie the phone was ringing as Philippa opened the door. Bessie's niece, who had been due to come to tea with her aunt but had had trouble with her car. She had phoned Bessie, but knew she was upset. Could Philippa possibly . . . ?

'Don't worry, I'll go up,' Philippa assured her. 'Of course it's no trouble.' But turning from the phone, she was taken aback to see Jon's face dark with anger.

'Go where? What's no trouble?' he demanded.

Philippa's heart sank. How could his good humour dissipate so swiftly? 'I have to make sure Bessie's all right. I won't be long.'

'Can't someone else run after these damned people?'

'There isn't anyone else.'

'The world can get along without you, you know. You don't have any special remit to run the whole show.'

Philippa flushed, but only said quietly, 'Bessie will be disappointed. She'll have got things ready.'

'Oh, spare me the details. She'd have managed all right if we hadn't come back. For Christ's sake, for once in your life can't you just leave them to it.'

She's my neighbour. She's old and half-blind. But there was no point in getting into an argument. 'I'll make tea for you before I go, and I'll only be—'

'I can make my own tea.' He couldn't believe that their happy intimacy and the promise of the evening ahead was being wrecked by something so trivial.

'Good.' Philippa would be conciliatory so far but no further.

She wasn't away long, though she wished she could have spared more time when she saw the trouble Bessie had taken, fumbling laboriously through such preparations as she could manage. Coming fast down the hill, she let herself believe that Jon would have recovered his temper by now. He'd been so marvellous today.

'Have you had tea?' she called cheerfully as she came through the kitchen, but received no answer. Instead, she walked into the worst storm yet.

Jon had taken his tea into the sitting-room, but had been too angry about Philippa leaving him on his own to settle down. He had prowled about the room, nursing his resentment, convincing himself that the moment had been perfect and was now destroyed. Then the events of the day returned, improving his mood a little, and, with all that he'd learned fresh in his mind, he looked about him with new eyes.

Those incongruously large pieces of furniture – had they come from Affran? Were there other clues and links? They proved easy to find once he began looking. He recognised the background to photographs in which he'd only looked at Philippa before; the watercolours he'd barely glanced at were of the fancy summerhouse and the loch below the slope of daffodils. The row of battered childhood books, on the lower shelf of the big bookcase, must have come from Affran too.

Awkwardly he bent to pull one out. 'To darling Pippa on

her eighth birthday, with love from Aunt Christian.' Christian! But as he turned the pages with a sort of bitter vicarious nostalgia, he found himself unable to despise something once so clearly treasured.

It would be a pity to spoil the day. He was tired, aching after the unaccustomed exercise; that was why he'd lost it for a minute. And he'd felt suddenly hopeless and disillusioned, he amended more honestly, recognising that, no matter how close he and Philippa appeared to be, there would always be people she'd put before him. Always lame dogs. Well, it was part of her, better get used to it.

Browsing along the shelves he came across *A Bridge Too Far*. Must read that again, he thought, taking it out, though its sequence of disasters hardly made cheerful reading. An envelope fell from between the pages, and he kept it out while dipping into a passage about XXX Corps' doomed race. About to put it back, he saw it was addressed to Flight Lieutenant P. L. Howard. Philippa's husband? But he was a wing commander, wasn't he? A flight lieutenant once, of course. But checking the postmark Jon saw that the date was too recent for that to fit. And Philippa's husband was called Richard.

It was the one deception Jon couldn't accept, by the one person he had truly trusted. She'd made a fool of him, was his first furious reaction. No wonder she'd been so much at home with the references when he'd indulged in service talk. No wonder she knew about ranks and mess bills and the rest. No wonder her shots were up to date and she had a goddam field dressing with arrow markings in her kitchen cupboard. He'd been pitching his stories at civilian level, when all the time . . .

And he'd passed himself off as a major, not only to someone who had been in the services, but to someone who'd been an officer. Though technically one in his present role, he was well aware that was little more than play-acting. How Philippa must have been laughing at him.

But beneath his surface anger and humiliation coiled something deeper. Jon felt Philippa had denied them something important – the chance to share a world to which they'd both belonged. He felt hurt, betrayed, in a way he could barely define.

Philippa had never faced or imagined the sort of rage he poured out on her. In his raw mortification he didn't care how brutal he was, and it shook her.

'I thought you'd mind if you knew I was an officer,' she attempted to explain. 'I did want to tell you, but it was hard to find a way.'

Useless. She'd tricked him. She, to whom he'd revealed more of his private self than he ever had to anyone. After the happy optimism of the day this revelation destroyed him. And he'd felt guilty for not telling her about June . . .

He let Philippa drive him to Keeper's Cottage, because he was desperate to get there and because she insisted with such stubbornness, as though to do this one last thing for him would somehow keep a door open between them for the future. She put together food for him, nearly blinded by tears, and would have packed his clothes if he hadn't ordered her roughly to leave them alone.

'But the water isn't even on,' she said, clutching at the hope that if he didn't go tonight they might be able to sort this out reasonably.

'More of your bloody meddling. Well, you'd better organise your mafia to get it on again.'

'At least stay until tomorrow, so that I can—'

'You must be joking. I'd rather walk.'

Even lying battered in Muirend Hospital, Jon hadn't looked to Philippa as utterly desolate as he did when she drove away from Keeper's Cottage, and in her rear-view mirror saw him standing there, propped on his crutches, his bag and the box of food at his feet. He hadn't so much as let her carry them in for him.

19

'I suppose it's no use asking Philippa to the Opening Picnic on the island,' Joanna Drummond said resignedly. This traditional event, which included the rebuilding of the dam to create a good pool for swimming in the river, had been recently revived. Most of their group, as well as friends and family staying in the Allt Farr cottages for the Easter holidays, turned up for it. 'She won't budge without this new man of hers.'

'Oh, he's gone.' Penny had come up for cuttings and seedlings. Since the Munro family had returned to their unwieldy stone pile, with its towers, draughts, ancient wiring and chancy plumbing, Joanna's contribution to their pooled resources had been to make the huge garden productive on a commercial basis. Though Penny was here primarily as a customer, as she was also staying for lunch she guessed she would have to face more searching questions from Grannie than dreamy Joanna would ever ask.

'Gone from the glen?' Joanna looked up from a plug she had prised from its nest to check its roots.

'No, from Achallie. He's back in Michael's cottage. He took it for a year, supposedly to find somewhere to buy though I haven't heard of him looking at anything.'

'You don't like him?'*

'I've never met him. That's the point, really. Ever since she met him Philippa seems to have vanished.'

'It was a bit surprising,' Joanna conceded, 'when she took him back to Achallie after his accident.'

'After his fight,' Penny said shortly. She knew she had mixed feelings about this new and obviously absorbing relationship of Philippa's. On the face of it, there was plenty to be dubious about, but there always remained the impression that Philippa had at last found something special, and Penny's own life, these days, was so dreadfully predictable. Predictable and not entirely satisfactory. Yet what more could she possibly want? She had her adored boys, and David and Barney were fit, cheerful teenagers who enjoyed life and had few hang-ups that she could see. She lived at Alltmore, the home she loved, and had an enviably comfortable lifestyle. And she had Andrew. Here she paused. What fault could she find in their marriage after more than twenty contented years? What was it that was lacking? But once in her life Penny had known something different, something she mostly succeeded in keeping firmly buried, and meeting Philippa lately she had known that she too had found something that mattered to her. She couldn't help fearing pain for a friend who had surely had enough loss and sadness in her life.

Joanna had looked up in mild surprise at the abrupt correction. 'Um, must meet this man.'

'Alec's going to be happier anyway,' Penny said more lightly, seeking safer ground.

'I'm sure he is.' But Joanna sounded doubtful. 'I know he's got these plans for Torglas, but do you honestly think that sort of thing will appeal to Pippa?'

'At least she'll see that he's making an effort. Oh, I know Alec's not ideal for her, but nobody would be more faithful and kind, or care more about her, and that's what she needs just now. Someone safe.' Precisely what she herself found less than fulfilling, an ironic voice reminded her.

'I know what you mean, in theory anyway.' Joanna's thoughts went to her own marriage. Her husband's death was now far enough away for her to admit at last that it had been, for her, second best. Ideal on paper, but leaving always that hidden ache of life having carried her away from something infinitely better. 'Does it ever work, totting up the advantages?' she asked, her hands idle. 'There's something about Philippa these days I've never seen before. I'd love her to be happy again.'

'Of course,' Penny protested. 'So would I.'

Joanna smiled at her affectionately. 'But you'd like best to see her with a husband like Andrew, a family, and a house like Alltmore. Though not like Affran.'

'God, no.' Penny shuddered. 'Do you remember how desolate it always felt? Sort of coldly splendid?'

'With the patches on the walls as the pictures were sold one by one, and the way everything seemed to moulder slowly where it stood.'

They laughed, but as the conversation moved on Penny was conscious of a nag of discomfort. Joanna had been right – she did want to see Philippa 'safe' in familiar, comprehensible circumstances. How far behind her she herself had left adventures. She pushed guilt away.

June had never undertaken such a terrifying drive before, but the panic Jack's letter had aroused in her, and her failure to find a phone number for the address he'd given, had impelled her to extreme measures. She had also been egged on by Teresa, fellow receptionist in the Thornton dental practice where June worked part-time to augment Jack's allowance. In spite of the tips Brian bragged about at the Ripon salon, he always needed more.

'I wouldn't stand for it, me. I'd go straight up there and tell him where he gets off. He can't throw you out of your own house. Some woman will have put him up to it.' Teresa had urged action at every lull in work, and the easy vengefulness of the uninvolved had readily chimed with the muddled aggrievement and anxiety the letter had awoken. One thing was clear to June – she must keep the house, the safe burrow beyond which loomed a daunting world she had never had to face. In it lay the only status she had, as a married woman whose husband's work 'took him away a lot'. Terror filled her at the idea of his depriving her of it.

The car terrified her too. It was Brian's, though Jack's money had bought it, after Brian had dreamed up the plan of telling him the roof needed fixing, getting phoney estimates from a couple of builders he knew. June had learned to drive when Brian lost his licence, but hadn't touched the car since he got it back. Good thing Brian was off in Spain this week on a spring break with that friend of his he never let her meet.

Nervous and sweating, she clung to the inside lane through the endless miles, missing chance after chance to take a break because she always left it too late. But she had to do this; she had to have it out with Jack, and see off this other woman Teresa was convinced was behind it all. If he'd got someone else she'd never see a penny from him, then how would she manage? It didn't occur to her, in spite of the years since Jack had appeared in Thornton, that turning up on his doorstep as the outraged wife might not achieve her ends. For the first time since leaving the Army he'd sent an address. That was enough for her.

Brian might have put her straight, but Brian, dead to the world beside the sweaty, snoring body of his lover, was sleeping the hours away till the bars and clubs came to life again.

Philippa, outwardly unruffled, appeared punctually to fulfil her various commitments. She looked rather peaky, people like Lady Hay vaguely thought, but she gave little away, and not even her closest friends were aware of her desperate unhappiness. It was an effort, all the same, to apply herself to work. The mixed emotions after Jon's departure had shaken her by their intensity, and behind them, never relenting, ached a hollow sense of loss.

Angry that Jon could have such an impact on her life, she would promise herself that she would never give him the chance to disrupt it again. Then, helplessly, she would find herself longing to see him. Nothing had ever been so good as being with him. There had been such a feeling of things beginning, of being on the brink of something wonderful. Now she would never know.

Going through her days with outward calm resolutely in place, she felt stretched thin, drawn with agonising slowness to some point where she must inevitably snap. Sometimes she thought that if she and Jon had slept together everything would have been all right. It was her boring caution that had ruined everything. Why had she made such a big deal of it? But what kind of answer would it have been? (A lovely and marvellous one, a wistful voice would suggest.)

Being Philippa, however, with her inconvenient sense of fairness, she could see that Jon had had grounds for being angry. She had misled him, and she could relate to his feeling that a service past was something they could have shared. How would she have felt, making a similar discovery about him, especially after a day of such accord as they'd spent at Affran? She could guess, from what he'd told her, how empty of trust his life had been, and it saddened her to think that he now saw her as behaving towards him exactly as everyone else had always done. Besides, an explosion of abusive rage meant little to him. He would have no idea of the effect it had had on her. He had wanted to hurt her and had simply used any weapons to hand.

How was he faring at Keeper's Cottage? His car was still at the Semples'. He might not even remember where she'd said it was. The food she'd provided wouldn't last long. Well, he had a phone, he could order what he needed. What about when he needed to get to hospital? They'd fetch him; he wasn't her responsibility. How callous to abandon him, though. What would he do with himself all day?

Stop thinking about him, she would order herself in exasperation, starting another garden job or going for another long walk, finding little comfort in either.

In the end she couldn't bear it. Compassion was stronger than pride. Picturing Jon imprisoned, immobile and unoccupied was too awful. Filling a box with what he might need, debating and hesitating, seeing every item through his eyes, Philippa did pause to ask herself why she wasn't phoning first to find out what he needed.

She didn't want him to slam down the phone, was the answer to that. She wanted to see him as much as she wanted to help him; and, if possible, make him understand why she'd withheld the one fact which had obviously mattered so much to him. Above and beyond any of this she knew, if there was the smallest chance that he was missing her as much as she was missing him, that she was prepared to face anything.

Jon's capacity for fuelling a grievance was far greater than Philippa's, but even for him need and regret soon replaced anger – simple need for the sight of her, for everything about her. Not practical need, for unexpected solutions had turned up. The water had been turned on within an hour of his arriving at the cottage, Annie at the Kirkton shop had agreed to send supplies and Postie brought them up.

When Michael Thorne called and chatted amiably over a beer, giving a landlord's eye to the roof and the state of the sheds while he was there, Jon drew the obvious ironic conclusion. They thought he and Philippa had got it together.

Staying at Achallie had been his passport into the charmed
circle. They were a bit behind the times, he thought bleakly.

  Although, as his anger waned, he could concede that
Philippa had done no more than he'd done himself, and
though he was the one who'd stormed out, he still saw it
as down to her to make the first move. But if she did, was
he really up for more of the good-mates business? Was he
ever. Life with Philippa in it, and life without her, were in
such stark contrast that every time he came to this point he
wanted to reach for the phone on the spot. Then he would
remember that she'd be at the hotel, or off on some job, or
running round with those damned friends of hers. She didn't
need him, more than probably never wanted to set eyes on
him again.

Philippa didn't recognise the car parked at Keeper's Cottage.
Nurse, health visitor? Or had Jon decided he could drive and
hired a car so wouldn't need anything? Balancing the laden
box on her raised knee, she gave a brief knock and went
in. The sitting-room door was open and the first thing she
noticed was the smell of cigarette smoke; then she was in the
doorway.

  A woman turned from the window, a woman strikingly
incongruous in these surroundings. June had made an all-
out effort for the trip. Although she preferred to live in
comfortable squalor, she liked to get dolled up when she
went out. Most of her money went on clothes and make-
up. And Jack had fancied her in the days when she took
care of herself. Today she was wearing a black skirt and
flesh-coloured polyester top with a sweetheart neck, over
which the temperature of Keeper's Cottage had forced her
to add a white nylon beaded cardigan. But unhealthy eating
habits and lack of exercise had long ago turned her round
little body into an uncheckable mound of flab, and these

cheap garments strained around it, while her ankles swelled above flimsy shoes. She was dripping with trinkets and her once pretty young-girl's face, now lost in puffy flesh, was heavily made-up. Her hair, specially done before setting off, was as lifeless as hay after years of perms and back-combing, bleaching and dyeing.

She was staring at Philippa with open aggression, but also with a kind of greedy satisfaction which Philippa couldn't interpret.

Jon was stretched in a chair by the fire. He didn't get up. Instead he watched Philippa with an expression she read as mocking. Had he found it rewarding to see her check, disconcerted, in the doorway?

The room was messy, objects tossed down on every chair, the saucers doing duty as ashtrays stained with yellow. On the table, half cleared after a meal, stood an uncapped bottle of gin and a pack of tonic water, its plastic wrapping raggedly torn.

Philippa, repelled, was nevertheless conscious of an instant, protesting conviction that this wasn't how the room would normally look. She hadn't been in Keeper's Cottage during Jon's occupancy, but she was sure that the preference for neatness and order which he'd revealed at Achallie was natural to him.

'You're making yourself at home, I must say,' the woman attacked shrilly, cutting across these thoughts. 'Who do you think you are, walking in here as if you owned the place?'

It was a startling reception from a complete stranger, and Philippa, groping for some clue as to who she could be, let her surprise show as she eyed her coolly across the box lid, declining to explain herself.

'Well, in case you don't know who I am,' the woman announced stridently, 'I'm June Holcombe. And this is Jack Holcombe, though I dare say he's been telling you something different. Yes, it's my husband you've been carrying on with, thank you very much.'

Jon, from his chair, endorsed the introduction with a sardonic bow, and Philippa felt her cheeks burn. This appalling creature with her gross body and querulous voice was Jon's wife – his *wife*. Philippa steadied herself against the door as shock spread through her. Then bracing anger overtook it. This nightmare female was actually gloating over her. Philippa straightened her spine and stepped forward to prop her cumbersome burden on the corner of the cluttered table.

'How do you do. I'm Philippa Howard.' She looked at June calmly, eyebrows raised, offering a challenge of a kind June had not anticipated.

June had readily believed that Jack was shacking up with someone – what other reason could he have for wanting to get rid of her? – but had taken it for granted that it would be some tart who could be routed in a satisfying screaming match, in which the heavy guns of marriage and status would be firmly on her own side. This woman was a shock, and in spite of herself June felt her confidence waver. Philippa, in faded well-cut jeans over polished tan boots, her skin clear and healthy against the navy of her cashmere sweater, hair pulled smoothly back in the dateless fashion of the class June pretended to despise but helplessly envied, looked a daunting adversary.

'You the one he's been carrying on with then?' she demanded, pulling herself together. But her voice sounded less assertive than she'd intended, and the term she would have liked to use remained unspoken.

Philippa looked at her, head tilted in polite enquiry, allowed a tiny pause and said calmly, 'Your husband' – and thank God this appalling woman would never know the effort that cost her – 'has been staying at my house, if that's what you mean.'

June goggled at her. She hadn't known this and couldn't believe Philippa was telling her, cool as cucumber. Floundering, she turned on Jon.

He raised his hands, refusing to be embroiled. 'You heard the lady.'

'You're admitting it then?' June's voice rose hysterically as she swung back to Philippa.

'He was there for two weeks,' Philippa said helpfully. Against her will, her eyes went back to Jon. Impossible, caught up in this repellent scene, to believe in the happiness of that time.

Jon was defeated rather than drunk, as Philippa supposed him to be, and recognised the courage and control she had summoned to see her through this. Once more he gave her that mocking little half-bow, a gesture of salute, but also of bitter farewell to something he knew would never be for him.

To Philippa it seemed he was enjoying her discomfiture, and that hurt. She must get out of here without delay, or she'd break down in front of them.

'Goodbye, Mrs Holcombe,' she said formally. 'As you're here Jon won't need these.' At least the wretched box gave her something to hold on to.

'Hang on a minute, you needn't think you're getting off that easy,' June rushed in indignantly. 'I've a few things to say to you, my lady.'

Philippa looked at her, glad of her extra inches. Then, 'I think not,' she said with calm authority, and turned away. She wished she could find the resolution to say goodbye to Jon but knew it was beyond her.

Cheated of her legitimate redress, baffled and angry, June puffed out after her.

'Don't you show your face here again, you hear?' she shouted, but the words lacked force and made no visible impression on Philippa, going steadily through the motions of stowing her redundant offerings in the back of the Mini, getting into the driving seat and fumbling for the key. Blinking hard, she turned without hitting June's car and found the track.

He didn't even tell me his real name.

Pain beginning to sear after the temporary numbness of the blow, she vowed, I'll never cry for him again.

June slammed the door with all her strength and waddled triumphantly back into the sitting-room.

'That saw *her* off,' she bragged, urgently needing to claw back some self-esteem. 'From now on you can keep your tarts out of the place.'

Jon heaved himself out of his chair with explosive violence. 'One more word,' he warned, 'and I'll break your neck.'

He looked entirely capable of it and June's face crumpled as he loomed over her. 'I was only—'

'Get out.'

'But, Jack—'

'Get out, anywhere out of my sight.'

June retreated in haste to the kitchen. What had she done? Did he really think she'd put up with his woman turning up like that, bold as brass? She'd make him something nice for his dinner, then he'd feel better.

Jon, back in his chair, hearing the clatter of pans across the corridor, felt hopelessness rise in him like a cold tide. He sank his head in his hands.

20

When Jon had heard a car revving hard up the slope in low gear, he'd known it couldn't be Philippa. Nor any local, in fact, making such a meal of it. Resenting the intrusion, he'd hobbled to the window, scowling to see some unknown fat woman heave herself out of the white Nissan. As she'd turned, staring uncertainly at the cottage, he'd wanted desperately to refuse recognition. It couldn't be happening. June couldn't be here, in this place. It had been like a horrible dream to see her start towards the door, eyes and mouth little o's of worry in the fleshy, over-made-up, middle-aged face.

But worse than her sudden appearance, her gone-to-seed bulk, her nervous flow of words in the release of tension after her journey, had been the sick feeling of inevitability which had overwhelmed him. She came like a manifestation of the past, bringing unwelcome reminders of everything he had hoped he'd left behind him, reminders reaching back to times before he even knew her – to the shifting rootlessness of his early years, as he fought his stubborn battle for personal survival, and to the loneliness of adolescence, when bitterness at his treatment at the hands of the Hinks had kept him going as much as his determination to profit from whatever they could offer him. And the longing for a home of his own had lured him into the trap of marriage with this woman.

He had felt, as complaints turned into accusations, that the past had triumphed and always would. Here, with this empty-headed, vulgar creature, he belonged. And he had let himself think he stood a chance with Philippa.

He had made June, though she protested shrilly about facing that horrible track again, go to the village for supplies. When she'd come back she had cooked supper, and the sight of the limp chips and the frizzled brown edges to the eggs had rolled back the years in a way which had filled him with a murderous, futile anger.

He had disabused her, with enough curtness to make her flounce and sniff, of any idea that she would share his bed, letting her make the best she could of the fusty dark room at the rear of the cottage. But during a long evening, despair settling on him like a sombre cloud, it had been June and not he who had turned for solace to the gin she had found unopened in the kitchen cupboard.

Then, unbelievably, Philippa had come, concerned about him in spite of everything. And he'd had to watch her walk, unsuspecting, into that ugly scene. He had understood, as June could never begin to understand, her shock and what it had cost her to hide it. Christ, that she should find out like that – he groaned to think of it. And he'd had the gall to blow his top because she hadn't told him she'd been in the Air Force. Even that, as he'd seen as soon as he took the time to think about it, had been done to protect him from something she'd thought he'd mind.

Bleak though his mood was after Philippa had gone, Jon didn't succumb, as he would have done a few weeks ago, to the depression which threatened to engulf him. He was in better shape now, both mentally and physically. Whether he fully recognised it or not, being with Philippa had begun to turn him back into the person he had been in his Army days, before the destruction of his last hope of being commissioned had started him on the dangerous downward spiral to his present situation.

This tentative return to half-forgotten responses and values proved enough to sway the balance. Gathering his resolution, he began to look for a way out of the pit he'd dug for himself. He might have lost Philippa, but at least he could get his life in order. He should have done it long ago; it had been too easy to let June stay where she was, looking after his precious house, the house which seemed oddly unimportant now. He had moved on from the need to know it was there. What this present contract brought him would buy another; might even enable him, at last, to make reality the dream he so often turned over in his mind. Or he wouldn't need a house at all.

First he must be free of June. He already felt free of Brian, long ago rejected, and any guilt at recognising that he was repeating the cycle of his own, unknown father's rejection of him he kept deeply buried. But June wasn't going to let him go without a fight, that was certain. Her hot-footing it up here because she was afraid the handouts were going to stop had shown as much.

All right, since she was here he'd make use of her. She could take him to the hospital when required, and take him to collect his car. Where was the car, come to that? Philippa had left it with friends. Good excuse to phone her. But, as the thought tempted, his well-trained memory clicked up the name. Well, he didn't intend to use excuses or pretexts with her again anyway. Clean slate. And a lot of good that will do you now, he told himself grimly.

Philippa, doggedly trying to focus on her normal occupations, did her best to rationalise the situation. She'd known it was madness to embark on a relationship with a man like Jon, so why should it be so devastating to find out that he had a wife? Because it made her shudder to think of him touching that woman, in bed with her, making love to her, *married* to her . . .

It was a relief to be busy. Shona Murray's mother was critically ill, Shona and Ian both away, so Philippa was putting in extra time at the hotel. Little fear that Jon would show up there, under the circumstances. But no matter how rushed or tired Philippa was, the thoughts could attack at any moment, without warning, harrowing her with longing for that 'something marvellous' she'd glimpsed with Jon. She often wished they'd made love, so that she could have that memory too. How petty and absurd her scruples on the point seemed now.

Jon embarked with energy on his campaign to rout June. First he had to convince her that nothing was going on between Philippa and himself, and the plot nearly came apart right there, since June was far too ready to agree that someone like Philippa couldn't possibly see anything in someone like him. However, with so much at stake, he managed to keep a grip on his temper.

Then, which he found even harder, he had to make June believe he was glad she'd come. He only succeeded because of her vanity, and her firmly rooted belief that, since he'd gone on sending her money, deep down he still fancied her. Also, seeing for herself that he needed looking after, she was satisfied for the moment to lumber round the cottage wiping all surfaces impartially with a damp cloth, or raising clouds of dust by sweeping the carpet with a broom because she was too lazy to get the hoover out. She stuffed the cupboards with junk food, daily bewailed the absence of a microwave and had the television on for every second that Jon would tolerate it.

Feeling like a man up to his knees in quicksand, he did his best not to remember the very different quality of life at Achallie, and Philippa's ease in achieving it. He tried not to think of Achallie at all. The very colour of the sunlight had seemed different there. Though he swore savagely at himself when such comparisons caught him unawares, even so, stuck in the frowsty room which June kept as hot as she dared, never opening a window, the smell of her cigarettes laced by the crude whiff of her scent, how could his mind help returning to such delights as breakfast in the garden at Achallie on sparkling mornings, the fresh exhilarating bite to the air?

And he had to convince this woman that he wanted her, was tired of being on his own and finally ready to settle down. One thing he couldn't bring himself to do, though the omission should have puzzled her, was to let her move into his room. He fobbed her off with a few random platitudes, solemnly delivered.

'We need to give ourselves time, take things slowly, make sure we get it right this time around. After all, there's a lot to think through. You know how it is . . .'

June wasn't sure that she did, but for the moment she was satisfied with having seen Philippa off and being so patently needed. Although her muddled feelings as she'd driven up had included a few anticipatory tremors at the thought of bed with Jack, now that she was here she found the prospect less attractive. Did she really want 'all that' again? Anyway, it would be a bit awkward, with his plaster and everything. Best wait, like he said.

Complaisant, she blundered through the housework, went back and forth to the shop, drove Jack to the hospital, and worried a lot about what Brian was going to say when she got back. Another thing, she'd taken more time off from work than she'd said; would they keep her on? Teresa would be popping into the house to water the plants, so that was all right at any rate.

Perhaps she wouldn't have to bother about a job, though, if she was with Jack again. Sometimes it did dimly occur to her to wonder what it would be like. He could be funny about things, just like he'd been before. He'd gone daft about her putting cigarette ends down the toilet. And that time she'd gone in and changed his bed . . .

Jon, enjoying the new freedom of a walking plaster, had returned from a short expedition up the burn, where he'd perched on a sun-warmed rock and indulged in the ache and pleasure of thinking about Philippa, and had found June in his room. The contrast between his dreaming thoughts and this reality had flared into such frustrated rage that June had thought for a moment he was going to hit her. Scrambling to escape, flustered and vocal, she had had to admit he was still the same old Jack.

After this Jon stepped up the action.

'Perhaps we'd better get someone in to look over the house,' he suggested idly that evening, having kept June's glass well topped up during and after supper. 'Did you leave a key with anyone?'

'A key?' she repeated stupidly.

One of those things you – but he controlled his exasperation. 'We ought to get things moving. There's no sense in hanging about and having the place on the market in the autumn. This is the best time for selling.'

'Selling?' June echoed blankly, staring at him with round alarmed eyes.

'You do realise we'll have to be up here now? But this part of the world isn't bad. You'll like it.'

'Here?' June could hardly find the breath to get the word out. A tide of red mottled her cheeks.

'Prices aren't bad at the moment.' Jon managed in spite of the maddening way she was repeating everything he said to keep his voice affable. 'And we've done quite a bit to the house. We'd have to get rid of most of the stuff though. No room here.' He glanced round with a rueful shrug he was rather proud of.

He'll find out the money he sent for the roof went on the car. He'll go mad, June thought in panic. Then the full meaning of what he'd said sank in.

'My things? You're not getting rid of my things! You'd never do that.'

'Where would we put them?' Jon asked reasonably.

'But you can't sell the house,' June protested wildly, her brain refusing to make sense of this.

'Not much point in having two. Can't afford it anyway. This place should do us quite well.'

June stared round, dismay filling her. Live here, in this poky, freezing cold cottage, stuck in the middle of nowhere? No one lived in places like this these days. Every atom of her longed for the familiar-smelling fug of her own lounge, her comfy chair pulled up close to the big television which pulsed out sound and reassurance all day long, people passing the window, the buses grinding round the tight turn at the bottom of the terrace.

'I'll get in touch with the estate agents first thing in the morning,' Jon said briskly.

It didn't take long after that. The house would be June's, on the undertaking that she would make no further claim on him. It wasn't difficult to impress her with the benefits of home ownership, long-term security, a hedge against inflation and the possibility of a mortgage if she ever needed ready cash. In fact, blatantly as he had manipulated her, when Jon recalled what that house had cost him in terms of determination and self-sacrifice, he thought she hadn't done too badly.

June, too, began to see that she might be getting a good deal. Owning the house without having Jack thrown in couldn't be bad. For, she had to admit, being with him again hadn't turned out to be a bed of roses.

But one thorn still festered.

'You going to go after that woman then?'

'I told you, there's nothing in that,' Jon snapped roughly. It was hard to say even now.

The news that the major's wife had turned up had flashed round the glen. Goodwill towards Jon sharply declined, and speculation ran high as to how Philippa must feel. Those who knew her less well felt that, though this must be a nasty slap in the face for her, or however they chose to phrase it, she would never have got it together with someone like Jon anyway. Those who knew her better, and who had seen her new, tentative happiness, were less sure this was something to write off so easily. Pleased as her friends might be, from a purely selfish point of view, to have her back in circulation, the more perceptive realised that they would have to tread carefully, and guessed she would need their sympathy and support.

For Alec Blaikie, trying to bear this in mind and not show his relief and satisfaction too openly, though fooling no one, the news was enough to galvanise him into activity. Now the daunting task of stirring Torglas from its quarter century of peaceful slumber, already put in hand with the help of Penny, Joanna, and Joanna's sister Harriet, though she tended to witter on too much to be much use, could surge forward. No half measures now. He had thought for a while that curtains and carpets might do it. New wallpaper in a couple of rooms, perhaps. He couldn't see much point in slathering paint over the untouched wood which everywhere prevailed; only have to keep painting it if you did that, damn silly idea.

However, his sketchy plans had led, at a speed which had left him giddy, to a nightmare period of floors being lifted, roof cavities explored, and being told he must not only treat wet rot, dry rot and woodworm, but lay drains and renew guttering and windows. Well, if that was what it took. He knew, though he would have found it hard to put into words, that the way he and his father had been content to live was not 'normal'. He looked at the lives of his friends and saw that they were richer, fuller and, he suspected, more satisfying. Images of sharing life at Torglas with Philippa, Philippa at the other end of the table where his father had sat, Philippa down at the river casting over the next pool on summer evenings, Philippa sharing a dram in the gunroom (the warmest place in Torglas apart from the enormous linen cupboard) after a long cold day after the stags, would, he vaguely supposed, expand into others. Philippa with children; a son to take out with his first gun, or discovering in his turn the haunts which had been so important to an only child; and people in the house, big, relaxed gatherings where Philippa would know just how to look after everyone . . .

There was still a long way to go, however, he would remind himself, with a frisson of trepidation but also with undeniable relief. More alarming than anything was the (staggeringly expensive) business of choosing colours and fabrics for the new Torglas. Though his usual approach would have been to let this hover somewhere in the future, with any luck ignoring it altogether in the end, so used to bare plaster and bare boards that he no longer saw them, now he saw his opportunity. He'd be subtle, however. It would be a bit obvious to ask Philippa to choose outright. Instead he'd round up the usual committee of faithfuls, including her, naturally, and – a master stroke, this – invite Joanna's mother too.

'Does he imagine that if I'm there Philippa won't know it's about her?' Grannie demanded when she received this appeal. 'Hopeless man. He'll have to sharpen his wits if he's really serious this time.'

'Oh, but he is serious,' her elder daughter Harriet hurried to protest. 'He's always adored her.'

Grannie snorted. 'It's not enough,' she said with finality. Though she was aware that many of their circle, such as

the Semples and Adèle Hay, believed that being safely settled with someone known, reliable and unexceptionable like
Alec would be the best possible thing for Philippa, Eleanor
Munro had known, briefly, love outside the safe, conventional
parameters, and she suspected that in Philippa lay the capacity
for feelings of the same scale and depth. And now this man
she'd become involved with, who, it must be said, sounded
less than desirable, had deceived her, and it was evident that
she was still recovering from the blow.

Watching her now across Alec's dining-table, strewn with
plans, swatches, colour charts and indecipherable notes in his
illiterate hand, Eleanor Munro saw that Philippa was hopelessly distanced from what was going on around her. Though
she roused herself from time to time to make some input,
the effort was obvious. She might as well, Grannie thought
with a mixture of impatience at the time they were wasting
and compassion for someone she admired and cared for,
have been mouthing at them from that wonderful Edwardian
phone booth, made of glass and hooped with brass like a
birdcage, which stood in the hall outside. (And someone
had better make sure Alec didn't do away with *that* in his
reforming zeal.)

Frowning, Grannie turned back to business, frightening
the wits out of Alec in the process. Her contribution towards
family survival at Allt Farr was to make luxurious patchwork
for an exclusive market. Indeed, she often felt that the only
thing keeping her sane was to be able to leave behind the dour
chill of the house for the warmth, vibrant colours and rich
textures of her workroom above the kitchen. Alec, blinking
at the glowing ochre, burnt sienna and ox-blood she flashed
before him, wished he'd had the courage to ask Philippa to
do her own choosing.

It was Penny, as conscious as Grannie of Philippa's abstraction, who took the chance, when Joanna and Harriet were in

the kitchen and Grannie, having pole-axed Alec by telling him what it would cost to re-cover the billiards table, had taken him off to argue the point with the evidence before them, to say quietly to Philippa, 'Things are pretty bad, aren't they? Want to talk some time?'

Philippa looked startled, then guilty. 'I thought I was doing rather well,' she said.

'You haven't been with us all evening.' Penny looked at her with sympathy, hesitating. 'It hurts?'

Philippa got her mouth under control. 'Terribly.'

'I'm so sorry.' But still Penny dreaded intruding. Philippa had always been reticent over the big things. This looked like being another of them. She must have found something special with this man, in spite of having admitted to Penny more than once that he was certain trouble. 'We're all here for you. Don't forget,' she said, laying a quick hand on Philippa's arm.

Philippa nodded, but couldn't speak.

Driving home, she decided she would marry Alec. Though she had been fond of Torglas as it was, like a familiar old friend in a shabby cardigan, it did need some attention. If the silver pantry was knocked through you'd have a really good utility room. The walled garden could be reclaimed; those blackcurrant bushes definitely ought to come out; Joanna could give her advice.

She tried not to look, not to see, as she headed for home, the single square of light at Keeper's Cottage away up on its hillside.

21

'Will he leave the glen, do you think?'

Joanna Drummond, phoning to make arrangements for her daughter Laura to spend a long weekend at Tynach with the Balfour children, wasn't surprised by Sue's question. Everyone who knew and cared about Philippa was asking the same.

'No one knows. His plaster's off, apparently, so that means he'll be able to drive again.'

'But his wife's still with him?'

'Yes, and she's ghastly. How a man married to a woman like that could ever have thought of Philippa . . .'

'Um, but she seems rather to have thought of him,' Sue reminded her. 'She was pretty cagey when she was here, you know how Philippa can be, but there was something about her I hadn't seen for ages. I really thought there was a chance . . . Have you met him?'

'No, but I gather he's pretty striking-looking. Not that looks would be enough for Philippa.'

'No, it must have been more than that. I suppose the worst thing would be if he stayed on in Michael's cottage with his wife. Or in the glen. Wasn't the original idea that he was looking for somewhere to buy?'

'Tough for Pippa if he does.'

'Do you honestly think Alec's in with a chance?'

'I'm not really sure that I want him to be.' Joanna was aware, as Sue returned to practical matters, of the small, persistent ache of might-have-been. She knew what it meant to see the one person who mattered in the world committed elsewhere, and she hoped, without being in a position to make any judgements about this Paulett man, that Philippa wouldn't follow her own mistaken course and settle for second best. That, Joanna was convinced, could never lead to happiness.

Jon sat in his car, parked in a field gateway off a quiet road above Muirend. The window was down and the sun hot on his arm. For the first time this year he noticed the sound of bees. Even high up the glen now, the green of new grass and new foliage was vivid after warm days of sun and showers. He savoured a sensation of lightness and freedom not unlike that of the moment when he'd handed in his ID card, carried for so many years on pain of punishment, and walked out of the guardroom and out of the Army.

His foot was out of plaster, his ribs mended, mobility and independence regained, and June, no longer useful to him after taking him to collect his car, had driven away, struggling with the groping suspicion that somehow, somewhere, things had gone terribly wrong.

But she had accepted his terms, and he was finally clear of all she represented in his life. A concrete fact to offer Philippa. For he was going to see Philippa; that much was definite. She must understand that he'd had no idea June would turn up here. But would she listen to him? He didn't know. He could only hold on to the thought that, in spite of his having walked out of Achallie in a rage, she had come to Keeper's Cottage to make sure that he was all right.

As he'd decided in the past, it would be too easy for her to fob him off if he phoned. Where might she be? He hated to be so out of touch with her movements. Better wait till evening. The cottage had to be sorted out anyway.

It was satisfying to turn out the room June had used, bin what she'd left in the kitchen cupboards, and enjoy the return of unrestricted movement as he reduced the cottage to the soldierly order which suited him best.

Philippa was pegging out a line for a row of seeds. It had been too hot to do the job earlier, but there was plenty of moisture in the soil; they should be all right. Impossible as it was to keep Jon out of her mind, she wasn't expecting to see him again, and didn't register the sound of the Subaru as it came up the hill.

When it turned in her whole body trembled, something she'd never experienced before. Her knees shook as she came to her feet. For one thankful, perfect moment she thought only, he's here – then the facts rushed back. The last time she'd seen him he'd been with his wife. Armour safely in place, she went to meet him.

God, she's lovely, Jon thought, almost startled, his eyes devouring her. Not a bone in her body. She was wearing denim shorts and a faded pink shirt tied across her midriff. Her flat belly was brown and so were her slim legs. Earth smudged her forehead and dusted her knees. Her chin was up, her back straight, her face politely enquiring. Jon wondered how he had ever imagined this would be easy. He half expected her to ask, 'Can I help you?' as she would of a guest at the hotel.

'Philippa.' His voice sounded as though he hadn't used it for a week.

Philippa waited, allowing her questioning look to deepen.

The evening sun was red-gold, birds beginning to sing after the heat of the day, the shadow of the house stretching black and solid up the grass. They were like actors on a well-lighted stage who'd forgotten their lines. Jon tried to clear the constriction in his throat.

'Can we talk?'

'Oh, no, I think not,' Philippa said very nicely.

'Right.' In spite of everything he hadn't expected that. 'Only, there are a couple of things I'd—'

'Best to leave it.' She sounded very calm. Still courteously, she made a movement towards his car, as though helping out a visitor unsure of how to leave.

'June's gone,' Jon said, not budging.

Philippa said nothing.

'She only came because I'd written to say I wanted a divorce.'

'Jon, there's no need for any of this.' Philippa's voice was light, disengaged. Just right, she thought.

Jon wanted to take her arm, make her look at him, make her listen to him, but knew any contact would be fatal. He felt he was already using his big guns, his shots bouncing harmlessly off her defences of impervious civility.

'It's not like you to refuse to listen,' he said, more aggressively than he had meant to, and immediately regretted it.

Philippa's eyes met his. 'No,' she agreed.

Even with so much at stake Jon found time to admire her coolness. Put her in front of an interrogation team and she'd play it by the book. 'Look, can't we at least put the record straight? There are some things—'

'Jon, I'm sorry, I don't want to talk to you. I want you to go.' Her big guns. Normally it would have been more than enough to make him walk away, but this was different.

'No, I'm going to say this, so *listen* to me.' He moved nearer, as a substitute for the grasp on her arm he knew he couldn't risk. His bulk, his insistence, and what she read as his anger, menaced her. 'June came here off her own bat. I let her stay so that I could make her agree to a divorce. For what it's worth, she had her own room while she was here. She means nothing to me, and I'll never see her again.'

Crowded and threatened, and for other reasons finding it

hard to deal with having him so near, Philippa stepped back, and saw in his eyes how much that hurt him. But she kept her voice steady.

'That really has nothing to do with me—'

'I lied to you. That's it, isn't it? I let you think I was free and, believe me, I regret it more than I've ever regretted anything in my life. But – don't you see, I felt I *was* free.' He was intent on getting through to her, his defences down. This woman meant a whole world to him, scarcely apprehended but incalculably precious, and he wasn't going to let it or her go without a fight. 'I'll never lie to you again.' Unable to help himself, hardly aware of doing it, he gripped her arms, looking closely into her face, his own revealing his feelings in a way he'd never come close to before, even with her.

But Philippa, shaken as she was, clung to her decision. Storms, misunderstandings, lies, were everyday life to him. I'll never cry for him again, she had vowed. She heard her own voice saying with an aloofness which sounded unintentionally patronising, 'I hardly think there's anything to be gained by discussion, do you?'

She felt Jon's disbelief in the relaxing of his grip, saw it in his face. Disbelief not at her decision, but that she had recognised his willingness to plead and had spurned it. Don't give in now, she warned herself in panic, though every instinct protested at what she had done. Don't give in. He'll destroy your life.

Jon gave her one last stunned look, as though he couldn't believe she would leave it there, then the shutters came down. He closed her out, wrote her off. He turned, got into his car and drove away without another word or glance.

Rooted where she stood, icy dismay filling her, Philippa felt the awful trembling begin again. She wanted to sink down, huddle herself together, let the tears come. Instead she went back to the vegetable patch, opened her packet of seeds – after a little trouble – and ran them along the drill with a wavering hand, smoothed the earth over them with the back of the rake, rolled up her line and put away her tools. She went into the kitchen and washed her hands. It was later than she'd thought. She would make an omelette for supper.

'I shall make an omelette,' she said aloud. She got out a bowl, cracked two eggs into it, added salt and ground in pepper. She reached for a fork and stabbed a yolk, then with a violent gesture swept the bowl away. It slammed against the cooker and bounced off. A trail of albumen glistened across the floor; the yolks spread in golden splatters. Running, she reached her room, her bed.

After a long time, shivering, she got up, pulled on warmer clothes and went out, unable to endure the silent house. She took the slope behind the cottage at a pace that made her heart thud. Cruel. She had been knowingly, deliberately cruel to another human being. It was like a physical sensation, leaving an after-taste of shame she had never known she could feel. She knew Jon had told her the truth. He had admitted a lie and made a promise. He had trusted her. He had presented the soft underbelly and she had kicked it unhesitatingly as hard as she could.

This image bringing her to a halt, she looked around her. She hadn't realised she'd come so far. The gloaming was deepening, but she took the descent from the ridge at a heedless pace and, reaching the high gate in the deer fence round a well-grown plantation, swarmed up and over without hesitation. It was dark among the trees, but a pale gap of sky showed where the fire-break cut down and she moved fast. Emerging into the open, she looked across the glen and saw a light at Keeper's Cottage. Skirting the field to avoid disturbing ewes and lambs settled for the night, she made for the nearest place where she could cross the river. She had no clear plan. She simply knew that what she'd done had been appalling.

She paused beneath the last rise to the cottage, but only to slow her breathing. She wouldn't change her mind now. As she passed the uncurtained window, she flinched at what she saw – Jon sitting at the table, a bottle of whisky and a glass in front of him. Then she realised that the bottle was untouched, the glass empty. Jon, motionless, had his head propped on his hands.

Remorse and compassion filled her. She went swiftly in (no time for memories of the last time she had walked in here), to stand in the doorway of the sitting-room. Jon's head came up and he stared at her in disbelief. Then his chair scraped back and he was up and coming towards her, amazed delight in his face, his arms out. Then, as abruptly, he halted, wariness returning.

'Jonnie, I'm sorry.' No choosing of words. This was what she'd come to say. She had no idea what she looked like, her jeans wet to the knee, hair straggling out of the band she'd pulled it into hours ago for gardening. 'I'm so sorry.' Her voice would have melted rocks, her eyes were full of tears.

'Christ, Philippa.'

She thought he would crush the life out of her as he seized her, then felt his renewed doubt as she tried to free herself.

'Just need to breathe,' she said, between tears and laughter, and he laughed too, beginning to believe she was really here. He bent his head over hers, gathering her to him. Her body felt weightless and fragile, shivering and nervous.

'It's OK,' he said. 'It's OK.' He cupped her head, pressing it against him. Her hair was a stringy mess, cold from the spring night. A loving acceptance of everything about her filled him as he hugged her close; a glimpse of what might be, lives interwoven, another being becoming an extension of himself. 'You're frozen.'

'Not too bad.' It seemed irrelevant.

'Come here.' He drew her to the big chair. He'd lit the fire when he came in then forgotten it, but it was still alive, and roused obligingly when he propped two or three small logs round its red core. 'Take your shoes off. God, you could wring the damn things out.' He wrapped his warm palm round one narrow, clammy foot, said, 'Stay there,' and went to ferret out a pair of thick white seaboot stockings (courtesy the Royal Navy), which he pulled on with an impersonal briskness that felt very good to Philippa. The dank wet cloth of her jeans no longer clung to her legs; warmth began to flow back.

Jon looked up and saw that she was smiling at him, relaxed, accepting all he did. His heart turned over. Resolutely prosaic, he went back to the bedroom and fetched a comb.

'Sit up.'

She levered herself up with her elbows, and sat straight, eyes closed, while Jon, muttering, got rid of the band and began with careful concentration to comb out her tangled hair, her acquiescence telling him more clearly than any overt sexual signal that she had committed herself.

I'll never let her go, he vowed, as he took in the candour and serenity of her face, anguish momentarily gripping him at the thought of what could yet come between them. He smoothed her hair with his hand, and as Philippa opened her eyes he read the happiness in them. Leaning forward he kissed her, and feeling her give herself up to the kiss without reserve he was aware of an intoxicating mixture of tenderness and fierce possessiveness. He swung her out of the chair and dropped into it with her in his arms. She fitted against him so neatly; he wanted to draw her right into his body.

Surprisingly, it was he who checked first, soothing them back to quietness. He didn't want their first loving to be merely a reaction after anger, nor did he want to sweep Philippa along too fast, risking regrets later. He told her so, a new confidence between them.

'Not part of the drama of tearing across hill and glen for a big reconciliation scene,' she agreed. 'I know, it has to stand on its own. Ah, might I have chosen a better phrase?'

'Hardly.'

'Also apt.'

It was good to laugh with her and gave Jon the courage to return to unfinished business, though Philippa was reluctant to spoil the moment by venturing onto dangerous ground. She didn't particularly care to be reminded that June had been here, in this room. But Jon needed the memories eradicated, not buried, and needed too to talk out some of his own sense of entrapment.

'I was so proud of you, the day you came here,' he told her presently.

'*Proud?*' The impression that he had been on June's side, almost enjoying the scene, had been one of Philippa's worst memories.

'Of course. You showed some guts, and I thought the world of you for it.'

'You were too drunk to think any such thing.'

'Drunk?' He was surprised, then his face grew dark as he recalled that day. 'I wasn't drunk, I was in despair.'

Philippa winced at the bleakness in his voice, and as they talked on took her own chance to say, 'I should have told you about being in the Air Force.'

It was hard to believe now that he'd walked out of Achallie for such a reason.

'I suppose I hated feeling I'd been made a fool of,' he said. 'No, it was more than that. I felt cheated out of something special that we had in common. Even as if we could have met.' She must have looked stunning in uniform. 'Anyway, no more of that. We'll talk. I can't promise no rows, but at least we'll have them out.'

'If we're going to talk we probably won't have rows,' Philippa said peacefully.

Holding her like this, welded so sweetly against him, Jon found it easy to believe. He felt desire storm up again, needing the release of making love but still afraid of second thoughts on her part afterwards.

'Philippa, look at me.'

She tipped back her head and he read the loving trust in her eyes. He drew in a breath, thinking incredulously, that's for *me*. Then he gathered her up and came to his feet, ignoring the mean twinge his ankle gave. Philippa, her arms round his neck, remembered that once Richard, seeing himself being macho, had done this, and sweeping her off to bed had banged her head on the doorpost. Jon, she knew, would do no such thing.

The air of the bedroom was as frigid as if winter had returned. Was it never warm in this damned country? Jon put on the heater and turned back to Philippa. As he slid his hands under her sweater and began to pull it up she raised her arms helpfully but he felt her mood was more amenable than passionate. With interest, he found that this made him feel not impatient but protective.

OK, no slow sexy undressing then. Philippa wasn't wearing the right sort of clothes for one thing and for another it was too fucking cold. Might I have chosen a better phrase . . . ? Remembering their laughter steadied him, though he would bet she didn't guess he needed reassurance too. He stripped off her jeans and sweater, the big socks, her shirt and pants. No bra; no surprise. He pulled back the bedclothes, and she gasped as her warm body hit the sheets.

Jon laughed. 'That bad? Don't worry, soon warm you up.'

But Philippa felt her body shrivel. The suspension of their intimacy by the fire, the cold air ghosting over her skin, the interval, empty of words, as Jon swiftly peeled off his clothes, combined to make her rigid with trepidation. Then he was diving in beside her, with a roar like a swimmer plunging into a mountain pool.

'*Jesus!* Where are you, come here, cuddle up . . .' His big body was gloriously warm and he drew her against him with a matter-of-factness which was just what she needed. 'God, you feel good.' He could hardly believe he had in his arms at last that silken-skinned body, so supple and spare, so unlike the soft-fleshed bodies of the past, and so full of promise that he felt for the moment more exuberant than amorous. 'Bloody hell, was that your foot? Not a bag of frozen peas or something?'

'Sorry,' said Philippa, hastily withdrawing it.

'Can't have that.' Tucking the bedclothes round her as he moved, he reached down to search the floor, coming up with the socks. 'Here, get 'em on.'

'Isn't that the wrong way round?' Philippa asked. '*Umm,* how did you know that's what I really wanted?'

'I'm just not a masochist,' he grumbled, yanking the blankets up round them again.

Rewrapped in his arms, comforted by this robust approach and the heat that flowed from him, Philippa felt her taut muscles begin to relax, her nervousness evaporate. Jon felt it too and a voice in his head sang, *yes,* it's going to be all right. As his hands, not surprisingly expert but surprisingly gentle, began to explore her body, she was aware of one last coherent and unexpected thought. He would look after her.

Afterwards Jon could have pinpointed exactly the moment when her brain and body said, I'm yours. He paced himself because, for the first time, a woman's pleasure mattered more to him than his own. He had always until now focused on his own need and satisfaction, and could hardly believe what he'd been missing. He was entranced by Philippa's body. She was so trim and flexible, in perfect running order, but there was also an honesty in her response which moved him more than he could have imagined possible. He realised almost humbly that when she caressed him she touched him with love. The word had not been spoken between them but it was there in her lips, her hands, the unreserved giving of her body. When he entered her he found himself, unbelievably, trembling. Don't let me hurt her, he thought in a panic of need to be certain of her pleasure, to be certain of this being right and forever right for them both.

With a tenderness that was quite new he watched her come slowly back to awareness of where she was.

'Hello, sweetheart.'

'Hello, Jonnie.' Her voice sounded drugged, dredged up from somewhere far away, and he laughed at her, filled with delight and gratitude. He settled them comfortably, though he thought her boneless limbs would have sunk contentedly anywhere and anyhow, and drew her close, not wanting to sleep yet, wanting instead to savour this sweetness of closeness after loving, something else he had unaccountably missed out on till now.

'So lovely,' Philippa mumbled into his neck. 'So lovely.'

And smiling against her hair, he felt thankful that she had found it so.

22

Philippa always found it hard, later, to unravel the sequence or time-scale of the weeks that followed. Everything and everyone in her life except Jon seemed to take a step back, part of some outside world. She supposed people who grew up in close, happy families were familiar with this; for Jon and for herself it was new. They were absorbed in one another, aggression and wariness on Jon's part, self-protective restraint on Philippa's, forgotten in an intensely aware inter-dependence.

Jon found perceptions heightened in every way. It seemed to him that he was observing the beauty of early summer for the first time. Seeing himself as an outdoor man, he began to realise that until now the natural world had been principally the backdrop to his own activities. This keener awareness made him feel that he was at last being given a slice of the cake he used to watch others eating as of right. The sense of exclusion had gone.

It was Philippa who gave him this, and his gratitude was expressed in a passion which sometimes almost carried him away. Once or twice, gathering up her limp, sated body after love-making, he would wonder with sharp anxiety if he had been too rough with her, but seeing her eyes open on his with that languid contented smile which he sometimes thought the sweetest part of their loving, he would read her happiness with an ache in his throat.

'Good thing you're a cross between an electric eel and a

rubber band,' he would comment gruffly, shaken with love for her.

''Tis lucky,' she would agree in her blurred, dopey voice of after-love.

He had never known a woman who became so completely unaware of her surroundings during sex as Philippa. It could take her moments to reorientate herself. Once she asked, squinting at a fold of duvet a few inches from her face, 'Why are there roses on the ceiling?'

'For God's sake,' Jon demanded, 'what are you on?' But her abandonment thrilled him every time.

The keener sense of his surroundings brought back memories of climbing and expedition training in the days when the Army had still satisfied him, when a commission had looked certain and the future full of promise. For the first time, knowing Philippa could relate to what he told her, he was able to admit that he, and not the system, had ruined his chances. He also talked, with more difficulty, of the years of living with the Hinks.

'It's hard to put a finger on how they were cruel,' he said, his face sombre. 'They didn't knock me about or lock me in the coalshed. Far from it, they prayed over me. On paper, I was damned lucky to end up with them after some of the places I'd been in. But they never, the whole time I was with them, spoke to me as if I were a real person. Every day, in ways hard to pin down, they spelled out the difference between me and their son.'

'It sounds awful. You did well to stick it out.'

'I suppose even then I knew it was the best chance I was likely to get. I had access to books, and a room of my own where I was left in peace.' Peace. Those endless lonely hours. 'I didn't stick it out long enough though. Couldn't stand it another day once I'd got a few O levels under my belt. I should have hung on.'

Cathartic as it was to release some of the pain of the past in talking to Philippa, he never found himself able to refer to his private dream for the future, centred on that tucked-away place on the West Coast which he and Mackay and others had occasionally used on jobs. Too many imponderables lay between him and that cherished image for him to expose it, even to her, though he knew they must talk, and soon, about what lay ahead. He mustn't risk her thinking he was concealing anything from her. Yet to touch upon ugly realities could so easily destroy this magic time they'd been granted. Dreading to mar its perfection, he gave himself a little longer.

During these precious days, he watched Philippa incessantly and hungrily. She looked so much at home in her landscape, tanned and fit, glowing with sun and sex and love, and he studied with ever-fresh delight the fine bone structure, the line of her throat, the tapering fingers, a curve of shoulder brown and smooth as a farmyard egg, the small high breasts and slender thighs.

Philippa was also aware of the fragile quality of their happiness, and knew she couldn't go on for much longer ignoring the truth of what Jon's life might be. With a lurch of apprehension whenever she thought of it, she would wonder if she'd be brave enough to accept what she learned and, clutching defiantly at the present, she too told herself it could wait.

To her surprise, Jon didn't suggest moving in with her, and she couldn't help feeling rebuffed when he made it clear that Keeper's Cottage would remain his base.

Jon saw the hurt and, in spite of regretting causing it, couldn't stifle a swift gratification that she had taken for granted that he would move into Achallie. But getting into the reasons for his decision would be the start of the road away from her. With the imminence of departure ever more on his mind, he was determined, whether it suited him or not, that

Philippa should as far as possible keep to her normal pattern of living. She would have to survive here after he'd gone, and though she seemed ready in her present euphoric state to pitch everything out of the window to spend time with him, he didn't intend, though the irony didn't escape him, to let her do so. He also believed that until he could offer her security, of permanence rather than in material terms (important as it was for a man of Jon's stamp to feel that he was the provider), he had no right to let her commit herself to him.

Finally, Keeper's Cottage was the place where he was supposed to be available. He, and the rent, were being paid on that basis, and with every passing week the likelihood of recall increased. He was aware that Philippa, knowing the lease ran for a year, still supposed in spite of his hints that he would stay roughly that long. He must at least make sure that she knew he might have to go at a moment's notice.

On one other point Jon was adamant. There must be no risk of Philippa conceiving. The thought of going off and leaving her pregnant was unendurable to him. This was primarily concern for her, but he also found, to his secret astonishment, that if there was ever to be the chance of a child with Philippa, then he wanted his full share in it.

Philippa had her own thoughts on the subject. She could never quite rid herself of the fear that Jon wouldn't come back. Not that he would be prevented from coming, but would decide not to. She knew if he suspected this he would be deeply wounded, and she didn't doubt his present feelings for her. But she had a pretty good idea of the kind of thing he was involved in, and couldn't help wondering whether, once back in that scene, he wouldn't find it the simplest, or most practical, option to write off the entire episode and put it out of his mind.

The thought of having his child tempted her powerfully – to be able to hold on to some part of him which could never

be taken away, a life to share hers, someone to care for and
love. But to betray Jon over something so crucial; to plan,
deliberately, to bring into the world a child who might grow
up without a father, or to hope that its existence might draw
Jon back to her – no.

When the mock-up music club cassettes began to arrive,
containing updates on the suspended operation, Jon knew he
had to find a way to talk to Philippa without further delay,
not dreaming that one of them would provide the trigger.

He and Philippa were sitting outside Keeper's Cottage one
morning when the post arrived.

'Didn't know you were into music,' Philippa said idly. 'Can
I look?' Not imagining there could be anything private about
it, she began to open the package.

'Give me that.' Jon plucked it from her hand, startling her
by both the brusque gesture and the anger in his face.

'Jonnie, I'm sorry. I didn't think you'd—'

'Mind your own bloody business.' He was on his feet, the
cassette in his hand, knowing he'd overreacted. What price
training? But this chance piece of bad timing had brought
the irreconcilable areas of his life into collision in a way he
couldn't for the moment handle. He turned and went into the
house, leaving Philippa open-mouthed. He came out again
after a couple of minutes with mugs of coffee, sitting down
at the old weathered table without meeting her eye.

Did he hope she'd let it go? 'That seemed a somewhat
excessive reaction,' she remarked. 'I dread to think what kind
of thing you're listening to.'

Jon grunted, trying to sound amused, but recoiling inwardly
at what he knew he must tell her.

Philippa raised her eyebrows and sipped her coffee. All
right, if he didn't intend to explain.

'It isn't music,' he said abruptly. 'It's tapes. Op info.'

For a moment her brain refused this, seeking something

else to focus on, the grain of the wood under her hand, the wind plastering a strand of hair against her cheek, the breadth of Jon's shoulders in the major's check shirt and green gilet – and his eyes watching her, narrowed, anticipating trouble.

'You've got to go.' Her voice was thin, almost unrecognisable as hers.

'Oh, God, Philippa.' Jon was round the table, pulling her up into his arms. 'It doesn't mean that yet. But we do have to talk.'

'I know.' She hid her face against him, clinging to him. Later she was glad he had told her there and not at Achallie. She remembered not wanting to sit down again, separate from him, not being warm enough as he talked but unwilling to interrupt by fetching a sweater. It was as if this had to be taken in a single stride or she wouldn't be able to face it. She remembered how hard the chair was, how the wind kept tugging free the hair she pushed behind her ear, that the backs of her legs were icy.

Jon was honest. He knew nothing else would serve. He didn't pretend that she wouldn't hate what he'd been involved in since coming out of the Army. He didn't prevaricate, as while he was in the house he had been briefly tempted to do, by saying he was acting on moral grounds. All he could offer her was the promise that once this job was over he would walk away. (And if a god exists anywhere, he prayed, let that be possible.)

Listening with painful attention, watching his face and seeing the almost desperate frankness in it, Philippa didn't doubt that he meant what he said. But what she had to deal with, now, at this moment, was the fact that he had been involved, was still involved, in a ruthless and possibly illegitimate type of warfare which many people found abhorrent.

'But where are you fighting?' she broke in to ask once. 'What's the political background? Can't you tell me more?'

She knew she was hoping to see his activities as justifiable, perhaps even condoned by world opinion.

Jon hesitated, his mouth grim. How he longed to wrap this up in fancy packaging like the tapes, painting a picture she might find half acceptable, glossing over the realities. It was tempting to fudge about his own role, offering generalities about political manoeuvring and the dubious clandestine motives of the international agencies in the background. But Philippa was no fool, and her military background gave her an insight which he had ignored to his cost on previous occasions.

'Look, it's better you don't know too much.' He was aware that he sounded unconvincing, and was angry with himself. 'I don't want to think of you reading stuff when I've gone, horror stories cooked up by the media.' Scanning accounts of revolution, massacre, genocide, searching for names, details . . . He tried a lighter tone. 'Our old friend need-to-know, yes?'

Philippa nodded slowly, and he realised with relief that her thoughts had run parallel with his. 'Yes. Probably better not to know where. I agree with that. It would be a nightmare to hear shreds, half-truths, of—' Of things too horrible to put into words. 'I think I'd like to know, though, that what you're doing won't be—' What? A crime against humanity? Her control wavered.

Jon saw it, and reached for her hands. 'I know what you're asking, and I know it's a nasty business, one I wish to God I'd never got into, but I can say this much – I do believe I'm fighting on the right side, in so far as there is one. And though I'm committed to completing this assignment, after it I shall never touch anything like it again as long as I live.'

Philippa, whose eyes had been on their tight-locked hands, looked up to meet his eyes, and couldn't doubt the sincerity she saw in them. She nodded slowly. He could have attempted to justify his choice in a dozen ways.

'How did you get into this?'

By the standard route, was the answer to that. Via jobs with civilian security firms, frequently run by former SAS officers, leading to a search for more colourful action only to be found by serving abroad. Compensating, as Jon had been aware even at the time, for the cock-up he'd made of his career. He had soon discovered, however, that the true professionals, ready to offer their skills and dedication to some foreign power, were disturbingly outnumbered by the mediocrities with a personal axe to grind, low achievers who had often been discharged from whichever service they'd belonged to for violence or uncontrollable behaviour.

'It's not all like Angola though,' he wound up, and heard the defensiveness which had crept into his voice in spite of himself. 'That's what everyone immediately thinks of, isn't it? But things have changed in twenty years. That whole thing was run by psychopaths. Three of the Paras involved had ended their Army careers in prison.' He shook off the thought that he and Mackay had more than once joked that the K of 'Colonel K' should stand for Callan. 'A good many ex-Army men have fought for governments they genuinely believed needed support. Stirling himself became a mercenary, in Rhodesia, because he believed in racial equality and the virtues of meritocracy and—'

Philippa wasn't buying it. 'It's not like that nowadays though, is it? It's what it says. Mercenary.'

Jon's face closed, and she recognised the moment as pivotal. Would he go on talking?

'Working for money, yes,' he conceded, after a tense pause, and Philippa was thankful, in spite of her distaste for the subject. 'But for a lot of men when they come out of the Army, men like myself, some civilian job just isn't enough. I had no ties, no future . . .'

Philippa didn't remind him that he'd had a wife. Nothing

could have told her more clearly how separate from June he felt himself to be.

'You felt your military life was somehow unfinished?'

He glanced at her gratefully. 'Something like that. I still had something to prove. Needed action.'

'And to give two fingers to the establishment.'

Those cool comments of hers, always so accurate. She surely could lay things on the line. 'That too.'

A longer silence fell between them. Philippa knew she had to decide, here and now, whether she could accept what Jon was doing, accept him in effect as he was. She had guessed, of course, what he was engaged in. She had told herself it was a trade like any other, and one for which he was supremely well fitted. But she still hated the thought of it, and that was what she had to deal with. Although she preferred not to know details, the fact that he never talked about it, and of his being virtually in hiding in the glen, wasn't reassuring. Instinctively repelled by what he did, could she still want him?

Another question was, would a man drawn to such a life ever be able to break free of it? And if he did, what could he find to put in its place which would satisfy him? But these issues, she knew, must be set aside for the moment. They had to do with a time so far ahead that it barely existed. She and Jon had never talked about the future, and this was why. What she had to decide was whether or not she accepted Jon himself.

Watching her, he was tempted to add he'd only get the final pay-off if he completed the job, but saw in time that Philippa wouldn't regard money as a factor.

'I do have to go,' he said, unable to bear her silence any longer.

'I know.' She looked up, and Jon felt a helpless anger with himself to have produced that stricken expression. She looked insubstantial and vulnerable, the freckles staring on her cold face, lips pinched, her hair whipped into rat's-tails, the bones of her hands sharply prominent as she held on to his.

'Oh, sweetheart, you're freezing. Come into—'

'When?' Philippa interrupted him.

He abandoned persuasion. 'I honestly don't know.'

'But you came for a year.' She knew in her heart that this time-scale had never meant anything.

Jon didn't answer.

'It could be – any time?'

He felt the effort it cost her to ask.

'Probably not right away.' The best he could do.

She shivered, then said in a rapid, muffled voice which he had to bend close to hear, 'Jon, I can't bear to talk about it any more just now. But I do accept that you have to go. And that you mean it when you say that after this it will be over. I also know,' with a croaky attempt at a laugh, 'that it's twelve o'clock in the morning, but do you think we could possibly go to bed? Not to make love if you don't want to, but to be close and warm. Could we?'

No invitation from a woman had ever moved him so much. She was prepared to take him as he was, had been, would be, and somewhere beyond the dark high barrier ahead there might, truly might, lie the possibility of winning the incredible prize.

23

There was an edge to everything now, a sense of time slipping at frightening speed through their fingers, accentuated by the way Jon pushed himself to build up fitness again. One result was that, filled with a new energy, he ate up any jobs he could find, obscurely wanting, though he knew it was absurd, to leave Philippa with everything he could possibly do for her in place.

Aware that he should spend time there, he also did some work at Keeper's Cottage, puttying windows, shoring up the sheds and reducing the ragged garden to order. Many jobs he and Philippa did together, levelling the flagstones in the sunny corner at Achallie, attacking the jungle in the further reaches of the garden, digging up yards of nettle and ground elder roots. Sometimes they took time off for what Philippa called real walks, as opposed to her four- or five-mile trots round the nearer skyline, coming back from that high wide world enriched and satisfied. Occasionally they went to Affran, where Philippa enjoyed showing Jon her favourite haunts. Once she borrowed a key, and took him miles out across the moor to a bothy in a windless hollow beside the ice-green pools and smooth rock slides of the Affran burn, where they swam and lay in the sun in the old childhood picnic place.

After days like this, returning to Achallie to cook dinner together, Jon would forget about staying near his own cottage, and would sleep with Philippa in the big attic room she now used – partly because it had a double bed but also because, though she never said so, she hoped there would be less pain, when she was alone once more, in not having too many memories of Jon in her own room.

Michael Thorne, Jon's landlord, who had not thought his tenant at Keeper's Cottage too attractive a character on first acquaintance, was ready by this time to look on him more favourably. Jon's attentions to the cottage hadn't gone unnoticed. Also, though the appearance of his wife had been unexpected, she seemed to be out of the picture now, and Michael had not only heard comments on Philippa's new happiness but had seen it for himself. Meeting her in the village, he'd been struck by the change in her. The look of resolutely putting disaster behind her had been replaced by a smiling serenity. Michael was not only very fond of Philippa, but he respected her judgement. Any man who could chase away that walking-wounded look must have something to recommend him. Maybe it was time to get to know him better.

Choosing a day when he knew Philippa would be at the hotel, Michael took himself up to Keeper's Cottage and was gratified to find Jon at work repairing the track below, where snow and rain had made their annual ravages. In fact Jon, having put a new exhaust on Philippa's Mini, didn't want his work wasted. Hearing a vehicle approach he looked up in annoyance at the interruption.

Friendly so-and-so, Michael thought as he pulled up, noting the carefully expressionless face, the unforthcoming message in Jon's whole stance. But he said pleasantly, 'Don't get too many tenants like you,' nodding at the mattock Jon was holding.

Not a muscle of Jon's face moved.

'There was something I wanted to have a word about,'

Michael went on, still pleasantly. There was no denying that this major fellow had looks, and an impressive physique (Jon was wearing shorts and desert boots and was deeply tanned), but might Philippa not prefer someone who opened his mouth occasionally? 'I wondered if you'd be interested in giving me a hand with a new fank I'm building. My so-called handyman was offered a job in Muirend and vanished at short notice. You'd be a damn sight more use than he was anyway, by the look of it,' he added, eyeing the tidy boulders Jon had shifted.

Jon surveyed him for a moment more, his face giving nothing away, then asked, 'Was this Philippa's idea?'

'Philippa's?' Michael let his surprise show, not caring for Jon's manner. 'She knows nothing about it.'

His cool tone wasn't lost on Jon. OK, so I should know by now that I can take these people at face value. He modified his approach slightly. 'So what's the job?'

'New dip, changing the layout for feeding sheep through and shedding. I've sketched out some plans but I'd be glad of a professional opinion. Want a look?'

A tempting project for a Sapper out to grass, and non-committal as Jon tried to be as he studied the plans Michael unrolled on the Land Rover bonnet, it wasn't difficult to see how tempted he was. An inspection of the existing fank won him over without a struggle.

Philippa, though wishing she was free to get more involved herself, was delighted to know not only that Jon would be happily occupied, but that he had made his own contact with a friend as close to her as Michael.

Later, that job would be one of the core memories Jon would call up when the ability to pin his mind to something meant the difference between survival or going under, running over every detail obsessively – the solitary hours when Michael was busy elsewhere, the satisfying physical exertion, the sun on his back or the cool air on his skin, the grass thick with wild flowers, the sound of the burn that fed the dip, the calls of peewits and curlews. Though after a while he could have done without the deepening call of the cuckoo, an unavoidable reminder of how swiftly time was passing.

Philippa came whenever she could, and Michael, who found plenty to enjoy in Jon's company once he'd thawed a bit, did more than his share. He and Jon, or the three of them together, established an easy working style, and trouble only arose on the day the job was finished, when Philippa, without consulting Jon, accepted Michael's invitation for them both to have dinner at Baldarroch.

'I thought you'd like it,' she said, taken aback by Jon's sharp protest as soon as they were on their own.

'Yes, well, I'd prefer to be given a choice.'

She saw the point and apologised. 'Sorry, Jonnie, of course I should have asked you. But it seems natural now for us to do things together.'

This should have mollified him but the actual, if unacknowledged, source of his resentment had been the feeling of being pushed against his will into an alien social scene, and he couldn't quite leave it. 'Can't stand these toffee-nosed bastards,' he muttered.

'You get on well with Michael.'

'Yes, mixing cement. That doesn't mean I want to sit down to dinner with him and a bunch of arrogant gits moaning about the fees at Eton and how they're all down to their last quarter million.'

Philippa thought her friends would be more likely to moan about the cost of mending the roof or tarring the drive, but she only said, 'You might enjoy it.'

'Enjoy it? Don't worry, I'm not going.'

'That's rather a shame. I'd love you to come. It's only one evening. Won't you really?'

He looked at her, frowning. Was she winding him up? But her tone convinced him. And Philippa rarely asked him for anything. 'It can't go on for ever, I suppose.'

'Pick you up at half seven then,' she said promptly, heading for the Mini before he could change his mind.

'Hey, hang on, can't you?' he shouted. 'What kind of do is it? What am I supposed to wear?'

'Jeans,' she called over her shoulder.

'Don't give me that,' he said, leaping after her.

'Honestly, jeans. Perhaps not those,' she added innocently, glancing at the pair he had on, through on both knees and white with cement dust.

'If you come back all tarted up I'll wring your neck,' he threatened.

Philippa laughed, giving him a quick hug. 'It won't be too awful, I promise.'

She was less ready to be reassuring, however, when he joined her in the Mini a couple of hours later, spruce in clean shirt and freshly ironed jeans, then grumbled and complained all the way down the track.

'Who'll be there anyway?'

'Not sure.'

'Well, for a start, who lives there?'

'Just Michael and Julie.'

'Yes, but there's bound to be a mob of their friends as well, screeching like parrots . . .'

That's my friends you're talking about, Philippa protested silently. Perhaps it was time for a small lesson. Taking the drive which led to the towering front of the castle, mutilated in Victorian times with much architectural embellishment in red sandstone, she swept round to halt before its high, iron-studded doors. Jon, who hadn't until now appreciated the scale of the building, hidden among its trees, was visibly rattled. Philippa allowed him a discomfited second or two, then accelerated away again, grinning wickedly, whirling him to a sunless courtyard crammed between a streaming cliff and the equally damp rear of the castle.

'What's going on?' Jon demanded.

'Come on, and stop belly-aching.'

She was off, picking a route through the hens' buckets, dogs' bowls, boots, brooms and flower-pots which occupied a doorstep as big as Jon's bedroom, pausing only to yank at a bell which came out fully eighteen inches on a curved brass arm. Jon decided to bide his time. Events were moving too rapidly for Philippa to get her come-uppance just yet.

A stone-flagged corridor, as densely cluttered as a junk shop, led into a hinterland of storerooms and pantries, through archways designed for troglodytes and past black recesses whose cold air reached trailing fingers to them as they passed.

'Anybody in?' yelled Philippa, making Jon jump, then swear at himself for jumping.

'Hello, love, good timing, come on in,' yelled back an unexpected voice in the uncompromising tones of Lancashire, as they turned a final corner and walked into a kitchen which made Jon blink. After the crowded corridor it seemed as big as a ballroom and as high as a church, and he saw that it had been extended by knocking through larders and sculleries so that their windows gave added light. In an angle, south-west to judge by the sunlight pouring in, a bay window had been built out (some job that must have been) and a cushioned bench seat fitted round the table in its curve.

Coming to meet them, wearing exercise sandals and a dingy jogging suit under some kind of tabard of maroon crushed velvet, was a short unprepossessing woman, a flop of grey hair in her eyes, cigarette in the corner of her mouth, a dripping ladle held aside in one hand.

'Nice to see you, love,' she said to Philippa, offering a puckered-up cheek as though she was prepared to submit to being kissed but wouldn't be doing any kissing herself. 'Glad you came,' she added to Jon, with an appraising upward glance and a curt nod, leaving him with the impression that she knew all about the banging on he'd been doing on the way here. Who was she?

'Julie, this is Jon Paulett. Jon, Julie.'

The Paulett reminded Jon that the major might come to his aid. 'How do you do, Mrs Thorne.'

'Mrs Somebody Else, actually, but Julie will do.' The scruffy little woman regarded him with an amused glint in her eye.

Philippa was going to regret this, Jon promised himself, shooting her a look which made her put a hand to her mouth in mock alarm.

Two black labradors with welcoming grins bustled in ahead of Michael who, Jon observed with relief, was still wearing the clothes he'd worn at the fank.

'Thank God you've come,' Michael greeted them. 'I can give up the unequal struggle with that accursed mower. I was ready to hurl it into the river. Some idiot's mixed the fuel again. Now, what will you have? Pippa?'

The kitchen, Jon saw, held most of the essentials of daily life, including an array of bottles and glasses on a long table, scrubbed to the ridged dark-yellow grain, which would have been at home in a butcher's shop.

'These are ready. Come on.' Julie headed for the table in the sunny window, clutching in the burned remnants of an ovencloth a warped and blackened baking tray dotted with plump golden sausage rolls. The noses of the labradors travelled after her, scent high. Julie dumped the tray on an ethnic mat, whose scorch marks gave evidence of much similar treatment, and accepted a huge gin and tonic from

Michael, who touched her cheek lightly with the back of his fingers as he gave it to her.

'Grab one,' Philippa said to Jon, helping herself to a sausage roll, juggling it in her fingers and blowing on it before biting into it. Julie put hers whole into her mouth then breathed round it, eyes bulging. Once she'd dealt with it, the plunge into talk was instant. Julie, give her her due, had to be the least self-conscious person he'd ever met, Jon decided, as the buttery perfection of the puff pastry fragmented in his mouth.

Michael, an easy-going but observant host, watched with satisfaction as Jon relaxed. And watched with even greater satisfaction the speed with which he related to Julie. She wasn't everybody's cup of tea, he acknowledged in her own words, lovingly.

It was some years now since, impelled by a growing certainty that for all the wrong reasons he had allowed himself to be deprived of the one thing which truly mattered to him, he had broken free of a meaningless marriage and gone in search of her. His only regret, he reflected, as Julie sent the baking tray winging floorwards over the heads of the dogs, who inched forward to explore its barren greasiness with eager tongues, was that he hadn't done it sooner. And now here was Philippa, clearly caught up, as he had been, in an attraction whose force she barely understood for someone who, superficially at least, could not be seen as 'suitable'. How the word had dogged the childhood of people like him. Penny Forsyth, and others who came readily to mind, was hooked on it still. Yet who could deny that there was something vital and vibrant between these two? Michael, who had spent more time than anyone with them, wondered how obvious it would be to Julie.

Julie, as indeed he might have known, had read it as they came in at the door and, like Michael, she saw Jon's readiness to despise everything he found here reluctantly evaporate. Her reaction, however, was one of sardonic amusement. Touchy bastard thought it was going to be posh. Only concentrating on himself. Never crossed his mind that Philippa was saying something by bringing him. She's going to have her hands full with this one. Serve him right if she had landed him somewhere a lot trickier to handle. But she'd known he'd be all right here. No social crap at Baldarroch; pure bloody waste of time.

So, to Jon's relief, no one else appeared and presently Michael, enquiring, 'Who's hungry?' ambled across to the Aga, took a simmering casserole from the oven and called, 'Eating irons, someone.' It was Philippa who got to her feet to help him. Julie was too busy expounding her views on nuclear testing to Jon, looking ready to climb over the table at him as he dropped in the odd military consideration to keep her going. She had paid him the compliment, unspoken naturally, of finding him a worthy adversary. Looks meant nothing to Julie; she could never understand why people got so excited about them. The whole package was what mattered, and this man, whether she had quite decided if she liked him or not, had a powerfully compelling quality about him.

Jon was sure she neither saw the food arrive nor was aware of starting to pitch it in. He was aware of it, however – young lamb with herbs and summer vegetables, braised to melting tenderness – and aware of the velvet glory of the claret Michael had produced.

'Don't know what it is,' Michael said, in answer to his question. 'Labels went when we had a burst pipe in the cellar a few years back. Father's instructions survived though.' He uncurled a stained luggage label for Jon to read. In blurred purple ink it said: Not to be squandered on the godly. 'He hated the church but couldn't imagine a time when the minister wouldn't come to Sunday lunch.'

It was a brand of upper-class humour which normally made Jon's hackles rise, but he found it hard to resent in this atmosphere. He felt at ease in his surroundings, relishing Julie's straight-to-the-jugular style, and the contrast between her caustic wit and the open affection which she and Michael showed for each other.

With the dogs banging the casserole against the table legs, Julie fetched a delicious concoction of fruit, cream and meringue from some cool hiding place – no sign of a fridge. Later Michael brought coffee and Kümmel and lit an oil lamp, whose smoke-darkened chimney spoke of frequent use. They didn't move from their comfortable corner, talking on as the last glimmer of sunset died in the black water sliding below, nothing breaking the mood. Michael's arm was round Julie. Touch was clearly essential to them, yet to Jon they made an incongruous couple – Michael with his lean patrician looks, his careless drawl, his expensive, conventional country clothes, hard-worn as they were; Julie with her harsh vowels, her uncouth garments and iconoclastic outlook.

In spite of the relaxed mood and the open sexuality wafting across the table, Jon didn't touch Philippa. His arm lay along the seat-back behind her, he was intensely aware of her and was certain she was tuned with equal awareness to him, but he was content with that. Before long that delicate supple body would be in his arms, a private and precious delight.

Philippa felt as he did, hugging to herself the sensuous pleasure of his nearness. She was glad that Michael and Julie so obviously found in Jon much of what she herself saw beneath the touchiness and aggression. He was at his best tonight, his dry humour sparked by Julie's acerbity, her range of interests finding a response in his own fund of knowledge and experience. How perfect, thought Philippa, mellow with food and wine and love, that soon he'll be taking me home to bed.

'One or two small points to be cleared up,' Jon reminded her, as he drove home in the summer dawn.

'You loved it,' she said, unrepentant.

'Mrs Somebody Else, huh?'

'Well, you were asking for it.'

But the next day, weeding the onion patch at Achallie, Jon returned to the subject of Julie.

'How did she turn up in the glen?'

'She was a waitress at the Cluny.'

'Come off it.'

'Honestly. She was doing a summer job there when she and Michael first met. Must be twenty years ago.'

'And Michael fancied her?' Even twenty years ago she couldn't have been much to write home about.

'He loved her so much that he was prepared to break his life apart for her,' Philippa said simply.

'Go on.' Jon had reasons of his own for wanting to hear the story.

'Michael was stuck in one of those obvious marriages no one ever questions. Margot grew up in a place exactly like Baldarroch, knew all about fading fortunes and catching your feet in the carpets and wrapping up two hundred Christmas presents for the estate people. She was quite sweet in a meaningless sort of way, only you never remembered a thing she said.'

'Pretty damning,' Jon remarked with a grin.

Philippa laughed, sitting back on her heels among the green spears of the onions. 'Can you imagine the contrast of Julie, straight out of LSE, brimming with energy, questioning everything, stumping about and bashing plates down in front of people in the hotel?'

'I might have stuck to Margot.'

'I doubt it. Anyway, Michael knew he'd found the only person he wanted, but Julie wasn't about to wreck his marriage, and there was Robin, Michael's son, about four at the time, so she took off. Michael carried on for a while then suddenly moved Margot out, with Robin, and set out to find Julie.'

'And Julie had married Mr Somebody Else?'

'Yes, in Khartoum, where they were both lecturing, but he'd walked out on her.'

'And Michael found her and she came back with him but they're not married?'

'She never bothered to get a divorce. But she did once tell me that she was never happy for a single day after she left Michael.'

'They're happy now anyway.'

'Totally. Never go off the estate. Julie buys things by post and cuts up old curtains for clothes. To satisfy what she calls her essential creativity she weaves, and sends the stuff to charity. She gardens strictly for food production, not a flower in sight. Everything we ate last night was produced on Baldarroch. They never see people, so we were extremely honoured, I'd have you know.'

'And she never wraps up Christmas presents for the estate people?'

'Regards them as a pack of predatory loafers.'

'Some lady.'

'So I'm forgiven for accepting?'

'No, you bloody well aren't. And those onions you're sitting on will never recover. Get weeding.'

Jon had a lot to think about.

24

'Your sheep fank's finished, then?'

Michael, long inured to resistant morning silence from Julie who, face screwed up and eyes remote, preferred to begin her day by communing with her cigarette than with the living world, looked up from his bacon and eggs in surprise. A simple 'Yes,' was all he risked, however.

Julie took a drag, meditated, exhaled. 'You'll be able to find other jobs though?'

'For Jon?'

A flicker of impatience tightened Julie's face. 'Chancy bugger,' she said after a moment, examining her cigarette tip with a scowl. 'Needs something to keep him busy.' Pause. 'It would help your precious Philippa too.'

Michael took the point, though he had no intention of expanding on it at this time of the morning. But he was glad Julie had liked Jon. Apart from anything else he would be glad to make use of those high-calibre skills for as long as they were available. There were several jobs he'd had in mind for some time, but hadn't dared tackle with the frequently costly help of his ex-handyman.

Michael was also glad, for reasons of his own, of the level of contact Julie actively sought, after that successful dinner, with Jon and Philippa. Though he didn't worry about it often, too content in his peaceful, eccentric life with her to have much time for introspection, he was well aware that Julie possessed a sharper brain and had wider interests than he did, and he had his moments of wondering whether their reclusive existence would always satisfy her.

Though Julie stuck to her rule of never eating in any house but her own, she clearly liked Jon and Philippa coming to the castle. When he looked back on that summer, Michael always felt that the friendship which developed among the four of them, as well as the jobs on which he kept Jon busy, did almost as much to help the latter back onto an even keel as the relationship with Philippa.

It was easy now to imagine Jon as the smartly turned out, competent Sapper, master of the multiple skills of his trade, absorbed in the regiment and the Army. Fit and trim, he even carried himself differently, head no longer thrust forward on hunched shoulders as though he was permanently spoiling for a fight. He rarely went to the Cluny Arms these days, except to join Philippa for lunch occasionally, and Michael saw no sign of the hard drinking which had been so much a part of the major's image when he first came to the glen.

Julie, surprising Michael once more, took another unprecedented step. She showed Jon her workroom, the former drawing-room and now her inviolate private space, where her big Swedish loom was set up, though Margot's orthodox striped Regency wallpaper and damask curtains, disregarded, still provided the décor.

'Go on, look from them to me with your gob open,' Julie mocked, as Jon took in the glowing colours of the length in progress and the heap of finished pieces on the long table filched from the unused dining-room.

He grinned, but didn't pretend he wasn't surprised. Julie rarely wore anything bright, and as he never saw her anywhere but in the cavernous kitchen, which he doubted had been decorated this century, or in her flowerless if fecund garden, he had had no hint of this side of her. Was bringing him here her way of saying she was willing to move on to a new level of communication?

'So tell me,' he said, bypassing the minefield of artistic expression, though his eyes remained on the richness of the careless pile before him, 'why this business of never going out of the gates?' It was something he often wondered about and now, looking up, he caught a glint in Julie's eye which told him she had expected the question, or one very like it, and knew exactly why he needed to ask it.

'It works,' was all she said. He waited for more, wringing a little grunt of amusement from her. 'All right, you canny so-and-so, I'll spell it out. I can't get along without Michael, and don't intend to ever again, but I've no time for the type of outdated, time-wasting socialising people up here go in for, or for killing poor bloody creatures either, which is all most of them seem to care about. Michael, however, sees Baldarroch as his lot in life, his job, his responsibility. He'd ditch the whole shooting match – how apt – if I asked him to, but what right do I have to do that? So we've worked around it, and come up with a compromise.'

'And you're happy.' He made it a statement rather than a question, but Julie knew quite well where he was coming from. She studied him with a gleam of affection in her shrewd eyes which no one but Michael usually saw. 'It could work,' she said.

Jon, not pleased to be read so easily, though he'd invited it, was half ready to see that gleam as amusement, still not finding it easy to shed defensiveness, and Julie, catching his frown, wondered if Philippa would be able to handle the rough patches there would certainly be with a character like this.

'There's a long way to go,' Jon said abruptly, after a pause so long that Julie was sure he'd thought better of pursuing the subject.

'Unfinished business?'

'Did Philippa tell you that?' His head came up, his eyes bored into hers, and the anger in them and way he rapped out the question were actually menacing.

Oops. But Julie kept her cool. 'She never discusses your affairs. You should know that.'

Jon grunted, visibly taking his temper in hand. 'I suppose I should,' he said, turning to prowl away down the long room, his thoughts busy. Julie was glad to have a bit of space between them. He had a big personality, this man, always with that hint of hidden forces lurking which even she, tough as she was, wouldn't care to unleash.

His back to her, one hand gripping the high marble mantelpiece, Jon said unexpectedly, 'You might as well know – I'm involved in something pretty unsavoury.'

'Illegal?' Are you mad, Julie asked herself.

'No, not illegal.' He swung round to face her, but stayed where he was, and Julie knew that, whatever was coming, talking about it went totally against the grain for him. 'But something – I'm not proud of.'

She surveyed him, mouth pursed, face set. 'Don't you mess Philippa about,' she warned.

Their eyes locked. It was Jon who relaxed first. 'I think we're on the same side, you know,' he said quietly, coming back towards her with his easy stride.

Julie in turn smoothed her feathers. 'Yes, well, Philippa's a bit special. She needs some protection from an evil bastard like you.'

'True,' he said. Then, making up his mind, 'I'll tell you this much. If I get back I'll be through. That'll be it. I'll never touch anything like it again.'

Julie searched his face, then nodded slowly. 'Right,' was all she said, but Jon was satisfied.

Julie kept this exchange to herself, feeling Michael would

see more in it to worry him on Philippa's behalf than otherwise. For herself, she was relieved to have Jon's promise,
which she believed he meant to keep, though it didn't alter
her original opinion that whatever happened he and Philippa
had a rocky road ahead.

She was not the only person whose thoughts were on them at
this time. The date was approaching for the barbecue always
held at Alltmore on the first Sunday after the Twelfth, and
Penny Forsyth was in a quandary.

'Don't be silly, of course invite them,' Andrew said
unsympathetically, having heard far too much of the subject.
'You can't not ask Philippa.'

'But I'll have to ask Alec as well. He always comes. How's
he going to feel?'

'As far as I'm concerned, Alec missed his chance. It was
all very fine knocking Torglas about, and I grant you it
was badly in need of it, but he had to do a bit more,
don't you think? Such as say something to Philippa? Anyway, he's had plenty of time to get used to the idea that
she's smitten by this Paulett character, and now it's up
to him to decide whether he can face meeting them or
not.'

'But are they going to stay in the glen?' Penny worried on.
'Though it would be awful for Pippa to have to move away
again. I'm sure she'd hate it.'

Andrew looked at her with exasperation but understanding.
It had done her no favours, he sometimes thought, to have
lived after marriage in the house she'd grown up in. In her
entire life she'd spent no more than eighteen months or so
away from it – a few months in Switzerland, learning how
to seat archbishops and the scions of deposed royal houses
round a dinner table (very useful in Glen Maraich), and a
few months after that playing at being someone's secretary,

which as far as he'd ever been able to gather meant changing the blotting paper every day.

'Just invite them,' he said, not unkindly. He didn't think old Alec would agitate himself nearly as much as Penny anticipated. Not the type.

There he was wrong. Alec, in his inarticulate, self-deprecatory way, went through agonies over the prospect of seeing Philippa with Jon. But staying away from an event so central to the glen year as the Alltmore barbecue would send up a distress signal he dreaded to think of all and sundry reading. He would go. He would probably be teased, he would certainly be hurt, but he would smile, say nothing, smile some more, and then come home to his altered, admirable, empty house, where the plumbing now worked, the roof no longer leaked, and long-familiar slothful comfort had been stripped away.

Philippa was amazed when Jon said he would go.

'Won't you hate it?' she asked incautiously.

Jon shot her a sardonic look. 'Oh, I dare say I'll be able to stand it, provided there's plenty of alcohol.'

'Fine,' Philippa said after a small pause. 'I'll tell Penny then.'

Jon hid his grin. He had his own agenda here. Time was passing (God, how fast), and more and more he found himself looking ahead, from Philippa's angle, to the days when he'd be gone. It was important to him to think of her reintegrating into the local scene, and he felt that the more people who'd met him, and accepted him even at a superficial level, the easier the process would be for her. Also Julie's support, however unflatteringly expressed, had given him more confidence than he knew.

Goodness, she's brought him, Penny thought, more alarmed than pleased when she saw them coming down the lawn together. In spite of Philippa having accepted for them both,

Penny had half convinced herself it wouldn't happen. And goodness, he's attractive, was her next thought. She had glimpsed Jon in the distance once or twice, but now, faced at close quarters with his height and breadth, and meeting the striking grey eyes, their expression at once guarded and unsettlingly appraising, it wasn't hard to see what had been keeping Philippa out of circulation in recent weeks. A pang of memory caught at her, to be pushed resolutely back into its lurking place.

'Umm, *yes*,' she said in Philippa's ear as she hugged her, and was rewarded by a quick flush of pleasure. 'Jon, I'm so pleased to meet you at last,' she added warmly, and if the 'at last' sent his hackles up for a second she remained serenely unaware of it. 'Now, what will you have to drink? We have some efficient butlers . . .' one of whom, aged about ten, appeared on cue under Jon's elbow.

'Most efficient.' Jon took a glass of white wine for Philippa (without needing to ask what she wanted, Penny noted with another pang which she knew was absurd) and lager for himself, with due care for the balance of the tray, flashing a smile at its bearer which made Penny reflect, as she turned reluctantly away to greet new arrivals, that really Alec had only himself to blame.

Knowing that everyone, on the whole kindly but some less ready to approve, would be speculating, assessing or at best intrigued, Philippa suddenly felt very proud of Jon for coming, and grateful that he'd done so, as she belatedly recognised, for her sake. She was impressed too by how readily he was drawn into the scene, guiltily aware that she had wondered how successfully it would work.

Jon, in his turn, had a few preconceived ideas to work through, not least about what people were wearing. Though he had no way of knowing that the barbecue was a modern version of the formal lunch party Penny's parents had traditionally given, and in spite of being by now used to the casual way Michael Thorne and Julie lived, he had still expected a certain amount of dressing up. He found instead a startling range of garb, from earth-stiffened cavalry twill trousers held up by gardening twine to dayglo-pink Lycra shorts, from Amy Semple's dipping Liberty silk in various shades of mauve to Eleanor Munro's dashing denim cap. The thing that struck him most, however, was how much they were all enjoying themselves, in the perfect setting of wide lawn, sheltered by mounds of rhododendrons backed by firs and birches, sloping to the loch, across whose silver shimmer the moors climbed away, hazy in the sunshine, silent in the Sunday truce.

It was Max Munro, always finding it easier to tolerate social gatherings – which ate into time he could usefully have spent about the estate – when he had something to do, who co-opted Jon into cooking, rightly appraising him as another person who preferred to be occupied. Getting to work without argument, Jon was unaware of Philippa's relief to see him so readily involved.

He was also unaware, fortunately, of one or two adroit moves on her part as the party hit its stride, such as heading off Colonel Arbuthnott of Dalquhat, whose favourite bedtime reading was the Army List, and keeping quiet about the fact that the elderly man in paint-spattered overalls who helped Jon to rig the dinghy was not, as Jon assumed, the Alltmore handyman, but Grannie's great chum Gilbert Rathlyn, a retired admiral.

'No wonder you've been keeping him to yourself!'

It wasn't the first time that had been said to Philippa today. In this case the words were accompanied by a big hug from Pauly Napier and Philippa, pleased as she was to see her, glanced over her shoulder and moved away a little, as though not wanting Jon to hear. In fact she wanted to get her out of Jon's eye-line. Pauly, her smooth skin nicely tanned, her mass of splendid hair wind-blown after a buzz up the hill behind Barney Forsyth on the shepherd's quad bike, was looking particularly voluptuous in a laced top that gave the impression she should be wearing at least one more layer over it. Jon could hardly miss the fact that she looked ready to burst out of it at any moment, and the sight had filled Philippa with a novel but unmistakable jealousy.

She suffered it again watching Jon, who had no inhibitions about believing he could outshoot any of these twits, even if they had been blasting away at Daddy's grouse since they were in nappies, raise his hands in amused defeat to the Hay granddaughter, clad in a frilly yellow sundress which Philippa also considered unnecessarily exiguous, who had wiped his eye at the clays. Philippa was startled to find herself thinking vengefully that he'd get a nasty shock if he found out she was a barrister.

Sexual jealousy, or jealousy in any form, was new to Philippa and, ashamed of the reaction, she tried to make a joke of it on the way home.

'Well, I'm never taking you anywhere again,' she announced, but found to her dismay that she hadn't achieved anything like the light note she'd intended.

Jon, confident all had gone well and rather proud of himself, was dumbfounded. 'What have I done?'

Seeing his outrage, Philippa assured him hastily, 'No, it's me. I had no idea I could be so jealous.'

'Jealous?' It was the last thing he'd expected. 'About what? What are you talking about?'

'I minded when you and Clarissa—'

'Clarissa? Who the hell's Clarissa?'

'At the clays. And then Pauly Napier—'

'Ah well.' He grinned. 'She's a bit special.'

'There, you see!' Philippa no longer felt like apologising.

'Oh, come on.' Jon was immensely gratified and didn't attempt to hide it. 'You can't be serious.'

Philippa managed to laugh, but knew she had learned something about herself today, and about her feelings for Jon, which it might have been easier not to know.

Though Philippa's friends, with the exception of Alec Blaikie, for whom the barbecue had been one long numb ordeal, had been glad to meet Jon, and he had made on the whole a favourable impression, the least perceptive of them saw him as a walking time bomb in Philippa's life. They had been sad for her when her father died and Affran was sold, and had stood helplessly by as her marriage to Richard headed so rapidly for disaster. Now, in spite of their reservations, they loyally did their best to make Jon welcome. He was offered fishing at Sillerton by Lady Hay and a couple of days at the Drumveyn grouse by Archie Napier. He and Philippa were included in a big lively crowd at the Kirkton Games, and went on with them to have dinner at Grianan, which Sally Buchanan, now that her Aunt Janey had died, intended to keep going as a hotel. They went more than once to Allt Farr, whose holiday cottages were overflowing with family and friends, for lunches which wound on all afternoon, and Jon found he had to keep his wits about him when Grannie took him on in verbal sparring matches even more challenging than those he enjoyed with Julie.

They also, though time together was increasingly precious, invited people to Achallie, and Jon found to his surprise that entertaining could be more enjoyable than being entertained, even if the part he still liked best was waving everyone off afterwards and shutting the door behind himself and Philippa. But though her friends were willing to see his good qualities, and none could deny the happiness he and Philippa shared, few could help wondering how precarious that happiness might be.

Awareness that everything could end at a stroke inevitably wound up the emotional pitch. Love-making sometimes had almost a hint of desperation in it, and quarrels could flare up over things which normally wouldn't have mattered – as when Jon came back from the village one day furiously angry, having found the Mini's brakes virtually non-existent. Philippa, shaken by the rage he loosed on her, fled to her room, and Jon knew, for she'd never done such a thing before, that he must go after her.

He was appalled to find her crouched sobbing beside her bed. In two strides he was across the room and had her in his arms. 'Sweetheart, don't. I only yelled because I couldn't bear the thought of what might have happened to you.' His own voice was unsteady.

'But to be so *angry*,' she gasped out.

'How do you suppose I felt? And why on earth hadn't you said the brakes were in that state?'

'It's such a waste to have you working on the car when I'm at home.'

'I never heard anything so stupid.' But, hugging her close, Jon knew he wouldn't forget in a hurry the bowel-loosening fear at the images that had filled his mind.

On his side, a similar possessive need for time with her could lead to trouble on the old grounds of her work. Though he knew she needed the stability of on-going jobs, he couldn't help resenting them. One evening when she came home exhausted after a hot and gruelling stint at the hotel, and he complained that she was late, she took him aback by turning on her heel and going straight out again.

Jon caught her up at the hill gate.

'Look, I'm sorry, I was out of order.'

'It's all right,' Philippa said. 'I'm just tired.' But she didn't look at him.

After a moment's hesitation, he gently turned her towards him, and to his relief felt her relax against him.

'It's been a long day,' she admitted. 'Sometimes I don't even know what I'm doing there. It seems so unimportant now . . .'

He didn't forget this lesson, and it prompted him to agree at once, one morning after he'd slept at Achallie, when Philippa suggested his coming out with her on a job. She had never done so before but, going to pack a shooting lunch into the Mini and finding the lawn white with ground frost, the air smelling unmistakably of autumn, she had dumped down her box and gone back into the house and upstairs.

'Come with me today,' she said without preamble.

Jon, emerging from a pleasant doze, took one look at her face, and said, 'OK by me.' Though if she smiles at me like that we won't be going anywhere, he at once amended. 'What time do we have to leave?'

'Now,' Philippa said firmly.

'That obvious?'

'And tempting.' But she had already whisked out of reach. 'Breakfast. Move yourself, soldier.'

It was a day both remembered when they had need of such memories. Philippa directed Jon up a tiny road which ended in a down-at-heel farmyard with round slated byres and railed kennels, their doors chewed half off by bored dogs. In a cart shed were piled trestle tables and chairs.

'Fine enough to be outside,' Philippa decreed, and led the way down a nettly path to a stretch of turf sheltered by rowans, their berries already half stripped by the birds, where a burn tipped down rocky falls and a wide view opened. Jon looked about him with satisfaction. If anyone wanted him today they could whistle for him.

In this mood he accepted cheerfully the cursing struggles with rickety tables, the squalor of the farm kitchen where Philippa heated up her stew, and the wily depredations of a couple of hungry collies, his good humour only wavering when the guns came tramping back in high spirits after a good morning and each in turn crushed Philippa into a tweedy embrace. The best bit of the day came when they'd gone off again, not quite so keen for action after their excellent lunch, and he and Philippa propped themselves against a boulder, polished off the sloe gin and basked in the mellow afternoon sunshine.

Autumn was definitely here. Tortoiseshell butterflies spun dizzily out of curtains drawn for the first time for months. Mushrooming for supper, Philippa would look with an ache of resistance at the pale barley stubble in the fields by the river. Cattle floats appeared on the road, stacks of potato boxes inside field gates. The swallows left, fieldfares and redwings came through, and exotic waxwings gorged on the cotoneaster berries.

Philippa woke one morning to hear the faint, high calling of geese going south and roused Jon without compunction. He, coming out of sleep to awareness of her need, made love to her with an unhesitating response which for the moment drove vague terrors from her mind. Leaning above her afterwards, his hands clamped round her head, he made her look at him. 'I'll come back to you, you know. Nothing will stop me coming back,' he said, and she knew that in that moment he believed it.

Walking above Keeper's Cottage one November afternoon they were caught in a mean shower driven on an easterly wind, and turned for home. Heads down, they moved fast, Philippa's thoughts on tea by the fire, Jon's on tea in bed, and they were almost at the cottage before they saw the car parked beside theirs. A car Philippa didn't know.

'God, not another wife,' she said cheerfully, then turned as Jon stopped short, his face like stone. Ever afterwards she would remember with terrible exactness the way fear spread through her. 'Jonnie?'

'Come on.'

As they reached the car a man got out. He didn't look at Philippa. 'Boss wants you,' he said, and Jon nodded, his face unreadable, and turned towards the house.

Philippa followed uncertainly, even in those few seconds feeling excluded, and stood by the fire while he gathered things together in the bedroom.

'Philippa.'

She went to the door, and Jon glanced up from the holdall he was filling. 'Could you get my washing kit?' Was that all he had to say to her? She went to the bathroom and brought it. He had already packed what he needed. 'Dump the rest,' he said with a glance round the room that was purely practical. He picked up his bag and for one cold moment Philippa thought he was going to walk straight past her. 'No fuss. Good girl,' he said, reaching a finger to lift her chin.

'Jonnie,' she said desperately, her throat hard.

She saw the pain in his face in the second before he crushed her to him. 'For the love of God, don't cry,' he begged in a muffled voice. Clinging to him, she concentrated all her resources on obeying, then he pushed her away, looking for one moment more into her face. But with those wide wretched eyes fixed on him he found himself incapable in this final moment of offering her any promise he wasn't sure of keeping.

'Don't come out,' was all he could manage.

Philippa nodded, shivering as she heard him cross the sitting-room, an engine rev impatiently, the Subaru's come to life, and both cars head fast down the track. I didn't say anything, she realised in anguish. Not a single word. I just let him go. The awfulness of that threatened to overwhelm her but an instinct of self-preservation held back the tears. If she cried now she would never cope with the loneliness ahead.

She looked round the room, already meaningless. She would empty the cottage later; she couldn't face it now. Going down the track she couldn't even convince herself that Jon's thoughts had been on her as he drove this way only moments ago. He had already moved on.

INTERLUDE

Into the emptiness and silence came one message, in the form of a call from Muirend station, to say a delivery was waiting for her which should be collected without delay. Mystified, thinking perhaps someone had sent her a present of game, Philippa drove down and was surprised to be led to the porter's own den.

There, on the dingy cushions of the chair, a long-coated retriever puppy was curled fast asleep, the remains of a luggage label sticking up rakishly behind one ear and most of the porter's cheese sandwiches swelling his belly.

'There must be some mistake,' Philippa said, bewildered, but longing to believe this had something to do with Jon.

'No mistake, I've his ticket here. And there's this label, though he's chewed most of it, the wee devil.'

Philippa crouched to examine it with painful eagerness and found not Jon's shapely hand but uncouth capitals, giving the portions of her address the puppy hadn't eaten, and adding laconically FOR A SURPRISE – KEEPE.

Keeper. Philippa bent over the small sleeping form to hide her face. 'Yes, he's for me,' she said. The puppy barely stirred as she lifted him in her arms, soft as a velvet bag but surprisingly solid. 'Thank you for looking after him so well. You don't happen to know where he was sent from?' Any shred of fact would mean so much.

'From Glasgow. Ach, never fear, he'll have been spoiled to death all the way . . .'

No word. If only there had been some word. But carrying the puppy out to the car, planning how she would manage for tonight until she could kit him out properly, Philippa was already comforted.

Then the silence became complete, turning into life itself and, as the months stretched out with aching slowness, she found she was unable to make herself believe any longer that Jon would ever come back.

25

When Jon found himself on the move again, as had been the pattern during the period after he was taken, but with dissension clearly growing now among his captors, the demands on his strength, reduced by months of poor diet and inactivity, were almost harder to deal with than the nerve-racking uncertainty about what they intended to do with him. If the disputes became violent, then a casual bullet in the back of his head would be the simplest and most likely way for them to be resolved.

Past and present merged confusedly in his mind as he forced himself to keep going, and often he seemed to be back in that earlier time, when they had never spent two nights in the same place and he and Mackay had been driven endlessly on through the punishing terrain in the heat and humidity, hands tied, guts to pieces on the starvation diet, and in his own case the wound in his arm throbbing painfully. Then, as now, he had tried to avoid meeting the dark, doped-up eyes, or making any move which would spark a reaction of casual brutality.

When they had shot Mackay, weakened by fever and no longer able to handle the pace, Jon, beaten off when he tried to help him, had had a disorientating feeling that he had died too, and been disposed of in the same heedless way. A feeling that it scarcely mattered any more whether the time before the inevitable end was long or short. It had made it hard to focus on the survival ploys he had been trained in, which depended on the concentration of mind and will.

One event which had brought some brief hope, though it had been terrifying at the time, had been the fierce altercation which had broken out when, joining up with other members of the same faction, including an officer of evident seniority, the man who had shot Mackay had been summarily executed. Jon had hoped this might mean that he himself was regarded as a valuable bargaining counter, which in turn suggested that, in spite of the failure of the engagement in which he and Mackay had been taken, the coup overall had been successful, and the forces holding him were now the rebels.

This interpretation was correct, though he wasn't to learn the details until much later. Colonel K, wounded in the same action, had later died, making Jon the most senior surviving mercenary officer. But he knew nothing of this and the hardest thing to endure, as the conditions of his captivity gradually became less harsh, had been the fact that there seemed no reason for his situation ever to change.

When the unit holding him had established permanent camp and he was able to conserve his strength, his health had improved. He had been left unmolested in a rough shelter, and regularly fed. The clearest indicator of the intention to keep him alive had been the fact that his wound had been treated and had eventually healed. Over time, familiarity had created a level of acceptance between captors and captive, and he had been allowed outside his hut so long as he stayed near it. The fear of imminent death had receded, but had left in its place the debilitating mental strain of solitude and absolute ignorance as to what would happen to him.

He had had no way of knowing whether anyone was aware that he was still alive and held hostage. He had no clue to the current political situation, any swing in which could mean that from one day to the next he would become expendable.

He had to call up every ounce of his reserves to discipline and occupy his mind, working obsessively through half-forgotten trivia, digging for facts, names, places, events. At first he had gulped down the memories wholesale, but over time had learned to piece them together with infinite care, making them last and last . . .

When a flurry of activity broke out one morning, radio messages coming in, urgency and excitement in the air, and the senior officer suddenly put in an appearance again, to Jon it was not only sinister but almost unwelcome, jolting him out of an existence he'd come to accept, routine, within his scope. Then, abruptly, the end came, and he found himself roused by shouted commands and prodded roughly towards a waiting jeep, hardly capable of making his shaking limbs obey him.

Later, trying to piece together the events of the next two days, he could remember little.

When he was led into an opulent office and saw behind its desk the colonel, now elevated to general and wearing full ceremonial uniform, who had previously acted as liaison officer between the indigenous forces and Colonel K, his stunned mind could only grope for answers, hopelessly baffled.

The explanations he was given were little help, but one thing he did grasp – he had become some kind of trophy. His recovery, it appeared, had been a matter of prestige for the present government, the government he had helped to bring to power. The group which had captured him, demanding amnesty if they gave him up, had threatened to release news of his whereabouts to the international media, and it was not considered desirable for them to be seen to be holding the one remaining ranking officer of a mercenary force recruited principally in Europe.

The exchange made, however, Jon's usefulness to either

side was over. He was, in effect, an embarrassment. Times were changing. Employing foreign mercenaries could give a regime a bad name. His good fortune in being repatriated, rather than being removed from the scene by less costly means, was, it seemed, purely at the whim of the present head of government, who, while detesting Colonel K, had admired Jon's professional skills.

The flight home was petrifying. Jon was quite unable to take in the fact that he was free, convinced that any careless move would slam the trap shut once more. He avoided all contact with such nervous resolve that he was marked down as suspect by the cabin crew, and ended up under the very surveillance he feared. After landing he didn't move from his seat until the last passenger had gone, awaiting orders, then wandered for hours around the terminal feeling alien and afraid, as though the activity around him was part of a world in which he no longer had a place. Gradually, however, the truth penetrated, and he began to wonder, not where he should go – there was only one answer to that, the place whose images had kept him sane – but how he should get there. He had been supplied with cash and basic personal requirements. All he had to do was get himself onto a Glasgow flight; he could surely manage that.

Philippa was planting early potatoes, a peaceful job once the hard work of preparation was done. The sun was warm on her back, the turned earth smelled good. Keeper was lying on the lawn, snapping lazily at flies.

She took no notice of the car coming up the hill. The days were long past when the hope that it might be Jon had flared and died. Life was ordered and busy once more, and though dreams could still torment her, dreams she spoke of to no one, she had learned to live with the anguish of not knowing and, in the end, of not hoping.

When the car turned in her only thought was, damn, half a row to go, it would have been nice to have finished the job. When did she know? She could never afterwards be sure, or recall the moments between straightening up and finding herself walking down the lawn.

She certainly didn't recognise at once the gaunt bearded man, in cheap dark clothes, getting out of the car with awkward movements. But when he stood, watchful and hesitant, a hand gripping the top of the car door, uncertainty in his whole stance, then she knew.

Something seemed to swell in her chest and nearly choke her. Shock and disbelief, joy and relief, tumbled in her brain, shot with a wild anger that he should turn up like this, without a word, as though he imagined . . .

Then he was moving round the open car door, slamming it shut, his eyes fixed on her. With movements as involuntary and probably unconscious as her own, he was coming over the grass towards her, and she knew that something was terribly wrong.

Her first thought (one which would shame her for a long time to come) was that he was drunk. To appear in this condition, when she hadn't seen him for a year and a half, hadn't heard from him . . . How dare he?

Then she saw the skeletal thinness of his big frame, the sunken eyes and hollow cheeks above the beard, the almost groping way he moved. He was ill. Sharp concern was added to the churning of other emotions. She became aware that Keeper, close at her side, was watching the stranger with a suspicion far from his usual friendliness.

'Jonnie.' The sound was thin, without carrying power. Jonnie, yes, but how altered, not only in appearance but in his whole aura and presence. What had happened to him?

Prison? It had seemed the second most likely possibility when the agonising silence had gone on and on. But his skin was darkly tanned; no prison pallor there. Anger rose again. Doubts, questions, exactly as before. How *dare* he let all this time go by without contact of any kind, then roll up so calmly?

But these thoughts seemed weightless, inconsequent, beside the one astounding fact, the fact that impelled her forward, brought hot tears to her eyes and half choked her, as he took the last couple of strides between them and seized her in a crushing embrace. He had come back. There was unbelievable comfort in feeling his arms round her, as though life made sense again, but in the same instant startled recoil too. This bony body felt quite different from the well-muscled strength she remembered, and he held her, not with the natural ease of the past, but clumsily, almost painfully, clinging to her with what felt like desperation. And the smell of his skin, so much part of his sexual appeal for her, was unfamiliar and distasteful.

'Oh, Jonnie, I've missed you so.' Later she was to be thankful that her first words, spoken from the heart, were these.

He said nothing, pressing his head against hers, and, emaciated as he was, she had to brace herself against his weight. It felt as though he was holding on to her for support rather than from delight to see her again, and she knew questions would have to wait; he needed her help.

'Come on, Jon. Come into the house.'

She was relieved to feel him muster his resources to obey her. Keeper stayed tight at Philippa's heels, ruff still up, as they went towards the house. The scent of this man carried messages he didn't care for, and there were new and disturbing emotions in the air.

They negotiated the doorway with some difficulty, and as Jon sank onto a kitchen stool Philippa realised that he still hadn't uttered a word. And he'd driven here. From where? The clothes he was wearing, black canvas trousers and T-shirt, denim jacket, looked foreign and had a smell of cheap shop newness about them.

Hastily she turned away to make tea. He clearly needed something to brace him, but she wasn't going to risk brandy. Keeper followed every movement she made, brow furrowed, with an air of being ready to do anything she required of him. Philippa smoothed his head and he pressed up against her hand, giving a sweep of his feathery tail but not reassured. This stranger, he felt in his soul, brought with him some obscure threat.

As Philippa stirred in sugar and brought the mug to the table, Jon began to look around him and take in his surroundings. But still he said nothing, seizing the mug from her as if it were miser's gold, hunching his shoulders over it, holding it close.

Philippa turned away, shaken and suddenly afraid. But she pushed alarm down. She must feed him. What did she have in the house? Or, more pertinently, what would it be all right to give him? He'd have to stay; that much was clear. She couldn't send him away in this state. The feeling that he was giving her no choice woke fresh frustration. He'd been back for five minutes and already he was spinning her life into chaos.

Jon gulped down a couple of biscuits, coughed at the crumbs, emptied his mug in a greedy draught.

'Sorry, Philippa,' he said, his voice hoarse, as if he hadn't used it for a while. 'Sorry to—' He made a helpless gesture, unable to complete the thought.

Compassion overriding every other concern, Philippa went to stand close to him, and he dropped his head against her with exhausted thankfulness.

'It's all right,' she said. 'It's all right.'

'Just need some sleep,' he mumbled, hardly able to shape the words.

'I know. Come on.'

Would he make it up the stairs? But Philippa knew that, whatever his need, she couldn't bring herself to put this man, with his stranger's body, his stranger's scent, into her own bed.

Prepared to help him out of his hideous clothes if necessary, she found there was no need. Jon swayed towards the bed, fell like a log across it and was instantly asleep. She pulled off his boots – US Army combat boots, she noted, but couldn't apply her mind to an explanation – then drew the duvet round him, and stood back to survey him. Nothing was going to disturb him now.

'Jon Paulett, you wretched man, does it have to be like this?' she demanded aloud.

Keeper was waiting for her, protective and anxious, at the turn of the stair. She was glad he was there.

Now, where there had been a peaceful, productive day, there was a turmoil of questions. How could she settle to anything with Jon upstairs; how could she go out and finish what she'd been doing, knowing he might wake and need her? We've been here before, she thought bleakly, as she went to fetch whatever luggage Jon had from the beat-up old Datsun, finding only a carrier bag containing the barest necessities. Was this all he now owned in the world? It appeared all too probable.

The hours waiting for him to wake seemed unreal, outside time, as she swung from incredulous joy that he was here, safe, nothing else mattering, to passionate anger that he hadn't let her know he was alive, that he had put her through such tortures of grief and loneliness. She passed most of the time curled up on the sofa, cold and shivery as the April dusk grew chilly, but almost afraid to move, as if any attempt to perform such ordinary acts as lighting the fire or cooking a meal would reveal how remote ordinariness already was.

She stirred herself in the end to feed Keeper, and give him a brief run. Checking on Jon before she went out, she found he hadn't stirred. It was disturbing to look into his haggard sleeping face, its lines deeply carved, and see it as that of an intimidating stranger, and at the same time see Jon there, the Jon she had loved.

After a night during which she barely slept, and a walk in the grey dawn, she was relieved, looking in on him again, when, hearing her, he woke. His reaction, however, drawing in his limbs in an instinctive movement of self-protection, was not reassuring. He had clearly been in captivity of some kind. Held in some jungle hide-out?

Images formed with grim readiness after all the news stories, impossible to avoid seeing, of hostages kept for months on end before being traded for ransom or some other demand. But in these instances the hostages had been returned to their homes and families under the eyes of the world and, though they'd had to face the ordeal of media attention, they had also received appropriate medical care. How many didn't make it, not valuable enough to trade? Diplomatic silence, presumably, covered their fate.

What had Jon been through? Well, whatever it was, this wasn't the moment to take a moral stand about it. They'd had that out long ago, and she'd made her decision. Was all this now behind him? But, however crucial the question was to her, she knew, waiting while Jon stumbled down to the bathroom and back again, it too would have to wait. She must hold on to the essential fact: given the choice between Jon coming back, in whatever state, or gone from her life for good, there was no choice. She wanted him here; and she committed herself, in that moment, to all that followed.

As sleep claimed Jon once more, she went out to the landing and took from a cupboard the clothes she had kept there. It was only when she rooted out a pair of his favourite desert boots that the memory of the day she had collected these things from Keeper's Cottage threatened to overwhelm her.

26

Standing in the doorway of Jon's room in the early evening Philippa knew he was awake, and she had the feeling that he'd been awake for some time. Why hadn't he called?

'Jonnie?' Her voice was uncertain, and she realised she was bracing herself as if to meet some challenge.

'Am I really here?' His voice rasped, exhausted still.

Philippa, without putting on the light, crossed to the bed. 'Yes, you're here, at Achallie. You came yesterday afternoon. You've been asleep ever since.'

'Yesterday? What day's this then?' He'd been trying to work it out.

'Sunday.'

He frowned, as though needing to relate this to something, but gave up. 'Philippa?'

Well, he remembers my name, she thought, preferring irony to the pain that he didn't reach to touch her.

'I shouldn't have pitched up like that.'

'It's all right,' she said and, helplessly, heard herself sounding polite, almost formal, giving no hint of the feelings it aroused to have him here again.

'Well, things change, don't they?' he said with an attempt at heartiness which didn't succeed.

Had changed for him? Philippa felt a chill of doubt. She hadn't thought of this. Was he merely using Achallie as a temporary refuge or staging post?

'No one objecting to my being here?' Jon went on in the same tone, when she said nothing.

She frowned in the dim light. Who could mind? Then she understood what he was asking, what he would of course need to ask. 'I'm still on my own,' she said. 'There's no one else.' Not, 'There's no one else here.'

'Christ,' Jon said on a long breath, drawing a hand down his face as though obliterating unwelcome visions. 'This room, you, in the dreams, then always waking—'

She knew he didn't mean the dreams she had dreamed. Gently she lifted his fleshless hand, folding it in both hers. With a harsh exclamation Jon pulled it free and heaving himself up crushed her roughly against him. Once more Philippa was perturbed to find the embrace clumsy and alien, waking no response. It wasn't only his angular frame which felt unfamiliar, but he seemed to have forgotten the knack, once so instinctive, of moulding a woman to him. When he found her lips his kiss was urgent, seeking, the taste of him startlingly different. Then abruptly he stopped kissing her, pressing his face into her neck, and she wondered with alarm if he found her equally unfamiliar or, worse, had felt her lack of response. Perhaps he had, for he released her and lay back, hands behind his head, staring at the ceiling.

Philippa took care to let a few moments pass before saying gently, 'Jonnie, you must be terribly hungry. You haven't eaten since you came. Would you like to come down and have supper, or shall I bring it up here?'

'I'll stay where I am,' Jon said after a second's hesitation. The steps involved in dressing, going downstairs and attempting to walk back into a past which now seemed hopelessly confused by the overworked, and in the end hallucinatory, memories to which he had clung to keep him sane, were too daunting to face.

'No problem, I'll fetch something.' Philippa guessed there

would be little point in asking what he'd like, and in any case didn't have much to offer, not having liked to leave him alone in the house while she went to the village. Nor had she wanted to meet anyone. In the kitchen, assembling a scratch meal, she hesitated over the tray. Would Jon mind if she left him to eat on his own, or would he think it odd if she stayed? Would he notice either way? Oh, come *on*, she exclaimed under her breath. Of all the things she had fantasised about, should Jon ever reappear, she had hardly imagined getting wound up about a decision so trivial.

'I couldn't let you know where I was,' Jon said abruptly, as they finished an uninspired supper which he'd gulped down in an odd mixture of voracious greed and blind indifference to what he put into his mouth.

Philippa felt a shiver of apprehension. Did she want to hear what was coming? She said nothing.

'What was going on, I mean.' Jon had plunged into this almost desperately, knowing he owed her some kind of explanation, but not sure he could give her any account she would find acceptable. But he had to go on now. 'It all went wrong. At least, we thought it had.' He still found it hard to take in that the faction they'd supported had gained power but had only now negotiated for his release. 'I got picked up, anyway. Taken hostage.' The enormity of remembering, in this quiet room he'd thought he would never see again, the struggle he'd gone through to hold on for so long without hope, threatened to overwhelm him. How could he make anyone, even Philippa, understand? He came closer to breaking down in that moment than he had in all the months of fear and deprivation. Closing his eyes, he summoned the familiar, hard-won stratagems to focus his brain only on what it could deal with.

Philippa looked at his shut face, gaunt in the light of the bedside lamp, and accepted in that moment that she would learn no more. But whatever had happened to this man he was still Jonnie. He had suffered and, whether he'd brought the suffering on himself or not, he needed her. Like him, however, she had one vital question to ask.

'Jonnie?' She saw him gather his resources. 'I need to know – do you have to go back?'

'Back?' He stared at her as though the word conveyed nothing. Then for the first time she saw awareness of her, and of what she might be feeling, awake. He seized her hand. 'Philippa, no, it's over, finished. I'm out of it. Don't ever think about it again.'

She wanted to ask, 'And will you stay?' but it was a very different question from 'Do you have to go back?' and her courage failed her. Well, he wasn't going anywhere tonight, that much was certain.

Nor was he going to expect – or want – to make love to her, that essential ending to every fantasy she had ever had about his return, beyond which it had been fatally easy never to look. It was a cold, sad moment when she accepted that the thought hadn't entered his mind.

On a different level, but important too in its own way, was the subject of Keeper. She had so often wanted to tell Jon how much his arrival had meant to her at that awful time. But when she broached the subject he only demanded irritably, 'What are you talking about?'

'The puppy you had delivered, after you left.'

Jon's mind groped back. 'I don't remember.'

'But the message, saying he was called Keeper . . .'

Could she have been wrong all along? Dismayed resistance filled her, as though something precious was being taken away from her.

'Keeper?' Jon frowned. 'Oh yes, that god-awful cottage.' It had figured in the dogged exercises of the mind; he didn't want to think about it now. 'Wait a minute, though, it's coming back to me. I gave some guy money. Never thought he'd do anything about it.'

So much for sentiment.

Jon, shrugging off the dimly recalled incident as too tedious to think about, noticed for the first time the clothes Philippa had laid over a chair. 'Is that my gear? You kept it?' His voice had sharpened. The discovery evidently had significance for him.

'Yes.'

'You were so sure I'd come back?'

How to answer that? 'I couldn't bear to get rid of them,' Philippa said simply. Those clothes of his, what they had meant to her – the numb misery of collecting them from cold, deserted Keeper's Cottage, her need to touch them, bury her face in them, and later her reluctance to wash them and remove the last lingering trace of him.

'You believed I'd come back,' Jon repeated.

'Well, there they are,' she agreed, trying to smile. They'll hang off him, she thought in distress. Seeing him in them will be almost worse than seeing him in those horrible clothes he arrived in yesterday.

It was strange to have Jon in the house. And how like him, Philippa couldn't help thinking, to turn up in a state so far from anything she could ever have imagined – a state which increasingly worried her, for it was clear his problems went far beyond physical debility. He had largely withdrawn into a world of his own and, though dependent on Philippa's presence, seemed to need it primarily for his own reassurance. But, as sleep and good food did their work, and the reality of freedom and safety sank in, other thoughts began to obsess him. Though for so long every other instinct had been subordinated to the main aim of survival, memories of Philippa had inevitably included sex.

And the more realistic memories which now began to stir included it too.

One evening when Philippa came up to make sure Jon was comfortable for the night, she was disconcerted to be met by the brusque question, 'Where are you sleeping?'

He knew the answer to that. 'Downstairs.'

'Not tonight. You're sleeping here.' But behind the forced jauntiness she caught doubt, amounting almost to dread. It wasn't hard to guess at the mixture of feelings prompting what had sounded more like a challenge than an invitation: a male desire to be in control again, longing, perhaps, for things to be as they had been, but above all a need for reassurance which she knew Jon would never put into words. She also knew the moment was pivotal – and that she had no choice.

It was awful. Deep down, she had believed that once she was finally in his arms Jon would re-create the old magic for them both, but in moments she realised they were a long, long way from that. She could have been anyone. Jon's hands, touching her, transmitted no message of pleasure to either of them. Instead she could feel only his helpless, baffled frustration.

Knowing better than to try to comfort him, she lay rigid, waiting for him to sleep, this separate, damaged stranger, and wishing she could wake in her own room, as she had done for so long, to thoughts of him rounded into something familiar and bearable, infinitely preferable to the emotional turbulence his presence brought.

All that mattered, she reminded herself over and over again during that long night, was to look after him and help him back to normality. She must accept his worrying, morose silences, and somehow get him through the much worse times when he jerked out of one of the nightmares which continued to beset him, sweating and trembling, and spilled out incoherent fragments of what he'd gone through. She was well aware that what he really needed was a period of rehabilitation under professional care, but could see no way of getting him to agree to it. The best she could offer was patience, reassurance and as much time as he needed.

One thing which surprised her was his reluctance to leave the house. She would have thought he would have valued the freedom to come and go above all else, but Jon chose to stay in bed for hours, then prowl about indoors, grim-faced and edgy. He wasn't interested in anything Philippa had done to the house or garden, and giving her a hand with anything was clearly not in his mind.

Though she cut back on jobs in order to spend as much time as possible with him, she was ashamed to find herself glad to be out of the house when she went off to those to which she felt committed. They couldn't go on living like this, she knew, but even so she wasn't prepared for Jon's demand that she give up work altogether.

'It's a good idea to have some money coming in, don't you think?' she said carefully, all too aware of what a source of contention this had been in the past.

'Peanuts,' Jon said dismissively. 'Anyway, you don't need it now I'm back.'

All very well, Philippa thought, but not one penny had he contributed since he arrived, though she had taken a wad of fifties from the pocket of the horrible trousers she'd thrown away.

'Are you going to get a job then?' she asked, doing her best to make the question sound conversational.

'No need.'

Had he somehow been paid, in spite of everything? But money's not the point, she wanted to protest. It's the future we should be discussing; how we feel, what we want.

It was a view shared by Philippa's friends, the majority of whom were less than thrilled to learn that Jon had reappeared.

It was easy to forget how happy Philippa had been with him when he was in the glen a couple of years ago, and during his absence they'd grown used to her filling her accepted niche in their lives once more.

'I know he was fearfully attractive,' Penny Forsyth said (did I know she thought that, Andrew wondered with passing interest), 'but I can't imagine him making her happy in the end, can you? And I think she might have told me. When I passed on the message about those new people at Balgowan wanting help with a house-warming, she only said she was too busy at present.'

This, Andrew knew, was what Penny really minded. She had heard about Jon's return from him, via Michael Thorne.

'Anyway,' Penny was saying, trying to be positive though still sounding aggrieved, 'at least Alec won't be upset by it, that's one good thing.'

Andrew hid a smile. He thought Alec had shown more sense than ever in his life before when, with a smartened-up house on his hands and a clear field after Jon's abrupt disappearance, he had unexpectedly abandoned his pursuit of Philippa and turned his attentions to a Heriot niece from Carhill, marrying her, to everyone's astonishment, six months later. Andrew would never know, and nor would anyone else, that Philippa, stunned and desolate though she had been after Jon left, had realised what Alec would read into her solitary state, and had taken the trouble to drive over to Torglas and tell him, as kindly as she could, that she would never marry him.

Only Michael and Julie, who had known how devastating Jon's departure had been for her, and had admired her courage as, step by painful step, she got her life together again, were more perceptive about what his return would mean. But even they had never imagined the state in which he would show up, or the difficulties Philippa would face because of it.

'Not good,' Michael reported worriedly, after running into her in the village. 'She looks as if she hasn't slept for a week, and she was on the defensive at once when I asked after Jon.'

'Did you ask them over?'

'I did, but she says he's not well at present.'

'Not well.' Julie snorted. 'Bugger's been banged up, I suppose. If he disappears again she's going to need us. Here, give me a hug.'

Michael knew the hug was not for her.

27

Busy juggling the demands of work and looking after Jon, Keeper, house and garden (planting vegetables for two?), but no matter how hard she tried always feeling she was short-changing someone, Philippa failed to grasp the true source of Jon's moods. It was like having an unknown person in the house, daunting and taciturn, and their former delight in each other, the talk and laughter as well as the loving, seemed impossible to recapture.

Outwardly, Jon was recovering, his beard gone, old sores and insect bites healed, his big frame filling out. He no longer slept away half the day and his dreams were less frequent and less harrowing. He would sit outside occasionally now, though he still disliked going far from the house. He had abandoned his efforts, however, to make love to Philippa – though any other term would have done, she would think forlornly, lying beside him in the big bed. She felt a return to her own room would make too explicit a statement and prove a hard step to reverse.

Though realising that Jon was suffering from post-traumatic stress, and prepared for recovery to be a long process, she missed the vital point. He felt superfluous. It was not merely that Philippa had managed perfectly while he'd been away or that, as far as he could see, she had taken his reappearance without missing a step, or that from morning to night nothing was required of him, but that, crucial to a man of his stamp, he

was incapable of reassuming the dominant male role natural
to him.

If only Philippa would have a go at him sometimes, he
would think helplessly, but she was always so damned tolerant,
accepting his surliness and inertia and inability to make love to
her with the same smiling equanimity. Sometimes he wanted
nothing more than to give up, drive away, forget the whole
thing. Or alternatively blast it apart, getting Philippa away
from this house where everything he looked at was hers.

Increasingly, his thoughts turned to the forsaken bothy on
the West Coast. He had always kept the idea tucked away
as a vague insurance against the future, and now Mackay's
words came temptingly back: 'Don't worry, no one else will
want it. The key's got your name on it.'

But going in search of that key would mean breaking the
news. Mackay's wife, like Philippa, would have been sitting
out the months without a word. Jon wasn't sure he could
handle facing her yet. Images of the remote little place
continued to haunt him, however. He had so often pinned
his mind, while still capable of such mental effort, on plans for
renovating it, that by this time it was hard to recall its original
condition. But it might, just might, be the answer he needed.
Alone at Achallie, restless and aimless, he allowed the images
to shape into an alluring vision, ignoring all obstacles.

Philippa, racing back after shopping in Muirend, turned in
just as Jon was throwing a bag into the back of the Datsun.
She had automatically pulled up out of his way before its
significance reached her. Getting out, she found her knees
were weak.

Jon, psyched up for action, saw none of her shock. 'Got a
few things to see to,' he said.

Philippa focused on extraneous details – the holdall Jon
had found was that freebie from Barclaycard, Keeper, left
in her car, was barking, the bones of Jon's hand stood out

as he gripped the door of the Datsun. Then she saw that he was watching her with a wariness she read as hostility. She had failed him. She had lost him. She would never see him again. She drew a breath so deep it made her dizzy.

'Fine,' she said, smiling brightly.

'Right then. I'll push off.'

Her instinct was to ask if he had everything he needed. For what, she asked herself bleakly.

Jon, his mind on what lay ahead, already had a foot in the car. Philippa stepped back, still smiling, and waited while he tried the starter, found the choke and turned with his elbow over the seat to back out. As the wheels turned he jumped at a sudden furious battering on the window, jerking round to see Philippa's raised fists and distraught face. For a hideous moment he thought he'd gone over her foot. Then he was out and had her in his arms.

'What in God's name—?'

She seemed unhurt but clutched at him desperately, and he folded her against him to still her shaking, bending his head to catch incoherent gasping words.

'. . . going away . . . I can't bear it again . . .'

'Philippa, I'll be back in a couple of days.'

'You won't, I know you won't. It was so awful, not hearing, not knowing. I can't bear it—'

'Of course I'll be back. What are you talking about?' But she only clung to him, her head pressed tight against him. 'Come on, come back inside. We'll sort this out.' He turned her towards the house. 'It's all right, I'm coming in too. I'm not leaving you like this.' He didn't notice that, now the need was there, he had taken charge without question. Neither of them heard Keeper's protests as he watched them go in.

'Sorry, Jonnie. Didn't know I was going to do that.' Philippa got her breathing under control and pushed back her hair, looking up at him with rueful apology.

'Don't be silly.' The moment's blind panic had told him more than all her patience and care since his return. Leading her into the sitting-room he drew her down beside him on the sofa. As he did so, an odd thought struck him – for the first time, he truly felt he was home.

'Right, now – are you paying attention? I have to go to Glasgow to see to some business—'

'You'd have gone without telling me.' She couldn't get past that.

'What's that on the table?' Jon made her turn to look, and she saw the note propped against the fruit bowl.

'What does it say?' she asked suspiciously, needing to be talked round.

Jon grinned. She was feeling better. 'It says I can't stand the food here any longer.'

As she turned back to him he saw the relief and laughter in her face. 'God, you're such a bastard.'

'True.' He caught her hands and held them. 'Now listen, I don't have to go today if you'd rather I didn't. What I have to do can wait.'

'Or I could come with you?' But Philippa saw his face instantly close at that, the face of a man choosing his excuse, and her voice sharpened in fear. 'Jonnie, you're not still involved, you're not going back to—'

'For Christ's sake, no.' Momentary anger flared that she didn't trust him. 'I've said, that's over and done with. There's something I have to do. Nothing dangerous and nothing dodgy, but – well, I can't tell you about it.' He felt a superstitious reluctance to talk about his private dream. About to put it to the test, he was all too aware of how nebulous it was.

Philippa, hearing that quick anger, knew she had to trust him, and show that she trusted him. 'All right, I won't ask. But you'll be careful, won't you? I really couldn't stand it if anything happened to you.'

He heard the break in her voice and it moved him.

'I'll be fine,' he said gruffly, pulling her head against him. Philippa distressed and needing reassurance radically altered the balance between them.

If he'd taken her to bed there and then, she was to think later, everything might still have been all right. But Jon, having geared himself up to the point of facing the outer world again, couldn't conceal his anxiety to be off. She could feel the hyped-up energy in him, and recognised that this was something he had to do.

The drive was an ordeal. When Jon had made the journey back to Scotland he'd been functioning on automatic, digging into his last reserves of will power to organise funds, get hold of wheels and head for Achallie. Now he sweated and cursed through the traffic, making with sick reluctance for places he'd hoped never to see again.

Mags was still in the old house. Need was there anyway, Jon thought, noting the state of it. Had the payment up front which they'd insisted on, those who'd survived to be recalled for the second phase, gone already? Thank God he'd had the sense to shove his share straight into the bank.

He hardly recognised fiery Mags. She had a tight-mouthed, defeated look about her which was new.

'Oh – you,' she said flatly, when she opened the door. Then she peered into his face, and a shoulder lifted. 'Yeah, right. Don't tell me. Damned man. I knew he shouldn't have went back. He was lucky to get out the first time.'

Damned man. Ronnie's epitaph.

'We had to go back.'

'Oh, aye.' She looked at Jon with an indifference edged with contempt. 'You'd best come in, I suppose.'

The gas fire was on, and the television, full bore. Two grubby children had their eyes glued to the screen. Jon pushed away reminders of June, of Brian.

'If you'd like to talk,' he began awkwardly. It occurred to him for the first time that he didn't have a single possession of Mackay's to give her. 'If there's anything I can tell you—' He broke off, glancing uncertainly at the children.

She followed his glance, and her mouth turned down. 'Don't worry about them. They wouldn't notice supposing a bomb went off. Anyway, what d'you reckon on telling me? That it was all over in a minute? He didn't feel a thing? Well, you can stick it. Beats me why he ever came out of the Army, it was all he ever cared about. I'm just as well off without him. You're all the same, the lot of you.'

'I wanted to make sure you were managing.' Jon had to find some way into the subject he'd come to broach.

'Managing?' Mags' face filled with weary scorn. 'Who's managing these days? But you made it back all right, I see. Got the full pay-off, did you?'

'No.' He kept his voice quiet. 'None of us did.'

'Don't give me that. There's always someone gets the pay-off. But not the poor sods like Ronnie.'

Time to open negotiations. Jon read the calculation in her eyes the moment he mentioned the bothy.

'There's plenty been after it,' she lied swiftly. 'Folk'll pay anything for a place up there.'

Jon was willing to bet she'd never been near it. He also knew, in that second, that she'd have sold it long ago had the option been open to her. So Mackay had tied it up somehow. For him? Was this really going to happen?

Alone at Achallie, Philippa clock-watched compulsively. If she had sometimes wondered, on bad days with Jon, if solitude wasn't preferable to the see-saw of emotions when he was around, she had her answer now. She missed him desperately. She also had far too much time to reflect on the similarities between his first appearance in the glen and this one. In both cases he had needed a period of recuperation after danger and disaster. Would the end also be the same? Memories of the grey November day when he had left before tormented her.

When the phone rang after she'd gone to bed she nearly didn't answer, feeling hardly capable either of discussing work or of chatting to some friend.

'Philippa.' In that one word the old Jon was back, exactly as she remembered him, fit and active, relaxed and loving, grey eyes teasing as he watched her with satisfaction and desire.

'Jonnie?' She cleared her throat and tried again, terrified he might vanish if she couldn't make him hear. 'Where are you?'

'Glasgow, I told you. Look, I just wanted to say – I'll have some great news for you when I get back.' He sounded exuberant and full of energy, the Jon she loved. She couldn't speak.

'Had you gone to bed?' he was asking.

'It doesn't matter.'

'Where are you sleeping?'

'Upstairs.' She was glad she hadn't gone back to her own room as she had been tempted to do.

'Good girl.'

'When will you be back?' The only thing that mattered.

'For Pete's sake.' But he didn't attempt to hide his gratification and she smiled, content. 'I've got one or two things to tie up but don't worry, I'll be there, day after tomorrow probably.'

That call changed everything, making his absence ordinary and bearable, and the next day Philippa had no difficulty in getting down to waiting jobs. She'd been asleep for a couple of hours when Keeper's barking woke her. She pitched herself down the stairs and into Jon's arms with all the old spontaneity and delight.

'God, that feels good,' he said, hugging her.

'But you said tomorrow—'

'Well, now I'm here.'

He was too buoyed up to go to bed, insisting on raking the fire together and opening a bottle of wine, while Philippa, elation unaccountably dying as she watched him, tried to ignore the feeling that something was coming which she wouldn't want to hear. Even so she couldn't for a second have imagined what it turned out to be.

Leave Achallie? Shock crystallised into those two disbelieving words, though she didn't utter them. What kept them back was Jon's confidence that she would be as delighted as he was at his news. It meant so much to see enthusiasm fill him again; how could she destroy it?

At least he didn't want her to live in Glasgow – and he was taking it for granted they would be together, which she hadn't always been certain, in recent days, that he would want. But more importantly, as he talked on, she saw that any hint of hesitation on her part would be fatal.

Jon had hauled himself out of his inertia and taken decisive action. That was impressive in itself. He was offering her all he had in his power to give. He was doing his best to take charge of his life again, and hers, which he saw as his role and his responsibility. High on optimism, he was a different man from the one who had driven away yesterday, and listening to his eager voice Philippa knew half measures wouldn't do. He needed her unconditional support, and she gave it, pushing away the nagging warning that he had no idea of what this step meant to her, or of her feeling – conscious of how far they still had to go to re-establish trust and communication – that it was a step she was taking very much alone.

28

They went to Shionach on a windblown day in early May, coming over the brow of the lane in a sparkling gap between showers, to see for the first time the pale curve of Drishaig Bay and the long finger of the rocky point beyond which the bothy lay. Exclaiming in delight, ready to forget all doubts, Philippa wound down her window as Jon drove slowly on, though most of the view was at once obscured by Keeper's head as he gulped in heady new scents of sea-wrack and salt air. The lane, patterned by blown sand, ran close above the shore, ending where a drive led up to the big yellow-harled house of Fassfern.

Mags Mackay, amazingly, had been able to produce the title deeds of the bothy, still in their tattered original envelope, but said she'd never seen a key. The Muirend solicitor had contacted Fassfern estate, which encircled the bothy, and been assured that one could be found which would fit. It was to be left in the mailbox at the drive end. It was there and Jon, hefting its cold weight in his hand, was gripped by an almost painful anticipation. Was this truly happening at last?

As they left the car and set off up the slope, he assessed the peaty hollows and rock ribs of the track with a dubious eye. That would need a bit doing to it.

But Philippa was thrilled with everything. 'Jonnie, it's fabulous! I always forget how glorious the west is. The light's so different over here.'

'Not bad.' Jon had other things on his mind. Then, seeing the vivid pleasure in her face, her loving generosity and willingness to be pleased by what she found, took him by the throat. He caught her hand and swung her towards him. 'And you're not bad yourself.'

She beamed, putting her hands flat on his chest as he held her loosely in the circle of his arms. Nowadays he rarely said anything so direct. 'This is going to be marvellous,' she said. 'I'm sure it is.'

'God knows what we'll find,' he warned her. Now that reality was close, the visions which had helped to keep him sane seemed to be slipping away, impossible to hold on to, sick fantasies, fabricated out of need.

'Well, we're only here to look,' Philippa said cheerfully. But Jon knew that in his mind he had gone much further. He had an irrational, almost panicky feeling that this place had to provide some answer for them. As with the Thornton house, he had insisted on everything being properly gone into. There must be no glitches over technicalities such as access, water, wayleave – or the possible upgrading of this track.

He fell silent as they approached the ridge. He and Mackay had come and gone each time by boat, at night, and had hardly moved from the bothy by day, so his memories of its surroundings were vague. The house itself had been basic, a mere place to camp. Since then it had stood empty, as far as he knew, buffeted by wind and weather, perhaps broken into by walkers or sailing people, or used by animals for shelter. If renovation wasn't feasible, what then? The question brought him face to face with a blank he hardly dared contemplate and, face grim, he tried to keep his mind on the present.

As they reached the spine of the headland a huge view opened before them, but the steep fall of ground below still hid any sign of the cottage. The track turned away above a scrubby wood of hazel, birch, rowan and oak.

'Hang on, the map shows another track going down the side of the wood, more or less following the burn.' They cast about and picked up the faint trace of it. Clearly it hadn't been used for some time.

'Come on.' Jon looked increasingly forbidding, and Philippa followed him in silence. She was beginning to realise that this place meant more to him than he'd revealed, and hoped he wasn't going to be disappointed. He had little resilience these days to deal with setbacks.

As they came to the lip of the drop they were at last able to see what lay below, and Jon checked. Sheltered from the wind, the tree-clad curve of the hill at its back repeated in the shingle beach before it, the whitewashed bothy stood on a slight rise of sheep-grazed turf looking out over the loch. It was flanked on one side by two rowans and further back stood a small stone outbuilding.

Jon stood transfixed. Better than all his dreams. At his shoulder Philippa drew in a breath of delight.

'What a place,' she whispered. 'What an absolutely perfect place.'

'How to get to it is the next question,' Jon grunted, doing his best to crush down rising hope.

'Roof's on anyway,' he said, deliberately prosaic, as they reached the foot of the slope and started towards the cottage.

Philippa didn't answer. Suddenly this mattered far too much, to both of them.

The thick stone walls had withstood the gales and rain of more than a century. Most of the slates were in place, though a few were crooked, but the windows were boarded up, mortar had crumbled from the chimneys and the rones were down, half buried by grass.

Jon stalked round the simple rectangle, his face showing nothing, and Philippa let him go. She had the impression he'd forgotten she was there. When he joined her again he was silent, hope that this might after all be possible tarnished by the associations of the past.

The door gave to his shoulder and he stepped over the threshold into darkness, reaching for his torch. Litter everywhere, the derelict remnants of furniture, a rust-streaked grate with two ovens, a nose-clogging smell of damp and dirt. The floor was through in one corner; a clump of rushes grew from the wall. A ladder led to the low-ceilinged loft where they had slept.

He tested its firmness. 'I'll check the roof.'

Philippa went back to the door, where Keeper waited uneasily, and gazed and gazed at the beauty on every side, loving the contrast between this sunny, tucked-away enclave – its spring grass bright with flowers, a sheet of yellow showing where flags grew near the burn – and the open miles of loch backed by the great rugged shapes of the western hills.

To live in such a place. Could it really work? The problems would be huge, but they wouldn't be hers to cope with single-handed. After being on her own for so long she was still getting used to that.

Jon's face as he came out gave nothing away. 'We'd better check the water catchment tank. At least the burn looks pretty reliable, and coming from that height there should be no worries about pressure.'

Watching him as he studied the flow of peat-gold water, Philippa was suddenly filled with love for him, knowing he'd dreaded encountering some insuperable obstacle, and understanding how deeply he needed to establish a foothold that was his. But when he turned to her she felt tension instantly knot, in spite of knowing this wasn't her decision. In her mind, she had already taken the step, if that was what he wanted, of leaving Achallie and the life she'd established there since her marriage ended. This place was about him. Making it work would depend on his determination and skill. There would be no better thereapy, she knew, if he could do it.

'We'd have to bring everything in by boat to start with,' he said – repressively, as though she had frivolously suggested moving in today.

'Jonnie?' She found she hardly dared to breathe.

'Would you come here?' Suddenly his attention was on her, focused and uncompromising. He wasn't interested in facile raptures about hidden cottages in idyllic secret nooks; he was interested in facts. 'We'd have to work bloody hard. Roof would have to come off, every inch of wood be renewed. Power to bring in. Plumbing from scratch. Then there's the small matter of the road.'

'I know it would be—' Philippa began, but he stopped her.

'Don't say anything yet. That's mere logistics, nuts and bolts. What really matters is—' But he couldn't go on, looking away from her across the loch, finding it beyond him, now that the moment had come, to summon the words he needed, unaware of how harsh and unequivocal he looked and sounded.

Philippa's heart began a slow, heavy thumping.

He turned back to her, making a huge effort. 'Look,' he said, 'we both know I've cocked up my life and been lucky to get away with it, and even luckier, God knows, to find you. What I need now is some project I can get my teeth into, commit to. At Achallie – I don't know – half the time I feel like the damned lodger . . .'

Philippa hid her hurt. She knew there was no room in his mind to consider how that might make her feel. He was intent on the future, and that was how it should be.

'I know I could find a job,' he went on before she could speak, 'and we could buy some bog-standard house and live quite decently. But this would be something to tackle together. And it would give us a chance to be on our own, sort ourselves out a bit—' He broke off, frowning, as though he had incautiously touched on a subject he wasn't ready to cope with yet, and Philippa slipped a hand into his, not sure he wanted her to speak.

'So what do you think?' he asked after a moment, and Philippa knew that, whatever her opinion of Shionach, if she wanted a future with Jon the answer had to be positive, and unhesitating. She thought of the glimpses he'd given her of his embattled childhood, and his rootlessness after leaving the Army; she thought of the condition he'd been in when he'd rolled up at Achallie, and his bitter moods and lack of motivation since. He needed this.

'I think we could do it,' she said quietly.

He looked into her face with penetrating enquiry, and the grip he took on her hand was painful. 'Not because it's pretty and the sun's shining?' He had to be sure.

'I don't think we could find anything that would suit our needs better.' She met his eyes squarely, and she meant what she said. She heard Jon catch his breath and then was seized in a quick hard hug. 'I'll do my best for you, you know,' he promised, his cheek against hers, his voice rough with emotion. 'I'll look after you.'

For one second, the need whirling up from nowhere, she wanted him to ask her to marry him, but knew nothing would be further from his mind at this moment. In fact, it occurred to her with a slight shock, she didn't even know if he was divorced. She was going to have to jump blind; nothing else would make him believe in the trust he needed.

'I know you will,' she said gently, for whatever the words meant to him she knew he was offering all he had.

When they called at Fassfern to return the key Philippa was careful to keep a low profile. Nick and Sue Balfour of Tynach were friends of the Campbells; in fact she seemed to recall that Neil Campbell was small Neil's godfather. If Jon thought for a moment she was going to plunge into a web of friendships here, exactly like the one he'd found it so hard to tolerate in Glen Maraich, she guessed that he'd turn his back on Shionach without hesitation, no matter what it cost him.

'It was unusual to have that slice carved out of the estate in the first place,' Neil was saying to Jon, as they studied the large-scale map on the estate-room wall. 'Shionach was a tied cottage, not even a crofting tenancy, yet my grandfather made it over unconditionally to the Mackay of the day. As thanks for a lifetime's service, though one can't help wondering what he did that was so special. In those days everyone on the place was expected to give a lifetime's service. Anyway, it worked for a generation, the next lot weren't interested and the present situation you know. This is the ground that goes with it.'

Philippa came to look as he traced a rough rectangle round the bothy, one long side being the shore.

'When was it last lived in?' Jon enquired.

'Oh, years ago. Ronnie took off as soon as he left school. His father was ill at the time and died a couple of years later, and his mother moved to the village.'

'Is she still alive?' Though Jon tried to sound casual Philippa heard in his voice the fear that after all some unforeseen claim could exist.

'No, she died soon after her husband. Ronnie was the only child. It was his to leave as he chose.'

'But you'd like to have got it back?' Philippa knew Jon had no idea of how challenging he sounded.

'Well, it's always preferable to keep an estate intact,' Neil said easily. What sort of neighbour would this touchy, hard-eyed character make? The girlfriend was another matter; lovely smile, lovely voice too. Philippa Howard. Didn't that ring a bell? Celia would know. 'Anyway,' he went on, turning from the map, 'I have to confess that I was responsible for boarding up the windows and keeping the roof on. Not strictly my business, but once people find a way in word gets round, and damage can swiftly result.'

'Good thing you did,' Jon said heartily, and Philippa hid a smile, having seen the expression which had crossed his face at the idea of anyone interfering with his property.

'What does the name mean?' she asked Neil, as they settled by the fire for tea.

'The field of the foxes, though the Gaelic's been rounded down a bit.'

'I like that,' she said.

Jon made no comment, but he liked it too. It felt oddly special to own a place whose name meant something, though he couldn't have put the feeling into words.

The news went down badly back in Glen Maraich.

'Obviously neither of you will rest till you've thrown over everything and everyone for each other,' was Julie's tart comment, while Michael begged, 'For heaven's sake, Pippa, don't sink every penny you've got into this. At least hang on to Achallie until you see how things work out.'

Philippa knew that by 'things' he didn't mean the work of renovation.

Max Munro, now married and viewing matters from that standpoint, was even more outspoken. 'Has he said how he proposes to make enough to support you both in that forsaken spot? No, I thought not. Well, my advice is, don't open a joint account. I mean it.'

Penny, who, on seeing Jon's changed appearance, had forgotten about being offended over not being told he was back, was more concerned by the absence of that glowing happiness in Philippa which had seemed to justify the relationship when Jon was here before. She too felt it would be sensible to hold on to Achallie.

'Can't you get someone to oversee the work, and go back and forth till it's finished? It doesn't seem a good idea to cut yourself off altogether.' She longed to ask if they were planning to marry, feeling she would be happier with some evidence of commitment on Jon's part.

To these concerned enquiries, and others, Philippa replied with an airiness bordering on prevarication. She didn't reveal that Shionach wouldn't be habitable for months, that Jon took it for granted she would sell Achallie or that marriage had never been mentioned. She was more preoccupied with other aspects of their future, which she could discuss with no one.

Jon gave no sign of understanding what this tearing apart of her life meant to her, and that could make her feel frighteningly alone. More importantly, they had still not recaptured the magic of their physical relationship, and sometimes dread would seize her that they never would. To launch into a new life together, in a place so primitive and isolated, with a problem so fundamental unresolved between them, would sometimes seem such madness that she could hardly believe she had agreed to it.

But whenever she reached the point of telling Jon that she'd changed her mind and couldn't go through with the plan, the thought of what it would do to him brought her up short. It was becoming increasingly clear to her that changing her mind wasn't an option.

29

Philippa wished she had said goodbye to Achallie when it was still untouched, possessions still in place, its peace undisturbed. Wandering through the stripped rooms, while Jon stuffed last oddments into the Shogun, which now replaced the two cars, she already felt a stranger in this little house she'd loved so much. Memories of the happiness once shared here with Jon had been overtaken by the uncertainties of the present. The only sure thing was that Jon took for granted a future together. It had to compensate for the absence of all reassurance, spoken or physical. Being desired does boost one's confidence, Philippa thought wistfully, standing at an upstairs window for a last look at the familiar view.

Then she turned to look at the big, hideous bed behind her, glad it was a fixture and not being stored with the rest of the furniture. Would new surroundings really make love-making good again? She knew Jon believed so. She found it hard to help him, afraid sympathy and consoling words would only underline his inability to perform. Hampered by her natural reticence, she did all she could to show she loved him, but felt she had failed him every time he turned from her in silent despair.

Accepting, painful as it was, that Achallie no longer meant anything to him, and glad for his sake that he now had a definite goal, she backed every decision regarding Shionach, hiding regrets and ignoring the concern she met on every side.

'Aye, well,' Ian Murray said heavily, when she told him she was leaving, 'that was to be expected, I suppose.' Grudging indeed after all her conscientious work. But he gave her one of the cashmere sweaters he sold in the hotel, a gift Jon could have no part in, accompanying it with a hard wordless embrace which told her he cared about what happened to her and made up for his disapproval.

Lady Hay said goodbye with a loving anxiety which dangerously threatened Philippa's self-control. 'We're all here, darling Pippa. You won't forget, will you?' It said very little for the trust they put in Jon.

When Penny and Andrew, finally understanding that she felt she must make an irreversible break with her present life for Jon's sake, saw that they weren't going to persuade her to keep Achallie, it was they, ironically enough, who found a buyer, a friend wanting a holiday cottage. It wasn't the fate Philippa would have chosen for it, but a private sale would be quick and that was what counted to Jon.

People less close to Philippa trotted out well-intentioned comments: 'Oh, the West Coast's beautiful, I'd love to live there myself . . . So rewarding, doing up an old property . . . It's no distance, you'll be able to come back often, and we'll all come over to visit.'

Only Julie and Michael had no truck with any of this. They said, 'You're right, love, all or nothing,' and, even more helpfully, 'Leave your things here till you're ready for them. We're hardly short of space.'

Jon accepted this offer because it came from them, but rejected Philippa's suggestion of asking an architect friend of hers for advice about planning permission and building warrants.

'I can sort the bumf out for myself,' he said tersely. 'Shouldn't be a problem anyway. It's an existing habitation. We don't need favours from your friends, thanks.'

Philippa didn't argue. Doing things his way was something he vitally needed at present.

She wasn't aware, pausing in the sitting-room doorway for a last look, that Jon, knowing how she must be feeling, had come in to find her then changed his mind and gone quietly out again, deciding it would be better after all not to butt in on her farewells. How grateful she would have been for any sign that he knew this was a bad moment for her. Her face was set as she turned her back on the empty room, went through the kitchen without a glance, locked the door behind her and pushed the key under the mat for Penny to pick up.

Jon, leaning against the jeep, took care to appear relaxed. She mustn't feel he was hurrying her. No tears, he saw, but then tears were rare for Philippa.

'Want a last look round the garden?' he called.

Philippa shook her head. The garden, after her hard work and the contented hours she'd spent in it, was almost harder to leave than the house.

She opened the jeep door. 'Better be on our way. Help, there are always more last-minute things than you think, aren't there? Poor Keeper can hardly move.'

'He'll be fine.' Jon didn't altogether care for the cheerful tone. He wanted to tell her to take as much time as she liked, this was a big wrench for her, but clinging to control was the way Philippa dealt with things and, though he wasn't happy, wanting to help her through the moment in any way he could, he let it go.

I've kept him waiting, Philippa thought guiltily, seeing his frown. He can't wait to get away. She pushed down apprehension at the prospect of driving off with him in this mood, into a future so deeply uncertain.

They had considered various ideas about where to live while they worked on Shionach – renting a cottage or caravan perhaps, or opting for bed and breakfast accommodation in

Drishaig. In the end they'd decided to camp in the byre till the house was habitable. If this proved too uncomfortable – or the midges drove them out – they could find some other alternative.

Jon had already spent a couple of days at Shionach, buying a boat, taking round basic materials and enlisting the help of one of the local men to make the byre weather-proof. He had also made some further arrangements of his own, which he hadn't mentioned to Philippa, and as the big vehicle, crammed as it was, made easy work of the steep pass above Bridge of Riach, his mind ran over them again.

Though he knew he was pinning an absurd degree of hope on their power to make her feel looked after and loved, he let himself hope that, when she saw the trouble he'd taken, Philippa would turn to him with all her old generous warmth, and he would find himself miraculously able to perform the one act which increasingly obsessed him. Not that he put it in quite those terms.

Philippa snatched last glimpses of the glen as they crossed the pass. There was Alltmore down on their left, a flash of sunlight catching the loch; and high to the right the new outline of Allt Farr, redesigned and partly rebuilt after last year's disastrous fire. It might have comforted her to know that Grannie's comment, on hearing the news that she was off to start a new life with Jon on the West Coast, had been a hearty, 'Good for her!'

She wished she could share the moment, so significant for her, with Jon. But his face was grim, his attention clearly elsewhere, and she said nothing.

Coming to Shionach for the first time by water she was thrilled all over again by its perfection, unaware of what her pleasure meant to Jon. He himself had never been prey to such nervous tension in his life, and was glad to have to concentrate on handling the laden boat. Philippa was impressed by his skill as they rounded the point against the powerful currents, and he brought them nosing neatly in to their own small beach.

'The overland route for me though, I think, if you're not there,' she remarked as she stepped ashore.

'Too right,' he said emphatically. 'I wouldn't dream of letting you out in the boat on your own.'

She registered his tone with a lift of her brows, but didn't really mind. It seemed natural that Jon should make a ruling on such a point.

She was totally unprepared for what she found in the byre. He had glazed the windows, put up shelves and hooks, brought over the gas cooker from the house and added a folding table, chairs and a thick Dunlopillo mattress which Keeper regarded with pleased interest.

'Don't even think about it, dog. So, what do you say?' Jon found a novel mixture of exuberance and trepidation filling him. 'We can run water across, and when I pull out the kitchen cupboards I can fit a couple in here.' He tried to sound matter-of-fact, but was watching her face with an eagerness he couldn't hide.

'Jonnie, it's amazing. I had no idea you were doing all this when you came over. We'll hardly be camping, it's a palace! You are good to take so much trouble.' She turned into his arms with a readiness she had rarely shown since his return and Jon, relief nearly suffocating him, whirled her up in a boisterous hug.

It's going to work, he thought elatedly as Keeper barked and leapt round them. We'll make a go of it. Philippa had left home, friends, everything, for him. She could look at this primitive little dwelling and be over the moon about it. He had never loved her so much.

Optimism filled them as they emptied the boat, were swept down the loch for a second load, and spent a couple of hours unpacking and disposing of what they'd brought. In a symbolic gesture, Jon wrenched the boards off the bothy windows to start their first fire, and they had supper beside it in the lingering light of early summer, its smoke keeping the midges at bay.

But when they rolled wearily onto the comfortable mattress the longed-for solution to their problem didn't follow. For Jon it mattered too much. He was too conscious of his own body, forgetting what he used to understand so well, that Philippa would need patience and tenderness. She wanted to plead with him for time, for words. She tried not to send signals of withdrawal, but in spite of herself her head turned from his hungry mouth, and Jon read the movement with despair, as he read the resistant dryness of her body about which she could do nothing.

He drew roughly away from her, in bitter anger and frustration, though the anger was with himself. Philippa couldn't know that and, though longing to comfort him, was afraid it would only add to his humiliation. It must be so much worse for him than it is for me, she told herself.

She hates me touching her, Jon thought helplessly. Why did I imagine everything would be all right here? What difference can it make where we are? Why have we committed ourselves to this? How can we get out of it now?

They lay still, apart, two people for whom everything in the world was unimportant except each other.

Next morning work began. The first job was to strip from the house anything which could be used to fit out the byre, which they soon considered they had brought to a high degree of comfort. Gutting the house came next, and endless trips to Drishaig and Fort William for materials, but as they began stripping the roof the worst weather they'd had since they came broke upon them. Jon wasn't fit to live with in his furious impatience, and Keeper found himself taken for many long wet walks by Philippa.

Though few people could have been more skilled than Jon in making the best of the conditions under which they lived, discomfort was inevitable. All food had to be kept in containers, mildew grew overnight, every garment they possessed was damp, while their mattress acquired a strange smell which added another element to Philippa's reluctance to go to bed. Huge waves thundered up the shingle and, though the house had been built well out of their reach, fetching and carrying was for the time being impossible, and Jon snarled and paced like a trapped animal.

Philippa, as much to get away from him as anything, finding confinement and inactivity harder to take than any physical discomfort, set out one day to take a rucksackful of washing to the Drishaig laundrette. It was a hard slog up the streaming track, and the wind met her with more force than she'd anticipated as she crossed the ridge, but with a bedraggled Keeper at her heels she reached the Shogun at last, thankful to be blasted warm, if not dry, by its efficient heater.

Parking at the end of the bay road on her return, she shivered at the prospect of leaving it. The rain and wind were still relentless, and she now had shopping to carry as well as washing. But she knew neither was the true source of her reluctance. She dreaded being cooped up once more with Jon in his present mood, knowing she was unable to help him. Hugging Keeper for comfort, she wondered miserably how things had come to this point.

Hearing a vehicle behind her, she glanced in her mirror to see a Range Rover turn into the Fassfern drive, then stop. Its driver got out, pulling up her Barbour hood over straggling fair hair, and ran back.

She didn't waste time on introductions. 'Come up to the

house,' she shouted as Philippa lowered her window. 'This weather's too ghastly for anything.'

The directness, the smile, the accent, added up to a comfortingly familiar message.

'Thanks, I will,' Philippa said, and the girl nodded and turned to hop long-legged across the puddles.

In the small sitting-room which Celia found the easiest place to keep warm at Fassfern, ordinary life engulfed Philippa with treacherous ease. The fire was lit, rain drummed against the windows, and the two liver-coloured pointers officiously checking out Keeper were called to order by five-year-old Tanera, one of whose socks had come off with her gumboot, and who was wearing scarlet dungarees with a tartan patch on the bottom and a nappy pin fastening one strap.

'Tanera, you won't mind if we move some of this, will you?' Celia asked courteously, reaching over a scatter of lively artwork to wake the slumbering fire. 'I often think of you over at Shionach,' she went on to Philippa. 'It must be a bit grim in this weather.'

'A bit,' Philippa conceded. 'Idyllic up to now.'

'Well, I'd been envying you too, I have to admit. No housekeeping. Bliss. Now, that's a respectable fire. Why don't we make toast? Who cares that it's supposed to be summer. You'd like that, wouldn't you, Tan?'

'So would the dogs,' Tanera warned, putting her felt pens in their wallet in the order she preferred.

'You know Sue and Nick Balfour, don't you?' Celia asked, as she held the first slice of bread to the fire on an elegant toasting fork with blackened prongs. At once the links were there, not only with the Balfours, but with Gilly Mainwaring, a member of the ubiquitous Hay clan who lived near Oban, and other friends and acquaintances. 'You must come to dinner soon so that I can meet Jon, and we'll catch up properly. I know you won't have clothes or anything, but I hardly ever have that kind of dinner party nowadays anyway. Wastes far too much time.'

Jon, Philippa knew, would dislike Celia on sight, resenting her undiluted upper-class voice and unselfconscious assurance. He didn't know what he was missing, she thought, wading into toast and home-made raspberry jam, chocolate cake and smoky Lapsang.

When Tanera returned to her drawing after tea, Celia noticed that she was using the back of a seven-day warning from a well-known agricultural supplier.

'Darling, I don't think that's such a good idea. You're drawing on one of Daddy's bills.'

'It's all right, he doesn't want it,' Tanera said. 'He threw it on the floor and said, "Bloody people".'

'Well, you've certainly made it look more cheerful,' Celia remarked, smoothing it out.

Jon wouldn't have laughed at that either, Philippa reflected, relaxing an hour later in the sybaritic luxury of a hot bath. She knew she was being unfair, but she felt back in her own world in this house, and especially in this big, splendid bathroom with its Victorian fittings, high ceiling and flower-painted loo, and it made her for the moment less sympathetic towards him.

Fighting her way home against the gusting wind, she knew she had also luxuriated in being with the people who belonged in that world. Then the image of Jon caught at her, Jon alone in the bothy, burning to get on with this project on which he'd pinned all his hopes, charged with energy which had nowhere to go. She was overcome by shame at her disloyalty. She didn't want to be anywhere else; or with anyone else.

If only she had said so. If only she had gone in on that wave of conviction and love and told Jon what she felt. But when at last she reached the byre he pointedly grabbed at the plans he was working on by the white glare of the Tilley, as she struggled to close the door against the wind, and demanded angrily, 'Where in God's name have you been till this hour?'

The moment was lost.

30

Philippa was much missed in Glen Maraich. Her friends found it very hard to come to terms with the fact that she had gone for good. Quite apart from being deprived of her company, and of the undeniable asset of having someone on hand who wasn't tied to the needs of a husband and children, few were convinced that she was going to be happy. It was only too easy to make the comparison with her marriage to Richard, though in many ways that had been easier to understand. Then she had been adrift; there had been nothing left for her here. This time she had wrenched apart a life that had appeared to satisfy her, sold the house which had given her so much pleasure, and gave every appearance of having gone beyond their reach.

This was the true source of concern. Though barely three hours' drive away, there was a general feeling that she had become inaccessible, and this was not merely because there was no telephone link or because, in her present circumstances, letter writing didn't come high on Philippa's agenda. It had to do with Jon. In most cases, she hadn't let her friends see enough of him, or of Jon and herself together, to give them much to reassure them. Her loneliness had been well concealed during his absence, and since his return there had been a disturbing withdrawal from contact, and an even more disturbing air of tension and reserve in Philippa when they did see her. Nor was there much to comfort anyone in the shreds of news which reached them via Celia Campbell and Sue Balfour about her present situation.

'All most unsatisfactory,' Lady Hay was more than once heard to pronounce, and this pretty well summed up the general view.

Philippa herself scarcely had time, or didn't give herself time, to dwell on the pangs of homesickness which occasionally assailed her. She had made her decision. It was easier to let work absorb energy, time and attention, making it a substitute for everything else. At this time of year it was light enough to go on late into the evening, and that was what Jon did, collapsing to sleep unmoving for a few hours, starting again as soon as he woke.

Philippa had taken it for granted that the essence of this new life would be tackling jobs together, as they had enjoyed doing in the past, but Jon, gnawed by a private urgency he could hardly have defined, had little patience these days with the level of help she could give. Instead he seemed increasingly to regard the whole enterprise as a personal battle of his own.

He was fast recovering his strength, and Philippa too was fit and trim. She couldn't guess at the helpless longing which the sight of her tanned, streamlined body roused in Jon, who was by now convinced that she had lost all interest in him sexually. Because, to her, it seemed hardly fair to show that she wanted him when he couldn't satisfy her, she was careful never to let him see the misery it was to lie close to his big, warm, powerful body night after night, and not be able to cuddle up against him and feel his arms go round her.

The strain produced by this state of impasse led inevitably to clashes, most of which were based on nothing. Doug McDonnell from Drishaig, who had helped Jon with the original work on the byre, put in the odd day's labouring

for them. He was casual about time and liked to do things
at his own pace, but he was a useful worker, always good-
humoured, and Philippa liked him. One evening he asked
if she'd like to go mackerel fishing with him and, glad to
supplement their diet, she accepted with pleasure. She was
shaken to be met by real anger from Jon when she got back,
and found it hard to accept the obvious explanation – that he
was jealous.

She was forced to believe it when he reacted in similar
fashion (he never gave Doug another day's work) to the
student he'd taken on to help with the roof. This time his
anger flared when, returning from a trip to Fort William to
collect an order for pipes and joints which had turned out
to be only half complete, he had found Philippa up on the
roof with Calum, chatting peacefully in the sunshine as they
worked, and wearing, as she often did in fine weather, bikini
top and shorts.

Jon shouted at her to come down and disappeared into the
byre so that she was obliged to follow him.

'What's wrong?'

A presumably unsatisfactory trip to town hardly seemed to
justify his hectoring manner as he demanded, 'What the hell
do you think you're playing at?'

'What do you mean?' She was baffled.

'What are you doing up there with Calum? I should have
thought you'd have had more sense.'

He thought she'd fall off the roof? Then Philippa remembered the episode with Doug. She also remembered that
Calum was within earshot. Saying nothing, she turned to
reach down a shirt and put it on.

Jon watched her, the muscles ridged in his jaw. He longed
to push her into open confrontation, but faced with this calm
compliance his anger had nowhere to go. If Philippa had
refused to let him get away with it he could have enjoyed

the release of one huge cathartic row. If that upset her he could have got hold of her and comforted her as he was so desperate to do. But Philippa, having done up the shirt buttons with fumbling fingers, only paused in polite enquiry to see if there was anything more he wished to say, then went past him, out of the door and back to work.

Calum kept his head down. The only sound was the crack and crash of the timber Jon set about sorting.

As Philippa had foreseen, he also had problems with her friendship with Celia Campbell, but in this case did have the sense to realise that, wherever they went in Scotland, they would run into the same scenario. Also he found Neil straightforward to deal with, and helpful about any work which affected the estate. That was a bonus too valuable to jeopardise.

Ordinary social contact with Fassfern never materialised, however, and Philippa knew it must wait till Jon felt more secure. For the same reason she refrained from asking her friends to visit, much as she was longing to see them by now. But, in spite of the growing tension with Jon, there was plenty to enjoy. Asking herself, as she sometimes did, whether given the chance she would want to be back at Achallie, her life unchanged, the answer was always an emphatic and reassuring no. One important factor was their surroundings. There could be no lovelier place to spend a summer, and the drawback they had anticipated, the scourge of the midges, had scarcely proved a problem. Philippa had never been troubled by them, and Jon also turned out to be one of the lucky people who didn't particularly attract them. Both cottage and byre stood well back from the water, high enough to catch any breeze there was, and the evening cooking fire was always a useful deterrent.

Also on a practical level, meeting no insuperable snags and reasonably confident of having the roof on before the autumn gales arrived, Jon's mood became less driven. A turning point was the blasting of the road, a job to delight the heart of any Sapper, and Philippa didn't need Neil's approving comments to realise how expertly Jon had accomplished it. Being able to drive in would remove many of the difficulties of day-to-day living and speed up progress on the house, but the roar of the detonations, the racket of the JCB, the raw patches of new metalling and the clearing of a turning place beside the house dispelled forever Shionach's enchanted solitude. Philippa, careful to give no hint of minding this, would have been surprised, and comforted, to learn that Jon felt exactly as she did.

The improvements to the track brought the move into the house a giant step closer. And then what? Neither was sure any longer how the other felt about it. Would they sell and move on, reclaiming some other semi-derelict dwelling, as they had once talked of doing as a means of living? Or would they make this their home, with Jon finding work locally? His reputation as 'a good man with his hands' was established and, though he was reckoned a chancy character, Philippa's friendly warmth adequately redressed the balance.

What secretly worried the latter, however, was that the image of finally moving into their own house had, during these demanding and uneasy months, become less alluring. It was hard not to picture the two of them as shut in there, goal achieved, occupation gone, the tension between them impossible to ignore.

Another worrying aspect was finding herself inescapably edged into the supporting female role. She tried to be reasonable about it, telling herself that now Jon was involved in the technical stuff like plumbing and wiring it made sense for her to do the running about, chase up orders, deal with suppliers and paperwork, keep the domestic side going. But it wasn't how things had been; it wasn't what she'd looked forward to.

Worst of all, accentuating this divergence of roles, was Jon's new habit of calling in at the Drishaig Inn whenever he passed. At first he went in search of contacts – like the quarryman who had supplied the explosives for the road – but it swiftly became a refuge from a situation he knew he had created but didn't know how to put right. He spent more time agonising over it than Philippa ever guessed.

He was still astounded by, and grateful for, the total commitment she had given him, and the way she had voiced none of the misgivings she must have felt, working without complaint harder than he would have believed any woman capable of. Even so, they were further apart than they had ever been. Underlying everything else was his sexual need for her, and he wasn't sure whether, with this crucial issue unresolved, he could go on living with her. Yet without her there was nothing worth living for.

They moved into Shionach on a grey autumn day, ahead of schedule, and the long-anticipated moment was quite meaningless. Almost in silence, each wondering bleakly where they went from here, they set up an arrangement similar to the one they'd had in the byre. The open-plan living space downstairs, with its fire, gave them all the space they needed. The empty rooms upstairs felt as remote as when they had yawned roofless. It would make a statement neither Jon nor Philippa was ready for to propose any alternative to sharing the (by now familiar and undeniably comfortable) mattress, newly laid out in warm, dry surroundings.

The sensation of being trapped grew with alarming speed, intensified by the evenings drawing in and winter looming. Though there was plenty of interior work to be done it hadn't reached the finishing stage, and there was little Philippa could help with, or Jon would let her help with, and she felt depressingly redundant.

In the evenings Jon, taking the Shogun, would disappear to Drishaig, staying later and later. This is where we came in, Philippa would think, remembering the watchful figure hunched at the bar at the Cluny Arms. This was Jon's life. The sharing and involvement of that first summer at Achallie had been nothing more than a temporary flirting with a different way of doing things.

While the undemanding hours in the Drishaig Inn became Jon's refuge from a situation he couldn't handle, Philippa turned to long walks with Keeper and endless reading, grateful for a supply of Fassfern books. She didn't grasp that Jon, seeing her so peacefully absorbed, curled up with Keeper in front of the fire, felt as superfluous as she did when he was busy on some job she couldn't share. This was how she had lived at Achallie, self-sufficient and at peace, before he came on the scene. This was how she'd lived while he was away.

They had one chance to break down the barriers. On a stormy afternoon Philippa went to Fort William to fetch the sink unit, in at last after endless delays. Things didn't go well. The plumber's yard, supposedly closed for lunch, remained obdurately locked until after three, and instead of cutting her losses and shopping, she made the mistake of waiting. When the plumber turned up it was found that the wrong unit had been delivered.

'Well, well, that's no' very clever,' was all he offered by way of apology.

All right, so it was the wholesaler's fault, but it would be nice to think, Philippa reflected wryly as she set off for home after racing through her list, that Jon would also remember that.

More immediate concerns soon took over, however, as even in the sturdy jeep the growing strength of the wind was making itself felt, and before she was halfway back sluicing rain began which the wipers could hardly cope with. Crawling at last round Drishaig Bay, she found giant breakers pounding to the top of the beach and hurling spray across the road. At the hill gate she pulled up in doubt, not sure she should attempt to cross the headland. Or was she being seduced by thoughts of warmth and comfort at Fassfern, and Celia's ready welcome? Besides, Jon would hardly be impressed if she left him stranded without a vehicle.

Going to open the gate, she was startled to find it snatched out of her hands by the wind and slammed back against the dyke. It hardly seemed possible that a few bars of wood could offer such resistance. Good thing the driver's door was on the lee side.

She made it, slowly and cautiously, over the ridge, though with a couple of ominous lurches in violent gusts on the slick, exposed slabs of its spine, and was drawing a breath of relief that the worst was over when disaster struck. For one second she lost sight of the track and couldn't remember which bend she was on. The steering wheel twisted out of her hands as the off-side sank into soft bog. The wind did the rest. The Shogun seemed to tip in slow motion, then it was over, in a blur of crashing sound and jolting pain.

Thank goodness I didn't bring Keeper, was Philippa's last thought. But she was out for no more than a couple of seconds, returning to dazed consciousness to find herself hanging in her seat belt, her face sticky with what she didn't realise was blood, her body aching all over, the lights out and the only sounds the screaming of the wind and the drumming of rain. Her first coherent thought was, oh God, what will Jon say? Her second, more usefully, was, what would Jon do if he were here?

She found the ignition and switched off, dislodging tins and packages as she moved. A square of grey light above her looked as distant as a ceiling. Somehow she would have to haul herself up there and crawl out. It took struggling seconds to free herself from her seat belt and locate the torch, which blessedly was still working. Pushing it, with some trouble, into her pocket to leave her hands free, she began the laborious climb.

As she heaved the door up a couple of inches the problem of getting it open was solved as the wind whipped it from her hands. If only it didn't blow back the other way, slamming on her head. The Shogun swayed alarmingly as she moved and she checked in terror, crouching on the sill. But she couldn't stay here all night. She'd have to jump, out not down, and hope there were no rocks waiting. The squelching bog was as welcome as a feather bed, and no mass of metal came toppling down to crush her into it.

It wasn't the last time she was to end up on her face in peaty slime. The wind tore at her as though she was made of straw, more than once lifting her off her feet, but as she reached the wood there was more protection, and she knew she was going to make it. It was only as she stumbled thankfully across the level ground, the lighted window of the house beckoning ahead, that she remembered once more how furious Jon was going to be.

Her first words, as he leapt up at the sight of her, were, 'Sorry, Jonnie, I've ditched the jeep. I know you'll be livid.'

'Philippa, for God's sake!' She looked appalling, her clothes soaked and filthy, hair flattened to her skull, the blood which the rain had checked beginning to flow again. 'Whatever happened?'

'I didn't just ditch it, actually,' she said, her mind still fixed on what she thought would concern him most. 'I turned it over. I really am sorry.'

'Forget the jeep. What about you?' He had her by the shoulders, examining her face with sharp anxiety. 'Come to the fire, let's have a look at you.'

Keeper circled round them, whining quietly, nudging against Philippa. Jon kneed him away.

'Lucky it was mostly wrapped-up shopping,' Philippa said, beginning to giggle weakly. 'No eggs. It all landed on top of me and—'

'Into the hysteria phase, I see.' Jon's voice might be carefully ironic, but his hands were far from steady as he gently lifted away the sodden hair to discover the extent of the damage. 'What a sight you are, woman.'

Shivering more now from delayed shock than cold, Philippa stood obediently, chin up and eyes closed, as he examined the gash, deciding with relief that it was superficial. She hadn't noticed, he was sure, that he was in boots and jacket, having already been out twice to look for her. Nor did he think her capable of making any comparison with those long-ago incidents when she had rolled the Mini in the snow, or fallen off her shed roof and gashed her arm so badly. But both those occasions, and how he had felt, were very much in his mind, and it seemed natural to revert to the footing of those times. Philippa appeared to accept that too, acquiescent as he briskly stripped off her clothes, cleaned and patched her up, chivvied her into bed and brought food, encouraging her, as he had done before, to talk out the dramas of the storm, of the slow-motion seconds as the jeep turned over, and the blind, buffeted struggle to get home.

Jon couldn't help remembering too the readiness with which she'd accepted his presence and his help on the bright sunlit day of her earlier crash. It had been, really, the beginning of everything. If only, now, that trust could be re-established.

His positive mood nose-dived briefly when he heard about the sink but Philippa, scrubbed and wholesome as a child, stuck about with elastoplast, was immune from his wrath tonight. Once he was beside her in bed, however, gathering her up gingerly, mindful of the bumps and bruises, it was she who wrecked things. To her, the renewed intimacy and tenderness between them seemed to offer a chance to get their problems into the open, and to summon the courage at last to explain that whether or not Jon could make love to her didn't change her feelings for him. What she said was, too fuddled by the after-effects of shock to think about how it would sound to him, 'Jonnie, look, about making love. It doesn't matter, you know. I really don't mind about it . . .'

Jon froze. Exactly as he had feared, it made no difference to her that he never touched her now. The passionate response of their early days, the marvellous, total relinquishment of self which he'd never known in a woman before, were lost for good. Very carefully, as though she were already asleep, he took his arms away from her and lay back.

Philippa curled her aching desolate body into a ball. As the tears oozed from tight-shut lids, she wished she could creep away and share Keeper's beanbag.

Next morning Neil Campbell was already surveying the overturned Shogun when Jon arrived on the scene. The roof had grazed down a jagged rock, inches from where Philippa's head had been. Jon took one look and his face went green. He turned and walked away, to stand for a few moments with his head up to the wind. When he came back both men were strictly business-like about the technicalities of recovery.

Telling Celia about the incident later, Neil added, 'He adores her, you know.'

'I do know,' Celia replied sadly. 'And she adores him. But somewhere, somehow, they've lost the way.'

'But do you think, honestly, that he's right for her?' Neil, in common with the other males of Philippa's acquaintance, tended to feel protective about her, more inclined to respond to her warm smile and natural courtesy of manner than the resolute, tough-fibred side of her.

'Right or wrong, he's the only one,' Celia said with certainty. 'But there's a great deal more to him than good looks and bad temper, you know.'

'I'll take your word for it.' But, evaluating Jon on merit, and taking Philippa for the moment out of the equation, Neil knew she was right. There were many qualities in Jon which he could only admire. That still didn't make the Shionach set-up reassuring, however.

31

Celia's thoughts were often on the small dwelling across the headland, and its occupants, during these weeks. Not only did a spell of vile weather set in, when for days on end the windows of Fassfern framed nothing but veils of rain sweeping down the loch in relentless sequence, making her wonder what on earth Jon and Philippa could find to do in their isolation, but the news she had of them was not reassuring. At least they had electricity in now, giving some degree of comfort, but she knew all was far from well between them and wondered, as other friends did, what would happen now the main work was finished.

The development that most worried both Neil and herself, on Philippa's account – though they reminded themselves and each other that it was none of their business – was the amount of time Jon had begun to spend not only at the Drishaig Inn, but at another haunt he'd found a couple of miles down the loch, a motel whose bar was open all day. Though Philippa had only once referred to Jon's drinking as a problem early in the relationship, it wasn't hard to imagine how difficult this must be for her to handle, or how many lonely hours she would have to get through. But invitations to lunch, to dinner, to stay overnight, were invariably refused, though sometimes Philippa would look in on her own. Even then, she was reticent about anything touching on her and Jon's private affairs, and always had one eye on the clock, never quite relaxing. Both Neil and Celia observed increasing signs of strain in her, but knew that it would be useless to expect to help her by eliciting confidences. And both had a good idea of how deeply unwelcome interference in any form would be to Jon.

'It would take a braver man than me to put an oar in there,' Neil said flatly. 'And it would hardly help Philippa if Jon decided as a result to up sticks and take off somewhere else.'

Jon wasn't in fact drinking much; that wasn't what his absences were about. But when Philippa realised, appalled, that she was beginning to welcome them, she knew they couldn't go on living like this. As she saw it, she had failed him. She had had the chance to bring out the good qualities she was convinced he possessed, not by changing him – she didn't want that and was too realistic to suppose it could ever happen anyway – but by giving him the sort of security he'd never had, the security of trust. It didn't matter if others didn't see what she saw in him; to her he still had a compelling attraction, waking responses no one else had so much as stirred. Now, however, he no longer appeared to need her. She had to accept that what she could give wasn't enough.

On a day when at last the mist rolled up like a blind and a draggled sun showed its almost forgotten face, she abandoned work and took Keeper out before it could vanish again. Following the ridge to the summit, turning to look over the expanse of the sea-lochs and islands of the west, she felt liberated, intoxicated by a beauty hardly glimpsed for weeks. It seemed ridiculous, in this mood, that she and Jon couldn't find a solution to their problems, and she turned for home filled with fresh determination to try to put things right.

She walked into a cauldron of anger. Jon hadn't been able to find the Shogun keys. The first thing Philippa saw as she came in was her bag tipped out on the table.

'Where the hell have you been?' Jon demanded the moment he saw her. 'And where are the keys? You know I'm fetching the paint today. Christ knows, we've been waiting for it long enough.'

Indignation was replaced by guilt as Philippa felt hastily in her pocket. 'Sorry, Jonnie, I've got them.'

He wasn't mollified. 'Going off walking whenever it suits you. There's still work to be done, you know.'

That was hardly fair; anyway, these weren't the only keys. 'Isn't the spare set on the hook?'

'Do you think I'd be standing here if it was?'

'But didn't you have them when you were towing that driftwood up the beach?' When he'd mislaid the others, which Philippa had later discovered in his jeans when she came to wash them. 'You were wearing your combat jacket.' She turned to where it hung behind the door and found the keys at once. She held them out, a lift of her brows suggesting that perhaps it was time he calmed down and apologised.

That cool look brought Jon, as unexpectedly for him as for Philippa, to flashpoint. Like her, he had come very close recently to accepting that things weren't going to work out between them, and the pain of it had gnawed at him. Now, rage seethed up and over. How could she always be so damned imperturbable? Without conscious decision, driven by the despairing conviction that matters were beyond him to retrieve, his hand came up and he delivered a stinging slap to that polite, contained face. The blow caught Philippa totally unawares and, though it wasn't particularly hard, it sent her reeling back.

Jon never forgot that moment, or the shock and disbelief in her eyes. But even in his horror at what he'd done the thought was there – surely now she would react? Surely this would trigger some outburst which would resolve the impasse between them?

He should have known her better. All Philippa's reserves of courage and self-discipline came to her aid. It didn't occur to her to be afraid, and she met his eyes with that impermeable control still in place.

He couldn't believe it. She must be angry, weep, storm, at least admit he'd hurt her. But she only gazed at him, not even raising a hand to her cheek, refusing to be intimidated. She knew the blow had been involuntary; she had seen in Jon's eyes his instant dismay at what he'd done. What she wanted was for him to get hold of her, swear he'd never meant to do that, break the deadlock which was destroying them.

Instead, defeated, Jon stared at her for a taut moment then flung round and went out. As Philippa heard the Shogun's engine roar into life, she sank trembling onto the nearest chair, and Keeper, who had slunk off to his beanbag as waves of anger rocked the room, came to push his head against her, whining quietly in distress. She clutched at him gratefully, leaning down to bury her face in his warm ruff for comfort.

'That's it,' she said to him, in a voice intended to be firm, but which sounded very tremulous in the silent house. 'We talk. We sort this out. No more dodging.'

Jon's anger over something so trivial had to be a symptom of a frustration and unhappiness as deep as her own. How could they have let things come to this?

Jon couldn't think about what he'd done, and what it must surely bring about. He drove straight to the motel at Lower Drishaig. Later he could remember little of the hours during which he drank alone, though he knew that later the bar had filled with familiar faces (for the first darts match of the winter league), and there had been music, singing, dancing. Had he danced? Certainly he had gone out, when the bar finally closed, to continue the party in one of the staff chalets. There had been a giggling crush of bodies on the narrow bunks;

there had been Pam the receptionist snuggling up against him; and there had been shadowy, distasteful reminders of the past to mock him.

He did know the next morning, having somehow got himself and the jeep safely over the headland, that not only was his head coming apart but his whole world. He had hit Philippa – that had to be put right, urgently, before anything else. But, faced by the courteous normality with which she was behaving, it was hard to find the words. At least she had the sense not to cook any breakfast for him, let alone embark on a discussion of anything more meaningful than whether or not he wanted toast. He watched her covertly as she gathered up the clothes he'd been wearing last night, and didn't know whether to be frustrated or thankful when she said she was going to the village and asked if he needed anything.

Receiving in reply no more than a curt shake of the head which produced in turn a wincing frown, Philippa left the house with relief. Her pretence of equanimity hadn't been easy to maintain. It had been after four when Jon came blundering in, and the hours since had been sleepless and miserable. She looked round for Keeper, but he was making his morning circuit of the bay. In her mirror she saw him lift his head when he heard the Shogun start, and come racing after it, but she didn't pause, needing urgently to be on the move.

In the shop Jockie was busy with a delivery, and impatience briefly surged up. But in truth she was in no hurry. Time spent here was time away from the tensions of Shionach; how sad to see it like that. When Jockie called to say that a box of books had come in yesterday if she wanted to look through them, she was glad of the excuse to linger. The box was on the floor behind the wobbly rack which knocked things off neighbouring shelves if you attempted to turn it. She was down on her knees sifting through mainly fantasy, sci-fi and Catherine Cookson when two women came in talking.

'That Jon Paulett from Shionach, you mean?'

'Aye, him, and he was well away last night, so Jim was saying. Him and Pate would have seen him home, the state he was in, but he wasn't having any of it.'

'Maybe he wasna for going home?'

'How do you mean?'

'He'd have been happy enough staying where he was, likely, the way he's been carrying on with yon Pam.'

'The lassie that works at the motel? Never.'

'It's been going on for weeks. He's never out of the place.'

As they pecked happily away at this treat something clicked into place in Philippa's brain. As well as the bar fumes clinging to Jon's clothes this morning there had been something else; a woman's scent, sickly and cloying. She hadn't even known she had registered it, but now the memory came vividly back, fitting in all too well with what the gossiping voices were saying.

'Now then, ladies, what's it to be?' Jockie, coming back from the storeroom, cut in, and Philippa, rigid with shock, didn't notice his warning nod in her direction.

Her mind was fixed on one thing only. Jon's rage yesterday had not been the release of a frustration equal to her own; he had simply been angry with a person he no longer cared about. Because he had found someone else. Of course that's what he'd do. How absurd she had been, with her naive ideas of giving him time and patience. He'd probably only let her stay because she'd sold Achallie and had nowhere else to go.

She walked out of the shop, oblivious to the silence and the watching eyes. So this was the end. She should have had the courage to face it long ago. She looked up and down the empty road, struggling to focus her thoughts. Round the corner came the Fort William bus. She waited, numbly, while two people got off, then she got on and was carried away.

Jon didn't blame her for going. He could hardly have expected her to stay after the way he'd treated her. Apart from nearly knocking her down, which no woman of Philippa's type would ever put up with, he hadn't made love to her for months, had showed her no affection, in cold fact had hardly spoken to her. The miracle was that she'd stayed as long as she had, if you also took into account the way he'd expected her to live.

Obvious as all that was, one or two things never seemed quite to add up. The first was that she hadn't told him she was going; it was so unlike Philippa not to be open and up-front about such a decision. He groaned to think that he'd done that to her. Even so, gut instinct didn't entirely relinquish hope of hearing from her, if only to spell out her reasons for going, and it was this shred of hope which made him continue work on the house, stubbornly putting in place every detail they'd agreed on. One thing he was thankful for, as through the endless days he wondered obsessively where Philippa was and what she was doing – that he had, in spite of the fears of people like Michael Thorne and Max Munro, insisted on her keeping the money from the sale of Achallie in her own account. Not a penny of it had been used for Shionach, so at least he knew she had funds. It was small comfort.

Then Shionach was finished, just as they had planned it, with one big light room the width of the house, kitchen and utility room behind equipped to the last detail, bathroom more luxurious even than Achallie's (ache of the joke unshared), bedrooms waiting bare and tenantless. No question now of bringing over the furniture from Baldarroch, yet Jon was reluctant to buy any for himself. With unwelcome irony, the only item which had arrived, ordered some time ago, was the big new bed. Jon continued to sleep on the mattress in front of the fire.

With nothing more to occupy him on the house he turned to local jobs, which he had no difficulty in finding, but as far as possible he stuck to those where he could work alone. He never went now to the Drishaig Inn or the motel, and gave the impression of wanting contact with no one, needing no one. Not even the least tactful risked asking after Philippa, and his privacy at Shionach was scrupulously respected.

One of the worst things was coping with Keeper, so surprisingly left behind – the other question concerning Philippa's flight which continued to nag at Jon. The big dog waited and listened for her in a way that was hard to bear and sometimes, when he lifted his head as though he'd heard something, only to girn quietly to himself for a minute or two then settle again with a sigh, Jon would decide that he couldn't endure having him in the house another day. Yet the dog's presence seemed to hold some tenuous promise that Philippa might return and eventually, as the weeks passed, Jon began to value his company for its own sake.

Oddly enough, the person he found himself able to talk to in the end was Celia Campbell. This unlikely development was brought about by Tanera, who greatly admired Jon and who, after some slight domestic unpleasantness over painting yellow sunbursts on the pointers, had packed a bag and set off over the headland to live with him.

When he returned her to Fassfern Celia took the chance to say, as only dread of intruding had prevented her from doing long before, 'Look, Jon, if ever you feel like company, do please come to us. Just look in whenever you like. We'd always be glad to see you. It must be so lonely for you over at Shionach.'

His mouth open to refuse, Jon looked at her, taking in the battered Barbour and muddy boots she'd had on to hunt for Tanera, the windblown hair, the eyes meeting his with such genuine kindness, and was searingly reminded of Philippa. He knew the invitation meant precisely what it said. These people, with their principles and their directness . . . Celia must have known there had been some reason for Philippa to take off as she had, yet was ready to offer friendship where she saw it was needed.

It was a beginning. When they met by chance in the village or on the bay road they stopped to speak; sometimes Celia walked with Tanera and the dogs over to Shionach, or Jon looked in at Fassfern to consult Neil on some point and stayed for a meal. Gradually a link was forged which comforted him more than he would ever have admitted.

Once, abruptly, after resisting putting the question a dozen times, he asked Celia if she knew where Philippa was.

'I don't,' she replied, with a little grimace of sympathy – then added candidly, 'and if I did I'm afraid I shouldn't be able to tell you.'

It sounded so like Philippa that Jon laughed, in spite of the pang to know this avenue was closed.

'I think you should look for her though,' Celia added unexpectedly, and he glanced at her frowning, taken by surprise.

'No point, is there?' he said, after a moment almost of hope, as though Celia had told him something concrete. 'It was her choice to go.'

Celia hesitated. 'Would you mind if I said something very personal?' she asked, blushing slightly.

'Go on.' But Jon's eyes had narrowed.

Not encouraging. Celia gathered her resolve. 'She wouldn't have gone, like that I mean, if she didn't really care about you. It was such an extreme sort of thing to do, for Philippa. I'm sorry, Jon, I know it's none of my business, but it seems such a waste – and so sad.'

He gazed at her, mouth grim, unable to speak. Then he nodded brusquely, tucking the words away, grateful for kindness which didn't take sides.

It was months before he learned the truth, and it was Jockie who let it slip, forgetting after so long that Jon was the one person who didn't know. The same women who had been gossiping in the shop that day went out as Jon came in, and Jockie remarked chattily, 'I've always thought it was a damn shame, Philippa hearing what that pair said. Some tongues they have on them . . .'

'What do you mean? Philippa hearing what?' The name jerked Jon sharply out of his thoughts.

'Well, just what everyone knew.' Jockie groped to work out the rights of it after all this time.

Jon took one step forward. He didn't clutch Jockie by a handful of his shirt and threaten violence, as Jockie later vowed he had, but there was enough menace in the movement to extract all the information he needed.

Driving home he was so shaken by what he'd heard that he pulled up to sort out the implications. Philippa had gone because she'd believed he was having it off with Pam. Christ, he could hardly remember who Pam was. But wait a minute, wait a minute, he warned himself, nearly stifling as the tide of excitement beat up – you hit her. That was why she went. Yes, and for months we'd never got it together in bed, don't forget. But this fell too sweetly into place. If she'd gone because he hit her she'd have gone there and then, taking Keeper, and she'd have left him in no doubt about her reasons.

As he reviewed all this Jon became more and more certain. She wouldn't have left him because he'd resorted to violence. She hadn't been intimidated. She might have decided it was a turning point, that they should change the plot, get help, whatever, but she wouldn't have walked away without a word. But this, the June situation, the Moira situation, all over again; this she wouldn't tolerate, wouldn't stop to discuss.

He must find her, though he scarcely hoped that if he did she would give him another chance. He'd had plenty of time by now to see what he'd put her through since he came back. But at least her decision would be based on the facts, and she could be spared the pain of thinking he'd been unfaithful to her. If that would still cause her pain. Panic washing through him, he realised he no longer knew what she would think or feel.

32

Jon crossed the pass into Glen Maraich in a stinging flurry of sleet, heading down between dark walls of rock under a lowering sky. How blindly confident he had been, coming over here in the opposite direction close on a year ago, believing that he and Philippa were leaving problems behind them.

Now he felt uncertain and vulnerable, dreading the impact of memories and associations. This morning he had kept his mind resolutely on practical matters, packing minimum needs for himself, with no idea of how long he might be away, and shutting down the cottage, surprised at how much he minded leaving it. He had left Keeper with Celia, and could still hear the dog's anguished howls when he realised he was being left behind. He had minded that too, more than he could ever have foreseen.

Now the past leapt upon him and he had no defences. The work on the bypass at Bridge of Riach was finished, the old road over its hump-backed bridge now leading only to Allt Farr and its farms at the head of the glen. Here was the turning to Affran, bringing images pouring back; then Alltmore where the big barbecue had been held; the bend where Philippa had gone down the bank in the Mini (a memory blending with the later picture of her stumbling into Shionach streaming blood and peaty water). Here was the village and the road to the Cluny Arms; across the river, as he drove on, the little box of Keeper's Cottage stood drab on its shelf of hillside.

Taking the main drive to Baldarroch, his stomach hollow, he found it harder and harder to hold on to the present. The rain had stopped but mist hung in the great beeches of the avenue. He felt as though he were driving under a nebulous dome which moved with him and would never release him to light and normality. The Philippa of their first spring together seemed suddenly so close, with her light step and ready smile and generous capacity for affection, that he felt she must be there waiting for him, at the end of this shrouded tunnel of trees. He shook his head angrily. He had changed that gentle happy girl for good. He had a bleak vision of her as he had last seen her, too thin, too quiet, no gloss or glow about her.

Emerging onto the gloomy sweep of gravel in front of the castle, a vivid memory came of her whirling him up to that monstrous door to teach him a lesson, because he'd been so grouchy about being dragged to dinner. When had she last teased him? With an ache of bitter loss he drove round to the courtyard under the streaming cliff.

Julie was standing at the kitchen table, sowing herbs in pots. When the bell pealed in the passage she paused with head cocked, making sure it was someone who knew the form, then went on dribbling seeds out of the side of her palm as steps approached.

When Jon came to a halt in the doorway, presenting himself as it were with a sort of defiant wariness, she looked at him for one moment of enquiry over her crooked half-moons and thought, at the end of his tether. She slid the remaining seeds back into their packet, dusted her hands down the front of her sweater and came round the table towards him.

'Well, my lad, and what have you got to say for yourself?' But the words didn't matter. Her shrewd eyes took in his shut face, his hard control, his need. 'Come on.' She slid an arm through his. 'Goodness, I'd forgotten what a big lump you are. Sit there.'

'Sorry to barge in on you like this.' He could hardly speak, shaken by nostalgia.

'Don't be daft.'

'Should have phoned.' He hadn't dared risk it. He hardly knew what he was saying, so overwhelming were the memories and the pain, as though he had never truly taken it in till now, of realising what he'd thrown away.

'Here, get this down you.' Julie held out a glass. She had sloshed in the brandy to a scale she deemed bracing for a man of Jon's habits.

'Bloody hell,' he protested when he saw it. He wouldn't have believed he could raise a smile at such a moment, but Julie's matter-of-fact reception had been more than he could have hoped for. 'Thanks, I need that. I hadn't expected – you know, the glen, this place—'

'You're softer than you look,' Julie told him, her tone unexpectedly approving, loving even.

'She's gone, you know that?'

Julie nodded, her expression becoming less friendly. 'I expected you before this.'

Jon was on the defensive at once. 'You don't know the whole story.'

'I don't know any of it,' she said tartly. 'You don't suppose Philippa had a lot to say, do you?'

Jon relaxed, grinning, feeling the gusty breeze of common sense shred the cloud of self-recriminations and doubts of the lonely months. 'I want to find her.'

'About time.'

'Do you know where she is?' The question he had come to ask.

'No, and I'd be surprised if anyone else does.'

Jon stared at her; she had wiped out so much hope in that

single sentence. But he should have known. If Philippa meant to make a clean break she wouldn't indulge in first telling, then binding people to secrecy.

Julie gazed at him, debating. 'She came for her passport,' she said abruptly, then pursed her lips as though not sure she had wanted to say so much.

Jon felt a vast dismay fill him. For some reason, he'd taken it for granted that Philippa would be in Scotland, somewhere like Glen Maraich, in the scene where, to him, she belonged. But abroad? She could be anywhere. He had her address book with him and had checked obsessively through the Scottish clues, ignoring the foreign ones. There'd been a lot of them, he recalled.

'You'll be wanting your own passport, then,' Julie remarked, seeing something of this in his face.

He shook his head, scarcely hearing her. From ingrained habit he'd kept his passport, part of the major's kit recovered at Achallie, with him when they moved to Shionach, and he had it with him now.

'Jesus,' he said blankly.

Julie moved to his side, squeezing his shoulder with her compost-ingrained claw.

The touch acted like a release button. Suddenly Jon was able to talk, had to talk, bursting through the dam of baggage, hang-ups and wrong turnings which had brought him to this point. He spilled out long-buried hurts that made Julie wince, details of the violence and fear which lay behind the terrors that could still haunt his dreams, and he put into words at last the admission that he'd wrecked his chances of a promising career in the Army through his own intransigence. Every time the opening had been there some flaw in him, some sense of being forever the loner, outside the pack, had slammed the door shut again. He talked about the corroding sense of failure he'd carried with him after leaving the Army, the terrible blank it had left in his life, and the route down which these two factors had led him. And at last he was able to talk about Philippa, releasing some of his guilt over the way he'd treated her.

He didn't see Michael appear in the doorway, to withdraw in silence at a signal from Julie. He was aware only of Julie giving him her total, focused attention, offering no sympathy, making no judgements.

When finally he fell silent, he returned to the present with groping slowness. He rubbed both hands down his face. 'God, I'm sorry,' he muttered. 'Don't know where that lot came from. You must think—'

'Never mind about that,' Julie said sharply.

'I've never talked about all this before. Philippa doesn't know half of it.'

'I should hope not.'

He grimaced at the asperity in her voice, but didn't resent it.

'Should I let her go?' he asked, not looking up.

For the first time Julie felt a flurry of alarm at what she'd got herself into, but pushed it away. Too late now. 'Will you be able to find her?' she asked.

'I'll find her. No matter how long it takes, I'll find her. But will that be best for her?'

'You're coming on,' Julie mocked.

From her he could accept it. 'You don't think I've blown it for good?'

'No,' she said, and suddenly her voice was gentle. 'I don't think you ever could, for her.'

It took a moment to deal with how that made him feel. 'Did she say anything?' he asked, clearing his throat.

'She barely opened her mouth when she was here – walking wounded, if you ask me.'

His mouth tightened and his eyes stung.

Julie got up to push the kettle onto the Aga hob.

'Julie, thanks for listening. You've been—'

'Oh, spare me, spare me. Now, I've a man to retrieve, and dogs to feed, and I only got half these blasted seeds in. Go and fetch your bag.'

'You're sure—?'

'Out.'

She had given Michael the gist of what Jon had told her by the time they sat down to dinner, and no one tried to avoid the reason behind his sudden appearance.

'Where's Keeper, by the way?' Michael enquired, as he delved under the rich crust of the hare pudding to find some extra goodies for Jon.

'With the Campbells at Fassfern. Do you know them?' Jon was getting used to the network by now.

'Neil Campbell? His brother married a distant cousin of mine. Nice little place in Knapdale.'

Even as Jon grinned he caught Julie's sardonic look, and knew it wasn't there merely because he'd got his lines right. She was gratified to hear that he'd accepted from Celia Campbell precisely the sort of favour he used to jib at Philippa giving and receiving. And he'd come here for help, to Philippa's friends, never seriously doubting his welcome. It was as though, in the wings, she could still give him the good things of life.

When Michael raised his glass and said quietly, 'To success, Jon,' and Julie jerked hers towards him with less formality but equal goodwill, he would willingly have hugged them both.

Waking next morning, a new optimism flooded him, even before he fully realised where he was. He would find Philippa; the larger decisions which loomed beyond that must wait. But as he hurriedly dressed in the icy, dusty room, anxiety and urgency gripped him again. He tried to tell himself it was a straightforward practical exercise he was embarking on. He had only to be methodical and patient. It was useless; nothing else he'd ever undertaken had made him feel like this.

At least he knew now that he'd be wasting his time trying Philippa's other friends in Glen Maraich. It didn't occur to him to wonder how they might have felt that she had come without telling them to Baldarroch. Penny Forsyth, for one, had been hurt by it. Was she now so set in her ways, so immovably conventional, that Philippa had thought her incapable of understanding the emotional havoc that loving a man like Jon could produce? Eleanor Munro, at Allt Farr, had received the news in sardonic silence. It disappointed her.

But Jon knew nothing of this. His mind was set on his mission, though Julie, not a morning person, was unresponsive today, crouched over a mug of herbal tea, her hair in tufts as it had left the pillow, her face screwed up discouragingly. Michael, relaxed and friendly as ever as he cooked breakfast, could feel the nervous tension coming off Jon in waves. In the light of day, he wasn't so sure that he wanted him to succeed. Jon was a tough character; no woman could expect an easy ride with him. Then he thought of his own determined search for Julie. Who was he to question what Jon was doing?

It occurred to Jon, doing his best with bacon and eggs he didn't want, that not far away along the stone passages stood the little huddle of Achallie furniture, Philippa's possessions, things he had used and shared with her. He shivered. He had no wish to see them.

Julie had one surprise for him. Going out with Michael and the dogs to see him off, she led him away for a moment to a walled corner jutting above the river. Thin sunlight reached it; oystercatchers, recently returned, flashed with their rippling calls above the water.

'It was her fault too, you know,' she said without preamble.

'Philippa's?' Jon was unprepared for that.

'Do you still make love?'

Winded, he stared at her then, about to tell her hotly to mind her own business, saw something in her face that checked him. She was so concerned, so deeply engaged in the problem.

'No, we never got it together, after I came back,' he said after a moment, awkwardly.

'She'd be all wrong, you see.'

'What the hell do you mean?'

She gave a little snort. 'Don't get huffy with me, you daft bastard. It's just sex we're talking about. Philippa would be too passive. All right then, too well brought up. She'd never think of making the moves, and you needed that, didn't you?'

'For Christ's sake,' Jon said in a muffled voice, looking away from her, but he didn't deny it.

'I was thinking about it in the night,' Julie pursued, and he made a small sound of involuntary amusement at the idea. 'I don't want you going off to find her thinking everything was down to you. These terribly polite people aren't the easiest in the world to deal with – and I should know. Put up with anything and smile and smile. You never know where you are. How long is it since you came back? A year, just about? And she let you snarl and sulk – yes, I can see by the look you've just given me how delightful you must have been – and she'd never have a row when you were busting for one. So when you finally clouted her what did she do, apologise for being in the way? Ah, so you did hit her.'

He made a show of protesting, but couldn't really mind. 'One of the things I love her for is her gentleness, remember,' he pointed out, and was startled to find himself clutched in a bumpy hug.

'You can't *think* how good it is to hear you say so,' Julie exclaimed. 'Just keep it firmly in your mind.'

Jon went down the drive feeling almost more mangled by emotion than when he had driven up it, but much comforted. Perhaps that gave him the courage to take the road past Achallie. Steeling himself against all sorts of pain, the last thing he was prepared for was the *For Sale* sign leaning crookedly above the dyke. Noting clinically that his hands were unsteady he pulled up and got out.

One year. Achallie looked as if it had been empty for ten. The uncut grass of the lawn, flattened and pale, was spongy under his feet. In the vegetable plot chickweed and speed-well flourished, nettles were creeping back. As he walked round the house, his face like granite, he saw the leaves drifted against the back door, the cotoneaster sagging down, the flagstones they'd levelled together nearly swallowed up by weeds.

Peering in at the window of Philippa's bedroom, he saw that the white walls had been covered with a heavy flowery paper. The sitting-room had been divided again, the big fire-place dwarfing one half. New frosted glass hid any changes that might have overtaken the bathroom, but he could see into the kitchen. It had been gutted, every inch fitted with units in blurred beige and white. Chicken-shit pattern, Jon thought.

He pressed his forehead against the pane, closing his eyes, remorse eating into him. He had done this, as surely as he had quenched the spark of happiness in Philippa. He pushed himself upright and turned away, before too many ghosts came crowding.

He was almost past Bessie's cottage before he registered the fact. Philippa would have stopped; Philippa would be pleased if he stopped. The form came back – tap on the window, call to say who it was, feel for the key on its hook to the right, the cat shooting out past his head as he took it down.

Bessie, unalarmed by anyone who followed this ritual, was as glad as ever to have company, though she kept enquiring for Philippa, plainly puzzled by her absence. She asked Jon if he would like tea, and he remembered how the system worked and made it for her.

'So you're back in Scotland, then?' the old woman asked, after a silence during which she conducted an absorbing chase down the front of her cardigan for a fragment of biscuit.

'Yes, I came back last year.' Jon wasn't sure how much time would mean to her.

'Not last year,' she said testily. 'You and Philippa, I mean, from abroad.'

His heart gave a jolted thump. 'From abroad?'

'Yon place Philippa sent me the card from. Not that Postie could make it out, some foreign language it was printed in. I thought she'd have put more news, mind.'

'Perhaps I could tell you what it said.' His voice sounded odd, but Bessie didn't appear to notice.

'That would be grand, though. It's there on the dresser with the rest. Bring them all, laddie, I like to look at my cards, such bonnie ones nowadays. And you'll need to find me my glasses, not that they're much use to me, it's just the one eye now . . .'

A slithering stack of robins and snow scenes and Christmas roses. He would read every one if he had to. He knew Philippa's the moment he came to it, like a loved face seen in a crowd, a fragment of some larger scene depicted on decorative blue and white tiles: the shepherds round the crib, chosen to please Bessie.

'Is that it?' Bessie asked as he slipped it out of the pile. 'Read me out what it says.'

'With lots of love and best wishes for a very happy

Christmas, and special love to Pattie.' (Pattie? That damned cat of course.) 'Keep warm and cosy, Philippa.'

The sight of her writing made reading aloud difficult.

'Aye, well,' Bessie sniffed, half pleased and half ready to find fault. 'I'm warm enough, I suppose. But what's that it says, the printed bit?'

'*Boas Festas, Joyeux Noel* . . . That's all it says, Merry Christmas in different languages.'

'Oh aye,' said Bessie, disappointed.

The first language would be the country of origin. Spanish? He turned the card over. '*Adoração dos Pastores. Muséu Nacional do Azulejo, Lisboa.*' Not Spanish, Portuguese. Had Bessie taken him a gigantic stride forward? Dutifully, he went through the rest for her, excitement tonguing up inside him.

'And will you be back at Achallie now?' she arrested him by enquiring, when he'd washed and put away the tea things and was making up the fire.

'At Achallie?' What was she asking? 'No, I don't think so.'

From the moment of seeing it was for sale he'd been wondering if Philippa knew. If she did, would she want to buy it back?

'Philippa should never have let it go, to my way of thinking,' Bessie grumbled. 'After all the work she'd put into it. It's a sad wee place now, they tell me.'

A sad wee place. Yes, it was, but even so Jon was glad he'd come this way. As he left, after gathering Bessie's frail old body into a grateful hug, he could hardly believe the reward one simple, disinterested act had brought him.

33

Jon had extracted all the Portuguese details by now, but couldn't resist taking out Philippa's red leather address book to read them in her own flowing hand. As far as he could judge, they seemed to belong to the period between her father's death and her going into the Air Force. He spent some time examining these and other entries, more for the sense of contact with her which they gave than in the hope of gleaning more information.

It was a relief to be on the way. Though he had instinctively gravitated to Glasgow as a jumping-off place – for one thing, he had somewhere there to leave the Shogun for as long as necessary, no questions asked – he was no longer comfortable in that scene, and he couldn't get out of it fast enough. He was glad to be able to travel as Jon Paulett, to search for Philippa as Jon Paulett. It was the name which belonged to his life with her.

To a future life with her? He dragged his mind away from the question. One step at a time. Philippa might not even be in Portugal by now. He had a long way to go. But he couldn't subdue his excitement as the flight neared its end, and he looked down on a neat country of red earth hazed with the green of spring, the piled and spreading white city with its warm pantiled roofs, the wide silver river wheeling as they came in to land.

Unusually for him, he took little note of his surroundings on the drive into the city. His mind was fixed, clutching them like a talisman, on the name and address he'd decided to try first. Desmond Latimer, rua Dr Carlos Almeida 29, with 'Lisbon Diary' scribbled beside it. Was that some sort of magazine or newspaper as he hoped? If so, even after so long an interval, there would probably be no better starting point.

He bought a map, and found that the street was in the Lapa district, in the western part of the city. It proved to be a quarter of handsome old houses, museums and art galleries, and quiet residential streets. In a tall house with ornate balconies and ochre plasterwork, he found the office, in fact part of a private flat, of the *Lisbon Diary*. Shaky with relief, he swore at himself for letting this get to him so badly.

Desmond Latimer, a gentle, stooping, untidy man, had run the little newspaper for many years, more as a hobby than anything, an undemanding, literary hobby which enabled him to keep a benevolent eye on the comings and goings of the ex-pat community. Though he wasn't sure he approved of some of its newer elements.

'Ah, yes, I did hear Philippa had come back.' Once Jon felt he could cut through the courteous ramblings, Latimer's first response seemed full of promise. 'Charming girl. She did one or two very adequate pieces for me when she was here before. Some time ago now, of course. It would be a pleasure to see her again, but I don't think she was here very long. Certainly not in Lisbon. Now let me see if I can find the addresses of people who may be able to assist you . . .'

Hope sank again, as Jon saw they were the addresses he already had. It was clear that any information he would extract here would be as out of date as Bessie's Christmas card. But the fact of having talked to someone who knew Philippa, someone who'd received him with helpful kindness, nevertheless made Jon feel he had made some kind of progress. The country no longer seemed blank territory. If he talked to Philippa's friends one by one someone would know something.

Following Desmond Latimer's directions, he set off next for the Bairro Alto. This old part of the city was clearly a young people's haunt, busy and vibrant. It came as no surprise to find that the apartment he wanted was occupied by three female students, who asked Jon in with a cheerful lack of caution that worried him, lavished smiles and wine on him and were no help at all. Since he was looking for someone who had lived here half their lives ago, the best they could offer was eager argument about the tenants immediately before them.

Houses with new owners, embassy staff who had finished their tours and gone home, a dressmaker, and a lifeguard living in the fishermen's quarter in Caparica (Jon intended to question Philippa at the first opportunity about the brawny character who opened the door to him), and the list for Lisbon and its environs was exhausted. By evening he was heading north.

He saw nothing of Oporto that night, except for an impression of climbing lights and wet black streets, but he was up and out early, impatient to get on with his quest. The Hammond address read perfunctorily Boa Vista, Oporto, giving no street name. Over a breakfast of strong coffee and freshly baked crusty rolls in a café near the wharfs he asked some workmen for help. He thought they looked at him oddly as he showed them the name.

'Up,' one of the men said. 'Up.' Well, in Oporto that made sense.

Jon found himself eventually in a cobbled cul-de-sac, blank-walled except for one massive pair of double doors. With an entrenched reluctance to park facing a dead end, he reversed out again and left the car in a leafy road bordered by large, prosperous-looking houses.

Back in the narrow lane, he found a bell beside the gates. No number, no name. He pressed it firmly. What are you doing to me, Philippa? A wicket gate opened and a square young man with the neat appearance of an indoor servant and the steely gaze of a security guard confronted him.

'May I see Miss Elissa Hammond?' Probably Mrs Somebody by now – or the Duchess of Somewhere, Jon amended, unsettled by a glimpse of a courtyard the size of a football pitch, with a fancy fountain in the middle and a vast honey-gold mansion round three sides.

'Mees Hammond is not at home, *senhor*.' At least the man spoke English, if the courtesy in his tone was minimal. Jon, in his usual jeans and desert boots, had been assessed and had not found favour.

'Mrs Hammond?' Jon was beginning to realise that turning up on foot, on spec, might not have been the most effective approach here.

'I see if the *senhora* is at home.' No title, then; he'd scraped through that one.

The man was waiting, his face impassive. '*O senhor* has a card?'

Bastard, Jon thought with admiration. 'Paulett – Major Jon Paulett.' Not that the major would cut much ice here. 'A friend of Miss Philippa Galbraith's. Mrs Howard.' When did the friendship date from?

'If the *senhor* will wait.' The man's eyes had glazed at the names and Jon cursed inwardly, wishing he'd written them down.

He was left in a corridor of polished marble, as wide as a room, stretching the length of the wing. Rejecting after one glance the hectically carved seat the footman had indicated, Jon crossed to gaze out at the courtyard and the corresponding wing opposite, its long row of windows shuttered. He was suddenly oppressed by the futility of turning up to look for Philippa in such a place.

Hearing returning footsteps and feeling his heartbeat quicken, he promised himself that one day she would pay for this. But it appeared that Major Paulett would be received. Good for him. He set off on the lengthy walk scarcely believing it was happening. Lacquered cabinets on gilded bases, polychrome statues of the saints, the remnants of collections of ivory and nineteenth-century Celadon jade, passed by him in a blur.

The room he was shown into was hideous, its perimeter sombre with heavy Portuguese furniture, its heart a chintzy English drawing-room with cushions decorated with spaniels' heads in gros-point and a sofa table covered with copies of *Country Life* and *The Field*. The view which gave the house its name was hidden behind partly lowered blinds. A bad-tempered-looking female was waiting for him, beaky of nose and tight of mouth, wearing a green silk blouse with a floppy bow and a skirt of hairy green tweed. Her face was very red.

Leila Hammond was permanently angry. She had married into one of the rich families of English descent in Portugal, her husband one of the few who had held on to a large portion of his wealth and possessions after the revolution and its aftermath in the seventies. She lived in a house which, though three-quarters of it was shut up, was still extremely beautiful. She had a husband who let her do more or less as she pleased, and a daughter a good deal prettier than she deserved. Yet she felt forever hard done by, exiled from the only landscape and way of life which meant anything to her – the flat fields and laid hedges of Leicestershire, the safe world of cubbing and hunting, with its poignant smells of saddle soap and wet dogs and root crops on frosty winter mornings.

In place of these delights, she had been obliged to spend her adult life surrounded by beautifully dressed, well-groomed women, attending or giving dinner parties where everyone else seemed able to switch from language to language in a way that still left her floundering after thirty years, while the swift, allusive chatter skimmed lightly over topics she never came across in *Horse and Hound*. Her husband had long ago given up on her, reserving his interest and his affection for their daughter.

This daughter, Elissa, was at present living in Funchal with the son of a lace-maker, working in a tourist shop and expecting a baby in the summer, though none of these facts had been revealed to her mother. It was solely in the hope that Jon, as a friend of Philippa's, might have news of her that Leila had agreed to see him.

It was a barren interview, Jon casting about, having used Philippa as his introduction, for some way of asking where she was, and Leila, bluffing crossly, trying to glean news of Elissa. Prolonging the skirmish was clearly fruitless, and soon Jon found himself marching down the marble vistas once more, hearing the wicket gate slam behind him with vengeful finality.

That left two addresses, both in the Alentejo. As he walked back to the car the first real doubt shook him. If neither of them produced anything . . .

The tawny-red dust of the track led into the red eye of the sunset. Muttering and shielding his eyes, Jon realised that he was very tired. He had driven hard, juggling endlessly in his mind whether to try first the Pereiras in Santa Paula, or the less native-sounding O'Hallorans in a place called Casas Velhas. As the miles passed, he had realised he was not only afraid that he wouldn't find Philippa, but almost equally afraid that he would. If he ran her to earth and she turned him down that would be the end, and it could be very close.

Seeing a sign to Casas Velhas he had swung into the narrow road without further debate, glad to have his mind made up for him. In the village, little more than a couple of streets of traditional low white cottages, many in the process of being done up, there had been no difficulty in obtaining directions to Monte da Rocha.

Another big house, but very different from Boa Vista. Wide and low, its tiled roof pitched nearly flat, it stood bare of adornment, ironwork grilles over the lower windows, wooden shutters folded back above. Its double doors were open. A battered and dusty jeep stood before them, a toy dump truck loaded with stones parked by its wheel.

Jon got out of the car stiffly, trying to assemble what facts he knew. Micky and Antonia O'Halloran. Three children. Philippa had listed names and dates of birth; he couldn't summon one of them. There was no bell. He knocked, his knuckles making a muted sound on the solid door, then gave a couple of thumps with the side of his fist. Peering into the gloom, half blinded after the brilliance of the evening light, he saw that the hall was empty of everything but a small table with a telephone on it. Then he heard the pad of canvas pumps on the tiles, and a woman in a navy overall over a dark-coloured skirt and blouse came smiling towards him.

'*Boa tarde, senhor, boa tarde,*' she greeted him in a friendly sing-song.

'Mrs O'Halloran?' How did the locals cope with that?

'*A senhora, sim, sim. No jardim.* Come, please.'

She led him along the front of the house, and into what looked like a huge abandoned vegetable garden, a tiny portion of which was now fenced off for use. She pointed to a path, saying '*O tanque.*'

A tank? A pool? The general air of the place hadn't promised such luxuries. Jon went at a carefully unhurried pace along the path under a neglected pergola, past a row of what had presumably once been workers' cottages.

He heard children's voices ahead, and sounds of splashing. In silhouette against the sky a skinny small girl squatted at the top of a grass bank, bringing Tanera Campbell to mind with a pang of association Jon could well have done without at this moment.

'Mummy, someone's come!' the child called in an up-market English voice. A smile creased her triangular face as she added to Jon, 'The steps are at the end.'

As he started up a girl appeared above him, brown, goblin thin, with pointed shoulders, pointed face and little pointed breasts under a child's T-shirt.

'Hi, come on up. I can't turn my back for a second, sorry. These wretched tanks don't have a shallow end.'

'I was looking for Mrs O'Halloran.'

'Me. How nice. I hope you can stand noise.'

She couldn't possibly be the mother of this horde. A frill of children, most practically invisible under inflated arm-bands and rings, clung along the rim of the old irrigation tank, staring fixedly at the visitor.

'I'm Jon Paulett.' He shook a skinny hand, watching her huge blue eyes for some reaction to the name. Nothing.

'Hello, I'm Antonia – oh, James, do be careful, let him breathe occasionally. That's with his mouth above water, remember. They will insist on coming with us,' she said to Jon, 'but they won't learn to swim and their parents get tetchy if we drown too many. I'll get them out then we can talk. Come on, you lot.'

Judging by the wail that went up this was understood by everyone. 'James, give him a hand. He can't get out on his own even if he is still alive.'

Jon bent to swing bodies out of the water and, deflating their support systems, found some of them very small indeed.

'Are they all out? None at the bottom? No you don't,' Antonia cried, making a grab at a darting figure. 'They always try to get away with something. Now buzz off.'

Screaming delightedly, 'Buzze off, buzze off,' eighty per cent of the mob scudded away in the direction of the village.

'That's cleared the decks a bit. It was time they came out anyway. They were all mad keen for us to fill the tank, but I don't know how they can bear it at this time of year. These are my three, James, Joe and Deborah. Go and ask Angelina for supper,' she said as the children greeted Jon, 'and take something in with you,' she shouted as they wheeled for the steps. She began to pitch any remaining objects into a rug, looking over her shoulder at Jon with a grin very like her daughter's. 'Formalities can now ensue.'

Jon found himself unexpectedly, exasperatingly, at a loss. He couldn't spin some tale to this girl who had accepted his appearance with such simplicity. He took a deep breath. 'I'm a friend of Philippa's—'

He got no further. Antonia O'Halloran rocketed to her feet. 'You haven't left her with Micky? Oh no, I'm not having that. He fancies her like mad. Come on.' She set off, ready to abandon rug, toys, towels, clothes.

'No, wait.' Jon caught her arm, noting as she swung back that she weighed little more than the children he'd fished out of the tank. 'Philippa isn't with me. I'm looking for her, in fact.'

'I thought you'd come over from the Pereiras' with her – though now I come to think of it she told me she'd be in Lisbon today and wouldn't be back till late. *Oh!*'

He assumed she was aghast at what she'd given away, but had no time to worry about that. It had happened; he'd found Philippa.

But Antonia was exclaiming, 'You must be the one! Wow. Thank goodness you've turned up.' Her skinny hands seized his arm in an excited clutch, then she was diving at the rug again, saying, 'Come on, quick, we must tell Micky. He's going to be *so* thrilled. I can't tell you how worried we've been about Philippa.'

34

As they walked back past the ex-farmworkers' cottages over-looking the old *horta*, now most years put down to hay or used as a handy lambing enclosure, Jon, still hardly able to believe that the search was over, took his chance to ask the most urgent question of all while he had Antonia to himself.

'Did – does – Philippa ever talk about me?'

'We're not big on soul-baring girlie chats, if that's what you mean,' she told him, then couldn't resist going on, with a look of lively interest, 'but you're the one, aren't you? The one she was living with in Scotland? Though how very indiscreet of me,' this time with an irrepressible giggle, 'if you're not.'

Jon found he couldn't mind, particularly when she paused to gaze at him with her wide, goggly eyes and added more gravely, 'She's been so wretched.'

Greedy for facts, Jon learned that Philippa had been staying with the Pereiras, the last address on his list, since she left Shionach. Years ago she had taught their daughter English; now, it seemed, she was staying with them as their guest and friend. It was hard to imagine her unoccupied.

Jon found that Antonia was taking it for granted he'd stay the night at Monte da Rocha. 'Of course you must stay. Micky would be furious if I let you go. A friend of Philippa's? I'd never hear the last of it.' Then she stopped short with a frown. 'Or am I being an idiot? You must be knocked sideways to realise that you've found her. Would you really rather be on your own?'

Jon smiled at her, but was unexpectedly moved. He could so clearly hear Philippa asking that.

'I'd like to stay, thanks, if you're sure that's all right. The only thing is, Philippa might not want to see me.' He felt obscurely that it was essential to have everything above board; was her influence reaching out to him already? 'I wouldn't want you to feel later that you'd aided and abetted the enemy.'

Antonia looked at him, her face serious, and he noticed the little knobs at the angles of her pointed jaw. The spikes of her hair were drying out orange. 'That's nice of you,' she said, nodding, 'but, whatever Philippa decides, you are not the enemy.'

He couldn't have been in better hands for these last hours. Even Julie would have been too astringent now. Antonia led him into a kitchen with a smoke-darkened, high-raftered roof, and a red tiled floor with a tidemark of dog baskets, toys, bones, laundry, sacks, bins, boots and bits of machinery round it. The children were sitting at a table in the middle of the room.

'Angelina said we needn't drink milk,' Deborah announced the moment her mother appeared.

'She didn't say we had to,' corrected James.

'That's the same.'

'No, it's not.'

Angelina smiled over her shoulder from the stove but didn't enter into the dispute. Joe, making himself a neat parcel of smoked sausage and bread, also said nothing.

Ignoring them, Antonia swept Jon through the empty hall and into a wide corridor with an intricately tiled floor and half a dozen doors on each side. A small frog hopped unhappily towards them.

'I'll deal with him in a minute,' Antonia said. 'They come in via the plumbing. Nightmare landscape for them once they're in, wouldn't you imagine? Here's your room.' She made no apology for the fact that it contained nothing beyond a bed with a high, dark-green headboard painted with flowers and a richly coloured woven cover. Here too, the floor was beautifully tiled, the ceiling was high and boasted ornate plasterwork, and the two long windows were covered by delicate ironwork grilles. It was just that no one seemed to have thought of furniture.

'Bathroom at the end of the corridor, sitting-room across the hall. Angelina or the children will get you anything you want. I'm off to find Micky – I can't wait to tell him about you.'

After his training at the hands of Tanera Campbell, Jon had no reservations about being looked after by the children, and half an hour later was comfortably sunk in a deep sofa with a hefty gin and tonic in his hand, Deborah on one side of him studying *Vogue*, James on the other flicking through a year-old copy of *Ireland's Own* and kindly sharing his favourite jokes. Joe, pressed well back in an armchair opposite, was unalterably silent.

The sitting-room, as Jon was coming to expect, contained no inessential items, but was a satisfying room all the same. Colour was provided by the warm terracotta wash of the walls, and a couple of handsome Coimbra rugs. A long row of books ran along the base of two walls. The fire was lit, its warmth welcome in the cool spring evening.

'These skirts are knickers,' Deborah stated, making up her mind.

The boys looked quickly at Jon.

'If the melons do well we're going to have a new tractor.' James obviously felt a more masculine topic would provide safer ground.

'Mummy caught nine frogs today,' Deborah said competitively.

'This week, you mean,' James said.

'This week beginning today.'

They found this funny. Not a flicker from Joe.

Firm steps came across the hall and Deborah and James flung aside their magazines, but Joe was before them, out of his chair and across the room to be swung up in his father's arms, his grave face transformed at last. The two dogs at Micky's heels inspected Jon briefly, then threw themselves down in front of the fire.

Jon had been expecting some male counterpart of the classy Antonia but this tough-looking individual, short and wiry, with a thin, alert, dark face, was a surprise, especially when he enquired after Jon's welfare in the unadulterated tones of Wicklow.

'So are they looking after you at all?' He sounded friendly and welcoming, but Jon was aware of assessment too, and recalled Antonia's words. Philippa would never go short of champions, that was certain.

'They've looked after me extremely well, thanks,' Jon replied, watching Micky pull James's head against him for a moment then scoop Deborah up in his free arm.

'And did anyone think to find you a bed? Ah, good lad, James, that's just what I've been dreaming of these past two hours. They did? Well, you're in luck, let me tell you. It's not the kind of detail that's always attended to in this house. And did you entertain our visitor with fine conversation, Joe?'

Joe smiled and his father laughed. 'He saves his breath for the only thing that matters, farming.'

Antonia appeared, now in dungarees the colour of her hair, worn over a yellow polo-neck. She refilled Jon's glass, perched briefly on the arm of Micky's chair, and vanished again.

'And don't think she's been popping some mouth-watering dish into the oven,' Micky warned Jon darkly when she came back. 'It's not meals we get in this house, it's food, and that's thanks to Angelina.'

'Been shutting up the ducks,' Antonia said briskly. 'And I'm now going to run Angelina home while you shut up the children.'

Jon could feel himself unwinding. I'm safe here, he thought absurdly, grateful to have been accepted with such ready friendliness, grateful for the absence of questions. He enjoyed watching the evening domestic scene pursue its unselfconscious course; enjoyed Micky's flow of talk, smooth as the whisky in his hand; liked seeing the shutters fold out the darkness. The feeling of time slowing, of doubt and tension being put on hold, was infinitely comforting. Nothing could be done or decided tonight.

They had dinner in the kitchen, warmed by its wood-burning stove, at the round table draped with a heavy floor-length cloth.

'You put your feet on the ledge,' Antonia explained, seeing Jon having trouble with it. 'The tray in the middle used to be for burning charcoal. They're all converted to electric heaters now, but the principle's the same.'

'Matey idea,' Micky commented, topping up the wine glasses. 'It had its own conventions too. You apologised to your neighbour if you let in a draught when you moved, and tucked the cloth round you as quickly as you could.'

'And you sang out if you smelled burning shoes,' Antonia said, 'though that can still happen. Oh look, how lucky, there's plenty to eat.'

Micky raised his eyes to heaven.

Jon learned, without great surprise, that Antonia's father owned a racing stable but, more surprisingly, that Micky had ridden for him till he had grown too heavy for the flat. He had stayed on, but his ambition had turned more and more to his other passion – some day, somehow, to own land.

Antonia's passion had been Micky, from childhood on.

'You know what they're like, these young girls,' Micky said resignedly to Jon. 'No shame at all. She was at me night and day, "Micky, could you come and look at this one's leg" – no, I can't remember what he was called, for the love of heaven – "Micky, I know I could manage him in a snaffle", "Micky, won't you tell Daddy that I don't *need* O levels". I was afraid to open my door in the mornings for fear I'd trip over her and that's the truth of it.'

Antonia gave him a smile as brilliant as her hair, a smile so full of love that Jon was sure for a moment that neither remembered he was in the room. Longing, apprehension and the ache of loss twisted in him.

'I hadn't a chance, I tell you. Though if I'd known she meant marriage I'd have been up and away . . .'

Antonia told Jon about the money her aunt had left her and the fight she'd had to make Micky use it. They talked about the problems they'd faced in building up the farm again after its appropriation during the revolution, its years of mismanagement and eventual abandonment, while the owners waged a lengthy legal battle for compensation. They talked about the current trend for Portuguese landowners, finding the younger generation uninterested in farming, to sell to Dutch farmers, heavily subsidised by their government, who were finding success with such crops as early potatoes and onions, or with dairy herds.

Gradually, seeing Jon look less grim and driven, they drew him on to tell them about Shionach, and he found himself in his turn confessing his long-held dream and what it had meant to him.

Going out with Micky to give the dogs a run (their peaceful

presence during the evening had stirred more than one thought of Keeper), he felt compelled to a more difficult honesty, perhaps prompted by an instinct to have the slate clean before he saw Philippa again.

'You may know, or may have guessed, that I was involved in something pretty—' He broke off, rejecting the words, realising he should have straightened out his thoughts more carefully before he began.

The abrupt plunge came as no surprise to Micky. Not that he knew any details; he had merely guessed that Jon needed to offload something.

'I earned my living as a mercenary,' Jon went on, his voice harsh. 'The last job was – things got a bit messy. I was picked up, held hostage. I was a useful bargaining chip, as it turned out. For a long time I didn't think I'd make it. Then when I did get back, I was pretty much to pieces. I couldn't – well, get it together with Philippa, couldn't talk to her any more, or get close to her. I behaved like a shit too.' He took a deep breath, strangely relieved that this was said.

He was aware, above their heads, of the dry clack and rustle of the three palm trees that stood at this end of the house. The dogs had vanished into the darkness.

'It wasn't altogether surprising that you ran into trouble,' Micky remarked easily. 'It would be like suffering from prison asthenia. Debility. It can take a long time to get over. Neither of you would realise what you were up against, with you coming straight back out of it that way.'

Jon felt an amazed, encompassing gratitude at this speech. Putting a label on his condition made it somehow ordinary, capable of solution. 'Philippa thought I was after someone else,' he was able to add. 'I wasn't, but that's why she went off. At least that was the crunch. I must have been hell to live with. She'd been incredibly patient about everything up till then.'

Micky didn't share Julie's view that Philippa's patience would not have helped. 'Good thing she was,' he said, 'or there'd have been bloody wars and no way back. As it is, all I can tell you is she's been desperately unhappy since she came here, so you may be all right yet.'

In the high painted bed, his clothes on the floor, Jon slept at once, warmed by the quality of the welcome he'd been given, knocked out by wine and emotion and a day which seemed to have gone on for ever.

His last thought as he slid into sleep was Antonia's delighted exclamation, 'You went and knocked on the door at Boa Vista? You met the dragon face to face? This I must hear . . .'

He woke early, dimly aware of sounds out of doors, the thought hitting him like a hammer: it's today. How to get through the next few hours?

A scuffling broke out at his door.

'You can't go in.'

'I'm not going in, I'm peeping.'

'You're not supposed to peep.'

'I want to know what he looks like.'

'You saw him last night.'

'I can't remember.'

'Deborah, don't. Mummy will be furious.'

'Hi,' said Jon.

'We didn't wake you,' Deborah said instantly.

'Come on in.'

In a soft slap of bare feet on the tiles the children were beside him.

'Let's have a bit of light on the subject.'

'Mummy said you were to sleep late,' reported conscientious James as he opened the shutters.

'I'm going to be in trouble then.' Jon smiled at the row of serious faces and immediately they all smiled back, even Joe, with their mother's creased goblin grin. 'Come up off that cold floor.'

'Will you be here when we come home?' Deborah asked, curling against him.

What would have happened by the time school was over, Jon wondered, but before he could reply Antonia was upon them. Three heads snapped round as if on a string; three pairs of eyes widened in alarm.

'I asked them in,' Jon said hastily, wondering what kind of temper went with that hair. Micky, he guessed, would maintain any even-handed calm there was.

'Felt lonely and went looking for them, I suppose,' Antonia said scathingly. 'Deborah, this has to be down to you.'

'I like him,' Deborah stated simply.

'These young girls, no shame at all,' Jon quoted slyly, and at once Antonia was laughing.

'Well, I don't suppose you'll get back to sleep now, so you might as well get up and make yourself useful.'

Jon understood, gratefully, that she wanted to fill the waiting time for him. He helped James and Joe to feed various animals, went with Deborah through the cool morning garden to the tank in search of a lost sandal, and found himself volunteered for the school run and collecting Angelina.

'We can have civilised breakfast now,' Antonia greeted him on his return. And as Micky chatted, giving no hint that, with the ground ready for sowing his sunflowers, he was itching to get onto his machinery dealer to ask yet again where the discs for the drill were, Jon had no way of knowing that normally he would never have sat for so long at this hour.

Talking about farm matters, Micky confided, man to man, 'I have to let Antonia help a bit. To make her feel needed, you know, seeing that she's little enough use in the house. Though her upbringing is against her, poor girl. She has to do it by the book. Sits on the pigsty wall reading out to the pigs what their weight should be, lifts the hens with one hand to see if they're sitting and turns to page two hundred with the other. And here am I without a clean shirt to my back or a meal to come home to . . .'

Jon recognised it as his litany of love, and seeing Antonia trail her fingers lightly across his shoulder as she passed he felt again the wrench of need and fear.

'I don't want to risk phoning,' he said abruptly, and they knew they could help him no more.

'No, Philippa's good sense can be a drawback,' Antonia agreed, reminding him of Julie.

'What would be a good time?'

'An hour or so yet, maybe,' Micky said.

'I'll get going, I think.'

They nodded.

'Come back if you want to. With Philippa or not. I mean it now.' Micky's eyes met his with an unmistakable message of sympathy and support.

Jon couldn't answer. And when he'd collected his things and they came out to say goodbye he was moved again by Antonia's fierce little half shake, half hug, as she said, 'Don't disappear, whatever happens.'

'Ah, put him down, woman, you're a disgrace,' Micky protested, so that Jon was able to leave them laughing, which he thought as he drove away was what Micky had intended.

35

Jon sat out the final hour parked beside the road, staring blindly at a patchwork of wild flowers: pink mallow, scarlet poppies, white camomile, something purple he didn't know. This must be the obligatory 'set aside' Micky had talked about. Beyond it the greyish green of olives, the red-brown of newly harrowed earth waiting for the sowing of summer crops, the young green of cereals, rolled in a neat pattern to the small border town of Santa Paula on its rocky height. Though a system of ancient fortifications still crammed the old town in its grip, modern white suburbs spread below them.

How would he be received in the Pereira household? Both Antonia and Micky had warned him that Philippa was regarded almost as a daughter of the family – and also that it was a house where a certain old-style formality still obtained. Well, it was too late now for such doubts. His face setting in an expression of grim determination, he started the car and swung back onto the road.

He had trouble finding a place to park, but even so he was still early as he came out into the *praça* below the cathedral. What difference could a few minutes make, he asked himself impatiently, but he couldn't overcome a superstitious reluctance to arrive before the time he'd decided on. He stood in the sunlight, astonished to find his skin clammy, feeling strangely cut off from the life of the town going on around him, the shopping women, the children playing on the swirling black and white mosaic patterns of the square, the old men nodding on benches under the Judas trees.

What was he doing here? Philippa had made her decision. To track her down like this was an invasion of privacy of the sort she hated most. The cathedral clock booming the hour made him jump. He had never felt more vulnerable as he headed for the Pereira house.

It was tall and narrow, with many balconies and a solid door without knob or handle. When he rang the bell a window opened above and a voice called questioningly. He stepped back, looking up, unaware of having announced himself as a stranger by not having done so at once. He hadn't expected to have to shout his business up to a third-floor window. But before he could marshall words the voice called, '*Momento, momento, por favor*,' and the window clicked shut.

The door was opened by a stooped and tiny old woman, who smiled up at him. '*Bom dia, senhor.*'

'Mrs Philippa Howard?' Jon was surprised that he could get the words out.

'*A Dona Filipa, sim, sim.*' Nodding and smiling she beckoned him in with an arthritic finger. Christ, it was real; Philippa was here. Jon tried to calm the thudding of his heart as he waited in the dark hall, its shadows deepened by contrast with the light from a high window which glowed on the honey-toned marble of the stairs.

Then light feet tapping, a loosening of his gut as he looked up at the sound, and there was Philippa at the turn of the stairs – a Philippa he scarcely recognised, a Philippa as alien and remote from him as the elegant females he'd seen on the pavements of Lisbon, the finished products of dressmaker, beautician and hairdresser. She was wearing a simply cut, light-coloured dress, high-heeled sandals and a heavy gold bracelet he didn't recall seeing before. She was very brown, very thin, and her hair was cut criminally, heart-breakingly short.

Jon saw her check, saw her hand grip the pierced marble banister. For a long moment he found himself incapable of words or movement.

'Jonnie.' It was the merest whisper. In the long sleepless nights this was the fantasy Philippa had tried so hard to put out of her mind: Jon appearing exactly like this, waiting in the dim hall, come to fetch her. Her knees began to shake and she pressed against the banister, feeling its icy coldness against her hip.

Jon crossed the hall and took the first two steps without conscious intention, then halted. He mustn't, whatever he did, assume too much.

'I'm sorry. I should have warned you—'

'But how did you know I was here?'

'Long story.' He couldn't face it now. 'I had to find you. I couldn't let you go without—'

'I can't believe you're here.' Her voice had no substance. 'Is Keeper with you?'

'Keeper?' Jon was momentarily thrown by the question. 'No, he's – in Scotland.'

'Stupid of me.' Philippa shook her head, annoyed with herself. 'But he's all right?'

'He's fine. He's with Celia at Fassfern.' He didn't remember that the information might surprise her.

They fell helplessly silent.

'I know I should have warned you,' Jon said again, after an aching pause which seemed to last for ever.

'It's all right. It's quite all right to call,' she amended, making the point a social one.

Questions, doubts and longing swirled in the quiet hall, the noonday sounds of the town muffled behind the heavy door.

'Can we talk? Will you talk to me, Philippa?'

Jon felt shaken by her nearness, by hearing her voice again, by the texture of her skin within reach of his hand but so impossible to touch, and above all by his need to reach the self within that shorn elegant head. She was wearing scent. Her hands, which he had loved as capable outdoor hands, rarely without a scratch or scar, were smooth and well-tended, the nails polished.

She was at once utterly familiar and a dazzling stranger, and he realised with half-amused dismay that he was having an erection. But the months apart, uncertainty about her present feelings, and the need to put the record straight, lay like some impossible no-man's land between them, and he knew that to seize her in his arms as he longed to do would be the worst course he could take.

All Philippa longed for was his arms. Not words, not explanations, just his arms to end the long desolation of being alone.

'You must come and meet the Pereiras,' she said.

Jon hesitated, unsure what to read into that. 'Couldn't you come out somewhere so that we can talk?'

'Lena will have told Sylvia you're here. She'll want to meet you. Then I'm afraid there's a lunch party and I ought to be here for that. I'm sorry, Jonnie.'

'That's all right. I understand.' Same damned stuff. Other people dragging her away from him. But he wasn't going to blow everything by arguing at this stage. 'So – how about if I come back after lunch?'

He wasn't keen to give her the chance for second thoughts, or consolidating her defences, but saw no alternative.

'Oh, don't go away!' Philippa surprised him by exclaiming, with such consternation that he felt a first spark of genuine hope.

'Don't worry, I'm not going anywhere.'

'Sylvia will want to invite you to lunch. Could you bear that?'

He would sit through ten lunches if it meant not losing sight of her.

He was welcomed kindly by Carlos and Sylvia Pereira, and introduced to what seemed like a dozen well-groomed courteous strangers as they arrived. The only name which didn't go straight over his head was that of Maria-Helena, Philippa's ex-pupil. She smiled at him from soft dark eyes fringed by the longest lashes he'd ever seen, and murmured seductively, 'My mother likes me to practise my English.'

He thought he could probably manage to get through this.

Though Lena, now nearly eighty, who had come into the house as a child and had had nowhere to go when the revolution more or less put an end to the custom of having living-in servants, pottered endlessly about, liking to be part of things, lunch was served as a buffet. Sylvia had shopped for it, as everyone now did, in the big supermarket outside the walls, and had prepared it with the help of Philippa and Maria-Helena.

Buffet notwithstanding, it seemed a long-winded affair to Jon, and he was beginning to feel it could go on for ever when he found Philippa at his side.

'I'm sure Sylvia would excuse us if you'd like to go, Jonnie.'

'Like to?' He pulled himself together to follow her round the circle, shaking hands and trying to find adequate answers to polite farewells, but he didn't think anyone was fooled. Rarely had he felt such a sense of pure release as when the front door closed behind them, and the penned heat of the narrow street engulfed them.

'We'll have the town to ourselves at this hour,' Philippa remarked. 'I thought you might like to see the old walls. The views are lovely.' Politely proposing a little sight-seeing to fill in an hour or two for the stranger. As Jon crossed the *praça* at her side, relief ebbed, and he felt as stifled by the constraint between them as by the blanketing somnolence of siesta.

It seemed so right and normal to have Philippa there beside him, yet, in this composed and impersonal mood, she was bafflingly inaccessible. How thin she was, he thought with fresh anxiety, noting the sharpness of her shoulder blades, the thinness of her neck without its familiar swing of glossy hair.

With appalling timing, June came into his mind. Once he'd believed he loved her, had greedily wanted her. Now he couldn't imagine touching her. Was it like that for Philippa? Was she walking at his side unaware of him, untroubled? Still in silence, they followed a narrow street which opened suddenly into one of those spaces, too small to be called a square, where the houses stood back and the street plunged away at a new angle. A couple of cars hugged the walls, and high above washing hung from a system of ropes and pulleys as complex as the rigging of a three-master.

A Mercedes was edging into the last available feet of space and Philippa halted suddenly in what Jon, hyper-sensitive where she was concerned, felt to be dismay.

'I'm sorry,' she said, her eyes on the man getting out of the car. 'I must just—' And she walked towards him with an oddly stiff step.

What was this about? Eyes narrowed, Jon watched with an anger that was basically a refusal to accept the obvious, as the man turned, a smile of pleasure lighting his face. He was youngish, well-set-up, prosperous-looking, sleek. He greeted Philippa with a charm which couldn't be mistaken, then, after a few brief words, and a glance and formal incline of the head in Jon's direction, disappeared down an alley.

Jon saw Philippa, as she came back to him, read the antagonism he had failed to hide, and he made a violent effort to push aside a reaction he knew he had no right to make so obvious. He was appalled at his own blind confidence. Of course there had to be someone else. He couldn't believe he hadn't been prepared for it. He had imagined Philippa hurt, betrayed, lonely he had dared to believe, and even, since Julie had expressed her views on the subject so cogently, thinking that she had failed him. But he had never thought of her in another relationship. You stupid, stupid bastard, he said blankly to himself.

'Sorry not to introduce you, Jonnie.' Though she apologised, Philippa offered no explanations, and turned at once to go on.

The old fortifications were as wide as the streets of the tight-cramped town, and afforded a long view over the miles of rolling farmland. It was of no interest to Jon, who was only thankful, as they wandered slowly on like sightseers who had run out of adjectives, to be clear of the claustrophobic gullies of stone.

Philippa, rocked by the chance meeting with Paulo, felt dismay increase at Jon's unnerving aloofness. Seeing him waiting in the shadows of the hall this morning, she had thought only one thing – he's come to take me home. But that first thrilled conviction had faded into wretched uncertainty. He hadn't touched her, hadn't referred to her leaving him, hadn't told her that he'd missed her, let alone loved her. He had been watchful and unrelaxed and, though almost alarmingly amenable on the surface, his behaviour had scarcely been that of a man come to play out some tender reconciliation scene.

Then why had he come? Well, people did visit Portugal for other reasons than to fall at the feet of Philippa Howard. She was merely someone he'd had an affair with, an affair they had failed to resurrect after a separation. He had never spoken of permanence or marriage. Was he even divorced? It seemed incredible now that she had never asked.

He'd never even agreed to having a joint account. This piece of bathos had been her way of dragging herself out of the dreary circling of these thoughts, but it didn't help today.

They came to a star-shaped redoubt at a corner of the walls, and leaned to look into the gardens below.

'We could go down and sit in the shade,' Philippa suggested. 'They built steps down the outside of the walls recently. The historians and purists raised a terrible hullabaloo, of course, but—'

'Philippa.' Jon couldn't bear another second of being a tourist. 'I had to come to find you. There's something you have to know.' He was rushing in too baldly, he knew, but he couldn't stop himself. 'When you went away, you had the wrong idea. There was nothing going on with anyone else. There never had been.'

Philippa stared at him as though she had no idea what he was talking about. As Julie had guessed, by this time she saw the failure of their relationship as almost entirely her fault. Jon had needed far more help than she'd given him when he came back to Achallie. She should have seen to it that he had proper counselling, or at least that they talked. She should have made him realise how much she loved him, and never have allowed them to drift apart. If he'd looked elsewhere for solace, that seemed by now no more than the logical consequence of her own lack of understanding and compassion.

'I found out what you heard in the shop, the day you left,' Jon was continuing doggedly. 'About Pam. But it was just idle gossip, Philippa. There was nothing in it, nothing whatsoever, I promise you.'

Pam? Philippa had to struggle to place the name.

'It doesn't matter,' she said truthfully.

'But I wasn't playing about,' Jon persisted. Indifference was the one thing he hadn't bargained for. 'You must believe that.'

Philippa unwillingly dredged up the details of that morning. 'Your shirt smelled of scent.'

He looked at her, confounded by this detail, groping back in his turn. 'We'd gone to one of the staff chalets, a whole crowd of us . . .'

'It doesn't matter,' Philippa repeated. It had hurt at the time. It wasn't important now.

'But that was what made you go, wasn't it?' Jon couldn't believe that putting this straight hadn't magically, instantly, resolved things between them.

'That's what made me get on the bus, I suppose,' Philippa said almost vaguely. 'I really went because I knew we'd never be happy.'

Jon's throat was dry. 'Is that what you believe?'

He still hasn't said one word about wanting me or missing me, Philippa cried inwardly, a chill spreading through her. He only came to clear this up, so that I wouldn't accuse him of something he hadn't done.

'It never really works, I suppose, to go back,' she said, with a supreme effort keeping her voice matter-of-fact. 'We thought we could recapture what we'd had that first summer, but we'd become different people.'

It sounded terrifyingly past tense and detached to Jon. He had the feeling of having arrived at the end of a long road and finding it ended in a chasm. 'That bloke we ran into back there. Are the two of you—?'

'Paulo?' What did he have to do with anything? 'We go out together, yes.' Philippa meant simply that. She and Paulo, whom she had known well when she was here before, often met at the Pereiras and at the houses of other friends, and also dined and danced occasionally.

To Jon the phrase conveyed something else. Keeping his voice carefully free of emphasis, he asked, 'So that's it?'

They looked at each for a long moment, the sun beating down into their high nook of stone, the world shut out, not existing for them.

'Well, I suppose it is.' Philippa's voice was so thin with held-down emotion that it sounded almost casual.

Silence.

'I'd better push off then.' Jon wondered if he was physically capable of walking away.

'I'm sure Sylvia would invite you to—'

Always the social crap, he thought with wild anger. 'For Christ's sake, Philippa!'

Silence again, taut and stretching. An old woman toiled up the steps from the gardens. Their eyes followed her but barely registered her. She looked at them as she passed with the inoffensive curiosity of her kind, recognising Philippa, admiring her tall handsome companion.

'You'll stay on here?' Jon asked.

'I think so. For the time being, anyway.' Where else was there to go? 'And you? You'll stay at Shionach?' That took some effort.

'God knows.' The thought of being there knowing that she had truly gone for good was appalling. 'What do you want me to do about Keeper?' The fact that Philippa hadn't thought of this herself should have told him something.

'Keeper! Oh, I should have – maybe Celia would keep him until – I'll write to her.' Of course Keeper wasn't Jon's responsibility. She had assumed too much by leaving the dog with him in the first place.

'Are you all right for cash?' Jon realised the moment he spoke that the instinct to look after her at this stage was absurd.

'Oh, yes, thank you.' She gave him a brilliant, brittle smile. Sharing had been an illusion she had wanted to believe in; she'd been on her own all along.

Of course she is, you fool. She's all right for cash, and in every other respect, and always has been.

'Then there's no point in hanging around, I suppose,' Jon said.

Thank goodness she hadn't given herself away when she saw him this morning, Philippa reflected. She tried to say goodbye but the word was beyond her. For one second more Jon waited, then with a brusque nod he turned away, swiftly putting distance between them with his familiar prowling stride.

Emptiness and silence settled after him.

36

Jon was well into the maze of streets before he made any attempt to get his bearings. Where the hell was the car? The morning seemed a year away, but at least the effort to focus on some immediate practical problem postponed agonising realisation. The town was shaking off the torpor of siesta, traffic on the move again. He found his way to the *praça*, and retraced his steps to the car from there. He had no idea where he would go, just out of here, away, anywhere.

He released some of his anger as he cursed the intricacies of the one-way system, beginning to feel that he would never be free of crowding walls. Then, turning a corner, he saw a pick-up slewed across the road ahead, a wheel off, its load of crates shed, blocking the space from wall to wall. He braked and slammed into reverse, but a car was close behind him, and its driver was already getting out to add his quota to the argument going on up front. Passers-by were gathering. Calls and laughter floated down from windows and balconies above.

Jon felt fury jet up. He was desperate to break free of this oppressive place, put his foot down, hurtle away from the end of his hopes with Philippa, which seemed to have been reached with such simple and astounding speed. How had it happened? Why hadn't he put up some kind of fight? Because he had pinned his faith on the impact the one essential revelation would make, and it had meant nothing to her.

She was right, of course. Their problems went far deeper than the question of whether or not he'd been involved with someone else. Reviewing their stilted conversation, he knew he'd been terrified of pushing too hard, fearing out-and-out rejection. He had also been shaken by the encounter with Paulo. And, needing reassurance himself, he'd forgotten Julie's warning that Philippa would feel she had been as much at fault as he had been for all that had gone wrong.

But what about Achallie? There had been no chance to tell her it was for sale. She might not know and, if she needed a refuge, what better place could there be?

Knowing that he was clutching at a straw, Jon made up his mind. The chaos in the street clearly wasn't going to sort itself out for a while. Cars were now bottled up in both directions. In the limited space left to him to manoeuvre, he squeezed the car hard against the wall and left it. Let these clowns get on with it.

He headed, as he thought, for the Pereira house but in seconds, not having allowed for the tortuousness of the one-way system, he found himself once more below the ramparts. Frustrated, he was trying to get his bearings when he heard an urgent voice. The old woman whom he and Philippa had seen coming up the steps from the gardens was gesturing and calling, apparently to him. An odd word or two penetrated as she hobbled towards him.

'. . . *casa Pereira . . . inglesa . . .*'

He turned back, and even in that moment the thought flicked across his mind that Philippa wouldn't appreciate the English bit. The woman was pointing in agitation, up to the walls. Icy panic gripped him, no room left for trivia. That sheer drop, the long slope of the glacis below, now innocently patterned with flower-beds and bright with forsythia and spiraea. Surely Philippa wouldn't . . . ? He could never afterwards remember the interval it took him to reach the redoubt.

Philippa was leaning there, as limp as if her dress were draped across the stone on its own, and she was crying. Philippa the cool and composed, obliviously abandoned to grief in this public place. He lifted her away from the parapet and into his arms, his brain registering even in that moment how worryingly thin she was. Her body felt weightless, without resilience. But what alarmed him more than anything was that she scarcely seemed to know he was there. Her eyes were shut, her breathing uneven, and though she clutched at the front of his shirt he didn't think she had any idea who he was.

'Philippa, sweetheart, it's all right, I'm here. Don't cry, everything's all right.'

Gradually she became calmer and, opening her eyes, asked in a croaky voice, 'Jonnie? You came back?'

'And I'm not going away again, believe me,' he said savagely against the top of her head, pulling her close, aware of an unfamiliar prickling in his eyes, a hard ache in his throat.

Philippa pressed against him, her fingers still twisted in his shirt.

'We'll talk,' he promised her, his voice rough. 'Not yet maybe, but in time. We'll say everything we want to say.'

'Will we go back to Shionach?'

'We'll go back to Shionach.'

They stayed there, close and quiet, as the evening light reddened the tawny land and the golden stone.

But matters weren't to be resolved quite so easily, as Jon discovered when he tried to draw Philippa back to immediate reality. Her disillusionment this morning when he hadn't taken her at once into his arms, the hard control to which she'd held fast all day, and this rare descent into helpless tears, had been preceded by months of unhappiness. During these months she had been sleeping badly, eating far from adequately in spite of Sylvia's anxious care, and growing more and more unsure of her capacity to deal with life on her own again. Now she clung to Jon so desperately that he wondered how he was going to get her as far as the car.

Perhaps he could find her somewhere to sit quietly and wait while he fetched it. But at the first hint that he might leave her, Philippa dissolved into tears, tears so unrestrained that he knew they were an involuntary physical reaction. He would have to take her home first, and sort out the car later.

Sylvia Pereira, taking one look at Philippa, turned questioningly, and with some authority, to Jon.

He met her eyes. 'She's all right,' he said, and saw by her nod that she accepted the underlying message in the words. 'But she could probably do with some sleep.'

'Oh, no,' Philippa instantly protested. 'Of course I don't need to sleep. Sylvia, I'm sorry to rush off without warning, but I must go back to Scotland with Jon. We could get to Lisbon for the overnight flight if we left at once. There are sure to be seats.'

'Not tonight,' Jon said, and the irony didn't escape him that it was he who was putting on the brakes, while Philippa was ready to set off there and then. 'No one's going anywhere tonight.'

'There is no question of such a thing,' Sylvia put in firmly. 'Naturally, Jon is our guest, for as long as he wishes to stay. But you, *querida*, you must go and rest, have a bath, arrange yourself. Please, go with Lena. Yes, you must do as I say.'

Lena, who had been hovering anxiously, led Philippa away with admonishing pats and clucks.

Sylvia turned to Jon. She had been increasingly concerned about Philippa's evident unhappiness as the months had passed, and none of the care and affection she could offer had seemed to have any effect. Though Philippa had said little to anyone about her reasons for leaving Scotland, when she had brought Jon into the salon this morning Sylvia had not needed to be told who he was. And when they had come in together just now she had recognised instantly, though they didn't look at each other or touch each other, that things between them had moved on. They were now a unit, indivisible, separate from the rest of the world.

'Philippa is nervous at present,' she said, then seeing Jon's frown caught herself up. 'Ah, how foolish of me. It is not the same in English. I mean that the nerves are not strong. I have been anxious for her. What she needs, you are right, is rest and quiet, but' – with a rueful lift of her shoulders – 'I'm afraid that once again we have guests this evening. Perhaps you will prefer to take Philippa out for dinner, so that you can be alone?'

'That sounds the best idea,' Jon agreed, 'if you don't mind? I don't think she could cope with much tonight. And I'd just like to say, I don't want to take her away if there are things she should be doing here. She's not thinking straight at the moment, but I know she'd hate to realise later that she'd let you down in any way. We're in no hurry.' He could hardly believe he was saying it, but he knew he was right. He didn't want guilt, on however minor a point, muddying the future.

'No, absolutely not. There is nothing. Philippa is here as our friend, and as company for Maria-Helena. We shall miss her, very much, but she has no commitments here.' She needs to be with you. But Sylvia wasn't brave enough to say that.

A group had already congregated in the salon when Jon came back after fetching the car, having a bath and digging out his last clean shirt. He felt his hackles rise to see that one of the dark-suited, affluent-looking men chatting glass in hand was Paulo. This was a facet of the situation he had allowed later events to push out of his mind, but he knew it couldn't be ignored.

Carlos was asking Jon what he'd like to drink when Philippa

appeared in the wide doorway, hesitating there with a ten-
tativeness so unlike her usual smiling confidence that Jon's
throat constricted. She was wearing another elegant dress, and
looked as chill and perfect as some spun-sugar confection,
and as fragile. In the thin face her eyes were too large and
dark, her generous mouth unbearably vulnerable.

She saw Jon and started at once towards him, ignoring
everyone else in the room. Understanding enough by now
of the style of the house to realise it was unthinkable to omit
the customary greetings, Jon moved to meet her, intending to
do the rounds with her if necessary.

But Paulo was before him. Taking a glass of sherry from
Lena's tray, he intercepted Philippa with smooth adroitness.
Jon saw her focus her attention on him as though wakened
from sleep-walking. Then, accepting the drink with a smile,
she stood listening obediently to what he was saying.

Growling inwardly, Jon suppressed his instinct to go and
rescue her, and his equally strong instinct to knock Paulo
through the wall, and turned back to Carlos, who, reading
this small scene without difficulty and not feeling entirely
confident that that would be the end of it, nevertheless moved
calmly into conversation on local topics. Jon might not wish
to hear about the mixed success of experiments in rice and
tomato growing along the Guadiana, but it would be politic
to give him time to pull himself together.

Paulo had known at once who Jon was, when he'd seen
him with Philippa that afternoon. He knew more than anyone,
though even that wasn't a great deal, of what had lain behind
Philippa's reappearance in Santa Paula. When he had first
met her, some years ago, he'd been deep in the stormy seas
of his marriage to a beautiful Venezuelan, and though he had
been attracted by Philippa's slender beauty and long legs, her
smile and the aura of happiness she carried with her, he had
at that period taken little more than a friendly interest in her.

But the years had passed. The acrimony of fights with his wife had outweighed the joys of making up, and he had recently emerged from a vengeful and costly divorce.

To Philippa's altered, more fine-drawn looks were now added a new elegance and maturity, and something else – an air of having been wounded and not quite understanding why – which he found very hard to resist. A side of himself that he hardly recognised found pleasure in feeling protective towards her and slowly building up her trust. Though recognising that he must give her more time, he fully intended to ask her to marry him, and he had let himself believe he would achieve his goal.

The arrival of this big, lowering, dangerous-looking character from her past, obviously the man who had brought her to her present state, had been a shock but, Paulo assured himself, he surely couldn't constitute any serious threat at this stage.

With no time to waste on being subtle, he turned his back on the room and, under the guise of taking a polite interest in Jon's unheralded appearance in Santa Paula, took the chance to remind Philippa that life with him had been so unsatisfactory that she'd been driven to flee from it. To be fair to Paulo, he knew from his own experience the profound relief of winning clear of a turbulent relationship, and he believed a more settled and contented one to be in his power to offer her.

It was like reasoning with someone under an anaesthetic. Philippa tried to listen, frowning with the effort to concentrate. She had no wish to hurt Paulo, who had been so good to her, but she found it impossible to give him her attention. The need to be near Jon filled her mind. She wasn't accustomed to being at the mercy of any feeling so powerful, and it frightened her.

Jon, responding disjointedly to a patient Carlos and wondering how soon they could leave, tried not to watch her too obviously, but couldn't help seeing her tension, her frowning, distracted look. What was that bastard saying to her? Was he trying to persuade her to stay after all?

Carlos talked on about the lack of local labour which had resulted in employers bringing in workers from the Ukraine, Roumania, Croatia . . . Maria-Helena worked her way unobtrusively towards Jon, with one eye on her mother, who was listening to a dissertation on the new laws governing the employment of minors and wishing fervently that Paulo hadn't been invited tonight. She must catch Jon's eye. He would make no mistake about a signal to take Philippa away.

Snatching another look at Philippa, Jon saw that she was standing as if holding herself from pain, her hands wrapped round her glass, her mouth tight. Paulo was speaking urgently, leaning close.

Carlos followed Jon's glance and he too disliked what he saw. Then he became aware that Sylvia was trying to catch Jon's eye. Jon wasn't looking. He had already started towards Philippa.

She, however, anticipated them all. Leaving Paulo in mid-sentence, putting down her glass on the first available surface and moving as though there wasn't another person in the room, she went to meet Jon, her eyes fixed on his face. When she reached him she said nothing, but took his arm in both hands and, closing her eyes, leaned her forehead lightly against him.

Jon put a reassuring hand over hers and bent his head to her. 'Don't worry, I'm here. Everything's fine.'

As conversation began to flow again after a small discon-certed check Paulo stood rooted, doing his best to refuse a great and final sense of loss. Maria-Helena gazed enraptured at Jon and Philippa. Sylvia Pereira, as she made her way towards them, outward serenity unalterably in place, blinked a tear from her beautifully made-up eyes.

'I'll take Philippa out now, I think,' Jon said.

Carlos had also discreetly closed ranks.

'Please, feel free to come and go as you wish,' he said quietly. 'Our house is yours.'

Jon was grateful for the genuine, understanding kindness which had smoothed over the awkward incident, and was making it easy for them to escape.

It was one of the bleakest moments of Paulo's life when they slipped away with no more than a general, formal good-bye from Jon. Philippa looked dazed, giving the impression that she knew there was something she should have said or done, but that it was beyond her to bring her mind to bear on it.

There's nothing of her, Jon thought with a stab of actual fear, keeping his arm round her as they went down the treacherous polished marble of the stairs. She felt not only insubstantial and frail, but unsteady on the high heels of her strappy sandals. Was this the Philippa who'd been able to give him a run for his money any day on the hills above Glen Maraich?

In the street he said, 'Sylvia mentioned some hotel. Is that where you'd like to go?'

'Oh, not the hotel,' she objected quickly. 'You'd hate it there.'

He didn't much care for what that said about him, or her perception of him. 'Where then? Is there some place you prefer?' Though not somewhere Paulo took her, for choice.

'There's a restaurant where I go with Micky and Antonia – friends who farm nearby. It's a bit scruffy, but nice and relaxed, and the food's good.'

It seemed incredible that she still didn't know the details of his journey to find her; and to think that only this morning he'd left Monte da Rocha.

As he turned into the entrance of the Quinta do Rosal he

had the impression of a big untidy garden reaching back into the shadows, with not only the roses of its name, still in bud, but honeysuckle climbing everywhere, its scent sweet on the evening air. At once he knew this was a place where Philippa would feel at home, the feeling reinforced by the cars parked outside, battered Fiat Unos or Renault 5s very much in the glen style, and a general air of laid-back shabbiness.

They found a table on the verandah, which looked as though it had been glassed-in as an afterthought on the cheap, and Jon was more resigned than irritated when Philippa was greeted by several people, one elderly man coming to his feet to bow to her, hand on heart.

'One of the Pereira farm men,' Philippa explained, after going across to greet him with a pleasure more natural, and more reassuring to Jon, than any response she had shown for some time. 'He still lives in his cottage there, which hardly anyone does now, looking after his vegetable plot, helping out at lambing time, and his wife occasionally does sewing for Sylvia . . .'

It was a glimpse of the Philippa he remembered, and Jon was content to let her talk about anything she liked, if it made her feel better.

The proprietor came beaming to their table, '*Filipa*, so long you don't come. Welcome, welcome. *E o senhor*,' he added, giving Jon a raking glance.

The entire male world still thinking it owned Philippa. But Jon couldn't resent it; in an odd way it brought her back to him as she had been.

'OK, get ordering,' he told her, 'and just remember I'm bloody starving. All this emotion is hungry work.'

She laughed and he felt a leap of delight and hope at the sound. At last, here, in this friendly, unpretentious place, they would be given privacy and time would slow down, time would be theirs.

37

It was easy to laugh over Jon's account of his search for her, particularly his infiltration of the stronghold of Boa Vista. Philippa was not so impressed by his comments on the pretty students of the Bairro Alto in Lisbon, while Jon put on hold for the time being any enquiries about the muscular Caparica lifeguard. His reaction to the news that Antonia's father was Lord Macken, a famous owner-trainer even he had heard of, Philippa definitely found rewarding. The starting point of his quest, however, his call on Bessie, brought them to matters he would gladly have deferred for a little longer.

'How's Achallie looking these days?' Philippa asked eagerly. 'Do the new owners use it much?'

She hadn't heard it was for sale, then. Was she so out of contact with friends at home? What would the discovery mean to her? And what bearing might it have on their future plans? Jon watched her carefully as he told her the news, and could almost see the thoughts begin to turn. She said nothing, however, and in the silence between them he was aware of no extraneous sounds.

'It makes no difference,' Philippa said after a moment, as though hearing the questions he wasn't asking. 'It doesn't change anything.'

She could still go straight to the heart of things, he thought with gratitude.

'Achallie had its place, for me and then for us both,' she

went on slowly. 'I'd never want to lose touch with everyone there, though I've found it difficult to write to people while I – this time—' Too difficult. She left that. 'But I wouldn't want to go back to live. It wouldn't be the answer for us now.'

He took her hands between his, too moved to look at her. This new factor could have altered everything.

'You said this afternoon you'd take me back to Shionach,' Philippa said, 'and that's what I want.'

'You're prepared to give it another go? With me?' He found it hard to add those two vital words.

'Of course I am,' she said gently.

In that instant, Jon felt the whole bright future laid before him, a marvellous gift. Then, insanely, he found himself asking, 'What about Paulo?' He hadn't intended to ask, had indeed formed the iron resolve not to do so, yet there was his voice harshly putting the question. He might at least have wrapped it up a bit.

'Oh, poor Paulo, I was so awful to him just now.'

Jon wasn't interested in that. 'Look, I know I don't have any right to ask, but what was the deal there?'

Philippa looked at him in surprise. 'With Paulo? Nothing. No deal.' The idea seemed extraordinary to her. Did Jon still not understand that she couldn't be even remotely interested in another man? 'I knew him years ago, when I was here before. His marriage has recently broken up. He's been kind to me.'

'He fancies you, you mean.'

'A bit perhaps. He's lonely. But I couldn't possibly – don't you see – I couldn't have—' She looked distressed again, afraid she wouldn't find the words to convince him, and Jon knew her regained calm was paper-thin.

He gave her hands, folded in his, a little shake. 'Hey, don't get upset. I shouldn't have asked.'

'Well, I'd have asked in your place,' Philippa said fairly,

sounding so like her old self that he allowed himself to be reassured.

Their oblivious intentness on each other was interrupted as the proprietor himself brought heaped and steaming plates of chicken and rice. Philippa smiled at him so brilliantly that he gave her a couple of affectionate little pats as he turned away.

'And he can keep his hands to himself as well,' Jon said darkly, and grinned when she laughed aloud.

He wanted her. Longing for the release of love-making, wiping out in that one assuaging act all the misunderstandings, the misery of the months apart, today's see-saw of hopes and fears, swept him. Doubt as to whether or not he'd be able to perform didn't enter his mind. The only problem was that any such physical and emotional release was almost certainly out of the question as long as they were at the Casa Pereira.

Then it occurred to him that it might be just as well. God knew what memories love-making would bring back for Philippa, and if this first, precious time wasn't good for her, then it would be better to face that problem in surroundings where he could take his time to soothe and comfort her. In any case he wasn't sure she was in any fit state for sex tonight. She was pretty well into the rag doll stage by now. The best way he could look after her would be to take her safely home.

How good, though, it would have been to have had that slight, weary body gathered up against his in sleep, he thought, as he climbed into his high, stately bed an hour later. But being a male who had had a long and taxing day, not sexual desire, love reaffirmed nor the marvellous promise of the future, could keep him awake for a second after his head hit the pillow.

For Philippa it was very different. Worries swarmed – about the journey, about packing, about loose ends which must be tied up before she left, minutiae over-shadowed by larger, treacherous, night-time fears about returning to Shionach with Jon and making a life with him there, fears she didn't have the courage to examine.

Then her thoughts turned inevitably to Paulo, and she winced to think how callous she had been to him. In the end she got up and started to pack, set aside small presents for the maids and write farewell notes.

Jon, seeing her face when she came to fetch him for breakfast, seriously wondered if she was capable of facing the journey home.

'You look exhausted. Why don't we have a couple of quiet days here, packing up, saying your goodbyes?' he suggested, taking in the bruised look of the circles under her eyes, the tense set of her mouth.

'Oh, no!' she protested. 'I couldn't bear it.'

He frowned at the consternation in her voice. 'OK, just a suggestion. We'll do whatever you want. Only you look like a bit of chewed string at present.'

Thankful that he'd given in without argument, she retorted with a touch of her old crispness, 'Delightfully put,' and he was glad to hear it.

He was a model of patience as they made farewell calls, returned borrowed books, collected a necklace whose clasp still needed mending and paid the dressmaker – a patience he was mildly aggrieved to realise Philippa scarcely noticed or appreciated. But when it seemed that the list was finally done, he wheeled her, in spite of her protests, into a dark little bar and ordered coffee.

'We don't have time,' Philippa objected. 'I haven't finished packing. There's still masses to do.'

'What are you dodging?' he asked flatly.

'I don't know what you're talking about—'

'How about Paulo?' *Am I saying this?* 'You can't go off without saying goodbye to him, can you?'

Philippa stared at him with miserable eyes.

'You know you can't disappear without seeing him again. And I am as sure as hell not having you come back here to apologise.'

She raised a smile at that. 'I thought you'd be angry if I suggested it.'

'I'll get over it,' he grunted, hiding the way her admission made him feel. 'So, where does he hang out?'

'Oh, Jonnie.' The grateful smile she flashed at him almost made it seem worthwhile.

Paulo felt one surge of hope when Philippa was shown into his office, then read the truth in her face. He acknowledged her courage and her generosity in coming, though he couldn't help reflecting how such qualities in her would have transformed his life. He came to take her hands, bending his head over them. When he raised it his eyes were wet.

'Oh, Paulo, don't,' Philippa begged.

'I wish only for your happiness, you know that,' he said. 'Are you truly sure this is what you want?'

Her face remorseful, she could only nod.

Jon, seeing how shaken she looked as she came down the steps, thought, I must get her out of here, she's had enough. He did what he could to help with the final packing, then had to fight down his impatience at the affectionate farewells from the Pereiras, the hugs and tears, the assurances that their house was hers, Sylvia abandoning the conventional *abraço* for a warm hug while Maria-Helena sobbed unrestrainedly.

In spite of how well Micky and Antonia had looked after him, Jon was thankful when Philippa resisted his proposal, which for her sake he felt duty bound to make, of calling at the Monte da Rocha.

'I couldn't face it just now,' she confessed.

'We'll come back for a holiday one day,' he promised, and heard his voice sounding too hearty as she gave him a small tired smile. It was hard to believe in the reality of such ordinary plans with her in this state. Urgency to get her home consumed him.

Throughout the journey she was passive, agreeing to whatever he decided. Met with this docile acquiescence at every turn, Jon could hardly bear to recall the Philippa he had first known, with her air of energy and enjoyment in life.

There was only one crisis. At the airport Philippa, not capable by now of paying much attention to her surroundings, came out of the loo by a different door from the one she'd gone in by and found no Jon outside. Luckily he was prowling up and down, and saw her gazing helplessly about her, drenched in tears. Drawing her to a seat and holding her close, he was shaken by the depth of her distress as she gasped out, 'I thought you'd gone, I thought I'd never see you again.'

He gathered her tighter against him, his face grim. Would there always linger in her mind the memory of that day when he'd left Keeper's Cottage, disappearing without a word, making no contact? Or the later occasion, when she'd found him about to drive away from Achallie without telling her, and had been so distraught? Would she ever feel totally sure of him?

It was plainly out of the question to go on to Shionach today; Philippa was exhausted. At least now they could sleep together, though Jon had never imagined that when at last he made love to her again it would be in a characterless, over-heated Glasgow hotel, with the background sounds of traffic and a faulty ballcock hissing behind a bathroom door which wouldn't shut properly.

He hadn't intended to make love at all, but once he had stripped off her clothes, swung her unresisting body onto the bed and joined her under a scanty duvet, there was no question about what would happen next. She turned to him with a warm silken welcome which seemed as natural as breathing. They were once more the people they had been in their first months together, who had known each other's bodies with delight and love.

When Jon woke to find Philippa still laminated against his side, just as she'd fallen asleep, he experienced one of the deepest moments of happiness of his life. When she woke and smiled drowsily at him he wanted her on the instant. It was impossible to believe there had ever been any hang-ups between them.

He didn't risk leaving her when he collected the Shogun, but suspected that she wasn't even vaguely aware of where he took her. As he drove away he knew, with a great and thankful certainty, that it was his last contact with the world which once had threatened to drag him down into violence and evil.

Then they were on their way, not hurrying, heading north on a spring evening of watery sunshine and changing light, Philippa's mind beginning to turn forward to Shionach at last.

'Did you really finish the kitchen?'

'Every last inch of it.' But Jon was suddenly attacked by doubt himself. He thought of the simplicity of the Achallie kitchen, full of character and colour. Would she be pleased with what he'd done?

'Is the clothes line still up?'

'What kind of question is that? You're talking to a Sapper, remember.'

But anxiety dragged at him. Did these random questions mean she was harking back to the weeks in the byre, and thinking that was where they'd be living now? Was she seriously confused?

'Shall we collect Keeper as we go by, or wait till tomorrow?' she asked next.

'Whatever you like.'

'Would tomorrow be best?' she said uncertainly.

'Look, Philippa,' he began, then hastily toned down the exasperation. 'Don't try to work out what I'd like. Let's leave that one behind for good. If you want to pick up Keeper today that's fine by me.'

He wasn't enthusiastic about the prospect of getting involved with other people, even the Campbells, at this stage, longing to get Philippa home, but he accepted that the dog was part of Shionach for her.

Philippa looked out of the window. 'They've finished this bit of road,' she commented, and for a moment Jon thought she was shelving the decision. Then she said, more briskly than she'd spoken for some time, 'We'll go for him tomorrow. We don't want to see anyone else tonight – and Keeper's not counting.'

'Good thinking,' Jon said with satisfaction. Though they ought to shop for food somewhere en route. It disturbed him that this hadn't occurred to Philippa, and that when he stopped in Crianlarich she trailed round the shop at his heels as he filled a basket, but didn't attempt to help. Did she feel Shionach was now his, and that she was coming there in some way as his guest? Nothing could have shown more clearly how off balance she was, and for the first time Jon wondered if after all he would be able to look after her adequately.

They were silent as he drove on, but Philippa was sitting as close to him as she could get, and Jon, as he swung the jeep up the curves of the Black Mount and started across the Rannoch Moor, decided that was good enough for now.

He looked, with a sense of homecoming which took him by surprise, at the silver sheen on the lochans, the fine pencilling of reeds and grasses, the dark humps of rocky islets and the shadowy moors stretching away to the black silhouettes of the hills to the west. 'The forty shades of grey,' he remarked. 'Beats the Alentejo any day, for my money.'

'Mine too,' Philippa agreed contentedly.

'It feels as though we've gone back a whole season,' he said, remembering the trapped heat in the streets of Santa Paula – God, was that only yesterday?

'Time we can have again,' she replied, and both added mentally, together.

Approaching Drishaig, uncertainty again began to gnaw at Jon, and he wondered how much more apprehensive, in her present frame of mind, Philippa must be feeling.

'What are you thinking about, sweetheart?' he asked, reaching for her hand.

'About driving along here the day we moved into Shionach, and wondering if you'd ever got divorced,' she answered readily, not capable at the moment of weighing her words.

Jon, startled, actually braked, and having braked decided to pull up. He switched off the engine and turned to stare at her in disbelief. 'What are you talking about? I got divorced years ago. You know that. I set the whole thing in motion when I was at Achallie, after I came out of hospital.'

'But then I never heard whether it had happened. So I thought when you said nothing about getting married it was because you were still married to June.'

The name seemed so incongruous here, when Jon's mind was focused on everything the next hour was going to mean to them, that he was literally speechless.

'I suppose really, though, you aren't the marrying type,' Philippa added matter-of-factly.

'Philippa, for God's sake.' But he could only laugh at her conversational tone as he did his best to marshall his thoughts. 'How could I ask you to marry me when I was in such a mess, and when our life together was turning into a disaster? Oh, I don't mean only not being able to get it together in bed, but the fact that we were drifting further and further apart every day. And I couldn't even be sure I'd be able to support you properly.' He made an impatient gesture with his hand, knowing such a consideration wasn't important here. 'But the divorce, that's history. It went through before I went abroad. I was sure you knew.'

'You never talked about marriage, though,' she repeated, very nicely.

'Jesus!' He seized her, shook her, crushed her against him. 'How could I talk about marriage when I did nothing but create havoc in your life?'

'You could talk about it now.'

'OK, I'm talking about it.' She's in no fit state to discuss this, common sense warned him. Bollocks, said the rest of him.

'OK, I'm answering.'

'Ah, but what are you saying?' Absurd, releasing laughter swept them up.

I might have planned this better, Jon thought ruefully, as the jeep came down off the headland in the dark.

But nothing could mar Philippa's delight.

'Remember when we came over here first? I'd forgotten the road was so smart now.'

'You hated me tearing up the landscape to do it.'

She was surprised. 'I never said that.'

'No, you didn't say it.'

They looked back as if at strangers to the two wary, hurting people of that time.

The waiting shell of the finished house moved Philippa to tears, tears which neither of them minded, and her delight was Jon's reward for every stubborn hour of work he'd put into it, when persisting had seemed futile but the hope he'd refused to relinquish had driven him on.

'And you never slept up here?' Philippa asked, standing in the doorway of the big bedroom and surveying the stark new bed. 'Poor Jonnie, how could I have done that to you?'

He knew then that they were going to be all right, that she was truly back with him. Better get a fire going, he decided, get some warm food into her. And get the wrapping off that bed without delay.

'We'll go across to Baldarroch and see Michael and Julie and arrange for the furniture to come over.'

'We'll collect Keeper first thing in the morning.'

'He'll be off his head with joy.'

But Jon was glad he wasn't here tonight. He wanted nothing to break into this mood of intense awareness of each other, or his pleasure in watching Philippa explore the house he had created for her.

The early light through the uncurtained window and the gabbling voices of the oystercatchers along the shore woke her. Not since Achallie, it seemed, had there been that light, that immense silence behind the voices of birds, that peace. They wouldn't move from here. Renovating and moving on might be lucrative but it didn't create homes. No other house could ever mean to them what this one did.

'We'll have to watch out for the children going too near the loch, though,' she said in a business-like manner as Jon stirred and reached for her.